"now!"

The general barked that one word, and the trumpeter instantly raised his horn to his lips. The loud bray of the call rang from atop the tower, blaring stridently across the fortress and ringing harshly against the ears of the slowly awakening human army.

A deep rumble shook the fortress as gatesmen released the great stone counterweights and the massive fortress gates swung open with startling swiftness. Immediately the elven riders kicked their steeds, startling the horses into explosive bursts of speed. Shouts and cries of excitement and encouragement whooped through the air as the riders surged forth.

Still the trumpet brayed its command, and now the elven infantry rushed from the gates, emerging from the dust cloud raised by stampeding horses. Kencathedrus, his lively mount prancing with excitement, indicated with his sword each company of foot soldiers, and, in turn, they followed but a pace or two behind the unit that rushed before.

In the camp of the humans, the surprise was almost palpable, jerking men from breakfast idylls, or for those who had had duty during the night, from sleep. Eleven months of placid siege-making had had the inevitable effect of lessening readiness and building complacency. Now the peace of a warm summer's morning exploded with the brash violence of war!

THE DRAGONLANCE® SAGA

Elven Nations Trilogy
Volume Two

®

Saga

the
Kinslayer
Wars

Douglas Niles

Cover Art
Brom

Interior Illustrations
Robin Raab

DRAGONLANCE® Saga
Elven Nations

Volume Two

The Kinslayer Wars

Distributed to the book trade in the United States by Random House, Inc., and in Canada by Random House of Canada, Ltd.

Distributed to the book and hobby trade in the United Kingdom by TSR Ltd.

Distributed to the toy and hobby trade by regional distributors.

Distributed to the book trade in the United Kingdom by Random Century Group.

Cover art by Gerald Brom. Interior art by Robin Raab.

First Printing: August 1991
Printed in the United States of America
Library of Congress Catalog Card Number: 90-71492

9 8 7 6 5 4 3 2 1

ISBN:1-56076-113-X

TSR, Inc.
P.O. Box 756
Lake Geneva, WI
53147 U.S.A.

TSR Ltd.
120 Church End, Cherry Hinton
Cambridge CB1 3LB
United Kingdom

For Allison and René
Alles Guets

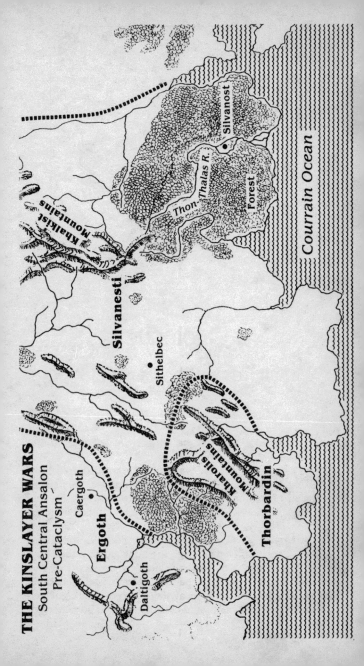

THE KINSLAYER WARS
South Central Ansalon
Pre-Cataclysm

Khalkist Mountains

Silvanost

Thon-Thalas R.

Forest

Courrain Ocean

Silvanesti

Sithelbec

Kharolis Mountains

Thorbardin

Ergoth

Caergoth

Daltigoth

⚘ Prologue ⚘

Winter, Year of the Ram, 2215 (PC)

"The emperor arrives—he enters the fortress at the South Gate!"

The cry rang from the walls of Caergoth, blared by a thousand trumpets and heard by a million ears. Excitement spread through the massive tent city around the great castle, while the towering fortress itself fairly tingled with anticipation.

The carriage of Emperor Quivalin Soth V, sometimes called Ullves, rumbled through the huge gates, pulled by a team of twelve white horses, trailed by an escort of five thousand men. From every parapet, every castellated tower top and high rampart in sprawling Caergoth, silk-gowned ladies, proud noblemen, and courtiers waved and cheered.

Sheer, gray-fronted walls of granite towered over the procession, dominating the surrounding farmlands as a mountain looms over a plain. Four massive gates, each formed from planks of vallenwood eighty feet long, barred the sides of the great structure against any conceivable foe—indeed, they proudly bore the scars of dragonbreath, inflicted during the Second Dragon War more than four centuries earlier.

The interior of Caergoth consisted of winding avenues, tall and narrow gates, stone buildings crowded together, and always the high walls. They curved about and climbed in terrace after terrace toward the heart of the massive castle, forming a granite maze for all who entered.

The carriage trundled through the outer gatehouse with imperial dignity and rolled along the streets, through open gates, and down the widest avenue toward the center of the fortress. Banners, in black and deep red and dark blue, hung from the ramparts. Everywhere the cheering of the crowds thundered around the emperor's coach.

Outside the walls, a vast sea of tents covered the fields around the fortress, and from these poured the men-at-arms of the emperor's army—some two hundred thousand in all. Though they did not mingle with the nobles and captains of the fortress, their joy was no less boisterous. They surged toward the castle in the wake of the emperor's procession, their shouts and hurrahs penetrating the heavy stone walls.

Finally the procession entered a broad plaza, cool and misty from the spray of a hundred fountains. Beyond, soaring to the very clouds themselves, arose the true wonder of Caergoth: the palace of the king. Tall towers jutted up from high walls, and lofty, peaked roofs seemed distant and unreachable. Crystal windows reflected sunlight in dazzling rainbows, filtering and flashing their colors through the shimmering haze of the fountains.

The coach rumbled down the wide, paved roadway to the gates of the palace. These portals, solid silver shined to mirrorlike brilliance, stood open wide. In their place stood the royal personage himself, King Trangath II, Lord of Caergoth and most loyal servant to the Emperor of Ergoth.

Here the royal coach halted. A dozen men-at-arms snapped their halberds to their chests as the king's own daughter opened the door of the gleaming steel carriage. The crowd surged across the plaza, even through the pools of the fountains, in an effort to see the great person who rode within. Around the plaza, from the surrounding walls and towers, teeming thousands shouted their adulation.

The emperor's green eyes flashed as he stepped from the high vehicle with a grace that belied his fifty years. His beard and hair now showed streaks of gray, but his iron will had hardened over his decades of rule until he was known, truthfully, as a ruthless and determined leader who had led his people into a prosperity they had never before known.

Now this regal leader, his robe of crimson fur flowing over a black silk tunic trimmed in platinum, ignored the King of Caergoth, stepping quickly to the three men who stood silently behind that suddenly embarassed monarch. Each of these was bearded and wore a cap and breastplate of gleaming steel plate. Tall boots rose above their knees, and each held a pair of gauntlets under his arm as he waited to greet the most powerful man in all of Ansalon.

The shrieks of the crowd reached a crescendo as the emperor seized each of these men, one after the other, in an embrace of deepest affection. He turned once more and waved to the masses.

Then Quivalin V led the three men toward the crystal doors of the king's palace. The portals parted smoothly, and when they closed, the hysteria beyond fell to a muted rumble.

"Find us a place where we can speak privately," the emperor commanded, without turning to look at King Trangath.

Immediately that royal personage scuttled ahead, bowing obsequiously and beckoning the emperor's party through a towering door of dark mahogany.

"I hope fervently that my humble library will suit my most esteemed lord's needs," the old king huffed, bowing so deeply he tottered for a moment, almost losing his balance.

Emperor Quivalin said nothing until he and the three men had entered the library and the doors had soundlessly closed behind them. A deep black marble floor stretched into the far corners of the huge room. Above them, the ceiling lofted into the distance, a dark surface of rich, brown wood. The only light came from high, narrow windows of crystal; it fell around them as beams of heat and warmth before its reflections vanished in the light-absorbent darkness of the floor.

Though several soft chairs stood along the walls, none of the men moved to sit. Instead, the emperor fixed each of the others with a stare of piercing strength and impelling command.

"You three men are my greatest generals," Quivalin V said, his voice surprisingly soft beneath the intensity of his gaze. "And now you are the hope and the future of all humankind!"

The three stood a little taller at his words, their shoulders growing a trifle more broad. The emperor continued. "We have borne the elven savagery long enough. Their stubborn refusal to allow humans their rightful place in the plains has become too much to bear. The racial arrogance of their Speaker has turned diplomacy into insults. Our reasonable demands are mocked. Silvanesti intransigence must be wiped out!"

Abruptly Quivalin's gaze flashed to one of the trio—the oldest, if his white beard and long hair of the same color were any indication. Lines of strain and character marked the man's face, and his short stature nevertheless bespoke a quiet, contained power.

"Now, High General Barnet, tell me your plans."

The older warrior cleared his throat. A veteran of four decades of service to this emperor—and to Quivalin IV before him—Barnet nevertheless couldn't entirely calm himself in the face of that august presence.

"Excellency, we will advance into the plains in three great wings—a powerful thrust from the center, and two great hooks to the north and south. I myself will command the central wing—a thousand heavy lancers and fifty thousand sturdy footmen with metal armor, shields, and pikes. Sailors and woodsmen from Daltigoth and the south, mainly, including ten thousand with crossbow.

"We shall drive directly toward Sithelbec, which we know is the heart of the elven defense—a place the elven general must defend. Our aim is to force the enemy into combat before us, while the northern and southern wings complete the encirclement. They will serve as the mobile hammers, gathering the enemy against the anvil of my own solid force."

High General Barnett looked to one of his co-commanders. "General Xalthan commands the southern wing."

Xalthan, a red-bearded warrior with bristling eyebrows and missing front teeth, seemed to glower at the emperor with a savage aspect, but this was simply an effect of his warlike appearance. His voice, as he spoke, was deferential. "I have three brigades of heavy lancers, Excellency, and as many footmen as Barnett—armored in leather, to move more quickly."

Xalthan seemed to hesitate a moment, as if embarrassed, then he plunged boldly ahead. "The gnomish artillery, I must admit, has not lived up to expectations. But their engineers are busy even as we speak. I feel certain that the lava cannons will be activated early in the campaign."

The emperor's eyes narrowed slightly at the news. No one saw the facial gesture except for Xalthan, but the other two noticed that veteran commander's ruddy complexion grow visibly pale.

"And you, Giarna?" asked the emperor, turning to the third man. "How goes the grandest campaign of the Boy General?"

Giarna, whose youthfulness was apparent in his smooth skin and soft, curling beard, didn't react to his nickname. Instead, he stood easily, with a casualness that might have been interpreted as insolence, except there was crisp respect reflected in his expression as he pondered his answer. Even so, his eyes unsettled the watchers, even the emperor. They were dark and full of a deep and abiding menace that made him seem older than his years.

The other two generals scowled privately at the young man. After all, it was common knowledge that Giarna's favored status with the emperor was due more to the Duchess Suzine des Quivalin—niece of the emperor, and reputed mistress to the general himself—than to any inherent military skill.

Still, Giarna's battle prowess, demonstrated against rebellious keeps across the Vingaard Plains, was grudgingly admitted even by his critics. It was his mastery of strategy, not his individual courage or his grasp of tactics, that had yet to be proven.

Under ordinary circumstances, General Giarna's army command skills would not have been tested on the battlefield for some years yet—until he was older and more seasoned. However, a recent rash of tragic accidents—a panicked horse bucking, a jealous husband returning home, and a misunderstood command to retreat—had cost the lives of the three generals who had stood in line for this post. Thus Giarna, youthful though he was, had been given his opportunity.

Now he stood proudly before his emperor and replied.

"My force is the smallest, Excellency, but also the fastest. I have twenty thousand riders—horse archers and lancers; and also ten thousand footmen each of sword and longbowmen. It is my intention to march swiftly and come between the Wildrunners and their base in Sithelbec. Then I will wait for Kith-Kanan to come to me, and I will shred his army with my arrows and my horsemen."

Giarna made his report coolly, without so much as a nod to his peers, as if the other two commanders were excessive baggage on this, the Boy General's first great expedition. The older generals fumed; the implication was not lost on them.

Nor on the emperor. Quivalin V smiled at the plans of his generals. Beyond the walls of the cavernous library, within the vast palace, the roar of the admiring crowd could still be heard.

Abruptly the emperor clapped his hands, the sound echoing sharply through the large chamber. A side door to the room opened, and a woman advanced across the gleaming marble. Even the two older generals, both of whom distrusted and resented her, would have admitted that her beauty was stunning.

Her hair, of coppery red, spiraled around a diamond-encrusted tiara of rich platinum. A gown of green silk conformed to the full outline of her breasts and hips, accented by a belt of rubies and emeralds that enclosed her narrow waist. But it was her face that was most striking, with her high cheekbones and proud, narrow chin and, most significant, her eyes. They glowed with the same vibrance as the emeralds on her belt, the almost unnatural green of the Quivalin line.

Suzine Des Quivalin curtsied deeply to her uncle, the emperor. Her eyes remained downcast as she awaited his questions.

"What can you tell us about the state of the enemy's forces?" asked the ruler. "Has your mirror been of use in this regard?"

"Indeed, Excellency," she replied. "Though the range to the elven army is great, conditions have been good. I have been able to see much.

"The elven general, Kith-Kanan, has deployed his forces in thin screens throughout the plain, well forward of the fortress of Sithelbec. He has few horsemen—perhaps five hundred, certainly less than a thousand. Any one of your army's wings will outnumber his entire force, perhaps by a factor of two or three."

"Splendid," noted Quivalin. Again he clapped, this time twice.

The figure that emerged from a different door was perhaps as opposite from the woman as was conceivable. Suzine turned to leave as this stocky individual clumped into the room. She paused only long enough to meet Giarna's gaze, as if she was searching for something in his eyes. Whatever it was, she didn't find it. She saw nothing but the dark insatiable hunger for war. In another moment, she disappeared through the same door she had entered.

In the meantime, the other figure advanced toward the four men. The newcomer was stooped, almost apelike in posture, and barely four feet tall. His face was grotesque, an effect accentuated by his leering grin. And where Suzine's eyes crowned her beauty with pride and dignity, the mad, staring eyes of the dwarf showed white all around the tiny pupils and seemed to dart frantically from person to person.

If he felt any repugnance at the dwarf's appearance, the emperor didn't show it. Instead, he simply asked a question.

"What is the status of Thorbardin's involvement?"

"Most Exalted One, my own dwarves of the Theiwar

Clan offer you their unequivocal support. We share your hatred of the arrogant elves and wish nothing more than their defeat and destruction!"

"Nothing more, unless it be a sum of profit in the bargain," remarked the emperor, his voice neutral.

The dwarf bowed again, too thick-skinned to be offended. "Your Eminence may take reassurance from the fact that loyalty purchased is always owed to the wealthiest patron—and here you have no competition in all of Krynn!"

"Indeed," Quivalin added dryly. "But what of the other dwarves—the Hylar, the Daergar?"

"Alas," sighed the Theiwar dwarf. "They have not been so open-minded as my own clan. The Hylar, in particular, seem bound by ancient treaties and affections. Our influence is great, but thus far insufficient to break these ties."

The dwarf lowered his voice conspiratorially. "However, your lordliness, we have an agent in place—a Theiwar—and should be able to ensure that little excess of comfort is delivered to your enemies."

"Splendid," agreed the emperor. If he was curious as to the precise identity of the Theiwar agent, he gave no sign. "A vigorous season of warfare should bring them to heel. I hope to drive them from the plains before winter. The elven cowards will be ready to sign a treaty by spring!"

The emperor's eyes suddenly glowed with dull fire, the calculated sense of power and brutality that had allowed him to send thousands of men to their deaths in a dozen of his empire's wars. They flamed brighter at the thought of the arrogance of the long-lived elves and their accursed stubbornness. His voice became a growl.

"But if they continue to resist, we will not be content to wage war on the plains. Then you will march on the elven capital itself. If it is necessary to prove our might, we will reduce Silvanost itself to ashes!"

The generals bowed to their ruler, determined to do his bidding. Two of them felt fear—fear of his power and his whim. Beads of sweat collected upon their foreheads, dripping unnoticed down cheeks and beards.

General Giarna's brow, however, remained quite dry.

PART 1:

a taste of killing

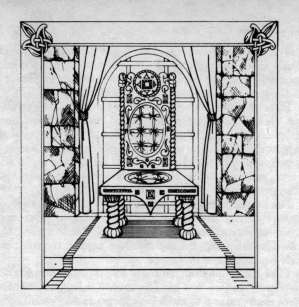

❧ 1 ❧

Late Winter, Year of the Raven, 2214 (PC)

The forest vanished into the distance on all sides, comfortingly huge, eternal, and unchanging. That expanse was the true heart, the most enduring symbol, of the elven nation of Silvanesti. The towering pines, with lush green needles so dark they were almost black, dominated, but glades of oak and maple, aspen, and birch flourished in many isolated pockets, giving the forest a diverse and ever-changing character.

Only from a truly exalted vantage—such as from the Tower of the Stars, the central feature of Silvanost—could the view be fully appreciated. This was where Sithas, Speaker of the Stars and ruler of Silvanesti, came to meditate and contemplate.

The sky loomed vast and distant overhead, a dome of black filled with glittering pinpoints of light. Krynn's moons had not yet risen, and this made the pristine beauty of the stars more brilliant, more commanding.

For a long time, Sithas stood at the lip of the tower's parapet. He found comfort in the stars, and in the deep and eternal woods beyond this island, beyond this city. Sithas sensed that the forest was the true symbol of his people's supremacy. Like the great trunks of forest giants, the ancient, centuries-living elves stood above the scurrying, scampering lesser creatures of the world.

Finally the Speaker of the Stars lowered his eyes to look upon that city, and immediately the sense of peace and splendor he had known dissipated. Instead, his mind focused on Silvanost, the ancient elven capital, the city that held his palace and his throne.

Faint traces of a drunken chant rose through the night air to disturb his ears. The song thrummed in the guttural basso of dwarves, as if to mock his concern and consternation.

Dwarves! They are everywhere in Silvanost! Everywhere, in the city of elves, he thought grimly.

Yet the dwarves were a necessary evil, Sithas admitted with a sigh. The war with the humans called for extremely careful negotiations with powerful Thorbardin, the dwarven stronghold south of the disputed lands. The power of that vast and warlike nation, thrown behind either human Ergoth or elven Silvanesti, could well prove decisive.

Once, a year earlier, the Speaker of the Stars had assumed the dwarves were firmly in the elven camp. His negotiations with the esteemed Hylar dwarf Dunbarth Ironthumb had presented a unified front against human encroachment. Sithas had assumed that dwarven troops would soon stand beside the elves in the disputed plainslands.

Yet, to date, King Hal-Waith of Thorbardin had not yet sent a single regiment of dwarven fighters, nor had he released to Kith-Kanan's growing army any of the great stocks of dwarven weapons. The patient dwarves were not about to be hurried into any rash wars.

So a dwarven diplomatic mission was a necessity in Silvanost. And now that war had begun, such missions required sizable escorts—in the case of the recently arrived dwarven general Than-Kar, some one thousand loyal axemen.

Surprising himself, Sithas thought with fondness of the previous dwarven ambassador. Dunbarth Ironthumb had fully possessed all the usual uncouthness of a dwarf, but he also had a sense of humor and was self-effacing, traits that had relaxed and amused Sithas.

Than-Kar had none of these traits. A swarthy-complected Theiwar, the general was rude to the point of belligerence. Impatient and uncooperative, the ambassador actually seemed to act as an impediment to communication.

Take, for example, the messenger who had arrived from Thorbardin more than a week ago. This dwarf, after his months-long march, must certainly have brought important news from the dwarven king. Yet Than-Kar had said nothing, had not even requested an audience with the Speaker of the Stars. This was the reason for the conference Sithas had scheduled for the morrow, peremptorily summoning Than-Kar to the meeting in order to find out what the Theiwar knew.

His mood as thick as the night, Sithas let his gaze follow the dark outlines of the river Thon-Thalas, the wide waterway surrounding Silvanost and its island. The water was smooth, and he could see starlight reflected in its crystal surface. Then the breeze rose again, clouding the surface with ripples and washing the chant of the dwarven axemen away.

Seeing the river, the Speaker's mind filled with a new and most unwelcome memory, a scene as clear in its every detail as it was painful in its recollection. Two weeks ago or more it was now, yet it might as well have been that very morning. That was when the newly recruited regiments had departed westward, to join Kith-Kanan's forces.

The long columns of warriors had lined the riverbank, waiting their turns to board the ferry and cross. From the far bank of the Thon-Thalas, they were about to begin their long march to the disputed lands, five hundred miles to the west. Their five thousand spears, swords, and longbows would prove an important addition to the Wildrunners.

Yet, for the first time in the history of Silvanesti, the elves had needed to be bribed into taking up arms for their

Speaker, their nation. A hundred steel bounty, paid upon recruitment, had been offered as incentive. Even this had not brought volunteers flocking to the colors, though after several weeks of recruitment regiments of sufficient size had finally been raised.

And then there had been the scene at the riverbank.

The cleric Miritelisina had just recently emerged from the cell where Sithas's father, Sithel, had thrown her for treason a year earlier. The matriarch of the faith of Quenesti Pah, benign goddess of healing and health, Miritelisina had voiced loud objections to the war with the humans. She had had the audacity to lead a group of elven females in a shrill, hysterical protest against the conflict with Ergoth. It had been a sickening display, worthy more of humans than of elves. Yet the cleric had enjoyed a surprisingly large amount of support from the onlooking citizens of Silvanesti.

Sithas had promptly ordered Miritelisina back to prison, and his guard had disrupted the gathering with crisp efficiency. Several females had been wounded, one fatally. At the same time, one of the heavily laden river craft had overturned, drowning several newly recruited elves. All in all, these were bad omens.

At least, the Speaker realized, the outbreak of war had driven the last humans from the city. The pathetic refugees of the troubles on the plains—many with elven spouses— had marched back to their homelands. Those who could fight had joined the Wildrunners, the army of Silvanost, centered around the members of the House Protectorate. The others had taken shelter in the great fortress of Sithelbec. Ironic, thought Sithas, that humans married to elves should be sheltered in an elven fortress, safe against the onslaught of human armies!

Still, in every other way, the city that Sithas loved seemed to be slipping further and further from his control.

His gaze lingered to the west, rising to the horizon, and he wished he could see beyond. Kith-Kanan was there somewhere under this same star-studded sky. His twin brother might even be looking eastward at this moment; at least, Sithas wanted to believe that he felt some contact.

For a moment, Sithas found himself wishing that his father still lived. How he missed Sithel's wisdom, his steady counsel and firm guidance! Had his father ever known these doubts, these insecurities? The idea seemed impossible to the son. Sithel had been a pillar of strength and conviction. He would not have wavered in his pursuit of this war, in the protection of the elven nation against outside corruption!

The purity of the elven race was a gift of the gods, with its longevity and its serene majesty. Now that purity was threatened--by human blood, to be sure, but also by ideas of intermingling, trade, artisanship, and social tolerance.

The nation faced a very crucial time indeed. In the west, he knew, elves and humans had begun to intermarry with disturbing frequency, giving birth to a whole bastard race of half-elves.

By all the gods, it was an abomination, an affront to the heavens themselves! Sithas felt his face flush, and his hands clenched. If he had worn a sword, he would have seized it then, so powerfully did the urge to fight come over him. The elves *must* prevail—they *would* prevail!

Again he felt his distance from the conflict, and it loomed as a yawning chasm of frustration before him. As yet they had received no word of battle, although he knew that nearly a month earlier, the great invasion had begun. His brother had reported three great human columns, all moving purposefully into the plainslands. Sithas wanted to go and fight himself, to lend his strength to winning the war, and it was all he could do to hold himself back. Inevitably his sense of reason prevailed.

At times, the war seemed so far away, so unreachable. Yet, other times, he found it beside him, here in Silvanost, in his palace, in his thoughts . . . in his very bedroom.

His bedroom. Sithas gave a rueful smile and shook his head in wonder. He thought of Hermathya, how months earlier his feelings for her had approached loathing.

Yet with the coming of war, a change had come over his wife as well. Now she supported him as never before, standing beside him every day against the complaints and pettiness of his people . . . and lying beside him every night as well.

He heard, or perhaps he felt, the soft rustle of silk, and then she was beside him. He breathed a deep sigh—a sound of contentment and satisfaction. The two of them stood alone, six hundred feet above the city, atop the Tower of the Stars, beneath the brilliant light shower of its namesake.

Her mouth, with its round lips so unusually full for an elf, was creased by the trace of a smile—a sly, secret smile that he found strangely beguiling. She stood beside him, touching a hand to his chest and leaning her head on his shoulder.

He smelled her hair, rich with the scent of lilacs, yet in color as bright as copper. Her smooth skin glowed with a milky luminescence, and he felt her warm lips upon his neck. A warm rush of desire swept through him, fading only slightly as she relaxed and stood beside him in silence.

Sithas thought of his volatile wife—how pleasant it was to have her come to him thus, and how rare such instances had been in the past. Hermathya was a proud and beautiful elfwoman, used to getting her own way. Sometimes he wondered if she regretted their marriage, arranged by their parents. Once, he knew, she had been the lover of his brother—indeed, Kith-Kanan had rebelled against his father's authority and fled Silvanost when her engagement to Sithas had been announced. Did she ever regret her choice? How well had she calculated her future as wife of the Speaker of the Stars? He did not know—perhaps, in fact, he was afraid to ask her.

"Have you seen my cousin yet?" she asked after a few minutes.

"Lord Quimant? Yes, he came to the Hall of Balif earlier today. I must say, he seems to have an excellent grip on the problems of weapon production. He knows mining, smelting, and smithing. His aid is much needed . . . and would be much appreciated. We are not a nation of weaponsmiths like the dwarves."

"Clan Oakleaf has long made the finest of elven blades," Hermathya replied proudly. "That is known throughout Silvanesti!"

"It is not the quality that worries me, my dear. It is in the quantity of weapons that we lag sadly behind the humans, and the dwarves. We cleaned out the royal armories in order to outfit the last regiments we sent to the west."

"Quimant will solve your problems, I'm certain. Will he be coming to Silvanost?"

The estate of Clan Oakleaf lay to the north of the elven capital, near the mines where they excavated the iron for their small foundaries. The clan, the central power behind House Metalline, was the primary producer of weapons-quality steel in the kingdom of Silvanesti. Lately its influence had grown, due to the necessity of increased weapons production brought on by the war. The mines were worked by slaves, mostly human and Kagonesti elves, but this was a fact Sithas had to accept because of his nation's emergency. Lord Quimant, the son of Hermathya's eldest uncle, was being groomed as the spokesman and leader of Clan Oakleaf, and his services for the estate were important.

"I believe he will. I've offered him chambers in the palace, as well as incentives for the Oakleaf clan—mineral rights, steady supplies of coal . . . and labor."

"It would be wonderful to have some of my family around again!" Hermathya's voice rose, joyful as a young girl's. "This can be such a *lonely* place, with all of your attention directed to the war."

He lowered his hand, sliding it along the smooth silk of her gown, down her back, his strong fingers caressing her. She sighed and held him tighter. "Well, maybe not *all* of your attention," she added, with a soft laugh.

Sithas wanted to tell her what a comfort she had been to him, how much she had eased the burdens of his role as leader of the elven nation. He wondered at the change that had come over her, but he said nothing. That was his nature, and perhaps his weakness.

It was Hermathya who next spoke.

"There is another thing I must tell you. . . ."

"Good news or bad?" he asked, idly curious.

"You will need to judge that for yourself, though I suspect you will be pleased."

He turned to look at her, holding both of his hands on her shoulders. That secret smile still played about her lips.

"Well?" he demanded, feigning impatience. "Don't tease me all night! Tell me!"

"You and I, great Speaker of the Stars, are going to have a baby. An heir."

Sithas gaped at her, unaware that his jaw had dropped in a most unelven lack of dignity. His mind reeled, and a profound explosion of joy rose within his heart. He wanted to shout his delight from the tower top, to let the word ring through the city like a prideful cry.

For a moment, he truly forgot about everything—the war, the dwarves, the logistics and weapons that had occupied him. He pulled his wife to him and kissed her. He held her for a long time under the starlight, above the city that had so troubled him earlier.

But for now, all was right with the world.

* * * * *

The next day Than-Kar came to see Sithas, though the Theiwar dwarf arrived nearly fifteen minutes after the time indicated in the Speaker's summons.

Sithas awaited him, impatiently seated upon the great emerald throne of his ancestors, located in the center of the great Hall of Audience. This vast chamber occupied the base of the Tower of the Stars, with its sheer walls soaring upward into the dizzying heights. Above, six hundred feet over their heads, the top of the tower stood open to the sky.

Than-Kar clumped into the hall at the head of a column of twelve bodyguards, almost as if he expected ambush. Twoscore elves of the House Protectorate—the royal guard of Silvanesti—snapped to attention around the periphery of the hall.

The Theiwar sniffed his nose loudly, the rude gesture echoing through the hall, as he approached the Speaker. Sithas studied the dwarf, carefully masking his distaste.

Like all Theiwar dwarves, Than-Kar's eyes seemed to stare wildly, with the whites showing all around the pinpoint pupils. His lips curled in a perpetual sneer, and despite his ambassadorial station, his beard and hair remained unkempt, his leather clothes filthy. How unlike Dunbarth Ironthumb!

The Theiwar bowed perfunctorily and then looked up at Sithas, his beady eyes glittering with antagonism.

"We'll make this brief," said the elf coldly. "I desire to know what word has come from your king. He has had time to reply, and the questions we have sent have not been formally answered."

"As a matter of fact, I was preparing my written reply when your courier interrupted me with this summons yesterday. I had to delay my progress in order to hasten to this meeting."

Yes, Than-Kar must have made haste, for he obviously hadn't taken time to run a comb through his hair or change his grease-spattered tunic, thought Sithas. The Speaker held his tongue, albeit with difficulty.

"However, insofar as I am here and taking up the speaker's valuable time, I can summarize the message that I have received from Thorbardin."

"Please, do," Sithas requested dryly.

"The Royal Council of Thorbardin finds that, to date, there is insufficient cause to support elven warmaking in the plains," announced the dwarf bluntly.

"What?" Sithas stiffened, no longer able to retain his impassive demeanor. "That is a contradiction of everything our meetings with Dunbarth established! Surely you—your people—recognize that the human threat extends beyond mere grazing rights on the plains!"

"There is no evidence of a threat to our interests."

"No threat?" The elf cut him off rudely. "You *know* humans. They will stretch and grab whatever they can. They will seize our plains, *your* mountains, the forest—*everything!*"

Than-Kar regarded him coolly, those wide, staring eyes seeming to gleam with delight. Abruptly Sithas realized that he was wasting his time with this arrogant Theiwar. Angrily he stood, half fearing that he would strike out at the dwarf and very much desiring to do just that. Still, enough of his dignity and self-control remained to stay his hand. After all, a war with the dwarves was the last thing they needed right now.

"This conference is concluded," he said stiffly.

Than-Kar nodded—smugly, Sithas thought—and turned to lead his escort from the hall.

Sithas stared after the dwarven ambassador, his anger still seething. He would not—he *could* not—allow this to be the final impasse!

But what else could he do? No ideas arrived to lighten the oppressive burden of his mood.

2

SPRING, 2214 (PC)

The horse pranced nervously along the ridgetop, staying within the protective foliage of the tree line. Thick, blue-green pines enclosed the mount and its elven rider on three sides. Finally the great stallion Kijo stood still, allowing Kith-Kanan to peer through the moist, aromatic branches to the vast expanse of open country beyond.

Nearby, two of the Wildrunners—Kith's personal bodyguards—sat alertly in their saddles, swords drawn and eyes alert. Those elves, too, were nervous at the sight of their leader possibly exposing himself to the threat in the valley below.

And what a threat it was! The long column of the human army snaked into the distance as far as the keen-eyed elves could see from their vantage on the ridgetop. The vanguard of the army, a company of heavily armored lancers riding huge, lumbering war-horses, had already passed them by.

Now ranks of spearmen, thousands upon thousands, marched past, perhaps a mile away down the gradually sloping ridge. This was the central wing of the massive Army of Ergoth, which followed the most direct route toward Sithelbec and presented the most immediate threat to the Wildrunners. Kith-Kanan turned with a grim smile, and Kijo pranced into the deeper shelter of the forest.

The commander of the Wildrunners knew his force was ready for this, the opening battle of his nation's first war in over four centuries. Not since the Second Dragon War had the elves of the House Protectorate taken to the field to defend their nation against an external threat.

The ring on his finger—the Ring of Balifor—had been given to his father as a reminder of the alliance between kender and elves during the Second Dragon War. Now he wore it and prepared to do battle in a new cause. For a moment, he wondered what this war would be named when Astinus took up his pen to scribe the tale in his great annals.

Though Kith-Kanan was young for an elf—he had been born a mere ninety-three years ago—he felt the weight of long tradition riding in the saddle with him. He knew no compelling hatred toward these humans, yet he recognized the threat they presented. If they weren't stopped here, half of Silvanesti would be gobbled up by the rapacious human settlers and the elves would be driven into a small corner of their once vast holdings.

The humans had to be defeated. It was Kith-Kanan's job, as commander of the Wildrunners, to see that the elven nation was victorious.

Another figure moved through the trees, bringing the bodyguards' swords swooshing forth, until they recognized the rider.

"Sergeant-Major Parnigar." Kith-Kanan nodded to the veteran Wildrunner, his chief aide and most reliable scout. The sergeant was dressed in leather armor of green and brown, and he rode a stocky, nimble pony.

"The companies are in place, sir—the riders behind the ridge, with a thousand elves of Silvanost bearing pike behind them." Parnigar, a veteran warrior who had fought in the Second Dragon War, had helped recruit the first wild elves into Kith-Kanan's force. Now he reported on their readiness to die for that cause. "The Kagonesti archers are well hidden and well supplied. We can only hope the humans react as we desire."

Parnigar looked skeptical as he spoke, but Kith suspected this was just the elf's cautious nature. The sergeant's face was as gray and leathery as an old map. His strapping arms rested on the pommel of his saddle with deceptive ease. His green eyes missed nothing. Even as he talked to his general, the sergeant-major was scanning the horizon.

Parnigar slouched casually in his saddle, his posture more like a human's than an elf's. Indeed, the veteran had taken a human wife some years before, and in many ways he seemed to enjoy the company of the short-lived race. He spoke quickly and moved with a certain restless agitation—both characteristics that tended to mark humans far more typically than elves.

Yet Parnigar knew his roots. He was an heir of the House Protectorate and had served in the Wildrunners since he had first learned to handle a sword. He was the most capable warrior that Kith-Kanan knew, and the elven general was glad to have him at his side.

"The human scouts have been slain by ambush," Kith-Kanan told him. "Their army has lost its eyes. It is almost time. Come, ride with me!"

The commander of the Wildrunners nudged Kijo's flanks with his knees, and the stallion exploded into a dash through the forest. So nimble was the horse's step that he dashed around tree trunks with Kith-Kanan virtually a blur. Parnigar raced behind, with the two hapless guards spurring their steeds in a losing struggle to keep pace.

For several minutes, the pair dashed through the forest, the riders' faces lashed by pine needles, but the horses' hooves landing true. Abruptly the trees stopped, exposing the wide, gently rolling ridgetop. Below, to the right, marched the endless army of humankind.

Kith-Kanan nudged Kijo again, and the stallion burst into view of the humans below. The elven general's blond hair trailed in the sun behind him, for his helmet remained lashed to the back of his saddle. As he rode, he raised a steel-mailed fist.

He made a grand figure, racing along the crest of the hill above the teeming mass of his enemy. Like his twin brother Sithas, his face was handsome and proud, with prominent cheekbones and a sharp, strong chin. Though he was slender—like every one of his race—his tall physique lifted him above the deep pommels of the saddle.

Instantly the trumpeters of Silvanost sprang to their feet. They had lain in the grass along this portion of the crest. Raising their golden horns in unison, they brayed a challenge across the rolling prairie below. Behind the trumpeters, concealed from the humans by the crest of the ridge, the elven riders mounted their horses while the bowmen knelt in the tall grass, waiting for the command to action.

The great column of humans staggered like a confused centipede. Men turned to gape at the spectacle, observing pennants and banners that burst from the woods in a riotous display of color. All order vanished from the march as each soldier instinctively yielded to astonishment and the beginnings of fear.

Then the human army gasped, for the elven riders abruptly swarmed over the ridgetop in a long, precise line. Horses pranced, raising their forefeet in a high trot, while banners unfurled overhead and steel lance tips gleamed before them. They numbered but five hundred, yet every human who saw them swore later that they were attacked by thousands of elven riders.

Onward the elven horsemen came, their line remaining parade-ground sharp. On the valley floor, some of the humans broke and ran, while others raised spears or swords, ready and even eager for battle.

From the front of the vast human column, the huge brigade of heavy lancers turned its mighty war-horses toward the flank. Yet they were two miles away, and their companies quickly lost coherence as they struggled around other regiments—the footmen—that were caught behind them.

The elven riders raced closer to the center of the column, the thunder of their hooves crashing and shaking the earth. Then, two hundred feet from their target, they stopped. Each of the five hundred horses pivoted, and from the dust of the sudden maneuver, five hundred arrows arced forth, over the great blocks of humans and then down, like deadly hawks seeking out their terrified victims.

Another volley ripped into the human ranks, and suddenly the elven riders retreated, dashing across the same ridge they had charged down mere moments before.

In that same instant, the humans realized they were going to be robbed of the satisfaction of fighting, and a roar of outrage erupted from ten thousand throats. Swords raised, shields brandished, men broke from the column without command of their captains, chasing and cursing the elven riders. The enraged mob swept up the slope in chaotic disarray, united only in its fury.

Abruptly a trumpet cry rang from the low summit, and ranks of green-glad elves appeared in the grass before the charging humans, as if they had suddenly sprouted from the ground.

In the next instant, the sky darkened beneath a shower of keen elven arrows, their steel tips gleaming in the sunlight as they arced high above the humans, then tipped in their inevitable descent. Even before the first volley fell, another rippled outward, as steady and irresistible as hail.

The arrows tore into the human ranks with no regard for armor, rank, or quickness. Instead, the deadly rain showered the mob with complete randomness, puncturing steel helmets and breastplates and slicing through leather shoulder pads. Shrieks and cries from the wounded rose in hysterical chorus, while other humans fell silently, writhing in mute agony or lying still upon the now-reddening grass.

Again and again the arrows soared outward, and the mob wavered in its onrush. Bodies littered the field. Some of these crawled or squirmed pathetically toward safety, ignored by the mindless rush of the others.

As more of them died, fear rose like a palpable cloud over the heads of the humans. Then, by twos and fives and tens, they turned and raced back toward the rest of the column. Finally they retreated in hundreds, harried back down the newly mud-covered slope by pursuing missile fire. As they vanished, so did the elven archers, withdrawing at a trot over the crest of the ridge.

At last the human heavy lancers approached, and a cheer

rose from the rest of the great army. A thousand bold knights, clad in armor from head to toe, urged their massive horses onward. The great beasts lumbered like monsters, buried beneath clanking plates of barding. A cloud of bright pennants fluttered over the thundering mass.

Kith-Kanan, still mounted upon his proud stallion, studied these new warriors from the ridgetop. Caution, not fear, tempered his hopes as the great weight of horses, men, and metal churned closer. The heavy knights, he knew, were the army's most lethal attack force.

He had planned for this, but only the reality of things would show whether the Wildrunners stood equal to the task. For a moment, Kith-Kanan's courage wavered, and he considered ordering a fast retreat from the field—a disastrous idea, he quickly told himself, for his hope now lay in steadfast courage, not flight. The knights drew nearer, and Kith-Kanan wheeled and galloped after the archers.

The great steeds rumbled inexorably up the slope, toward the gentle crest where the elven riders and archers had disappeared. They couldn't see the foe, but they hoped that the elves would be found just beyond the ridgetop. The knights kicked their mounts and shouted their challenges as they crested the rise, springing with renewed speed toward the enemy. In their haste, they broke their tight ranks, eager to crush the deadly archers and light elven lancers.

Instead, they met a phalanx of elven pikemen, the gleaming steel tips of the Wildrunners' weapons arrayed as a bristling wall of death. The elves stood shoulder to shoulder in great blocks, facing outward from all sides. The riders and archers had taken shelter in the middle of these blocks, while three ranks of pikemen—one kneeling, one crouching, and one standing—kept their weapons fixed, promising certain death to any horse reckless enough to close.

The great war-horses, sensing the danger, turned, bucked, and spun, desperate to avoid the rows of pikes. Unfortunately for the riders, each horse, as it turned, met another performing a similar contortion. Many of the beasts crashed to the ground, and still more riders were thrown by their panicked steeds. They lay in their heavy armor, too weighted down even to climb to their feet.

Arrows whistled outward from the Wildrunners. Though

the shortbows of the elven riders were ineffective against the armored knights, the longbows of the foot archers drove their barbed missiles through the heaviest plate at this close range. Howls of pain and dismay now drowned out the battle cries among the knights, and in moments the cavalry, in mass, turned and lumbered back across the ridgetop, leaving several dozen of their number moaning on the ground almost at the feet of the elven pikemen.

"Run, you bastards!" Parnigar's shout was a gleeful bark beside Kith-Kanan.

The general, too, felt his lieutenant's elation. They had held the knights! They had broken the charge!

Kith-Kanan and Parnigar watched the retreat of the knights from the center of the largest contingent. The sergeant-major looked at his commander, gesturing to the fallen knights. Some of these unfortunate men lay still, knocked unconscious by the fall from horseback, while others struggled to their knees or twitched in obvious pain. More humans lay at the top of the slope, their bodies punctured by elven arrows.

"Shall I give the order to finish them?" Parnigar asked, ready to send a rank of swordsmen forward. The grim warrior's eyes flashed.

"No," Kith-Kanan said. He looked grimly at his sergeant's raised eyebrows. "This is the first skirmish of a great war. Let it not be said we began it with butchery."

"But—but they're knights! These are the most powerful humans in that entire army! What if they are healed and restored to arms? Surely you don't want them to ride against us again?" Parnigar kept his voice low but made his arguments precisely.

"You're right—the power of the heavy knights is lethal. If we hadn't been fully prepared for their assault, I'm not certain we could have held them. Still . . ."

Kith-Kanan's mind balked at the situation before him, until a solution suddenly brightened his expression. "Send the swordsmen forward—but not to kill. Have them take the weapons of the fallen knights and any banners, pennants, and the like that they can find. Return with these, but let the humans live."

Parnigar nodded, satisfied with his general's decision. He

raised a hand and the line of pikemen parted, allowing the sergeant-major's charger to trot forward. Selecting a hundred veterans, he started the task of stripping the humans of their badges and pennants.

Kith turned, sensing movement behind him. He saw the pikemen parting there, too, this time to admit someone—a grimy elven rider straddling a foaming, dust-covered horse. Through the dust, Kith recognized a shock of hair the color of snow.

"White-lock! It's good to see you." Kith swung easily from his saddle as the Kagonesti elf did the same. The general clasped the rider's hand warmly, searching the wild elf's eyes for a hint of his news.

White-lock rubbed a hand across his dust-covered face, revealing the black and white stripes painted across his forehead. Typical of the wild elves, he was fully painted for war—and covered by the grit of his long ride. A scout and courier for the Wildrunners, he had ridden hundreds of miles to report on the movements of the human army.

Now White-lock nodded, deferentially but coolly, toward Kith-Kanan. "The humans fare poorly in the south," he began. "They have not yet crossed the border into elven lands, so slowly do they march."

White-lock's tone dripped with scorn—a scorn equal to that Kith had heard him use when describing the "civilized" elves of crystalline Silvanost. Indeed, the wild elves of Kagonesti in many cases bore little love for their cousins in the cities—antipathy, to be sure, that mirrored the hatred and prejudice held by the Silvanesti elves for *any* race other than their own.

"Any word out of Thorbardin?"

"Nothing reliable." The Kagonesti continued his report, his tone revealing that dwarves ranked near the bottom on his list of worthwhile peoples. "They promise to assist us when the humans have committed sufficient provocation, but I won't believe them till I see them stand and fight."

"Why does the southern wing of the Ergothian army march so slowly?" Kith-Kanan, through his Wildrunner scouts, had been tracking the three great wings of the vast Caergoth army, each of which was far greater in size than his entire force of Wildrunners.

"They have difficulties with the gnomes," White-lock continued. "They drag some kind of monstrous machine with them, pulled by a hundred oxen, and it steams and belches smoke. A whole train of coal wagons follows, carrying fuel for this machine."

"It must surely be some type of weapon—but what? Do you know?"

White-lock shook his head. "It is now mired in the bottomlands a few miles from the border. Perhaps they will leave it behind. If not . . ." The Kagonesti elf shrugged. It was simply another idiocy of the enemy that he could not predict or fathom.

"You bring good news," Kith noted with satisfaction. He planted his hands on his hips and looked at the ridgeline above, where Parnigar and his footmen were returning. Many waved captured human banners or held aloft helmets with long, trailing plumes. Every so often he saw a dejected and disarmed human scuttling upward and disappearing over the ridge as if he still feared for his life.

Today Kith and the Wildrunners had directed a sharp blow against the central wing of the human army. He hoped the confusion and frustration of the elven attack would delay their march for several days. The news from the south was encouraging. It would take months for a threat to develop there. But what of the north?

His worries lingered as the Wildrunners quickly reformed from battle into march formation. They would pass through partially forested terrain, so the elven army moved in five broad, irregular columns. They followed parallel routes, with about a quarter of a mile between columns. If necessary, they could easily outdistance any human army, whether mounted or on foot.

Kith-Kanan, with Parnigar and a company of riders, remained behind until sunset. He was pleased to see the human army encamp at the scene of the attack. In the morning, he suspected, they would send forth huge and cumbersome reconnaissances, none of which would find any trace of the elves.

Finally the last of the Wildrunners, with Kith in the lead, turned their stocky, fast horses to the west. They would leave the field in possession of the foe, but a foe a little more bewildered, a little more frightened, than the day before.

The elven riders passed easily along forest trails at a fast walk, and at a canter through moonlit meadows. It was as they crossed one of these that movement in the fringe of the treeline pulled Kijo up sharply. A trio of riders approached. Kith recognized the first two as members of his guard.

"A messenger, sir—from the north!" The guards pulled aside as Kith stared in shock at the third rider.

The elf slumped in his saddle like a corpse that had been placed astride a horse. As he looked toward Kith-Kanan, his eyes flickered with a momentary hope.

"We tried to hold them back, sir—to harass them, as you commanded!" the elf reported in a rush. "The human wing to the north moved onto the plain, and we struck them!"

The scout's voice belied his looks. It was taut and firm, the voice of a man who spoke the truth and who desperately wanted to be believed. Now he shook his head. "But no matter how quickly we moved, they moved more quickly. They struck at *us*, sir! They wiped out a hundred elves in one camp and routed the Kagonesti back to the woods! They move with unbelievable stealth and speed!"

"They advance southward, then?" Kith-Kanan asked, instinctively knowing the answer, for he immediately understood that the human commander of the northern wing must be an unusually keen and aggressive foe.

"Yes! Faster than I would have believed, had I not seen it myself! They ride like the wind, these humans. They have surrounded most of the northern pickets. I alone escaped."

The messenger's eyes met Kith's, and the elf spoke with all the intensity of his soul. "But that is not the worst of it, my general! Now they sweep to the east of my own path. Already you may be cut off from Sithelbec!"

"Impossible!" Kith barked the denial. The fortress, or city, of Sithelbec was his headquarters and his base of operations. It was far to the rear of the battle zone. "There can't be any humans within a hundred miles of there!"

But again he looked into the eyes of the messenger, and he had to believe the terrible news. "All right," he said grimly. "They've stolen a march on us. It's time for the Wildrunners to seize it back."

🍂 3 🍂

that night, in the army of ergoth

The sprawling tent stood in the center of the vast en-
campment. Three peaks stood high, marking the poles that
divided the shelter into a trio of chambers. Though the
stains of the season's campaign marked its sides, and seams
showed where the top had been mended, the colorless canvas structure had a certain air about it, as if it was a little
more important, a little more proud than the tents flowing
to the horizon around it.

The huge camp was not a permanent gathering, and so
the rows of straight-backed tents ran haphazardly, wherever the rolling ground, crisscrossed by numerous ravines,
allowed. Green pastures, feeding grounds for twenty thousand horses, marked the fringes of the encampment. As

dusk settled, the army's shelters lined up in gray anonymity, except for this high, three-peaked tent.

The inside of that structure, as well, would never be mistaken for the abode of some soldier. Here cascades of silken draperies—deep browns, rich golds, and the iridescent black that was so popular among Ergothian nobles—covered the sides, blocking any view of the harsh realities beyond the canvas walls.

Suzine des Quivalin sat in the tent, studying a crystal glass before her. Her coppery hair no longer coiled about the tiara of diamond-studded platinum. Instead, it gathered in a bun at the back of her head, though its length still cascaded more than a foot down her back. She wore a practical leather skirt, but her blouse was of fine silk. Her skin was clean, making her unique among all these thousands of humans.

Indeed, captains and sergeants and troopers alike grumbled about the favors shown to the general's woman—hot water for bathing! A luxurious tent—ten valuable horses were required just to haul her baggage.

Still, though grumbling occurred, none of it happened within earshot of the commander. General Giarna led his force with skill and determination, but he was a terrifying man who would brook no argument, whether it be about his tactics or his woman's comforts. Thus the men kept the remarks very quiet and very private.

Now Suzine sat upon a large chair, cushioned with silk-covered pillows of down, but she didn't take advantage of that softness. Instead, she sat at the edge of the seat, tension visible in her posture and in the rapt concentration of her face as she studied the crystal surface before her.

The glass looked like a normal mirror, but it didn't show a reflection of the lady's very lovely face. Instead, as she studied the image, she saw a long line of foot soldiers. They were clean-shaven, blond of hair, and carried long pikes or thin, silver swords.

She watched the army of Kith-Kanan.

For a time, she touched the mirror, and her vision ran back and forth along the winding column. Her lips moved silently as she counted longbows and pikes and horses. She watched the elves form and march. She noted the precision with which the long, fluid columns moved across the plains, retaining their precise intervals as they did so.

But then her perusal reached the head of the column, and here she lingered. She studied the one who rode at the head of that force, the one she knew was Kith-Kanan, twin brother to the elven ruler.

She admired his tall stance in the saddle, the easy, graceful way that he raised his hand, gesturing to his outriders or summoning a messenger. Narrow wings rose to a pair of peaks atop his dark helmet. His dark plate mail looked worn, and a heavy layer of dust covered it, yet she could discern its quality and the easy way he wore it, as comfortably as many a human would wear his soft cotton tunic.

Her lips parted slightly, and she didn't sense the pace of her breathing slowly increase. The lady did not hear the tent flap move behind her, so engrossed was she in her study of the handsome elven warrior.

Then a shadow fell across her, and she looked up with a sharp cry. The mirror faded until it showed only the lady, her face twisted in an expression of guilt mixed with indignation.

"You could announce your presence!" she snapped, standing to face the tall man who had entered.

"I am commander of the camp. General Giarna of Ergoth need announce his presence to no one, save the emperor himself," the armor-plated figure said quietly. His black eyes fixed upon the woman's, then shifted to the mirror. Those eyes of the Boy General frightened her—they were hardly boyish, and not entirely human, either. Dark and brooding, they sometimes blazed with an internal fire that was fueled, she sensed, by something that was beyond her understanding. At other times, however, they gaped, black and empty. She found this dispassionate void even more frightening than his rage.

Suddenly he snarled and Suzine gasped in fright. She would have backed away, save for the fact that her dressing table blocked any retreat. For a moment, she felt certain he would strike her. It would not be the first time. But then she looked into his eyes and knew that, for the moment, anyway, she was safe.

Instead of violent rage, she saw there a hunger that, while

frightening, did not presage a blow. Instead, it signaled a desperate yearning for a need that could never be satisfied. It was one of the things that had first drawn her to him, this strange hunger. Once she had felt certain that she could slake it.

Now she knew better. The attraction that had once drawn her to Giarna had waned, replaced for the most part by fear, and now when she saw that look in his eyes, she mostly pitied him.

The general grunted, shaking his head wearily. His short black hair lay sweaty and tousled on his head. She knew he would have had his helmet on until he entered the tent, and then taken it off in deference to her.

"Lady Suzine, I seek information and have been worried by your long silence. Tell me, what have you seen in your magic mirror?"

"I'm sorry, my lord," replied Suzine. Her eyes fell, and she hoped that the flush across her cheeks couldn't be noticed. She took a deep breath, regaining her composure.

"The elven army countermarches quickly—faster than you expected," she explained, her voice crisp and efficient. "They will confront you before you can march to Sithelbec."

General Giarna's eyes narrowed, but his face showed no other emotion. "This captain . . . what's his name?"

"Kith-Kanan," Suzine supplied.

"Yes. He seems alert—more so than any human commander I've faced. I would have wagered a year's pay that he couldn't have moved so fast."

"They march with urgency. They make good time, even through the woods."

"They'll have to stick to the forests," growled the general, "because as soon as I meet them, I shall rule the plains."

Abruptly General Giarna looked at Suzine inquiringly. "What is the word on the other two wings?"

"Xalthan is still paralyzed. The lava cannon is mired in the lowlands, and he seems unwilling to advance until the gnomes free it."

The general snorted in amused derision. "Just what I expected from that fool. And Barnet?"

"The central wing has gone into a defensive formation, as

if they expect attack. They haven't moved since yesterday afternoon."

"Excellent. The enemy comes to me, and my erstwhile allies twiddle their thumbs!" General Giarna's black beard split apart as he grinned. "When I win this battle, the emperor cannot help but realize who his greatest warrior is!"

He turned and paced, speaking more to himself than to her. "We will drive against him, break him before Sithelbec! We have assurances that the dwarves will stay out of the war, and the elves alone cannot hope to match our numbers. The victory will be *mine!*"

He turned back to her, those dark eyes flaming again, and Suzine felt another kind of fear—the fear of the doe as it trembles before the slavering jaws of the wolf. Again the general whirled in agitation, pounding his fist into the palm of his other hand.

Suzine cast a sidelong glance at the mirror, as if she feared someone might be listening. The surface was natural, reflecting only the pair in the tent. In the mirror, she saw General Giarna step toward her. She turned to face him as he placed his hands on her shoulders.

She knew what he wanted, what she would—she *must*—give him. Their contact was brief and violent. Giarna's passion contorted him, as if she was the vent for all of his anxieties. The experience bruised her, gave her a sense of uncleanliness that nearly brought her to despair. Afterward, she wanted to reach out and cover the mirror, to smash it or at least turn it away.

Instead, she hid her feelings, as she had learned to do so well, and then lay quietly as Giarna rose and dressed, saying nothing. Once he looked at her, and she thought he was going to speak.

Suzine's heart pounded. Did he know what she was thinking? She thought of the face in the mirror again—that *elven* face. But General Giarna only scowled as he stood before her. After several moments, he spun on his heel and stalked from the tent. She heard the pacing of his charger without, and then the clatter of hooves as the general galloped away.

Hesitantly, inevitably, she turned back to the mirror.

4

In Pitched Battle

*The two armies wheeled and skirmished across the flat-*lands, using the forests for cover and obstruction, making sharp cavalry sweeps and sudden ambushes. Lives expired, men and elves suffered agony and maiming, and yet the great bodies of the two armies did not contact each other.

General Giarna's human force drove toward Sithelbec, while Kith-Kanan's Wildrunners countermarched to interpose themselves between the Ergothian army and its destination. The humans moved quickly, and it was only the effort of an all-night forced march that finally brought the exhausted elves into position.

Twenty thousand Silvanesti and Kagonesti warriors finally gathered into a single mass and prepared a defense, tensely awaiting the steadily advancing human horde. The elven warriors averaged three to four hundred years of age, and many of their captains had seen six or more centuries. If they survived the battle and the war, they could look forward to more centuries, five or six hundred years, perhaps, of peaceful aging.

The Silvanesti bore steel weapons of fine craftsmanship, arrowheads that could punch through plate mail and swords that would not shatter under the most crushing of blows. Many of the elves had some limited proficiency in magic, and these were grouped in small platoons attached to each company. Though these elves, too, would rely upon sword and shield to survive the battle, their spells could provide a timely and demoralizing counterpunch.

The Wildrunners also had some five hundred exceptionally fleet horses, and upon these were mounted the elite— lancers and archers who would harass and confuse the enemy. They wore the grandest armor, shined to perfection, and each bore his personal emblem embroidered in silk upon his breast.

This force stood against a human army of more than fifty thousand men. The humans averaged about twenty-five years of age, the oldest veterans having seen a mere four or five decades of life. Their weapons were crudely crafted by elven standards, yet they possessed a deep strength. The blade might grow dull, but only rarely would it break.

The human elite included riders, numbering twenty thousand. They bore no insignia, nor did they wear armor of metal. Instead, they were a ragged, evil-looking lot, with many a missing tooth, eye, or ear. Unlike their elven counterparts, almost all were bearded, primarily because of a disdain of shaving, or indeed grooming of any kind.

But they carried within them an inner thirst for a thing uniquely human in character. Whether it be called glory or excitement or adventure, or simply cruelty or savagery, it was a quality that made the short-lived humans feared and distrusted by all the longer-lived races of Krynn.

Now this burning ambition, propelled by the steel-bladed drive of General Giarna, pushed the humans toward Sithelbec. For two days, the elven army appeared to stand before them, only to melt away at the first sign of attack. By the third day, however, they stood within march of that city itself.

Kith-Kanan had reached the edge of the tree cover. Beyond lay nothing but open field to the gates of Sithelbec, some ten miles away. Here the Wildrunners would have to stand.

The reason for falling back this far became obvious to elf and human alike as the Wildrunners reached their final position. Silver trumpets blared to the eastward, and a column of marchers hove into view.

"Hail the elves of Silvanost!"

Cries of delight and welcome erupted from the elven army as, with propitious timing, the five thousand recruits sent by Sithas two months earlier marched into the Wildrunners' camp. At their head rode Kencathedrus, the stalwart veteran who had given Kith-Kanan his earliest weapons training.

"Hah! I see that my former student still plays his war games!" The old veteran, his narrow face showing the strain of the long march, greeted Kith before the commander's tent. Wearily Kencathedrus lifted a leg over his saddle. Kith helped him to stand on the ground.

"I'm glad you made it," Kith-Kanan greeted his old teacher, clasping his arms warmly. "It's a long march from the city."

Kencathedrus nodded curtly. Kith-Kanan would have thought the gesture rude, except that he knew the old warrior and his mannerisms. Kencathedrus represented the purest tradition of the House Royal—the descendents, like Kith-Kanan and Sithas, of Silvanos himself. Indeed, they were distant cousins in some obscure way Kith had never understood.

But more than blood relative, Kencathedrus was in many ways the mentor of Kith-Kanan the warrior. Strict to the point of obsession, the teacher had drilled the pupil in the instinctive use of the longsword and in the swift and repetitive shooting of the bow until such tasks had become second nature.

Now Kencathedrus looked Kith-Kanan up and down. The general was clad in unadorned plate mail, with a simple steel helmet, unmarked by any sign of rank.

"What about your crest?" he asked. "Don't you fight in the name of Silvanos, of the House Royal?"

Kith nodded. "As always. However, my guards have persuaded me that there's no sense in making myself a target. I dress like a simple cavalryman now." He took Kencathedrus's arm, noting that the old elf moved with considerable stiffness.

"My back isn't what it used to be," admitted the venerable captain, stretching.

"It's likely to get some more exercise soon," Kith warned him. "Thank the gods you arrived when you did!"

"The human army?" Kencathedrus looked past the elves, lined up for battle. Kith told the captain what he knew.

"A mile away, no more. We have to face them here. The alternative is to fall back into the fortress, and I'm not ready to concede the plains!"

"You've chosen a good field, it seems." Kencathedrus nodded at the stands of trees around them. The area consisted of many of these thick groves, separated by wide, grassy fields. "How many stand against us?"

"Just a third of the entire Ergoth army—that's the good news. The other two wings have bogged down—more than a hundred miles away right now. But this one is the most dangerous. The commander is bold and adventurous. I had to march all night to get in front of him, and now my troops are exhausted as he prepares his attack."

"You forget," Kencathedrus chided Kith, almost harshly. "You stand with elves against a force of mere humans."

Kith-Kanan looked at the old warrior fondly, but he shook his head at the same time. "These 'mere' humans wiped out a hundred of my Wildrunners in one ambush. They've covered four hundred miles in three weeks." Now the leader's voice took on a tone of authority. "Do not underestimate them."

Kencathedrus studied Kith-Kanan before nodding his agreement. "Why don't you show me the lines," he suggested. "I presume you want us ready at first light."

*   *   *   *   *

As it happened, General Giarna gave Kith's force one more day to rest and prepare. The human army shifted and marched and expanded, all behind the screen of several groves of trees. Kith sent a dozen Kagonesti Wildrunners to spy, counting on the natural vegetation that they used so well to cover them.

Only one returned, and he to report that the human sentries were too thick for even the skilled elves to pass without detection.

The elven force took advantage of the extra day, however. They constructed trenches along much of their front, and in other places, they laid long, sharp stakes in the earth to form a wall thrusting outward. These stakes would protect much of the front from the enemy horsemen Kith knew to number in the thousands.

Parnigar supervised the excavation, racing from site to site, shouting and cursing. He insulted the depth of one trench, the width of another. He cast aspersions on the lineage of the elves who had done the work. The Wildrunners leaped to obey out of respect, not fear. All along the line they dug in, proving that they used the pick and the spade as well as the longsword and pike.

Midafternoon slowly crept toward dusk. Kith restlessly worked his way back and forth along the line. Eventually he came to the reserve, where the men of Silvanost recovered from their long march under the shrewd tutelage of Kencathedrus. That captain stepped up to Kith-Kanan as the general dismounted from Kijo.

"Odd how they work for him," noted the older elf, indicating Parnigar. "My elves wouldn't even look at an officer who talked to them like that!"

Kith-Kanan looked at him curiously, realizing that he spoke the truth. "The Wildrunners here on the plains are a different kind of force than you know from the city," he pointed out.

He looked at the reserve force, consisting of the five thousand elves who had marched with Kencathedrus. Even at ease, they lounged in the sun in neat ranks across the grassy meadows. A formation of Wildrunners, Kith reflected, would have collected in the areas of shade.

The teacher nodded, still skeptical. He looked across the

front, toward the trees that screened the enemy army. "Do you know their deployments?" asked Kencathedrus.

"No," Kith admitted. "We've been shut off all day. I'd fall back if I could. They've had too much time to prepare an attack, and I'd love to set those preparations to waste. Your old lesson comes to mind: 'Don't let the enemy have the luxury of following his plan!' "

Kencathedrus nodded, and Kith nearly growled in frustration as he continued. "But I *can't* move back. These trees are the last cover between here and Sithelbec. There's not so much as a ditch to hide behind if I abandon this position!"

All he could do was to deploy a company of skirmishers well to each flank of his position and hope they could provide him with warning of any sudden flanking thrust.

It was a night of restlessness throughout the camp, despite the exhaustion of the weary troops. Few of them slept for more than a few hours, and many campfires remained lit well past midnight as elves gathered around them and talked of past centuries, of their families—of anything but the terrible destiny that seemed to await them on the morrow.

Dew crept across the land in the darkest hours of night, becoming a heavy mist that flowed thickly through the meadows and twisted around the trunks in the groves. With it came a chill that woke every elf, and thus they spent the last hours of darkness.

They heard the drums before dawn, a far-off rattle that began with shocking precision from a thousand places at once. Darkness shrouded the woods, and the mists of the humid night drifted like spirits among the nervous elves, further obscuring visibility.

Gradually the dark mist turned to pale blue. As the sky lightened overhead, the cadence of a great army's advance swelled around the elves. The Wildrunners held to their pikes, or steadied their prancing horses. They checked their bowstrings and their quivers, and made certain that the bucklings on their armor held secure. Inevitably the blue light gave way to a dawn of vague, indistinct shapes, still clouded by the haze of fog.

The beat of the drums grew louder. The mist drifted across the fields, leaving even nearby clumps of trees nothing more than gray shadows. Louder still grew the precise tapping, yet nothing could be seen of the approaching force.

"There—coming through the pines!"

"I see them—over that way!"

"Here they come—from the ravine!"

Elves shouted, pointing to spots all along their front where shapes began to take form in the mist. Now they could see great, rippling lines of movement, as if waves rolled through the earth itself. The large, prancing figures of horsemen became apparent, several waves of them flexing among the ranks of infantry.

Abruptly, as suddenly as it had started, the drumming ceased. The formations of the human army appeared as darker shapes against the yellow grass and the gray sky. For a moment, time on the field, and perhaps across all the plains, across all of Ansalon, stood still. The warriors of the two armies regarded each other across a quarter-mile of ground. Even the wind died, and the mist settled low to the earth.

Then a shout arose from one of the humans and was echoed by fifty thousand voices. Swords bashed against shields, while trumpets blared and horses whinnied in excitement and terror.

In the next instant, the human wave surged forward, the roaring sound wave of the attack preceding it with terrifying force.

Now brassy notes rang from elven trumpets. Pikes rattled as their wielders set their weapons. The five hundred horses of the Wildrunner cavalry nickered and kicked nervously.

Kith-Kanan steadied Kijo. From his position in the center of the line, he had a good view of the advancing human tide. His bodyguards, increased to twelve riders today, stood in a semicircle behind him. He had insisted that they not obstruct his view of the field.

For a moment, he had a terrifying vision of the elven line's collapse, the human horde sweeping across the plains and forests beyond like a swarm of insects. He shuddered in the grip of the fear, but then the swirl of events grabbed and held his attention.

The first shock of the charge came in the form of two thousand swordsmen, brandishing shields and howling madly. Dressed in thick leather jerkins, they raced ahead of their metal-armored comrades, toward the block of elven pikes standing firm in the center of Kith's line.

The clash of swordsmen with the tips of those pikes was a horrible scene. The steel-edged blades of the pikes pierced the leather with ease as scores of humans impaled themselves from the force of the charge. A cheer went up from the Wildrunners as the surviving swordsmen turned to flee, leaving perhaps a quarter of their number writhing and groaning on the ground, at the very feet of the elves who had wounded them.

Now the focus shifted to the left, where human longbowmen advanced against an exposed portion of the Wildrunner line. Kith's own archers fired back, sending a deadly shower against the press of men. But the human arrows, too, found marks among the tightly packed ranks, and elven blood soon flowed thick in the trampled grass.

Kith nudged Kijo toward the archers, watching volleys of arrows arc and cross through the air. The humans rushed forward and the elves stood firm. The elven commander urged his steed faster, sensing the imminent clash.

Then the human advance wavered and slowed. Kith saw Parnigar, standing beside the archers.

"Now!" cried the sergeant-major, gesturing toward a platoon of elves standing beside him. A few dozen in number, these elves wore swords at their sides but had no weapons in their hands. It was their bare hands that they raised, fingers extended toward the rushing humans.

A bright flash of light made Kith blink. Magic missiles, crackling blasts of sorcerous power, exploded from Parnigar's platoon. A whole line of men dropped, slain so suddenly that members of the rear ranks tripped and tumbled over the bodies. Again the light flashed, and another volley of magic ripped into the humans.

Some of those struck screamed aloud, crying for their gods or for their mothers. Others stumbled back, panicked by the sorcerous attack. A whole company, following the decimated formation, stopped in its tracks and then turned to flee. In another moment, the mass of human bowmen streamed away, pursued by another volley of the keen elven arrows.

Yet even as this attack failed, Kith sensed a crisis on his left. A line of human cavalry, three thousand snorting horses bearing armored lancers, thundered through the rapidly thinning mist. The charge swept forward with a momentum that made the previous attacks look like parade-ground drills.

Before the horsemen waited a line of elves with swords and shields, soft prey for the thundering riders. To the right and left of them, the sharp stakes jutted forward, proof against the cavalry attack. But the gaps in the line had to be held by troops, and now these elves faced approaching doom.

"Archers—give cover!" Kith shouted as Kijo raced across the lines. Companies of elven longbow wheeled and released their missiles, scoring hits among the horsemen. But still the charge pounded foward.

"Fall back! Take cover in the trees!" he shouted to the captains of the longsword companies, for there was no other choice.

Kith cursed himself in frustration, realizing that the human commander had forced him to commit his pikes against the initial charge. Now came the horses, and his companies of pikes, the only true defense against a wave of cavalry, were terribly out of position.

Then he stared in astonishment. As more arrows fell among the riders, suddenly the horsemen wheeled about, racing away from the elven position before the defenders could follow Kith's orders to withdraw. The astonished elven swordsmen watched the horses and the riders flee, pursued by a desultory shower of arrows. The elven defenders could only wonder at the fortuitous turn of events.

In the back of Kith's mind, something whispered a warning. This had to be a trick, he told himself. Certainly the arrows hadn't been thick and deadly enough to halt that awe-inspiring charge. Less than fifty riders, and no more than two dozen horses, lay in the field before them. His scouts had given him a good count of the human cavalry. Though he had not been able to study these, he suspected he had seen only about half the force.

* * * * *

"Our men fall back as you ordered," reported Suzine, her eyes locked upon the violent images in her mirror. The glass rested on a table, and she sat before it—table, woman, and mirror, all encased in a narrow shroud of canvas, to keep the daylight from the crucial seeing device. She never lost view of the elven commander, who sat straight and proud in his saddle, every inch the warrior of House Royal.

Behind her, pacing in taut excitement, General Giarna looked over her shoulder.

"Excellent! And the elves—what do you see of them?"

"They stand firm, my lord."

"What?" General Giarna's voice barked violently against her, filling the small canvas shelter where they observed the battle. "You're *wrong!* They must *attack!*"

Suzine flinched. The image in the mirror—a picture of long ranks of elven warriors, holding their positions, failing to pursue the bait of the human retreat—wavered slightly.

She felt the general's rage explode, and then the image faded. Suzine saw only her own reflection and the hideous face of the man behind her.

* * * * *

"My lord! Let us hit them now, while they fall back in confusion!" Kith turned to see Kencathedrus beside him. His old teacher rode a prancing mare, and the weariness of the march from Silvanost was totally gone from his face. Instead, the warrior's eyes burned, and his gauntleted fist clung tightly to the hilt of his sword.

"It has to be a trick," Kith countered. "We didn't drive them away that easily!"

"For the gods' sakes, Kith-Kanan—these are *humans!* The cowardly scum will run from a loud noise! Let's follow up and destroy them!"

"No!" Kith's voice was harsh, full of command, and Kencathedrus's face whitened with frustration.

"We do not face an ordinary general," Kith-Kanan continued, feeling that he owed further explanation to the one who had girded his first sword upon him. "He hasn't failed to surprise me yet, and I know we have seen but a fraction of his force."

"But if they fly they will escape! We *must* pursue!" Kencathedrus couldn't help himself.

"The answer is no. If they are escaping, so be it. If they attempt to pull us out of our position to trap us, they shall not."

Another roar thundered across the fields before them, and more humans came into view, running toward the elves with all manner of weaponry. Great companies of longbowmen readied their missiles, while bearded axemen raised their heavy blades over their heads. Spearmen charged with gleaming points extended toward the enemy, while swordsmen banged their swords against their shields, advancing at a steady march.

Kencathedrus, shocked by the fresh display of human might and vigor, looked at the general with respect. "You *knew?*" he said wonderingly.

Kith-Kanan shrugged and shook his head. "No—I simply suspected. Perhaps because I had a good teacher."

The older elf growled, appreciating the remark but annoyed with himself. Indeed, they both realized that, had the elves advanced when Kencathedrus had desired, they would have been swiftly overrun, vulnerable in the open field.

Kencathedrus rejoined his reserve company, and Kith-Kanan immersed himself in the fight. Thousands of humans and elves clashed along the line, and hundreds died. Weapons shattered against shields, and bones shattered beneath blades. The long morning gave way to afternoon, but the passing of time meant nothing to the desperate combatants, for whom each moment could be their last.

The tide of battle surged back and forth. Companies of humans turned and fled, many of them before their charging ranks even reached the determined elves. Others hacked and slew their way into the defenders, and—occasionally—a company of elves gave way. Then the humans poured through the gap like the surging surf, but always Kith-Kanan was there, slashing with his bloody sword, urging his elven lancers into the breach.

Wave after wave of humans surged madly across the

trampled field, hurling themselves into the elves as if to shatter them with the sheer momentum of their charges. As soon as one company broke, one regiment fell back depleted and demoralized, another block of steel-tipped humanity lunged forward to take its place.

The Wildrunners fought until total exhaustion gripped each and every warrior, and then they fought some more. Their small, mobile companies banded together to form solid lines, shifted to deflect each new charge, and flowed sideways to fill gaps caused by their fallen or routed comrades. Always those plunging horses backed them up, and each time, as the line faltered, the elven cavalry thundered against the breakthrough, driving it back in disorder.

Those five hundred riders managed to seal every breach. By the time the afternoon shadows began to lengthen, Kith noticed a slackening in the human attacks. One company of swordsmen stumbled away, and for once there was no fresh formation to take their place in the attack. The din of combat seemed to fade somewhat, and then he saw another formation—a group of axemen—turn and lumber away from the fight. More and more of the humans broke off their attacks, and soon the great regiments of Ergoth streamed across the field, back toward their own lines.

Kith slumped wearily in his saddle, staring in suspicion at the fleeing backs of the soldiers. Could it be over? Had the Wildrunners won? He looked at the sun—about four good hours of daylight remained. The humans wouldn't risk an encounter at night, he knew. Elven nightvision was one of the great proofs of the elder race's superiority over its shorter-lived counterparts. Yet certainly the hour was not the reason for the humans' retreat, not when they had been pressing so forcefully all along the line.

A weary Parnigar approached on foot. Kith had seen the scout's horse cut down beneath him during the height of the battle. The general recognized his captain's lanky walk, though Parnigar's face and clothes were caked in mud and the blood of his slain enemies.

"We've held them, sir," he reported, his face creasing into a disbelieving smile. Immediately, however, he frowned and shook his head. "Some three or four hundred dead, though. The day was not without its cost."

Kith looked at the exhausted yet steady ranks of his Wildrunners. The pikemen held their weapons high, the archers carried bows at the ready, while those with swords honed their blades in the moments of silence and respite. The formations still arrayed in full ranks, as if fresh and unblooded, but their ranks were shorter now. Organized in neat rows behind each company, covered with blankets, lay a quiet grouping of motionless forms.

At least the dead can rest, he thought, feeling his own weariness. He looked again to the humans, seeing that they still fled in disorder. Many of them had reached the tree line and were disappearing into the sheltering forest.

"My lord! My lord! Now is the time. You *must* see that!"

Kith turned to see Kencathedrus galloping up to him. The elven veteran reined in beside the general and gestured at the fleeing humans.

"You may be right," Kith-Kanan had to agree. He saw the five thousand elves of Silvanost gathered in trim ranks, ready to advance the moment he gave the word. This was the chance to deliver a *coup de grace* that could send the enemy reeling all the way back to Caergoth.

"Quickly, my lord—they're getting away!" Impatiently, his gray brows bristling, Kencathedrus indicated the ragged humans running in small clumps, like sheep, toward the sheltering woods in the distance.

"Very well—advance and pursue! But have a care for your flanks!"

* * * * *

"They *must* come after us now!" General Giarna's horse twisted and pitched among the ranks of retreating humans, many of whom were bleeding or limping, supported by the shoulders of their sturdier comrades. Indeed, the Army of Ergoth had paid a hideous price for the daylong attacks, all of which were mere preliminaries to his real plan of battle.

The general paid no attention to the human suffering around him. Instead, his dark eyes fixed with a malevolent stare on the elven positions across the mud-spattered landscape. No movement yet—but they must advance. He felt this with a certainty that filled his dark heart with a bloodthirsty anticipation.

For a moment, he cast a sharp glance to the rear, toward the tiny tent that sheltered Suzine and her mirror. The gods should damn that bitch! How, in the heat of the fight, could her powers fail her? Why *now*—today?

His brow narrowed in suspicion, but he had no time now to wonder about the unreliability of his mistress. She had been a valuable tool, and it would be regrettable if that tool were no longer at his disposal.

Perhaps, as she had claimed, the tension of the great conflict had proven too distracting, too overpowering for her to concentrate. Or maybe the general's looming presence had frightened her. In fact, General Giarna *wanted* to frighten her, just as he wanted to frighten everyone under his command. However, if that fear was enough to disrupt her powers of concentration, than Suzine's usefulness might be seriously limited.

No matter—at least for now. The battle could still be won by force of arms. The key was to make the elves believe that the humans were beaten.

General Giarna's pulse quickened then as he saw a line of movement across the field.

* * * * *

"Elves of Silvanost, advance!" The captain had already turned away from his commander. The reserve companies started forward at a brisk march, through the gaps in the spiked fence of the elven line. The companies of the Wildrunners, battered and weary, cleared the way for the attackers, whose gleaming spearpoints and shining armor stood out in stark contrast to the muddy, bloody mess around them. Nevertheless, the Wildrunners raised a hearty cheer as Kencathedrus led his troops into the attack.

"On the double—charge!" His horse prancing eagerly beneath him, Kencathedrus brandished his sword and urged his complement forward. The troops needed no prodding. All day they had seen their fellow countrymen die at the hands of these rapacious savages, and now they had the chance to take vengeance.

The panicked humans cast down weapons, shields,

helmets—anything loose and cumbersome—in their desperate flight. They scattered away from the charging elves, racing for the shelter of any clump of trees or thick brush they could find.

The warriors of Silvanost, disciplined even at their steady advance, remained in close-meshed lines. They parted at the obstacles, while several who were armed with shortswords pressed into the grove, quickly dispatching the hapless humans who sought refuge there.

But even so, it was clear that the great bulk of the routed troops would escape, so rapid was their flight. The close ranks of the elves could not keep pace. Finally Kencathedrus slowed his company to a brisk walk, allowing the elves to catch their breath as they approached the first large expanse of forest.

"Archers, stand forward to the flanks." Kith-Kanan didn't know why he gave the order, but suddenly he saw how vulnerable were the five thousand elves, in the event that he *had* been tricked. Kencathedrus and his regiment had already avanced nearly half a mile ahead of the main army, while the fleeing humans seemed to melt away before them.

Two blocks of elves—his keenest longbows, some thousand strong each—trotted ahead.

"Pikes—in the middle, quickly!" One more unit Kith-Kanan sent forward, this one consisting of his fiercest veterans, armed with their deadly, fifteen-foot weapons with razor-sharp steel tips. They advanced at a trot, filling some of the gap between the two blocks of longbows.

"Horsemen! To me!" A third command brought the proud elven cavalry thundering to their commander. It seemed to Kith-Kanan that Kencathedrus and his company were now in terrible danger. He had to catch up and give them support.

Flanked by his mounted bodyguards, the commander led his horsemen through the lines, in a wide sweep toward the right of Kencathedrus's company. The elven archers carried their weapons ready. Pikes rattled behind them. Had he done everything that he could to protect the advance?

Kith sensed something in the air as the late afternoon seemed to grow sinister around him. He listened carefully;

his eyes studied the opposite tree line, scanned to the right and left to the limits of his vision.

Nothing.

Yet now some of his elves sensed the same thing, the indefinable inkling of something terrible and awesome and mighty. Warriors nervously fingered their weapons. The Wildrunners' horses moved restlessly, shaking off the weariness of many hours' battle.

Then a rumble of deep thunder permeated the air. It began as a faint drumming, but in Kith-Kanan's mind, it grew to a deafening explosion within a few seconds.

"Sound the withdrawal!" He shouted at the trumpeters as he looked left, then right—*where*, by all the gods?

He saw them appear, like a wave of brown grass on the horizon, to *both* sides—countless thousands of humans mounted on thundering horses, sweeping around the patches of woods, across the open prairie, pounding closer with all the speed of the wind.

The horns blared, and Kith saw that Kencathedrus had already sensed the trap. Now the elves of Silvanost retired toward the Wildrunners' lines at a quick pace. But all who looked on could see that they would be too late.

The archers and pikemen advanced, desperate to aid their countrymen. They showered the human cavalry with arrows, while the long pikes bristled before the archers, protecting them from the charge.

But the elves of Silvanost had no such protection. The human cavalry slammed into them, and rank after rank of the elven infantry fell beneath the cruel hooves and keen, unfeeling steel.

The pikemen and archers fell back slowly, carefully, still shredding the cavalry with deadly arrows, felling the horsemen by the hundred with each volley. Yet thousands upon thousands of the humans trampled across the plain, slaughtering the stranded regiment.

Kith-Kanan led his riders into the flank of the human charge, little caring that there were ten or twenty humans for every one of his elves. With his own sword, he cut a leering, bearded human from the saddle. Horses screamed and bucked around them, and in moments, the two companies of cavalry mingled, each man or elf fighting the foe he found close at hand.

More blood flowed into the already soaked ground. Kith saw a human lancer drive a bloodstained lance toward his heart. One of his loyal bodyguards flung himself from his saddle and took the weapon through his own throat, deflecting the blow that would have surely been fatal. With a surge of hatred, Kith spurred Kijo forward, chopping savagely through the neck and striking the lancer's head from his shoulders. Spouting blood like an obscene geyser, the corpse toppled from the saddle, lost in the chaos of the melee before it struck the ground.

Kith saw another of his faithful guards fall, this time to a human swordsman whose horse skipped nimbly away. The fight swirled madly, flashing images of blood, screaming horses, dying men and elves. If he had paused to think, he would have regretted the charge that brought his riders out here to aid Kencathedrus. Now, it seemed, *both* units faced annihilation.

Desperately Kith-Kanan looked for a sign of the elves of Silvanost. He saw them through the melee. Led by a grim-faced Kencathedrus, the elven reserve force struggled to break free of the deadly trap. Finally they tore from their neat ranks in a headlong dash through the sea of human horsemen toward the safety of the Wildrunner lines.

Miraculously, many of them made it. They scrambled between the thick wall of stakes, into the welcoming arms of their comrades, while the stampeding cavalry surged and bucked just beyond. By the dozens and scores and hundreds, they limped and dodged and tumbled to safety, until more than two thousand of them, including Kencathedrus, had emerged. The captain tried to turn and lunge back into the fray in a foredoomed effort to bring forth more of his men, but he was restrained in the grasp of two sergeants-major.

The archers, too, fell back, and then it was only the riders caught on the field. Isolated pockets of elven cavalry twisted away from the sea of human horsemen, breaking for the shelter of their lines. Kith-Kanan himself, however, after having led the charge, was now caught in the middle of the enemy forces.

His arm grew leaden with fatigue. Blood from a cut on his

forehead streamed into his eyes. His helmet was gone, knocked from his head by a human's bashing shield. His loyal guards—the few who still lived—fought around him, but now the outlook was grim.

The humans fell back, just far enough to avoid the slashing elven blades. Kith-Kanan and a group of perhaps two dozen elven riders gasped for breath, surrounded by a ring of death—more than a thousand human lancers, swordsmen, and archers.

With a groan of despair, he cast his sword to the ground. The rest of the survivors immediately followed his example.

* * * * *

As darkness finally closed about them, the humans turned back from the elven line. Kencathedrus and Parnigar knew that it was only nightfall that had prevented the complete collapse of their position. They knew, too, that the exhausted army would have to retreat—now, even before the darkness was complete.

They would have to take shelter in Sithelbec early the following day, before the deadly human cavalry could catch them in the open. The entire force of the Wildrunners could suffer the fate of the unblooded elves of Silvanost.

It seemed to the elven leaders that the day couldn't have been any more disastrous. Despair settled around them like a bleak cloud as they considered the worst news of all: Kith-Kanan, their commander and the driving force behind the Wildrunners, was lost—possibly captured, but more likely killed.

The army marched, heads down and shambling, toward the security—and the confinement—of Sithelbec.

Sometime after midnight, it started to rain, and it continued to pour throughout the night and even past the gray, featureless dawn. The miserable army finally reached Sithelbec, closing the gates behind the last of the Wildrunners, sometime around noon of the following gray, drizzling day.

❧ 5 ❧

After the Battle

Suzine awakened to a summons from the general, delivered by a bronze-helmed lieutenant of crossbows. The woman felt vague relief that General Giarna hadn't come to her in person. Indeed, she hadn't seen him since before the battle's climax, when his trap had snared so much of the elven army.

Her relief had grown from the previous night, when she had feared that he would desire her. General Giarna frightened her often, but there was something deeper and more abiding about the terror he inspired after he had led his troops in battle.

The darkness that seemed always to linger in his eyes became, in those moments, like a bottomless well of despair and hopelessness, as if his hunger for killing could never be sated. The more the blood flowed around him, the greater his appetite became.

He would take her then, using her like he was some kind of parasite, unaware and uncaring of her feelings. He would hurt her and, when he was finished, cast her roughly aside, his own fundamental needs still raging.

But after this battle, his greatest victory to date, he had stayed away from her. She had retired early the night before, dying to look into her mirror, to ascertain Kith-Kanan's whereabouts. She felt a terrible fear for his safety, but she hadn't dared to use her glass for fear of the general. He mustn't suspect her growing fascination with Kith-Kanan.

Now she dressed quickly and fetched her mirror, safe in a felt-lined wooden case, and then allowed the officer to lead her along the column of tents to General Giarna's shelter of black silk. The lieutenant held the door while she entered, blinking for a moment as she adjusted to the dim light.

And then it seemed that her world exploded.

The file of muddy elven prisoners, many of them bruised, stood at resentful attention. There were perhaps a score of them, each with a watchful swordsman right behind him, but Suzine's eyes flashed immediately to *him*.

She recognized Kith-Kanan in the instant that she saw him, and she had to forcibly resist an urge to run to him. She wanted to look at him, to touch him in all the ways she could not through her mirror. She fought an urge to knock the sword-wielding guard aside.

Then she remembered General Giarna. Her face flushed, she felt perspiration gather on her brow. He was watching her closely. Forcing an expression of cool detachment, she turned to him.

"You summoned me, General?"

The commander seemed to look through her, with a gaze that threatened to wither her soul. His eyes yawned before her like black chasms, menacing pits that made her want to hurriedly step back from the edge.

"The interrogation continues. I want you to witness their testimony and gauge the truth of their replies." His voice was like a cold gust of air.

For the first time, Suzine noticed an additional elven form. This one stretched facedown on the carpeted floor of the tent, a tiny hole at the base of his neck showing where he had been stabbed.

Numbly she looked back. Kith-Kanan stood second from the end of the line, near where the killing had occurred. He paid no attention to her. The elf between him and the dead one looked in grimly concealed fear at the human general.

"Your strength!" demanded General Giarna. "How many troops garrison your fortress? Catapults? Ballistae? You will tell us about them all."

The final sentence was a demand, not a question.

"The fortress is garrisoned by twenty thousand warriors, with more on the way!" blurted the prisoner beside the corpse. "Wizards and clerics, too—"

Suzine didn't need the mirror to see that he lied; neither, apparently, did General Giarna. He chopped his hand once, and the swordsman behind the terrified speaker stabbed at the doomed elf. His blade severed the elf's spinal cord and then plunged through his neck, emerging under the unfortunate warrior's chin in a gurgling fountain of blood.

The next swordsman—the one behind Kith-Kanan—prodded his charge in the back, forcing him to stand a little straighter, as the general's eyes came to rest upon him. But only for a moment, for the human leader allowed his scornful gaze to roam across the entire row of his captives.

"Which of you holds rank over the others?" inquired the general, casting his eyes along the line of remaining elves.

For the first time, Suzine realized that Kith-Kanan wore none of the trappings of his station. He was an anonymous rider among the elven warriors. Giarna didn't recognize him! That revelation encouraged her to take a risk.

"My general," she said quickly, hearing her voice as if another person was speaking, "could I have a word with you—away from the ears of the prisoners?"

He looked at her, his dark eyes boring into her. Was that annoyance she saw, or something darker?

"Very well," he replied curtly. He took her arm in his hand and led her from the tent.

She felt the mirror's case in her hand, seeking words as she spoke. "They are obviously willing to die for their cause. But perhaps, with a little patience, I can make them useful to us . . . alive."

"You can tell me whether they speak the truth or not—but what good is that when they are willing to die with lies in their mouths?"

"But there is more to the glass," she said insistently. "Given a quiet place and some time—and some close personal attention to one of these subjects—I can probe deeper than mere questions and answers. I can see into their minds, to the secret truths they would never admit to such as you."

General Giarna's black brows came together in a scowl. "Very well. I will allow you to try." He led her back into the tent. "Which one will you start with?"

Trying to still the trembling in her heart, Suzine raised an imperious hand and indicated Kith-Kanan. She spoke to the guard behind him. "Bring this one to my tent," she said matter-of-factly.

She avoided looking at the general, afraid those black eyes would paralyze her with suspicion or accusation. But he said nothing. He merely nodded to the guard behind Kith and the swordsman beside him, the one who had just slain the fallen elf. The pair of guards prodded Kith-Kanan forward, and Suzine preceded him through the silken flap of General Giarna's tent.

They passed between two tents, the high canvas shapes screening them from the rest of the camp. She could feel his eyes on her back as she walked, and finally she could no longer resist the urge to turn and look at him.

"What do you want with me?" he asked, his voice surprising her with its total lack of fear.

"I won't hurt you," she replied, suddenly angry when the elf smiled slightly in response.

"Move, you!" grunted one of the guards, stepping in front of his companion and waving his blade past Kith-Kanan's face.

Kith-Kanan reached forward with the speed of a striking snake, seizing the guard's wrist as the blade veered away from his face. Holding the man's hand, the elf kicked him sharply in the groin. The swordsman gasped and collapsed.

His companion, the warrior who had slain the elf in the tent, gaped in momentary shock—a moment that proved to be his last. Kith pulled the blade from the fallen guard's hand and, in the same motion, drove the point into the swordsman's throat. He died, his jaw soundlessly working in an effort to articulate his shock.

The dead guard's helmet toppled off as he fell, allowing his long blond hair to spill free when he collapsed, face first, on the ground.

Kith lowered the blade, ready to thrust it through the neck of the groaning man he had kicked. Then something stayed his hand, and he merely admonished the guard to be silent with a persuasive press of the blade against the man's throat.

Turning to the one he had slain, Kith looked at the body curiously. Suzine hadn't moved. She watched him in fascination, scarcely daring to breath, as he brushed the blond hair aside with the toe of his boot.

The ear that was revealed was long and pointed.

"Do you have many elves in your army?" he asked.

"No—not many," Suzine said quickly. "They are mostly from the ranks of traders and farmers who have lived in Ergoth and desire a homeland on the plains."

Kith looked sharply at Suzine. There was something about this human woman. . . .

She stood still, paralyzed not so much by fear for herself as by dismay. He was about to escape, to leave her!

"I thank you for inadvertently saving my life," he said before darting toward the corner of a nearby tent.

"I—I know who you are!" she said, her voice a bare whisper.

He stopped again, torn between the need to escape and increasing curiosity about this woman and her knowledge.

"Thank you, too, then, for keeping the secret," he said, with a short bow. "Why did you . . . ?"

She wanted to tell him that she had watched him for a long time, had all but lain beside him, through the use of her mirror. Suzine looked at him now, and he was more glorious, prouder, and taller than she had ever imagined. She wanted to ask him to take her away with him—right now—but, instead, her mouth froze, her mind locked by terror.

In another moment, he had disappeared. It was several

moments longer before she finally found the voice to scream.

* * * * *

The elation Kith-Kanan felt at his escape dissipated as quickly as the gates of Sithelbec shut behind him and enclosed him within the sturdy walls of the fortress. His stolen horse, staggering from exhaustion, stumbled to a halt, and the elf swung to the ground.

He wondered, through his weariness, about the human woman who had given him his chance to flee. The picture of her face, crowned by that glory of red hair, remained indelibly burned into his mind. He wondered if he would ever see her again.

Around him loomed the high walls, with the pointed logs arrayed along the top. Below these, he saw the faces of his warriors. Several raised a halfhearted cheer at his return, but the shock of defeat hung over the Wildrunners like a heavy pall.

Sithelbec had grown rapidly in the last year, sprawling across the surrounding plain until it covered a circle more than a mile in diameter. The central keep of the fortress was a stone structure of high towers, soaring to needlelike spires in the elven fashion. Around this keep clustered a crowded nest of houses, shops, barracks, inns, and other buildings, all within other networks of walls, blockhouses, and battle platforms.

Expanding outward through a series of concentric palisades, mostly of wood, the fortress protected a series of wells within its walls, ensuring a steady supply of water. Food—mostly grain—had been stockpiled in huge barns and silos. Supplies of arrows and flammable oil, stored in great vats, had been collected along the walls' tops. The greater part of Kith-Kanan's army, through the alert withdrawal under Parnigar, had reached the shelter of those ramparts.

Yet as the Army of Ergoth moved in to encircle the fortress, the Wildrunners could only wait.

Now Kith-Kanan walked among them, making his way to the small office and quarters he maintained in the gatehouse of the central keep. He felt the tension, the fear that approached despair, as he looked at the wide, staring eyes of his warriors.

And even more than the warriors, there were the women and children. Many of the women were human, their children half-elves, wives and offspring of the western elves who made up the Wildrunners. Kith shared their sorrow as deeply as he felt that of the elven females who were here in even greater numbers.

They would all be eating short rations, he knew. The siege would inevitably last into the autumn, and he had little doubt the humans could sustain the pressure through the winter and beyond.

As he looked at the young ones, Kith felt a stab of pain. He wondered how many of them would see spring.

🌿 6 🌿

autumn, year of the Raven

Lord Quimant came to Sithas in the hall of audience. His wife's cousin brought another elf—a stalwart-looking fellow, with lines of soot set firmly in his face, and the strapping, sinewy arms of a powerful wrestler—to see the Speaker of the Stars.

Sithas sat upon his emerald throne and watched the approaching pair. The Speaker's green robe flowed around him, collecting the light of the throne and diffusing it into a soft glow that seemed to surround him. He reclined casually in the throne, but he remained fully alert.

Alert, in that his mind was working quickly. Yet his thoughts were many hundreds of miles and years away.

Weeks earlier, he had received a letter from Kencathedrus

describing Kith-Kanan's capture and presumed loss. That had been followed, barely two days later, by a missive from his brother himself, describing a harrowing escape: the battle with guards, the theft of a fleet horse, a mad dash from the encampment, and finally a chase that ended only after Kith-Kanan had led his pursuers to within arrow range of the great fortress of Sithelbec.

Sithelbec—named for his father, the former Speaker of the Stars. Many times Sithas had reflected on the irony, for his father had been slain on a hunting trip, practically within sight of the fortress's walls. As far as Sithas knew, it had been his father's first and only expedition to the western plains. Yet Sithel had been willing to go to war over those plains, to put the nation's future at stake because of them. And now Sithas, his firstborn, had inherited that struggle. Would he live up to his father's expectations?

Reluctantly Sithas forced his mind back to the present, to his current location. He cast his eyes around his surroundings to force the transition in his thoughts.

A dozen elven guards, in silver breastplates and tall, plumed helmets, snapped their halberds to attention around the periphery of the hall. They stood impassive and silent as the noble lord marched toward the throne. Otherwise the great hall, with its gleaming marble floor and the ceiling towering six hundred feet overhead, was empty.

Sithas looked at Quimant. The elven noble wore a long cloak of black over a silk tunic of light green. Tights of red, and soft, black boots, completed his ensemble.

Lord Quimant of Oakleaf was a very handsome elf indeed. But he was also intelligent, quick-witted, and alert to many threats and opportunities that might otherwise have missed Sithas's notice.

"This is my nephew," the lord explained. "Ganrock Ethu, master smith. I recommend him, my Speaker, for the position of palace smith. He is shrewd, quick to learn, and a very hard worker."

"But Herrlock Redmoon has always handled the royal smithy," Sithas protested. Then he remembered: Herrlock had been blinded the week before in a tragic accident, when he had touched spark to his forge. Somehow the kindled coal had exploded violently, destroying his eyes beyond the abilities of Silvanost's clerics to repair. After seeing that the loyal smith was well cared for and as comfortable as possible, Sithas had promised to select a replacement.

He looked at the young elf before him. Ganrock's face showed lines of maturity, and the thick muscle of his upper torso showed proof of long years of work.

"Very well," Sithas agreed. "Show him the royal smithy and find out what he needs to get started." He called to one of his guards and told the elf to accompany Ganrock Ethu to the forge area, which lay in the rear of the Palace of Quinari.

"Thank you, Your Eminence," said the smith, with a sudden bow. "I shall endeavor to do fine work for you."

"Very good," replied the Speaker. Quimant lingered as the smith left the hall.

Lord Quimant's narrow face tightened in determination as he turned back to Sithas.

"What is it, my lord? You look distressed." Sithas raised a hand and bade Qiumant stand beside him.

"The Smelters Guild, Your Highness," replied the noble elf. "They refuse—they simply *refuse*—to work their foundries during the hours of darkness. Without the additional steel, our weapon production is hamstrung, barely adequate for even peacetime needs."

Sithas cursed quietly. Nevertheless, he was thankful that Quimant had informed him. The proud heir of Clan Oakleaf had greatly improved the efficiency of Silvanost's war preparations by spotting details—such as this one—that would have escaped Sithas's notice.

"I shall speak to the smelter Kerilar," Sithas vowed. "He is a stubborn old elf, but he knows the importance of the sword. I will *make* him understand, if I have to."

"Very good, Excellency," said Lord Quimant, with a bow. He straightened again. "Is there news of the war?"

"Not since the last letter, a week ago. The Wildrunners remain besieged in Sithelbec, while the humans roam the disputed lands at will. Kith has no chance to break out. He's now surrounded by a hundred thousand men."

The lord shook his head grimly before fixing Sithas with a hard gaze. "He must be reinforced—there's no other way. You know this, don't you?"

Sithas met Quimant's gaze with equal steadiness. "Yes—I do. But the only way I can recruit more troops is to conscript them from the city and the surrounding clan estates. You know what kind of dispute that will provoke!"

"How long can your brother hold his fort?"

"He has rations enough for the winter. The casualties of the battle were terrible, of course, but the remainder of his force is well disciplined, and the fortress is strong."

The news of the battlefield debacle had hit the elven capital hard. As the knowledge spread that two thousand of the city's young elves—two out of every five who had marched so proudly to the west!—had perished in the fight, Silvanost had been shrouded in grief for a week.

Sithas learned of the battle at the same time as he heard that his brother had fallen and was most likely lost. For two days, his world had been a grim shroud of despair. Knowing that Kith had reached safety lightened the burden to some extent, but their prospects for victory still seemed nonexistent. How long would it be, he had agonized, before the rest of the Wildrunners fell to the overwhelming tide around them?

Then gradually his despair had turned to anger—anger at the shortsightedness of his own people. Elves had crowded the Hall of Audience on the Trial Days, disrupting the proceedings. The emotions of the city's elves had been inflamed by the knowledge that the rest of the Wildrunners had suffered nowhere near the size of losses inflicted upon the elves of Silvanost. It was not uncommon now to hear voices raised in the complaint that the western lands should be turned over to the humans and the Wildrunner elves, to let them battle each other to extinction.

"Very well—so he can hold out." Quimant's voice was strong yet deferential. "But he *cannot* escape! We *must* send a fresh army, a large one, to give him the sinew he needs!"

"There are the dwarves. We have yet to hear from them!" Sithas pointed out.

"Pah! If they do anything, it will be too late! It seems that Than-Kar sympathizes with the humans as much as with us. The dwarves will never do anything so long as he remains their voice and their ears!"

Ah—but he is not their voice and ears. Sithas had that

thought with some small satisfaction, but he said nothing to Quimant as the lord continued, though his thoughts considered the potential of hope. *Tamanier Ambrodel, I am depending upon you!*

"Still, we must tolerate him, I suppose. He is our best chance of an alliance."

"As always, good cousin, your words are the mirror of my thoughts." Sithas straightened in his throne, a signal that the interview drew to a close. "But my decision is still to wait. Kith-Kanan is secure for now, and we may learn more as time goes on."

He hoped he was right. The fortress *was* strong, and the humans would undoubtably require months to prepare a coordinated assault. But what then?

"Very well." Quimant cleared his throat awkwardly, then added, "What is the word of my cousin? I have not seen her for some weeks now."

"Her time is near," Sithas offered. "Her sisters have come from the estates to stay with her, and she has been confined to bed by the clerics of Quenesti Pah."

Quimant nodded. "Please give her my wishes when next you see her. May she give birth speedily, to a healthy child."

"Indeed."

Sithas watched the elegant noble walk from the hall. He was impressed by Quimant's bearing. The lord knew his worth to the throne, proven in the half-year since he had come to Silvanost. He showed sensitivity to the desires of the Speaker and seemed to work well toward those ends.

He heard one of the side doors open and looked across the great hall as a silk-gowned female elf entered. Her eyes fell softly on the figure seated upon the brilliant throne with its multitude of green, gleaming facets.

"Mother," said Sithas with delight. He didn't see much of Nirakina around the palace during these difficult days, and this visit was a pleasant surprise. He was struck, as she approached him, by how much older she looked.

"I see you do not have attendants now," she said quietly to Sithas, who rose and approached her. "So often you are busy with the affairs of state . . . and war."

He sighed. "War has become the way of my life—the way all Silvanost lives now." He felt a twinge of sadness for his mother. So often Sithas looked upon the death of his father as an event that had placed the burden of rule on his own shoulders. He tended to forget that it had, at the same time, made his mother a widow.

"Take a moment to walk with me, won't you?" asked Nirakina, taking her son by the arm.

He nodded, and they walked in silence across the great hall of the tower to the crystal doors reserved for the royal family alone. These opened soundlessly, and then they were in the Gardens of Astarin. To their right were the dark wooden buildings of the royal stables, while before them beckoned the wondrous beauty of the royal gardens. Immediately Sithas felt a sense of lightness and ease.

"You need to do this more often," said his mother, gently chiding. "You grow old before your time." She held his arm loosely, letting him select the path they followed.

The gardens loomed around them—great hedges and thick bushes heavy with dewy blossoms; ponds and pools and fountains; small clumps of aspen and oak and fir. It was a world of nature, shaped and formed by elven clerics—devotees of the Bard King, Astarin—into a transcendent work of art.

"I thank you for bringing me through those doors," Sithas said with a chuckle. "Sometimes I need to be reminded."

"Your father, too, needed a subtle reminder now and then. I tried to give him that when it became necessary."

For a moment, Sithas felt a wave of melancholy. "I miss him now more than ever. I feel so . . . unready to sit on his throne."

"You are ready," said Nirakina firmly. "Your wisdom is seeing us through the most difficult time since the Dragon Wars. But since you are about to become a father, you must realize that your life cannot be totally given over to your nation. You have a family to think about, as well."

Sithas smiled. "The clerics of Quenesti Pah are with Hermathya at all times. They say it will be any day now."

"The clerics, and her sisters," Nirakina murmured.

"Yes," Sithas agreed. Hermathya's sisters, Gelynna and Lyath, had moved into the palace as soon as his wife's pregnancy had become known. They were pleasant enough, but Sithas had come to feel that his apartments were somehow less than his own now. It was a feeling he didn't like but that he had tried to overlook for Hermathya's sake.

"She has changed, Mother, that much you must see. Hermathya had become a new woman even before she knew about the child. She has been a support and a comfort to me, as if for the first time."

"It is the war," said Nirakina. "I have noticed this change you speak of, and it began with the war. She, her clan of Oakleaf, they all thrive upon this intensity and activity." The elven woman paused, then added, "I noticed Lord Quimant leaving before I entered. You speak with him often. Is he proving himself useful?"

"Indeed, very. Does this cause you concern?"

Nirakina sighed, then shook her head. "I—no—no, it doesn't. You are doing the right thing for Silvanesti, and if he can aid you, that is a good thing."

Sithas stopped at a stone bench. His mother sat while he paced idly below overhanging branches of silvery quaking aspen that shimmered in the light breeze.

"Have you had word from Tamanier Ambrodel?" Nirakina asked.

Sithas smiled confidentially. "He has arrived at Thorbardin safely and hopes to get in touch with the Hylar. With any luck, he will see the king himself. Then we shall find out if this Than-Kar is doing us true justice as ambassador."

"And you have told no one of Lord Ambrodel's mission?" his mother inquired carefully.

"No," Sithas informed her. "Indeed, Quimant and I discussed the dwarves today, but I said nothing even to him about our quiet diplomat. Still, I wish you would tell me why we must maintain such secrecy."

"Please, not yet," Nirakina demurred.

A thin haze had gradually spread across the sky, and now the wind carried a bit of early winter in its caress. Sithas saw his mother shiver in her light silken garment.

"Come, we'll return to the hall," he said, offering his arm as she rose.

"And your brother?" Nirakina asked tentatively as they turned back toward the crystal doors. "Can you send him more troops?"

"I don't know yet," Sithas replied, the agony of the decision audible in his voice. "Can I risk arousing the city?"

"Perhaps you need more information."

"Who could inform me of that which I don't already know?" Sithas asked skeptically.

"Kith-Kanan himself." His mother stopped to face him as the doors opened and the warmth of the tower beckoned. "Bring him home, Sithas," she said urgently, taking both of his arms in her hands. "Bring him home and talk to him!"

Sithas was surprised at his own instinctive reaction. The suggestion made surprisingly good sense. It offered him hope—and an idea for action that would unite, not divide, his people. Yet how could he call his brother home now, out of the midst of a monstrous encircling army?

* * * * *

The next day Quimant again was Sithas's first and primary visitor.

"My lord," began the adviser, "have you made a decision about conscription of additional forces? I am reluctant to remind you, but time may be running short."

Sithas frowned. Unbidden, his mind recalled the scene at the riverbank when the first column departed for war. Now more than half those elves were dead. What would be the city's reaction should another, larger force march west?

"Not yet. I wish to wait until . . . " His voice trailed off. He had been about to mention Ambrodel's mission. "I will not make that decision yet," he concluded.

He was spared the necessity of further discussion when Stankathan, his palace majordomo, entered the great hall. That dignified elf, clad in a black waistcoat of wool, preceded a travel-stained messenger who wore the leather jerkin of a Wildrunner scout. The latter bore a scroll of parchment sealed with a familiar stamp of red wax.

"A message from my brother?" Sithas rose to his feet, recognizing the form of the sheet.

"By courier, who came from across the river just this morning," replied Stankathan. "I brought him over to the tower directly."

Sithas felt a surge of delight, as he did every fortnight or so when a courier arrived with the latest reports from Kith-

Kanan. Yet that delight had lately been tempered by the grim news from his brother and the besieged garrison.

He looked at the courier as the elf approached and bowed deeply. Besides the dirt and mud of the trail, Sithas saw that the fellow had a sling supporting his right arm and a dark-stained bandage around the leggings of his left knee.

"My gratitude for your efforts," said Sithas, appraising the rider. The elf stood taller after his words, as if the praise of the speaker was a balm to his wounds. "What was the nature of your obstacles?"

"The usual rings of guards, Your Highness," replied the elf. "But the humans lack sorcerers and so cannot screen the paths with magic. The first day of my journey I was concealed by invisibility, a spell that camouflaged myself and my horse. Afterward, the fleetness of my steed carried me, and I encountered only one minor fray."

The Speaker of the Stars took the scroll and broke the wax seal. Carefully he unrolled the sheet, ignoring Quimant for the time being. The lord stood quietly; if he was annoyed, he made no visible sign of the fact.

Sithas read the missive solemnly.

I look out, my brother, upon an endless sea of humanity. Indeed, they surround us like the ocean surrounds an island, completely blocking our passage. It is only with great risk that my couriers can penetrate the lines—that, and the aid of spells cast by my enchanters, which allow them some brief time to escape the notice of the foe.

What is to be the fate now of our cause? Will the army of Ergoth attack and carry the fort? Their horses sweep in great circles about us, but the steeds cannot reach us here. The other two wings have joined General Giarna before Sithelbec, and their numbers truly stun the mind.

General Giarna, I have learned, is the name of the foe we faced in the spring, the one who drove us from the field. We have taken prisoners from his force, and to a man they speak of their devotion to him and their confidence that he will one day destroy us! I met him in the brief hours I was prisoner, and he is a terrifying man. There is something deep and cruel about him that transcended any foe I have ever encountered.

Will the dwarves of Thorbardin march from their stronghold and break the siege from the south? That, my brother, would be a truly magnificent feat of diplomacy on your part. Should you bring such an alliance into being, I could scarce convey my gratitude across the miles!

Or will the hosts of Silvanost march forth, the elves united in their campaign against the threat to our race? That, I am afraid, is the least likely of my musings—at least, from the words you give me as to our peoples' apathy and lack of concern. How fares the diplomatic battle, Brother?

I hope to amuse you with one tale, an experience that gave us all many moments of distraction, not to mention fear. I have written to you of the gnomish lava cannon, the mountain vehicle pulled by a hundred oxen, its stony maw pointed skyward as it belches smoke and fire. Finally, shortly after my last letter, this device was hauled into place before Sithelbec. It stood some three miles away but loomed so high and spumed so furiously that we were indeed distraught!

For three days, the monstrous structure became the center of a whirlwind of gnomish activity. They scaled its sides, fed coal into its bowels, poured great quantities of muck and dust and streams of a red powder into its maw. All this time, the thing puffed and chugged, and by the third day, the entire plain lay shrouded beneath a cloud from its wheezing exhalations.

Finally the gnomes clambered up the sides and stood atop the device, as if they had scaled a small mountain. We watched, admittedly with great trepidation, as one of the little creatures mixed a caldron at the very lip of the cannon's interior. Eventually he cast the contents of the vessel into the weapon itself. All of the gnomes fled, and for the first time, we noticed that the humans had pulled back from the cannon, giving it a good half-mile berth to either side.

For a full day, the army of Ergoth huddled in fright, staring at their monstrous weapon. Finally it appeared that it had failed to discharge, but it was not until the following day that we watched the gnomes creep forward to investigate.

Suddenly the thing began to chug and wheeze and belch. The gnomes scurried for cover, and for another full day, we all watched and waited. But it was not until the morning of the third day that we saw the weapon in action.

It exploded shortly after dawn and cast its formidable ordnance for many miles. Fortunately we, as the targets of the attack, were safe. It was the gathered human army that suffered the brunt of flaming rock and devastating force that ripped across the plains.

We saw thousands of the humans' horses (unfortunately a small fraction of their total number) stampede in panic across the plain. Whole regiments vanished beneath the deluge of death as a sludgelike wave spread through the army.

For a brief moment, I saw the opportunity to make a sharp attack, further disrupting the encircling host. Even as I ordered the attack, however, the ranks of General Giarna's wing shouldered aside the other humans. His deadly riders ensured that our trap remained effectively closed.

Nevertheless, the accident wreaked havoc among the Army of Ergoth. We gave thanks to the gods that the device misfired; had its attack struck Sithelbec, you would have already received your last missive from me. The cannon has been reduced to a heap of rubble, and we pray daily that it cannot be rebuilt.

My best wishes and hopes for my new niece or nephew. Which is it to be? Perhaps you will have the answer by the time you read this. I can only hope that somehow I will know. I hope Hermathya is comfortable and well.

I miss your counsel and presence as always, Brother. I treat myself to the thought that, could we but bring our minds together, we could work a way to break out of this stalemate. But, alas, the jaws of the trap close about me, and I know that you, in the capital, are ensnared in every bit as tight a position as I.

Until then, have a prayer for us! Give my love to Mother!

Kith

Sithas paused, realizing that the guards and Quimant had been studying him intently as he read. A full range of emotions had played across his face, he knew, and suddenly the knowledge made him feel exceedingly vulnerable.

"Leave me, all of you!" Sithas barked the command, more harshly perhaps than he intended, but he was nevertheless gratified to see them all quickly depart from the hall.

He paced back and forth before the emerald throne. His brother's letter had agitated him more than usual, for he knew that he had to do something. No longer could he force the standoff at Sithlebec into the back of his mind. His mother and his brother were right. He needed to *see* Kith-Kanan, to *talk* with him. They would be able to work out a plan—a plan with some hope of success!

Remembering his walk with Nirakina, he turned toward the royal doors of crystal. The gardens—and the stables—lay beyond.

Resolutely Sithas stalked to those doors, which opened silently before him. He emerged from the tower into the cool sunlight of the garden but took no note of his surroundings. Instead, he crossed directly to the royal stable.

The stable was in fact a sprawling collection of buildings and corrals. These included barns for the horses and small houses for the grooms and trainers, as well as stocks of feed. Behind the main structure, a field of short grass stretched away from the Tower of the Stars, covering the palace grounds to the edges of the guildhouses that bordered them.

Here were kept the several dozen horses of the royal family, as well as several coaches and carriages. But it was to none of these that the speaker now made his way.

Instead, he crossed through the main barn, nodding with easy familiarity to the grooms who brushed the sleek stallions. He passed through the far door and crossed a small corral, approaching a sturdy building that stood by itself, unattached to any other. The door was divided into top and bottom halves; the top half stood open.

A form moved within the structure, and then a great head emerged from the door. Bright golden eyes regarded Sithas with distrust and suspicion.

The front of that head was a long, wickedly hawklike

beak. The beak opened slightly. Sithas saw the great wings flex within the confining stable and knew that Arcuballis longed to fly.

"You must go to Kith-Kanan," Sithas told the powerful steed. "Bring him out of his fort and back to me. Do this, Arcuballis, when I let you fly!"

The griffon's large eyes glittered as the creature studied the Speaker of the Stars. Arcuballis had been Kith-Kanan's lifelong mount until the duties of generalship had forced his brother to take a more conventional steed. Sithas knew that the griffon would go and bring his brother back.

Slowly Sithas reached forward and unlatched the bottom half of the door, allowing the portal to swing freely open. Arcuballis hesitantly stepped forward over the half-eaten carcass of a deer that lay just inside the stable.

With a spreading of his great wings, Arcuballis gave a mighty spring. He bounded across the corral, and by his third leap, the griffon was airborne. His powerful wings drove downward and the creature gained height, soaring over the roof of the stable, then veering to pass near the Tower of the Stars.

"Go!" cried Sithas. "Go to Kith-Kanan!"

As if he heard, the griffon swept through a turn. Powerful wings still driving him upward, Arcuballis swerved toward the west.

It seemed to Sithas as if a heavy burden had flown away from him, borne upon the wings of the griffon. His brother would understand, he knew. When Arcuballis arrived at Sithelbec, as Sithas felt certain he would, Kith-Kanan would waste no time in mounting his faithful steed and hastening back to Silvanost. Between them, he knew, they would find a way to advance the elven cause.

"Excellency?"

Sithas whirled, startled from his reverie by a voice from behind him. He saw Stankathan, the majordomo, looking out of place among the mud and dung of the corral. The elf's face, however, was knit by a deeper concern.

"What is it?" Sithas inquired quickly.

"It's your wife, the Lady Hermathya," replied Stankathan. "She cries with pain now. The clerics tell me it is time for your child to be born."

❦ 7 ❧

Three Days Later

The oil lamp sputtered in the center of the wooden ta-
ble. The flame was set low to conserve precious fuel for the
long, dark months of winter that lay ahead. Kith-Kanan
thought the shadowy darkness appropriate for this bleak
meeting.

With him at the table sat Kencathedrus and Parnigar.
Both of them—as well as Kith, himself—showed the gaunt-
ness of six months at half rations. Their eyes carried the dull
awareness that many more months of the same lay before
them.

Every night during that time, Kith had met with these
two officers, both of them trusted friends and seasoned veterans. They gathered in this small room, with its plain table

and chairs. Sometimes they shared a bottle of wine, but that commodity, too, had to be rationed carefully.

"We have a report from the Wildrunners," Parnigar began. "White-lock managed to slip through the lines. He told me that the small companies we have roaming the woods can hit hard and often. But they have to keep moving, and they don't dare venture onto the plains."

"Of course not!" Kencathedrus snapped.

The two officers argued, as they did so often, from their different tactical perspectives. "We'll never make any progress if we keep dispersing our forces through the woods. We have to gather them together! We must mass our strength!"

Kith sighed and held up his hands. "We all know that our 'mass of strength' would be little more than a nuisance to the human army—at least right now. The fortress is the only thing keeping the Wildrunners from annihilation, and the hit-and-run tactics are all we *can* do until . . . until something happens."

He trailed off weakly, knowing he had touched upon the heart of their despair. True, for the time being they were safe enough in Sithelbec from direct attack. And they had food that could be stretched, with the help of their clerics, to last for a year, perhaps a little longer.

In sudden anger, Kencathedrus smashed his fist on the table. "They hold us here like caged beasts!" he growled. "What kind of fate do we consign ourselves to?"

"Calm yourself, my friend." Kith touched his old teacher on the shoulder, seeing the tears in the elven warrior's eyes. His eyes were framed by sunken skin, dark brown in color, that accentuated further the hollowness of the elf's cheeks. By the gods, do we all look like that? Kith had to wonder.

The captain of Silvanost pushed himself to his feet and turned away from them. Parnigar cleared his throat awkwardly. "There is nothing we can accomplish by morning," he said. Quietly he got to his feet.

Parnigar, alone of the three of them, had a wife here. He worried more about her health than his own. She was human, one of several hundred in the fort, but this was a fact that they carefully avoided in conversation. Though Kith-Kanan knew and liked the woman, Kencathedrus still found the interracial marriage deeply disturbing.

"May you rest well tonight, noble elves," Parnigar offered before stepping through the door into the dark night beyond.

"I know your need to avenge the battle on the plains," Kith-Kanan said to Kencathedrus as the latter turned and gathered his cloak. "I believe this, my friend—your chance will come!"

The elven captain looked at the general, so much younger than himself, and Kith could see that Kencathedrus wanted to believe him. His eyes were dry again, and finally the captain nodded gruffly. "I'll see you in the morning," he promised before following Parnigar into the night.

Kith sat for a while, staring at the dying flame of the lantern, reluctant to extinguish the light even though he knew precious fuel burned away with each second. Not enough fuel . . . not enough food . . . insufficient troops. What did he have *enough* of, besides problems?

He tried not to think about the extent of his frustration—how much he hated being trapped inside the fortress, cooped up with his entire army, at the mercy of the enemy beyond the walls. How he longed for the freedom of the forests, where he had lived so happily during his years away from Silvanost.

Yet with these thoughts, he couldn't help thinking of Anaya—beautiful, lost Anaya. Perhaps his true entrapment had begun with her death, before the war started, before he had been made general of his father's—and then his brother's—army.

Finally he sighed, knowing that his thoughts could bring him no comfort. Reluctantly he doused the lantern's flame. His own bunk occupied the room adjacent to this office, and soon he lay there.

But sleep would not come. That night they had had no wine to share, and now the tension of his mood kept Kith-Kanan awake for seeming hours after his two officers left.

Eventually, with the entire fortress silent and still around him, his eyes fell shut—but not to the darkness of restful sleep. Instead, it was as though he fell directly from wakefulness into a very vivid dream.

He dreamed that he soared through the clouds, not upon the back of Arcuballis as he had flown so many times before, but supported by the strength of his own arms, his own feet. He swooped and dove like an eagle, master of the sky.

Abruptly the clouds parted before him, and he saw three conical mountain peaks jutting upward from the haze of earth so far below. These monstrous peaks belched smoke, and streaks of fire splashed and flowed down their sides. The valleys extending from their feet were hellish wastelands of crimson lava and brown sludge.

Away from the peaks he soared, and now below him were lifeless valleys of a different sort. Surrounded by craggy ridges and needlelike peaks, these mountain retreats lay beneath great sheets of snow and ice. All around him stretched a pristine brilliance. Gray and black shapes, the forms of towering summits, rose from the vast glaciers of pure white. In places, streaks of blue showed through the snow, and here Kith-Kanan saw ice as clean, as clear as any on Krynn.

Movement suddenly caught his eye in one of these valleys. He saw a great mountain looming, higher than all the others around. Upon its face, dripping ice formed the crude outlines of a face like that of an old, white-bearded dwarf.

Kith continued his flight and saw movement again. At first Kith thought that he was witnessing a great flock of eagles—savage, prideful birds that crowded the sky. Then he wondered, Could they be some kind of mountain horses or unusual, tawny-colored goats?

In another moment, he knew, as the memory of Arcuballis came flooding back. These were griffons, a whole flock of them! Hundreds of the savage half-eagle, half-lion creatures were surging through the air toward Kith-Kanan.

He felt no fear. Instead, he turned away from the dwarfbeard mountain and flew southward. The griffons followed, and slowly the heights of the range fell behind him. He saw lakes of blue water below him and fields of brush and mossy rock. Then came the first trees, and he dove to follow a mountain rivulet toward the green flatlands that now opened up before him.

And then he saw her in the forest—Anaya! She was painted like a wild savage, her naked body flashing among the trees as she ran from him. By the gods, she was fast! She outdistanced him even as he flew, and soon the only trace of her passage was the wild laughter that lingered on the breeze before him.

Then he found her, but already she had changed. She was old, and rooted in the ground. Before his eyes, she had become a tree, growing toward the heavens and losing all of the form and the senses of the elfin woman he had grown to love.

His tears flowed, unnoticed, down his face. They soaked the ground and nourished the tree, causing it to shoot farther into the sky. Sadly the elf left her, and he and his griffons flew on farther to the south.

Another face wafted before him. He recognized with shock the human woman who had given him his escape from the enemy camp. Why, now, did she enter his dream?

The rivulet below him became a stream, and then more streams joined it, and the stream became a river, flowing into the forested realm of his homeland.

Ahead he finally saw a ring of water where the River Thon-Thalas parted around the island of Silvanost. Behind him, five hundred griffons followed him homeward. A radiant glow reached out to welcome him.

He saw another elfwoman in the garden. She looked upward, her arms spread, welcoming him to his home, to her. At first, from a distance, he wondered if this was his mother, but then as he dove closer, he recognized his brother's wife, Hermathya.

Sunlight streamed into his window. He awoke suddenly, refreshed and revitalized. The memory of his dream shone in his mind like a beacon, and he sprang from his bed. The fortress still slumbered around him. His window, on the east wall of a tower, was the first place in Sithelbec to receive the morning sun. Throwing a cloak over his tunic and sticking his feet into soft, high leather boots, he laced the latter around his knees while he hobbled toward the door.

A cry of alarm suddenly sounded from the courtyard. In the next moment, a horn blared, followed by a chorus of trumpets blasting a warning. Kith dashed from his room, down the hall of the captain's quarters and to the outside. The sun was barely cresting the fortress wall, and yet he saw a shadow pass across that small area of brightness.

He noted several archers on the wall, turning and aiming their weapons skyward.

"Don't shoot!" he cried as the shadow swooped closer and he recognized it. "Arcuballis!"

He waved his hand and ran into the courtyard as the proud griffon circled him once, then came to rest before him. The lion's hindquarter's squatted while the creature raised one foreclaw—the massive, taloned limb of an eagle. The keen yellow eyes blinked, and Kith-Kanan felt a surge of affection for his faithful steed.

In the next moment, he wondered about Arcuballis's presence here. He had left him in charge of his brother back in Silvanost. Of course! Sithas had sent the creature here to Kith to bring him home! The prospect elated him like nothing else had in years.

* * * * *

It took Kith-Kanan less than an hour to leave orders with his two subordinates. Parnigar he placed in overall command, while Kencathedrus was to drill and train a small, mobile sortie force of cavalry, pikes, and archers. They would be called the Flying Brigade, but they were not to be employed until Kith-Kanan's return. He cautioned both officers on the need to remain alert to any human strategem. Sithelbec was the keystone to any defense on the plains, and it must remain impregnable, inviolate.

"I'm sure my brother has plans. We'll meet and work out a way to break this stalemate!" The autumn wind swirled through the compound, bringing the first bite of winter.

He climbed onto the back of his steed, settling into the new saddle that one of the Wildrunner horsemen had cobbled for him.

"Good luck, and may the gods watch over your flight," Kencathedrus said, clasping Kith's gloved hand in both of his own.

"And bring a speedy return," added Parnigar.

Arcuballis thrust powerful wings, muscular and stout enough to break a man's neck, toward the ground. At the same time, the leonine hindquarters thrust the body into the air.

Several strokes of his wings carried Arcuballis to the top of a building, still inside the fortress wall. He grasped the peaked roof with his eagle foreclaws, then used his feline rear legs to spring himself still higher into the air. With a squawk that rang like a challenge across the plain, he soared over the wall, climbing steadily.

Kith-Kanan was momentarily awestruck at the spectacle of the enemy arrayed below him. His tower, the highest vantage point in Sithelbec, didn't convey the immense sprawl of the Army of Ergoth—not in the way that Arcuballis's ascending flight did. Below, ranks of human archers took up their weapons, but the griffon already soared far out of range.

They flew onward, passing above a great herd of horses in a pasture. The shadow of the griffon passed along the ground, and several of the steeds snorted and reared in sudden panic. These bolted immediately, and in seconds, the herd had erupted into a stampede. The elf watched in wry amusement as the human herdsmen raced out of the path of the beasts. It would be hours, he suspected, before order was restored to the camp.

Kith looked down at the smoldering remains of the lava cannon, now a black, misshapen thing, like a burned and gnarled tree trunk leaning at a steep angle over the ground. He saw seemingly endless rows of tents, some of them grand but most simple shelters of oilskin or wool. Everywhere the flat ground had been churned to mud.

Finally he left the circular fortress and the larger circle of the human army behind. Forests of lush green opened before him, dotted by ponds and lakes, streaked by rivers and long meandering meadows. As the wild land surrounded him, he felt the agony of the war fall away.

* * * * *

Suzine des Quivalen studied the image in the mirror until it faded into the distance, beyond the reach of her arcane crystal. Yet even after it vanished, the memory of those powerful wings carrying Kith-Kanan away—away from *her*—lingered in her mind.

She saw his blond hair, flying from beneath his helmet.

She recalled her gasp of terror when the archers had fired, and her slow relaxation as he gained height and safety. Yet a part of her had cursed and railed at him for leaving, and that part had wanted to see a human arrow bring him down. She didn't want him dead, of course, but the idea of this handsome elf as a prisoner in her camp was strangely appealing.

For a moment, she paused, wondering at the fascination she found for this elven commander, mortal enemy of her people and chief opponent of the man who was her . . . lover.

Once General Giarna had been that and more. Smooth, dashing, and handsome, he had swept her off her feet in the early days of their relationship. With the aid of her powers with the mirror, she had given him information sufficient to discredit several of the emperor's highest generals. The grateful ruler had rewarded the Boy General with an ever-increasing array of field commands.

But something had changed since those times. The man who she thought had loved her now treated her with cruelty and arrogance, inspiring in her fears that she could not overcome. Those fears were great enough to hold her at his side, for she had come to believe that flight from General Giarna would mean her sentence of death.

Here on the plains, in command of many thousands of men, Giarna had little time for her, which was a relief. But when she saw him, he seemed so coldly controlled, so monstrously purposeful, that she feared him all the more.

With an angry shake of her head, she turned from the mirror, which slowly faded into a reflection of the Lady Suzine and the interior of her tent. She rose in a swirl of silk and stalked across the rich carpets that blanketed the ground. Her red hair swirled in a long coil around her scalp, rising higher than her head and peaking in a glittering tiara of diamonds, emeralds, and rubies.

Her gown, of blood-red silk, clung to the full curves of her body as she stalked toward the tent flap that served as her door. She stopped long enough to throw a woolen shawl over her bare shoulders, remembering the chill that had settled over the plains in the last few days.

As soon as she emerged, the six men-at-arms standing at

her door snapped to attention, bringing their halberds straight before their faces. She paid no attention as they fell in behind her, marching with crisp precision as she headed toward another elegant tent some distance away. The black stallion of General Giarna stood restlessly outside, so she knew that the man she sought was within.

The Army of Ergoth spread to the horizons around her. The massive encampment encircled the fortress of Sithelbec in a great ring. Here, at the eastern arc of that ring, the headquarters of the three generals and their retinues had collected. Amid the mud and smoke of the army camp, the gilded coaches of the noble lancers and the tall, silken folds of the high officers' tents, stood out in contrast.

Before Suzine arose the tallest tent of all, that of General Barnet, the overall general of the army.

The two guards before that tent stepped quickly out of the way to let her pass, one of them pulling aside the tent flap to give her entrance. She passed into the semidarkness of the tent, and her eyes quickly adjusted to the dim light. She saw General Giarna lounging easily at a table loaded with food and drink. Before him, sitting stiffly, was General Barnet. Suzine couldn't help but notice the fear and anger in the older general's eyes as he looked at her.

Beyond the two seated men stood a third, General Xalthan. That veteran's face was deathly, shockingly pale. He surprised Suzine by looking at her with an expression of pleading, as if he hoped that she could offer him succor for some terrible predicament.

"Come in, my dear," said Giarna, his voice smooth, his manner light. "We are having a farewell toast to our friend, General Xalthan."

"Farewell?" she asked, having heard nothing of that worthy soldier's departure.

"By word of the emperor—by special courier, with an escort. Quite an honor, really," added Giarna, his tone mocking and cruel.

Instantly Suzine understood. The disaster with the lava cannon had been the last straw, as far as the emperor was concerned, for General Xalthan. He had been recalled to Daltigoth under guard.

To his credit, the wing commander nodded stiffly, retaining his composure even in the face of Giarna's taunts. General Barnet remained immobile, but the hatred in his eyes now flashed toward Giarna. Suzine, too, felt an unexpected sense of loathing toward the Boy General.

"I'm sorry," she said to the doomed wing commander quietly. "I really am." Indeed, the depths of her sorrow surprised her. She had never thought very much about Xalthan, except sometimes to feel uncomfortable when his eyes ran over the outlines of her body if she wore a clinging gown.

But the old man was guilty of no failing, she suspected, except an inability to move as quickly as the Boy General. Xalthan stood in the path of Giarna's desire to command the entire army. General Giarna's reports to the emperor, she felt certain, had been full of the information she had provided him—news of Xalthan's sluggish advance, the ineptness of the gnomish artillerymen, all details that could make a vengeful and impatient ruler lose his patience.

And cause an old warrior who deserved only a peaceful retirement face instead a prospect of torture, disgrace, and execution.

The knowledge made Suzine feel somehow dirty.

Xalthan looked at her with that puppylike sense of hope, a hope she could do nothing to gratify. His fate was laid in stone before them: There would be a long ride to Daltigoth, perhaps with the formerly esteemed officer bound in chains. Once there, the emperor's inquisitors would begin, often with Quivalen himself in attendance.

It was rumored that the emperor received great pleasure from watching the torture of those he felt had failed him. No tool was too devious, no tactic too inhumane, for these monstrous sculptors of pain. Fire and steel, venoms and acids, all were the instruments of their ungodly work. Finally, after days or weeks of indescribable agony, the inquisitors would be finished, and Xalthan would be healed—just enough to allow him to be alert for the occasion of his public execution.

The fact that her cousin was the one who would do this to the man didn't enter into her considerations. She accepted, fatalistically, that this was the way things would happen. Her role in the court family was to be one who remained docile and sensitive to her duties, useful with her skills as seer. She had to play that role and leave the rest to fate.

Just for a moment, a nearly overwhelming urge possessed her, a desire to flee this army camp, to flee the gracious life of the capital, to fly from all the darkness that seemed to surround her empire's endeavors. She wanted to go to a place where troubles such as this one remained concealed from delicate eyes.

It was only when she remembered the blond-haired elf who so fascinated her that she paused. Even though he had gone, flown from Sithelbec on the back of his winged steed, she felt certain he would return. She didn't know why, but she wanted to be here when he did.

"Farewell, General," she said quietly, crossing to embrace the once-proud warrior. Without another glance at Giarna, she turned and left the tent.

Suzine retreated to her own shelter, anger rising within her. She stalked back and forth within the silken walls, resisting the urge to throw things, to rant loudly at the air. For all her efforts at self-control, her vaunted discipline seemed to have deserted her. She could not calm herself.

Suddenly she gasped as the tent flap flew open and her general's huge form blocked out the light. Instinctively she backed away as he marched into her shelter, allowing the flap to fall closed behind him.

"That was quite a display," he growled, his voice like a blast of winter's wind. His dark eyes glowered, showing none of the amusement they had displayed at Xalthan's predicament.

"What—what do you mean?" she stammered, still backing away. She held her hand to her mouth and stared at him, her green eyes wide. A trace of her red hair spilled across her brow, and she angrily pushed it away from her face.

Giarna crossed to her in three quick strides, taking her wrists in both his hands. He pulled her arms to her sides and stared into her face, his mouth twisted into a menacing sneer.

"Stop—you're hurting me!" she objected, twisting powerlessly in his grip.

"Hear me well, wench," he growled, his voice barely

audible. "Do not attempt to mock me again—ever! If you do, that shall be the end your power . . . the end of *everything!*"

She gasped, frightened beyond words.

"I have chosen you for my woman. That fact pleased you once; perhaps it may please you again. Whether it does or not is irrelevant to me. Your skills, however, are of use to me. The others wonder at the great intelligence I gain concerning the elven army, and so you will continue to serve me thus.

"But you will *not* affront me again!" General Giarna paused, and his dark eyes seemed to mock Suzine's terrified stare.

"Do I make myself perfectly clear?" Giarna demanded, and she nodded quickly, helplessly. She feared his power and his strength, and she could only tremble in the grip of his powerful hands.

"Remember well," added the general. He fixed her with a penetrating gaze, and she felt the blood drain from her face. Without another word, he spun on his heel and stalked imperiously from the tent.

* * * * *

The flight to Silvanost took four days, for Kith allowed Arcuballis to hunt in the forest, while he himself took the time to rest at night on a lush bed of pine boughs amid the noisy, friendly chatter of the woods.

On the second day of his flight, Kith-Kanan stopped early, for he had reached a place that he intended to visit. Arcuballis dove to earth in the center of a blossom-bright clearing, and Kith dismounted. He walked over to a tree that grew strong and proud, shading a wide area, far wider than when he had last been here a year before.

"Anaya, I miss you," he said quietly.

He rested at the foot of the tree and spent several hours in bittersweet reflection of the elfwoman he'd loved and lost. But he didn't find total despair in the memory, for this was indeed Anaya beside him now. She grew tall and flourished, a part of the woods she had always loved.

She had been a creature of the woods, and together with

her "brother" Mackeli, the forest's guardian as well. For a moment, the pain threatened to block out the happier memories. Why did they die? For what purpose? Anaya killed by marauders. Mackeli slain by assassins—sent, Kith suspected, by someone in Silvanost itself.

Anaya hadn't really died, he reminded himself. Instead, she had undergone a bizarre transformation and become a tree, rooted firmly in the forest soil she loved and had strived to protect.

Then a disturbing vision intruded itself into Kith's reminiscences, and the picture of Anaya, laughing and bright before him, changed slightly. A beautiful elven woman still teased him, but now the face was different, no longer Anaya's.

Hermathya! The image of his first love, now his brother's wife, struck him like a physical blow. Angrily he shook his head, trying to dispel her features, to call back those of Anaya. Yet Hermathya remained before him, her eyes bold and challenging, her smile alluring.

Kith-Kanan exhaled sharply, surprised by the attraction he still felt for the Silvanesti woman. He had thought that impulse long dead, an immature passion that had run its course and been banished to the past. Now he imagined her supple body, her clinging, low-cut gown tailored to show enough to excite while concealing enough to mystify. He found himself vaguely ashamed to realize that he still desired her.

As he shook his head in an effort to banish the disturbing emotion, a picture of still a third woman insinuated itself. He recalled again the red-haired human woman who had given him his chance to escape from the enemy camp. There had been something vibrant and compelling about her, and this wasn't the first time he had remembered her face.

The conflicting memories warred within him as he built a small fire and ate a simple meal. He camped in the clearing, as usual making himself a soft bed. The night passed in peace.

He took to the air at first light, feeling as if he had somehow sullied Anaya's memory, but soon the clean air swept through his hair, and his mind focused on the day's journey. Arcuballis carried him swiftly and uneventfully eastward.

After his third night of sleeping in the woods, he felt as if his strength had been doubled, his wit and alertness greatly enhanced.

His spirits soared as high as the Tower of the Stars, which now appeared on the distant horizon. Arcuballis carried him steadily, but so far was the tower that more than an hour passed before they reached the Thon-Thalas River, border to the island of Silvanost.

His arrival was anticipated; boatmen on the river waved and cheered as he flew overhead, while a crowd of elves hurried toward the Palace of Quinari. The doors at the foot of the tower burst open, and Kith saw a blond-haired elf, clad in the silk robe of the Speaker of the Stars, emerge. Sithas hurried across the garden, but the griffon met him halfway.

Grinning foolishly, Kith leapt from the back of his steed to embrace his brother. It felt very good to be home.

PART II:

SCIONS OF SILVANOS

❧ 8 ❧

mɪᴅᴀᴜᴛᴜᴍɴ, 2214 (ᴘᴄ)

"By Quenesti Pah, he's beautiful!" Kith-kanan cautiously took the infant in his arms. Proudly Sithas stood beside them. Kith had been on the ground for all of five minutes before the Speaker of the Stars had hurried him to the nursery to see the newest heir to the throne of Silvanesti.

"It takes a while before you feel certain that you won't break him," he told his brother, based on his own extensive paternal experience, a good two months' worth now.

"Vanesti—it's a good name. Proud, full of our heritage," Kith said. "A name worthy of the heir of the House of Silvanos."

Sithas looked at his brother and his son, and he felt better than he had in months. Indeed, he knew a gladness that hadn't been his since the start of the war.

The door to the nursery opened and Hermathya entered. She approached Kith-Kanan nervously, her eyes upon her child. At first, the elven general thought that his sister-in-law's tension resulted from the memory of them together. Kith and Hermathya's affair, before her engagement to Sithas, had been brief but passionate.

But then he realized that her anxiety came from a simpler, more direct source. She was concerned that someone other than herself held her child.

"Here," said Kith, offering the silk-swathed infant to Hermathya. "You have a very handsome son."

"Thank you." She took the child, then smiled hesitantly. Kith tried to see her in a different light than he did in his memories. He told himself that she looked nothing like the woman he had known, had thought he loved, those few years earlier.

Then the memories came back in a physical rush that almost brought him to his knees. Hermathya smiled again, and Kith-Kanan ached with desire. He lowered his eyes, certain that his bold feelings showed plainly on his face. By the gods, she was his brother's wife! What kind of distorted loyalty tortured him that he could think these thoughts, feel these needs.

He cast a quick, apprehensive glance at Sithas and saw that his brother looked only at the baby. Hermathya, however, caught his eye, her own gaze sparking like fire. What was happening? Suddenly Kith-Kanan felt very frightened and very lonely.

"You should both be very happy," he said awkwardly.

They said nothing, but each looked at Vanesti in a way that communicated their love and pride.

"Now let's take care of business," said Sithas to his brother. "The war."

Kith sighed. "I knew we'd have to get around to the war sooner or later, but can we make it a little bit later? I'd like to see Mother first."

"Of course. How stupid of me," Sithas agreed. If he had noticed any of the feelings that Kith had thought showed so plainly on his face, the Speaker gave no sign. His voice dropped slightly. "She's in her quarters. She'll be delighted to see you. I think it's just what she needs."

Kith-Kanan looked at his brother curiously, but Sithas did not elaborate. Instead, the Speaker continued in a different vein.

"I've had some Thalian blond wine chilled in my apartment. I want to hear everything that's happened since the start of the war. Come and find me after you've spoken to Nirakina."

"I will. I've got a lot to tell, but I want to know how things have fared in the city as well." Kith-Kanan followed Sithas from the nursery, quietly closing the door. Before it shut, he looked back and saw Hermathya cuddling the baby to her breast. The elf-woman's eyes looked up suddenly and locked upon Kith's, making an electric connection that he had to force himself to break.

The two elves, leaders of the nation, walked in silence through the long halls of the Palace of Quinari. They reached the apartments of their mother, and Kith stopped as Sithas walked silently on.

"Enter" came her familiar voice in response to his soft knock.

He pushed open the door and saw Nirakina seated in a chair by the open window. She rose and swept him into her arms, hugging him as if she would never let him go.

He was shocked by the aging apparent in his mother's face, an aging that was all the more distressing because of the long elven life span. By rights, she was just reaching middle age and could look forward to several productive centuries before she approached old age.

Yet her face, drawn by cares, and the gray streaks that had begun to silver her hair reminded Kith of his grandmother, in the years shortly before her death. It was a revelation that disturbed him deeply.

"Sit down, Mother," Kith said quietly, leading her back to her chair. "Are you all right?"

Nirakina looked at him, and the son had trouble facing his mother's eyes. So much despair!

"Seeing you does much to bring my strength back," she replied, offering a wan smile. "It seems I'm surrounded by strangers so much now."

"Surely Sithas is here with you."

"Oh, when he can be, but there is much to occupy him. The affairs of war, and now his child. Vanesti is a beautiful baby, don't you agree?"

Kith nodded, wondering why he didn't hear more pleasure in his mother's voice. This was her first grandchild!

"But Hermathya thinks that I get in the way, and her sisters are here to help. I have seen too little of Vanesti." Nirakina's eyes drifted to the window. "I miss your father. I miss him so much sometimes that I can hardly stand it."

Kith struggled for words. Failing, he took his mother's hands in his own.

"The palace, the city—it's all changing," she continued. "It's the war. In your absence, Lord Quimant advises your brother. It seems the palace is becoming home to all of Clan Oakleaf."

Kith had heard of Quimant in Sithas's letters and knew his brother considered him to be a great assistance in affairs of state.

"What of Tamanier Ambrodel?" The loyal elf had been his mother's able aide and had saved her life during the riots that had rocked the city before the outbreak of war. Sithel had promoted him to lord chamberlain to reward his loyalty. His mother and Tamanier had been good friends for many years."

"He's gone. Sithas tells me not to worry, and I know he has embarked upon a mission in the service of the throne. But he has been absent a long time, and I cannot help but miss him."

She looked at him, and he saw tears in her eyes. "Sometimes I feel like so much excess baggage, locked away in my room here, waiting for my life to pass!"

Kith sat back, shocked and dismayed by his mother's despair. This was so unlike the Nirakina he had always known, an elfwoman full of vigor, serene and patient against the background of his father's rigid ideas. He tried to hide his churning emotions beneath a lighthearted tone.

"Tomorrow we'll go riding," he said, realizing that sunset approached quickly. "I have to meet Sithas tonight to make my reports. But meet me for breakfast in the dining hall, won't you?"

Nirakina smiled, for the first time with her eyes as well as her lips. "I'd like that," she said. But the memory of her lined, unhappy face stuck with him as he left her chambers and made his way to his brother's library.

"Come in," announced Sithas, as two liveried halberdiers of the House Protectorate snapped to attention before the silver-plated doors to the royal apartment. One of them pulled the door open, and the general entered.

"We wish to be alone," announced the Speaker of the Stars, and the guards nodded silently.

The pair settled into comfortable chairs, near the balcony that gave them an excellent view of the Tower of the Stars, which rose into the night sky across the gardens. The red moon, Lunitari, and the pale orb of Solinari illuminated the vista, casting shadows through the winding passages of the garden paths.

Sithas filled two mugs and placed the bottle of fine wine back into its bucket of melting ice. Handing one mug to his brother, he raised his own and met Kith's with a slight clink.

"To victory," he offered.

"Victory!" Kith-Kanan repeated.

They sat and, sensing that his brother wanted to speak first, the army commander waited expectantly. His intuition was correct.

"By all the gods, I wish I could be there with you!" Sithas began, his tone full of conviction.

Kith didn't doubt him. "War's not what I thought it would be," he admitted. "Mostly it's waiting, discomfort, and tedium. We are always hungry and cold, but mostly bored. It seems that days and weeks go by when nothing happens of consequence."

He sighed and paused for a moment to take a deep draft of his wine. The sweet liquid soothed his throat and loosened his tongue. "Then, when things do start to happen, you're more frightened than you ever thought was possible. You fight for your life; you run when you have to. You try to stay in touch with what's going on, but it's impossible. Just as quickly, the fight's over and you go back to being bored. Except now you have the grief, too, knowing that brave companions have died this day, some of them because you made the wrong decision. Even the right decision sometimes sends too many good elves to their deaths."

Sithas shook his head sadly. "At least you have some control over events. I sit here, hundreds of miles away. I send those good elves to live or die without the slightest knowledge of what will befall them."

"That knowledge is slim comfort," replied his brother.

Kith-Kanan told his brother, in elaborate detail, about the battles in which the Wildrunners had fought the Army of Ergoth. He talked of their initial small victories, of the plodding advance of the central and southern wings. He described the fast-moving horsemen of the north wing and their keen and brutal commander, General Giarna. His voice broke as he related the tale of the trap that had ensnared Kencathedrus and his proud regiment, and for a moment, he lapsed into a miserable silence.

Sithas reached out and touched his brother on the shoulder. The gesture seemed to renew Kith-Kanan's strength, and after drawing a deep breath, he began to speak again.

He told of their forced retreat into the fortress, of the numberless horde of humans surrounding them, barring the Wildrunners against any real penetration. The wine bottle emptied—it may as well have been by evaporation, for all the notice the brothers took—and the moons crept toward the western horizon. Sithas rang for another bottle of Thalian blond as Kith described the state of supplies and morale within Sithelbec and talked about their prospects for the future.

"We can hold out through the winter, perhaps well into next year. But we cannot shake the grip around us, not unless something happens to break this stalemate!"

"Something such as what? More reinforcements—another five thousand elves from Silvanost?" Sithas leaned close to his brother, disturbed by the account of the war. The setbacks suffered by the Wildrunners were temporary—this the speaker truly believed—and together they had to figure out some way to turn the tide.

Kith shook his head. "That would help—*any* reinforcements you can send would help—but even twice that many elves would not turn the tide. Perhaps the Army of Thorbardin, if the dwarves can be coaxed from their mountain retreat . . ." His voice showed that he placed little hope in this possibility.

"It might happen," Sithas replied. "You didn't get to know Lord Dunbarth as did I, when he spent a year among us in the city. He is a trustworthy fellow, and he bears no love for the humans. I think he realizes that his own kingdom will be next in line for conquest unless he can do something now."

Sithas described the present ambassador, the intransigent Than-Kar, in considerably less glowing terms. "He's a major stumbling block to any firm agreement, but there still might be some way around him."

"I'd like to talk to him myself," Kith said. "Can we bring him to the palace?"

"I can try," Sithas agreed, realizing how weak the phrase sounded. Father would have ordered it! he reminded himself. For a moment, he felt terribly ineffective, wishing he had Sithel's steady nerves. Angrily he pushed the sensation of doubt away and listened to his brother speak.

"I'll believe in dwarven help when I see their banners on the field and their weapons pointed *away* from us!"

"But what else?" pressed Sithas. "What other tactics do we have?"

"I wish I knew," his brother replied. "I hoped that you might have some suggestions."

"Weapons?" Sithas explained the key role Lord Quimant was playing to increase the munitions production at the Oakleak Clan's forges. "We'll get you the best blades that elven craftsmen can make."

"That's something—but still, we need more. We need something that cannot just stand against the human cavalry but break it. Drive it away!"

The second bottle of wine began to vanish as the elven lords wrestled with their problem. The first traces of dawn colored the sky, a thin line of pale blue on the horizon, but no ready solution came to mind.

"You know, I wasn't certain that Arcuballis could find you," Sithas said after a pause of several minutes. The frustration of their search for a solution weighed upon them, and Kith welcomed the change of conversation.

"He never looked so good to me," Kith-Kanan replied, "as when he came soaring into the fortress compound. I didn't realize how much I missed this place—how much I missed you and mother—until I saw him."

"He's been there in the stable since you left," Sithas said, shaking his head with a wry grin. "I don't know why I didn't think of sending him to you shortly after you were first besieged."

"I had a curious dream about him—about an entire flock of griffons, actually—on the very night before he arrived. It was most uncanny." Kith described his strange dream, and the two brothers pondered its meaning.

"A flock of griffons?" Sithas asked intently.

"Well, yes. Do you think it significant?"

"If we had a flock of griffons . . . if they all carried riders into combat . . . could that be the hammer needed to crack the shell around Sithelbec?" Sithas spoke with growing enthusiasm.

"Wait a minute," said Kith, holding up his hand. "I suppose you're right, in a hypothetical sense. In fact, the horses of the humans were spooked as I flew over, even though I was high, out of bowshot range. But who ever heard of an army of griffons?"

Sithas settled back, suddenly realizing the futility of his idea. For a moment, neither of them said anything—which was how they heard the soft rustling in the room behind them.

Kith-Kanan sprang to his feet, instinctively reaching for a sword at his hip, forgetting that his weapon hung back on the wall of his own apartment. Sithas whirled in his seat, staring in astonishment, and then he rose to his feet.

"*You!*" the Speaker barked, his voice taut with rage. "What are you doing here?"

Kith-Kanan crouched, preparing to spring at the intruder. He saw the figure, a mature elf cloaked in a silky gray robe, move forward from the shadows.

"Wait," said Sithas, much to his brother's surprise. The speaker held up his hand and Kith straightened, still tense and suspicious.

"One day your impudence will cost you," Sithas levelly as the elf approached them. "You are not to enter my chambers unannounced again. Is that clear?"

"Pardon my intrusion. As you know, my presence must remain discreet."

"Who is this?" Kith-Kanan demanded.

"Forgive me," said the gray-cloaked elf before Sithas cut him off.

"This is Vedvedsica," said Sithas. Kith-Kanan noted that his brother's tone had become carefully guarded. "He has . . . been helpful to the House of Silvanos in the past."

"The pleasure is mine, and it is indeed great, honored prince," offered Vedvedsica, with a deep bow to Kith-Kanan.

"Who are you? Why do you come here?" Kith demanded.

"In good time, lord—in good time. As to who I am, I am a cleric, a devoted follower of Gilean."

Kith-Kanan wasn't surprised. The god was the most purely neutral in the elven pantheon, most often used to justify self-aggrandizement and profit. Something about Vedvedsica struck him as very self-serving indeed.

"More to the point, I know of your dream."

The last was directed to Kith-Kanan and struck him like a lightning bolt between the eyes. For a moment, he hesitated, fighting an almost undeniable urge to hurl himself at the insolent cleric and kill him with his bare hands. Never before had he felt so violated.

"Explain yourself."

"I have knowledge that the two of you may desire— knowledge of griffons, hundreds of them. And even more important, I may have knowledge as to how they can be found and tamed."

For the moment, the elven lords remained silent, listening suspiciously as Vedvedsica moved forward. "May I?" inquired the cleric, gesturing to a seat beside their own.

Sithas nodded silently, and all three sat.

"The griffons dwell in the Khalkist Mountains, south of the Lords of Doom." The brothers knew of these peaks— three violent volcanoes in the heart of the forbidding range, high among vast glaciers and sheer summits. It was a region beyond the ken of elven explorers.

"How do you know this?" asked Sithas.

"Did your father ever tell you how he came to possess Arcuballis?" Again the cleric fixed Kith-Kanan with his gaze, then continued as if he already knew the answer. "He got him from me!"

Kith nodded, reluctant to believe the cleric but finding

himself unable to doubt the veracity of his words.

"I purchased him from a Kagonesti, a wild elf who told me of the whereabouts of the pack. He encountered them, together with a dozen companions. He alone escaped the wrath of the griffons, with one young cub—the one given by me to Sithel as a gift, and the one that he passed along to his son. To you, Kith-Kanan."

"But how could the flock be tamed? From what you say, a dozen elves perished to bring one tiny cub away!" Kith-Kanan challenged Vedvedsica. Despite his suspicions, he felt his own excitement begin to build.

"*I* tamed him, with the aid and protection of Gilean. I developed the spell that broke him to halter. It's a simple enchantment, really. Any elf with a working knowledge of the Old Script could have cast it. But only I could bring it into being!"

"Continue," said Sithas urgently.

"I believe that spell can be enhanced, developed so that many more of the creatures could be brought to heel. I can inscribe it onto a scroll. Then one of you can take it in search of the griffons."

"Are you certain that it will work?" demanded Sithas.

"No," replied the cleric frankly. "It will need to be presented under precise circumstances and with a great force of command. That is why the person who casts the spell must be a leader among elves—one of you two. No others of our race would have the necessary traits."

"How long would it take to prepare such a scroll?" pressed Kith. A cavalry company mounted on griffons, flying over the battlefield! The thought made his heart pound with excitement. They would be unstoppable!

Vedvedsica shrugged. "A week, perhaps two. It will be an arduous process."

"I'll go," Kith volunteered.

"Wait!" said Sithas sharply. "*I* should go! And I will!"

Kith-Kanan looked at the Speaker in astonishment. "That's crazy!" he argued. "You're the Speaker of the Stars. You have a wife, a child! More to the point, you're the leader of all Silvanesti! And you haven't ever lived in the wilderness before like I have! I can't allow you to take the risk!"

For a moment, the twins stared at each other, equally stubborn. The cleric was forgotten for the moment, and he melted into the shadows, discreet in his withdrawal.

It was Sithas who spoke.

"Do *you* read the Old Script?" he asked his brother bluntly. "Well enough to be certain of your words, when you know that the whole future of the realm could depend upon what you say?"

The younger twin sighed. "No. My studies always emphasized the outdoor skills. I'm afraid the ancient writing wouldn't make much sense to me."

Sithas smiled wryly. "I used to resent that. You were always out riding horses or hunting or learning swordsmanship, while I studied the musty tomes and forgotten histories. Well, now I'm going to put that learning to use.

"We'll both go," Sithas concluded.

Kith-Kanan stared at him, realizing the outcry such a plan would raise. Perhaps, he had to admit, this was the reason the scheme appealed to him. Slowly Kith relaxed, settling back into his chair.

"The trip won't be easy," Kith warned sternly. "We're going to have to explore the largest mountain range on Ansalon, and winter isn't far away. In those heights, you can be sure there's already plenty of snow."

"You can't scare me off," answered Sithas purposefully. "I know that Arcuballis can carry the two of us, and I don't care if it takes all winter. We'll *find* them, Kith. I know we will."

"You know," Kith-Kanan said ironically. "I must still be dreaming. In any event, you're right. The sons of Sithel ought to make this quest together."

With a final mug of wine, as the sky grew pale above them, they began to make their plans.

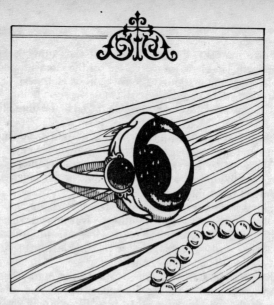

9

Next Morning

Kith-Kanan and his mother rode through the tree-lined streets of Silvanost for several hours, talking only of fond memories and pleasant topics from many years before. They stopped to enjoy the fountains, to watch the hawks dive for fish in the river, and to listen to the songbirds that clustered in the many flowered bushes of the city's lush gardens.

During the ride, it seemed to the elven warrior that his mother slowly came to life again, even to the point of laughing as they watched the pompous dance of a brilliant cardinal trying to impress his mate.

In the back of Kith's mind lurked the realization that his mother would soon learn of her sons' plans to embark on a dangerous expedition into the Khalkist Mountains. That news could wait, he decided.

"Are you going to join your brother at court?" asked Nirakina as the sun slid past the midafternoon point.

Kith sighed. "There'll be enough time for that tomorrow," he decided.

"Good." His mother looked at him, and he was delighted to see that the familiar sparkle had returned to her eyes. She spurred her horse with a sharp kick, and the mare raced ahead, leaving Kith with the challenge of her laugh as he tried to urge his older gelding into catching up.

They cantered beneath the shade of towering elms and dashed among the crystal columns of the elven homes in a friendly race toward the Gardens of Astarin and the royal stables. Nirakina was a good rider, with the faster horse; though Kith tried to spur the last energy from his own steed, his mother beat him through the palace gates by a good three lengths.

Laughing, they pulled up before the stables and dismounted. Nirakina turned toward him, impulsively pulling him into a hug. "Thank you," she whispered. "Thank you for coming home!"

Kith held her in silence for some moments, relieved that he hadn't discussed the twins' plans with her.

Leaving his mother at her chambers, he made his way to his own apartments, intending to bathe and dress for the banquet his brother had scheduled for that evening. Before he reached his door, however, a figure moved out of a nearby alcove.

Reflexively the elven warrior reached for a sword, a weapon that he did not usually carry in the secure confines of the palace. At the same time, he relaxed, recognizing the figure and realizing that there was no threat—at least, no threat of harm.

"Hermathya," he said, his voice oddly husky.

"Your nerves are stretched tight," she observed, with an awkward little laugh. She wore a turquoise gown cut low over her breasts. Her hair cascaded over her shoulders, and as she looked up at him, Kith-Kanan thought that she seemed as young and vulnerable as ever.

He forced himself to shake his head, remembering that

she was neither young nor vulnerable. Still, the spell of her innocent allure held him, and he wanted to reach out and sweep her into his arms.

With difficulty, he held his hands at his sides, waiting for Hermathya to speak again. His stillness seemed to unsettle her, as if she had expected him to make the next move.

The look in her eyes left him little doubt as to what response he was hoping for. He didn't open the door, he didn't move toward his room. He remained all too conscious of the private chambers and the large bed nearby. The aching in his body surprised him, and he realized with a great deal of dismay that he wanted her. He wanted her very badly indeed.

"I—I wanted to talk to you," she said. He understood implicitly that she was lying.

Her words seemed to break the spell, and he reached past her to push open his door. "Come in," he said as flatly as possible.

He walked to the tall crystal doors, pulling the draperies aside to reveal the lush brilliance of the Gardens of Astarin. Keeping his back to her, he waited for her to speak.

"I've been worried about you," she began. "They told me you had been captured, and I feared I would go out of my mind! Were they cruel to you? Did they hurt you?"

Not half so cruel as you were once, he thought silently. Half of him wanted to shout at her, to remind her that he had once begged her to run away with him, to choose him over his brother. The other half wanted to sweep her into his arms, into his bed, into his life. Yet he dared not look at her, for he feared the latter emotion and knew it was the worst treachery.

"I was only held prisoner for a day," he said, his voice hardening. "They butchered the other elves that they held, but I was fortunate enough to escape."

He thought of the human woman who had—unwittingly, so far as he knew—aided his flight. She had been very beautiful, for a human. Her body possessed a fullness that was voluptuous, that he had to admit he found strangely attractive. Yet she was nothing to him. He didn't even know her name. She was far away from him, probably forever. While Hermathya . . .

Kith-Kanan sensed her moving closer. Her hand touched his shoulder and he stood very still.

"You'd better go. I've got to get ready for the banquet." Still he did not look at her.

For a second, she was silent, and he felt very conscious of her delicate touch. Then her hand fell away. "I . . ." She didn't complete the thought.

As he heard her move toward the door, he turned from the windows to watch her. She smiled awkwardly before she left, pulling the door closed behind her.

For a long time afterward, he remained motionless. The image of her body remained burning in his mind. It frightened him terribly that he found himself wishing she had chosen to remain.

* * * * *

Kith-Kanan's reentry into the royal court of Silvanost felt to him like a sudden immersion into icy water. Nothing in his recent experience bore any resemblance to the gleaming marble-floored hall, and the elegant nobles and ladies dressed in their silken robes, which were trimmed in fur and silver thread and embellished with diamonds, emeralds, and rubies.

The discussions with his family, even the banquet of the previous night, had not prepared him for the full formality of the Hall of Audience. Now he found himself speaking to a faceless congregation of stiff coats and noble gowns, describing the course of the war to date. Finally his report was done, and the elves dissolved smoothly into private discussions.

"Who's that?" Kith-Kanan asked Sithas, indicating a tall elf who had just arrived and now made his way to the throne.

"I'll introduce you." Sithas rose and gestured the elf forward. "This is Lord Quimant of Oakleaf, of whom I have spoken. This is my brother, Kith-Kanan, general of the elven army."

"I am indeed honored, my lord," said Quimant, with a deep bow.

"Thank you," Kith replied, studying his face. "My brother tells me that your aid has been invaluable in supporting the war effort."

"The Speaker is generous," the lord said to Kith-Kanan modestly. "My contribution pales in comparison to the sacrifices made by you and all of your warriors. If we can but provide you with reliable blades, that is my only wish."

For a moment, Kith was struck by the jarring impression that Lord Quimant, in fact, wished for a great deal more out of the war. That moment passed, and Kith noticed that his brother seemed to place tremendous confidence and warmth in Hermathya's cousin.

"What word from our esteemed ambassador?" asked Sithas.

"Than-Kar will attend our court, but not until after the noon hour," reported the lord. "He seems to feel that he has no pressing business here."

"That's the problem!" snapped the Speaker harshly.

Quimant changed the topic. To Sithas and Kith-Kanan, he described some additional expansions of the Clan Oakleaf mines, though the general paid little attention. Restlessly his eyes roamed the crowd, seeking Hermathya. He felt a vague relief that she was not present. He had felt likewise when she didn't attend the previous night's banquet, pleading a mild illness.

The evening passed with excruciating slowness. Kith-Kanan stood tersely as he was plied with invitations to banquets and hunting trips. Some of the ladies gave him other types of invitations, judging from the suggestive tilts of their smiles or the coy lowerings of demure eyelashes. He felt like a prize stag whose antlers were coveted for everybody's mantel.

Kith found himself, much to his astonishment, actually looking back with fondness on the grim, battle-weary conversations he had most nights with his fellow warriors. They might have squatted around a smoky fire for illumination, caked with mud and smelling of weeks of accumulated grime, yet somehow that all seemed so much more real than did this pompous display!

Finally the fanfare of trumpets announced the arrival of the dwarven ambassador and his retinue. Kith-Kanan stared in surprise as Than-Kar led a column of more than thirty armed and armored dwarves into the hall. They marched in a muddy file toward the throne, finally halting to allow their leader to swagger forward on his own.

The Theiwar dwarf bore little resemblance to the jovial Dunbarth Ironthumb, of the Hylar Clan, whom Kith-Kanan had met years before. He found Than-Kar's wide eyes, with their surrounding whites and tiny, beadlike pupils, disturbing—like the eyes of a madman, he thought. The dwarf was filthy and unkempt, with a soiled tunic and muddy boots, almost as if he had made a point of his messy appearance for the benefit of the elven general.

"The Speaker has demanded my presence, and I have come," announced the dwarf in a tone ripe with insolence.

Kith-Kanan felt an urge to leap from the Speaker's platform and throttle the obscene creature. With an effort, he held his temper in check.

"My brother has returned from the front," began Sithas, dispensing with the formality of an introduction. "I desire for you to report to him on the status of your nation's involvement."

Than-Kar's weird eyes appraised Kith-Kanan, while a smirk played on the dwarf's lips. "No change," he said bluntly. "My king needs to see some concrete evidence of elven trustworthiness before he will commit dwarven lives to this . . . cause."

Kith felt his face flush, and he took a step forward. "Surely you understand that all the elder races are threatened by this human aggression?" he demanded.

The Theiwar shrugged. "The humans would say that *they* are threatened by elven aggression."

"*They* are the ones who have marched into elven lands! Lands, I might add, that border firmly against the northern flank of your own kingdom!"

"I don't see it that way," snorted the dwarf. "And besides, you have humans among your own ranks! It almost seems to me that it is a family feud. If they see fit to join, why should dwarves get involved?"

Sithas turned in astonishment to Kith-Kanan, though the speaker remained outwardly composed.

"We have no humans fighting on the side of our forces. There are some—women and children, mostly—who have taken shelter in the fortress for the siege. They are merely innocent victims of the war. They do not change its character!"

"More to the point, then," spoke the ambassador, his voice an accusing hiss, "explain the presence of elves in the Army of Ergoth!"

"Lies!" shouted Sithas, forgetting himself and springing to his feet. The hall erupted in shouts of anger and denial from courtiers and nobles pressing forward. Than-Kar's bodyguards bristled and raised their weapons.

"Entire ranks of elves," continued the dwarf as the crowd murmured. "They resist your imperial hegemony—"

"They are traitors to the homeland!" snapped Sithas.

"A question of semantics," argued Than-Kar. "I merely mean to illustrate that the confused state of the conflict makes a dwarven intervention seem rash to the point of foolishness."

Kith-Kanan could hold himself in check no longer. He stepped down from the platform and stared at the dwarf, who was a foot or more shorter than himself. "You distort the truth in a way that can only discredit your nation!"

He continued, his voice a growl. "Any elves among the ranks of Ergoth are lone rogues, lured by human coin or promises of power. Even the likes of you cannot blur the clear lines of this conflict. You spout your lies and your distortions from the safety of this far city, hiding like a coward behind the robes of diplomacy. You make me sick!"

Than-Kar appeared unruffled as he stepped aside to address Sithas. "This example of your general's impetuous behavior will be duly reported to my king. It cannot further your cause."

"You set a new standard for diplomatic excess, and you try my patience to its limits. Leave, *now!*" Sithas hissed the words with thick anger, and the hall fell deathly silent.

If the dwarf was affected by the speaker's rage, however, he concealed his emotions well. With calculated insolence, he marched his column about and then led them from the Hall of Audience.

"Throw open the windows!" barked the Speaker of the Stars. "Clear the stench from the air!"

Kith-Kanan slumped to sit on the steps of the royal dais,

ignoring the surprised looks from some of the stiff-backed elven nobles. "I could have strangled him with pleasure," he snarled as his brother came to sit beside him.

"The audience is over," Sithas announced to the rest of the elves, and Kith-Kanan sighed with concern as the last of the anonymous nobles left. The only ones remaining in the great hall were Quimant, the twins, and Nirakina.

"I know I shouldn't have let him get under my skin like that. I'm sorry," the general said to the Speaker.

"Nonsense. You said things I've wanted to voice for months. It's better to have a warrior say them than a head of state." Sithas paused awkwardly. "What he *did* say—how much truth was there to it?"

"Very little," sighed Kith-Kanan. "We are sheltering humans in the fortress, most of them the wives and families of Wildrunners. They would be slain on sight if they fell into the hands of the enemy."

"And are elves fighting for *Ergoth?*" Sithas couldn't keep the dismay from his voice.

"A few rogues, as I said," Kith admitted. "At least, we've had reports of them. I saw one myself in the human camp. But these turncoats are not numerous enough that we have taken notice of them on the field."

He groaned and leaned backward, remembering the offensive and arrogant Theiwar dwarf. "That *lout!* I suppose it's a good thing I didn't have my sword at my side."

"You're tired," said Sithas. "Why don't you relax for a while. This round of banquets and courts and all-night meetings, I'm sure, takes an adjustment. We can talk tomorrow."

"Your brother is right. You *do* need rest," Nirakina added in a maternal tone. "I'll have dinner sent to your apartments."

* * * * *

The dinner arrived, as Nirakina had promised. Kith-Kanan guessed that his mother had sent orders to the kitchen, and someone in the kitchen had communicated the situation to another interested party. For it was Hermathya who knocked on his door and entered.

"Hello, Hermathya," he said, sitting up in the bed. He wasn't particularly surprised to see her, and if he was honest with himself, neither was he very much dismayed.

"I took this from the serving girl," she said, bringing forward a large silver tray with domed, steaming dishes and crystal platters. Once again he was struck by her air of youth and innocence.

Memories of the two of them together. . . . Kith-Kanan felt a sudden resurgence of desire, a feeling that he thought had been gone for years. He wanted to take her in his arms. Looking into her eyes, he knew that she desired the same thing.

"I'll get up. We can dine near the windows." He didn't want to suggest they go to the balcony. He felt there was something furtive and private about her visit.

"Just stay there," she said softly. "I'll serve you in bed."

He wondered what she meant, at first. Soon he learned, as the dinner grew cold upon a nearby table.

ᴥ 10 ᴥ

The Morning After

Hermathya slipped away sometime during the middle of the night, and Kith-Kanan felt profoundly grateful in the morning that she was gone. Now, in the cold light of day, the passion that had seized them seemed like nothing so much as a malicious and hurtful interlude. The flame that had once drawn them together ought not to be rekindled.

Kith-Kanan spent most of the day with his brother, touring the stables and farriers of the city. He forced himself to maintain focus on the task at hand: gathering additional horses to mount his cavalry forces for the time when the Wildrunnners took to the offensive. They both knew that they would, they *must*, eventually attack the human army. They couldn't simply wait out the siege.

During these hours together, Kith found that he couldn't meet his brother's eyes. Sithas remained cheerful and enthusiastic, friendly in a way that twisted Kith-Kanan's gut. By midafternoon, he made an excuse to leave his twin's company, pleading the need to give Arcuballis some exercise. In reality, he needed an escape, a chance to suffer his guilt in solitude.

The following days in Silvanost passed slowly, making even the bleak confinement in beseiged Sithelbec seem eventful by comparison. He avoided Hermathya, and he found to his relief that she seemed to be avoiding him as well. The few times he saw her she was with Sithas, playing the doting wife holding tightly to her husband's arm and hanging upon his every word.

In truth, the time dragged for Sithas as well. He knew that Vedvedsica was laboring to create a spell that might allow them to magically ensnare the griffons, but he was impatient to begin the quest. He ascribed Kith-Kanan's unease to similar impatience. When they were together, they spoke only of the war and waited for a message from the mysterious cleric.

That word did not come for eight days, and then, oddly, it arrived in the middle of the night. The twins were wide awake, engaged in deep discussion in Sithas's chambers, when they heard a rustling on the balcony beyond the open window. Sithas drew the draperies aside, and the sorcerous cleric stepped into the room.

Kith-Kanan's eyes immediately fell upon Vedvedsica's hand, for he carried a long ivory tube, the ends capped by cork. Several arcane sigils, in black, marked its alabaster surface.

The cleric raised the object, and the twins instinctively understood, even before Vedvedsica uncorked the end and withdrew a rolled sheet of oiled vellum. Unrolling the scroll, he showed them a series of symbols scribed in the Old Script.

"The spell of command," the priest explained softly. "With this magic, I believe the griffons can be tamed."

* * * * *

The twins planned to depart after one more day of final preparations. With the scroll at last a reality, a new urgency marked their activity. They met with Nirakina and Lord Quimant shortly after breakfast, a few hours after Vedvedsica had departed.

The four of them gathered in the royal library, where a fire crackled in the hearth to disperse the autumnal chill. Sithas brought the scroll, though he placed his cloak over it as he set it on the floor. They all sat in the great leather-backed chairs that faced the fire.

"We have word of a discovery that may change the course of the war—for the better," announced Kith.

"Splendid!" Quimant was enthusiastic. Nirakina merely looked at her sons, her concern showing in the furrowing of her brow.

"You know of Arcuballis, of course," continued the warrior. "He was given to Sithel—to father—by a 'merchant' from the north." According to the strategy he and Sithas had developed, they would say nothing about the involvement of the gray cleric. "We have since learned that the Khalkist Mountains are home to a great herd of the creatures—hundreds of them, at least."

"Do you have proof of this, or is it merely rumor?" asked Nirakina. Her face had grown pale.

"They have been seen," explained Kith-Kanan, glossing over the question. He told Quimant and Nirakina of his dream on the night before he departed Sithelbec. "Right down to the three volcanoes, it bears out everything we've been able to learn."

"Think of the potential!" Sithas added. "A whole wing of flying cavalry! Why, the passage of Arcuballis alone sent hundreds of horses into a stampede. A sky full of griffons could very well rout the whole Army of Ergoth!"

"It seems a great leap," Nirakina said slowly and quietly, "from the knowledge of griffons in a remote mountain range to a trained legion of flyers, obeying the commands of their riders." She was still pale, but her voice was strong and steady.

"We believe we can find them," Sithas replied levelly. "We leave at tomorrow's sunrise to embark upon this quest."

"How many warriors will you take?" asked Nirakina,

knowing as they all did the legends of the distant Khalkists. Tales of ogres, dark and evil dwarves, even tribes of brutish hill giants--these comprised the folklore whispered by the average elf regarding the mountain range that was the central feature of the continent of Ansalon.

"Only the two of us will go." Sithas faced his mother, who appeared terribly frail in her overly-large chair.

"We'll ride Arcuballis," Kith-Kanan explained quickly. "And he'll cover the distance in a fraction of the time it would take an army—even if we *had* one to send!"

Nirakina looked at Kith-Kanan, her eyes pleading. Her warrior son understood the appeal. She wanted him to volunteer to go alone, leaving the Speaker of the Stars behind. Yet even as this thought flashed in her eyes, she lowered her head.

When she looked up, her voice was firm again. "How will you capture these creatures, assuming that you find them?"

Sithas removed his cloak and picked up the tube from the floor beside his chair. "We have acquired a spell of command from a friend of the House of Silvanos. If we can find the griffons, the spell will bind them to our will."

"It is a more powerful version of the same enchantment that was used to domesticate Arcuballis," added Kith. "It is written in the Old Script. That is one reason why Sithas must go with me—to help me cast the spell by reading the Old Script."

His mother looked at him, nodding calmly, more out of shock than from any true sense of understanding.

Nirakina had stood beside her husband through three centuries of rule. She had borne these two proud sons. She had suffered the news of her husband's murder at the hands of a human and lived through the resulting war that now engulfed her nation, her family, and her people. Now she faced the prospect of her two sons embarking on what seemed to her a mad quest, in search of a miracle, with little more than a prayer of success.

Yet, above all, she was the matriarch of the House of Silver Moon. She, too, was a leader of the Silvanesti, and she understood some things about strength, about ruling, and about risk-taking. She had made known her objections, and she realized that the minds of her sons were set. Now she would give no further vent to her personal feelings.

She rose from her chair and nodded stiffly at each of her sons. Kith-Kanan went to her side, while Sithas remained in his chair, moved by her loyalty. The warrior escorted her to the door.

Quimant looked at Sithas, then turned to Kith-Kanan as he returned to his chair. "May your quest be speedy and successful. I only wish I could accompany you."

Sithas spoke. "I shall entrust you to act as regent in my absence. You know the details of the nation's daily affairs. I shall also need you to begin the conscription of new troops. By the end of winter, we will have to raise and train a new force to send to the plains."

"I will do everything in my power," pledged Quimant.

"Another thing," added Sithas casually. "If Tamanier Ambrodel returns to the city, he is to be given quarters in the palace. I will need to see him immediately upon my return."

Quimant nodded, rose, and bowed to the twins. "May the gods watch over you," he said, then left.

* * * * *

"I *have* to go. Don't you understand that?" Sithas challenged Hermathya. She stomped about their royal bedchambers before whirling upon him.

"You can't! I forbid it!" Hermathya's voice rose, becoming shrill. Her face, moments before blank with astonishment, now contorted in fury.

"Damn it! *Listen* to me!" Sithas scowled, his own anger rising. Stubborn and untractable, they stared into each other's eyes for a moment.

"I've told you about the spell of bonding. It's in the Old Script. Kith doesn't have the knowledge to use it, even if he found the griffons. *I'm* the only one who can read it properly." He held her shoulders and continued to meet her eyes.

"I have to do this, not just for the good it will do our nation, but for *me! That's* what you have to understand!"

"I *don't* have to, and I won't!" she cried, whirling away from him.

"Kith-Kanan has always been the one to face the dangers and the challenges of the unknown. Now there's something that *I* must do. I, too, must put my life at risk. For once, I'm not just sending my brother into danger. I'm going myself!"

"But you don't *have* to!"

Hermathya almost spat her anger, but Sithas wouldn't budge. If she could see any sense in his desire to test himself, she wouldn't admit it. Finally, in exhaustion and frustration, the Speaker of the Stars stormed out of the chambers.

* * * * *

He found Kith-Kanan in the stables, instructing the saddlemaker on modifications to Arcuballis's harness. The griffon would be able to carry the two of them, but his flight would be slowed, and they would be able to take precious little in the way of provisions and equipment.

"Dried meat—enough for only a few weeks," recited Kith-Kanan, examining the bulging saddlebags. "A pair of waterskins, several extra cloaks. Tinder and flint, a couple of daggers. Extra bowstrings. We'll carry our bows where we can get at them in a hurry, of course. And twoscore arrows. Do you have a practical sword?"

For a moment, Sithas flushed. He knew that the ceremonial blade he had carried for years would be inadequate for the task at hand. Cast in a soft silver alloy, its shining blade was inscribed with all manner of symbols in the Old Script, reciting the glorious history of the House of Silvanos. It was beautiful and valuable, but impractical in a fight. Still, it rankled him to hear his brother speak ill of it. "Lord Quimant has procured a splendid longsword for me," he said stiffly. "It will do quite nicely."

"Good." Kith took no notice of his brother's annoyance. "We'll have to leave our metal armor behind. With this load, Arcuballis can't handle the extra weight. Have you a good set of leathers?"

Again Sithas replied in the affirmative.

"Well, we'll be ready to go at first light, then. Ah . . . " Kith hesitated, then asked, "How did Hermathya react?" Kith knew that Sithas had put off telling Hermathya that he would be gone for weeks on this journey.

"Poorly," Sithas said, with a grimace. He offered no elaboration, and Kith-Kanan did not probe further.

They attended a small banquet that night, joined by Quimant and Nirakina and several other nobles. Hermathya was conspicuously absent, a fact for which Kith was profoundly grateful, and the mood was subdued.

He had found himself anxious throughout these last days that Hermathya would tell her husband about her dalliance with his brother. Kith-Kanan had tried to put aside the memory of that night, treating the incident as some sort of waking dream. This made his guilt somewhat easier to bear.

After dinner, Nirakina handed Sithas a small vial. The stoneware jar was tightly plugged by a cork.

"It is a salve, made by the clerics of Quenesti Pah," she explained. "Miritelisina gave it to me. If you are injured, spread a small amount around the area of the wound. It will help the healing."

"I hope we won't need it, but thank you," said Sithas. For a moment, he wondered if his mother was about to cry, but again her proud heritage sustained her. She embraced each of her sons warmly, kissed them, and wished them the luck of the gods. Then she retired to her chambers.

Both of the twins spent much of the night awake, taut with the prospect of the upcoming adventure. Sithas tried to see his wife in the evening and again before sunrise, but she wouldn't open her door even to speak to him. He settled for a few moments with Vanesti, holding his son in his arms and rocking him gently while night gave way to early dawn.

11

Day of Departure, Autumn

They met at the stables before dawn. As they had requested, no one came to see them off. Kith threw the heavy saddle over the restless griffon's back, making sure that the straps that passed around Arcuballis's wings were taut. Sithas stood by, watching as his brother hoisted the heavy saddlebags over the creature's loins. The elf took several minutes to make sure that everything was secure.

They mounted the powerful beast, with Kith-Kanan in the fore, and settled into the specially modified saddle. Arcuballis trotted from the stable doors into the wide corral. Here he sprang upward, the thick muscles of his legs propelling them from the ground. His powerful wings beat the still air and thrust downward. In a single fluid motion, he leaped again and they were airborne.

The griffon labored over the garden and then along the city's main avenue, slowly gaining altitude. The twins saw the towers of the city pass alongside, then slowly fall behind. Rosy hues of dawn quickly brightened to pink, then pale blue, as the sun seemed to explode over the eastern horizon into a crisp and cloudless day.

"By the gods, this is fantastic!" cried Sithas, overcome with the beauty of their flight, with the sight of Silvanost, and perhaps with the exhilaration of at last escaping the confining rituals of his daily life.

Kith-Kanan smiled to himself, pleased with his brother's enthusiasm. They flew above the Thon-Thalas River, following the silvery ribbon of its path. Though autumn had come to the elven lands, the day was brilliant with sunshine, the air was clear, and a brilliant collage of colors spread across the forested lands below.

The steady pulse of the griffon's wings carried them for many hours. The city quickly fell away, though the Tower of the Stars remained visible for some time. By midmorning, however, they soared over pristine forestland. No building broke the leafy canopy to indicate that anyone— elf, human, or whatever—lived here.

"Are these lands truly uninhabited?" inquired Sithas, studying the verdant terrain.

"The Kagonesti dwell throughout these forests," explained Kith. The wild elves, considered uncouth and barbaric by the civilized Silvanesti, did not build structures to dominate the land or monuments to their own greatness. Instead, they took the land as they found it and left it that way when they passed on.

Arcuballis swept northward, as if the great griffon felt the same joy at leaving civilization behind. Despite the heavy packs and his extra passenger, he showed no signs of tiring during a flight that lasted nearly twelve hours and carried them several hundred miles. When they ultimately landed to make camp, they touched earth beside a clear pool in a sheltered forest grotto. The two elves and their mighty beast spent a peaceful night, sleeping almost from the moment of sunset straight through until dawn.

Their flight took them six days. After the first day, they

took a two-hour interval at midday so that Arcuballis could rest. They passed beyond the forests on the third day, then into the barren plains of Northern Silvanesti, a virtual desert, uninhabited and undesired by the elves.

Finally they flew beside the jagged teeth of the Khalkist Range, the mountainous backbone of Ansalon. For two full days, these craggy peaks rose to their left, but Kith-Kanan kept them over the dry plains, explaining that the winds here were more easily negotiable than they would be among the jutting summmits.

Eventually they reached the point where they had to turn toward the high valleys and snow-filled swales if they expected to find any trace of their quarry. Arcuballis strained to gain altitude, carrying them safely over the sheer crests of the foothills and flying above the floor of a deep valley, following the contours of its winding course as steep ridgelines rose to the right and left, high above them.

They camped that night, the seventh night of their journey, near a partially frozen lake in the base of a steep-sided, circular valley. Three waterfalls, now frozen into massive icicles, plunged toward them from the surrounding heights. They chose the spot for its small grove of hardy cedars, reasoning correctly that firewood would be a useful, and rare, commodity among these lofty realms.

Sithas helped his brother build the fire. He discovered that he relished the feel of the small axeblade cutting the wood into kindling. The campfire soon crackled merrily, and the warmth on his hands was especially gratifying because his work had provided the welcome heat.

Thus far, their journey seemed to the Speaker of the Stars to be the grandest adventure he had ever embarked upon.

"Where do you think the Lords of Doom lie from here?" he asked his brother as they settled back to gnaw on some dried venison. The three volcanoes were rumored to lie at the heart of the range.

"I don't know exactly," Kith admitted. "Somewhere to the north and west of here, I should say. The city of Sanction lies on the far side of the range, and if we reach it, we'll know we've gone too far."

"I never knew that the mountains could be so beautiful, so majestic," Sithas added, gazing at the awesome heights around them. The sun had long since left their deep valley, yet its fading rays still illumined some of the highest summits in brilliant reflections of white snow and blue ice.

"Forbidding, too."

They looked toward Arcuballis as the griffon curled up near the fire. His massive bulk loomed like a wall.

"Now we'll have to start searching," Kith commented. "And that might take us a long time."

"How big can this range be?" asked Sithas skeptically. "After all, we can fly."

*　*　*　*　*

Fly they did, for day after grueling, bone-chilling day. The pleasant autumn of the lowlands swiftly became brutal winter in these heights. They pressed to the highest elevations, and Sithas felt a fierce exultation as they passed among the lofty ridges, a sense of accomplishment that dwarfed anything he had done in the city. When the snow blew into their faces, he relished the heavy cloak pulled tight against his face; when they spent a night in the barren heights, he enjoyed the search for a good campsite.

Kith-Kanan remained quiet, almost brooding, for hours during their aerial search. The guilt of his night with Hermathya gnawed at him, and he cursed his foolish weakness. He longed to confess to Sithas, to ask for his forgiveness, but in his heart, he sensed that this would be a mistake— that his brother would never forgive him. Instead, he bore his pain privately.

Some days the sun shone brightly, and then the white bowls of the valleys became great reflectors. They both learned, the first such day, to leave no skin exposed under these conditions. Their cheeks and foreheads were brutally seared, yet ironically the cold air prevented them from feeling the sunburn until it had reached a painful state.

On other days, gray clouds pressed like a leaden blanket overhead, cloaking the highest summits and casting the vistas in a bleak and forbidding light. Then the snow would fly, and Arcuballis had to seek firm ground until the storm passed. A driving blizzard could toss the griffon about like a leaf in the wind.

Always they pushed through the highest summits of the range, searching each valley for sign of the winged creatures. They swung southward until they reached the borders of the ogrelands of Bloten. The valleys were lower here, but they saw signs of the brutish inhabitants everywhere—forestlands blackened by swath burning, great piles of tailings. Knowing that the griffons would seek a more remote habitat, they turned back to the north, following a snakelike glacier higher and higher into the heart of the range.

Here the weather hit them with the hardest blow yet. A mass of dark clouds appeared with explosive suddenness to the west. The expanse covered the sky and swiftly spread toward them. Arcuballis dove, but the snow swirled so thickly they couldn't see the valley floor.

"There—a ledge!" shouted Sithas, pointing over his brother's shoulder.

"I see it." Kith-Kanan directed Arcuballis onto a narrow shelf of rock protected by a blunt overhang. Sheer cliffs dropped away below them and climbed over their heads. Winds buffeted them even as the griffon landed, and further flight seemed suicidal. A narrow trail seemed to lead along the cliff face, winding gradually downward from their perch, but they elected to wait out the storm.

"Look—it's flat and wide here," announced Sithas, clearing away some loose rubble. "Plenty of space to rest, even for Arcuballis."

Kith nodded.

They unsaddled the creature and settled in to wait as the winds rose to a howling crescendo and the snow flew past them.

"How long will this last?" asked Sithas.

Kith-Kanan shrugged, and Sithas suddenly felt foolish for the question. They unpacked their bedrolls and huddled together beside the warm flank of the griffon and the cold protection of the cliff wall. Their bows, arrows, and swords they placed within easy reach. Just beyond their feet, the slope of the mountainside plummeted away, a sheer precipice vanishing into the snow-swept distance.

They coped, on their remote ledge, for two solid days as the blizzard raged around them and the temperature dropped. They had no fuel for a fire, so they could only huddle together, taking turns sleeping so that they didn't both drift into eternal rest, blanketed by a deep winter cold.

Sithas was awake at the end of the second day, shaking his head and pinching himself to try to remain alert. His hands and feet felt like blocks of ice, and he alternated his position frequently, trying to warm some part of his body against the bulk of Arcuballis.

He noticed the pace of the griffon's breathing change slightly. Suddenly the creature raised his head, and Sithas stared with him into the snow-obscured murk.

Was there something there, down the path that they had seen when they landed, the one that seemed to lead away from this ledge? Sithas blinked, certain his eyes deceived him, but it *had* seemed as if something moved!

In the next instant, he gaped in shock as a huge shape lunged out of the blowing snow. It towered twice as high as an elf, though its shape was vaguely human. It had arms and hands—indeed, one of these clutched a club the size of a small tree trunk. This weapon loomed high above Sithas as the creature charged forward.

"Kith! A giant!" He shouted, kicking his brother to awaken him. At the same time, purely by instinct, he picked up the sword he had laid by his side.

Arcuballis reacted faster than the elf, springing toward the giant with a powerful shriek. Sithas watched in horror as the monster's club crashed into the griffon's skull. Soundlessly Arcuballis went limp, disappearing over the side of the ledge like so much discarded garbage.

"No!" Kith-Kanan was awake now and saw the fate of his beloved steed. At the same time, the twins saw additional shapes, two or three more, materializing from the blizzard behind the first giant. Snarling with hatred, the elven warrior grabbed his blade.

The monster's face, this close, was more grotesque than Sithas had first thought. Its eyes were small, bloodshot, and very close-set while its nose bulged like an outcrop of rock. Its mouth was garishly wide. The giant's maw gaped open as the beast fought, revealing blood-red gums and stubs of ivory that looked more like tusks than teeth.

A deep and pervasive terror seized Sithas, freezing him in

place. He could only stare in horror at the approaching menace. Some distant part of his mind told him that he should react, should fight, but his muscles refused to budge. His fear paralyzed him.

Kith-Kanan rose into a fighting crouch, menacing the giant with his sword. Tears streaked Kith's face, but grief only heightened his rage and his deadly competence. His hand remained steady. Seeing him, Sithas shook his head, finally freeing himself from his immobility.

Sithas leaped to his feet and lunged at the monster, but his foot slipped on the icy rocks, and he fell to the rocks at the very lip of the precipice, slamming the wind from his lungs. The giant loomed over him.

But then he saw his brother, darting forward with incredible agility, raising his blade and thrusting at the giant's belly. The keen steel struck home, and the creature howled, lurching backward. One of its huge boots slipped from the ice-encrusted ledge, and with a scream, the monster vanished into the gray storm below.

Now they saw that the three other giants approached them, one at a time along the narrow ledge. Each of the massive creatures carried a huge club. The first of these lumbered forward, and Kith-Kanan darted at him. Sithas, recovering his breath, climbed to his feet.

The giant stepped back, then swung a heavy blow at the dodging, weaving elf. Kith danced away, and then struck so quickly that Sithas didn't see the movement. The tip of the sword cut a shallow opening in the giant's knee before the elf skipped backward.

But that cut was telling. Sithas watched in astonishment as the giant's leg collapsed beneath it. Thrashing in futility with its hamlike hands, the giant slid slowly over the edge, vanishing with a shriek that was quickly lost in the howling of the storm.

While the other two giants gaped in astonishment, Kith-Kanan remained a dervish of motion. He charged the massive creatures, sending them slipping and sliding backward along the ledge to avoid his keen blade, a blade that now glistened with blood.

"Kith, watch out!" Sithas found his voice and urged his brother on. Kith-Kanan appeared to stumble, and one of the giants crashed his heavy club downward. But again the elf moved too quickly, and the club splintered against bare stone. Kith rolled toward this one, rising into a crouch between its stumplike legs. He stabbed upward with all the strenth in his powerful arms and shoulders, and then dove out of the way as the mortally wounded giant bellowed its pain.

Sithas raced toward his brother, recognizing Kith's danger. He saw his twin slip as he tried to hug the cliff wall between the dying giant and its sole remaining comrade.

The latter swung his club with strength born of desperate terror. The loglike beam, nearly a foot thick at its head, crashed into Kith-Kanan's chest and crushed his body against the rough stone wall behind him. Sithas saw his brother's head snap back and blood explode from his skull. Slowly the elf sank to the ledge.

The wounded giant collapsed, and Sithas sent it toppling from the brink. The last of the brutes looked at the charging elf, the twin of the warrior he had just felled, and turned away. He bounded along the narrow ledge, descending across the face of the mountain, away from the niche that had sheltered the twins. In seconds, he disappeared into the distance.

Sithas paid no further attention to the monster. He knelt at Kith's side, appalled at the blood that gushed from his brother's mouth and nose, staining and matting his long blond hair.

"Kith, don't die! Please!" He didn't realize that he was sobbing.

Gingerly he lifted his brother, surprised at Kith's frailty— or perhaps at his own desperate strength. He carried him to their niche. Every cloak, every blanket and tunic that they carried, he used to cushion and wrap Kith-Kanan. His brother's eyes were closed. A very faint motion, a rising and falling of his chest, gave the only sign that Kith lived.

Now night fell with abruptness, and the wind seemed to pick up. The snow stung Sithas's face as sharply as did his own tears. He took Kith's cold hand in his and sat beside his brother, not expecting either of them to be alive to greet the dawn.

12

dawn

Somehow Sithas must have dozed off, for he suddenly noticed that the wind, the snow—indeed, the entire storm—had vanished. The air, now still, had become icy cold, with an absolute clarity that only comes in the highest mountains during the deepest winter frosts.

The sun hadn't risen yet, but the Speaker could see that all around him towered summits of unimaginable heights, plumed with great collars of snow. Gray and impassive, like stone-face giants with thick beards of frost, they regarded him from their aloof vantages.

The brothers' ledge perched along one of the two steep sides of the valley. To the south, on Sithas's left as he looked outward, the valley stretched and twisted toward the low, forested country from which they had come. To the right, it appeared to end in a cirque of steep-walled peaks. At one place, he saw a saddle that, while still high above him, seemed to offer a lone, treacherous path into the next section of the mountain range.

Kith-Kanan lay motionless beside him. His skin had the paleness of death, and Sithas had to struggle against a resurgence of despair. He couldn't allow himself to abandon hope; he was their only chance for survival. The quest for the griffons, the excitement and adventure of the journey he had known before, were all forgotten now, overwhelmed by the simple and basic wish to continue living.

The valley below him, he saw, was not as deep as they had guessed when the storm struck. Their shelf was a bare hundred feet above level ground. He leaned out to look over the edge, but all he saw was a vast drift of snow piled against the cliff. If the bodies of the giants or of gallant, fallen Arcuballis remained down there somewhere, he had no way to know it. No trees grew in this high valley, nor did he see any signs of animal life. In fact, the only objects that met his eyes, in any direction, were the bedrock of the mountain range and the snowy blanket that covered it.

With a groan, he slumped back against the cliff. They were doomed! He could see no possibility of any fate other than death in this remote valley. His throat ached, and tears welled in his eyes. What good was his court training in a situation like this?

"Kith!" he moaned. "Wake up! *Please!*"

When his brother made no response, Sithas collapsed facedown on his cloak. A part of him wished that he was as unconscious of their fate as Kith-Kanan.

For the whole long day, he lay as if in a trance. He pulled their cloaks about them as night fell, certain that they would freeze to death. Kith-Kanan hadn't moved—indeed, he barely breathed. Broken by his own anguish, the speaker finally tumbled into restless sleep.

It was not until the next morning that he regained some sense of purpose. What did they need? Warmth, but there was no firewood in sight. Water, but their skins of the liquid had frozen solid, and without fire, they couldn't melt snow. Food, of which they had several strips of dried venison and some bread. But how could he feed Kith-Kanan while his brother remained unconscious?

Again the feeling of hopelessness seized him. If only Arcuballis were here! If only Kith could walk! If only the giants . . . He snarled at himself in anger, realizing the idiocy of his ramblings.

Instead, he pushed himself to his feet, suddenly aware of a terrible stiffness in his own body. He studied the route along the narrow ledge that twisted its way from their niche to the valley floor. It looked negotiable—barely. But what could he do if he was lucky enough to reach the ground?

He noted, for the first time, a dark patch on the snow at the edge of the flat expanse. The sun had crested the eastern peaks by now, and Sithas squinted into the brightness.

What caused the change of coloration in the otherwise immaculate surface of snow? Then it dawned on him— water! Somewhere beneath that snow, water still flowed! It soaked into the powder above, turning it to slush and causing it to settle.

With a clear goal now, Sithas began to act. He took his own nearly empty waterskin, since Kith's contained a block of ice that would be impossible to remove. As he turned away from the sun, however, he had another idea. He set Kith's waterskin in the sunlight, on a flat stone. He found several other dark boulders and placed them beside the skin, taking care that they didn't block the sunlight.

Then he started down the treacherous ledge. In many places, the narrow path was piled with snow, and he used his sword to sweep these drifts away, carefully probing so that he did not step off the cliff.

Finally he reached a spot where he was able to drop into the soft snow below. He pushed his way through the deep fluff, leaving a trench behind him as he worked his way toward the dark patch of slush. The going was difficult, and he had to rest many times, but finally he reached his goal.

Pausing again, he heard a faint trill of sound from beneath the snow, the gurgling of water as it babbled along a buried stream. He poked and pressed with his sword, and the surface of snow dropped away, revealing a flowage about six inches deep.

But that was enough. Sithas suspended his skin from the

tip of his sword and let it soak in the stream. Though it only filled halfway, it was more water than they had tasted in two days, and he greedily drained the waterskin. Then he refilled it, as much as possible with his awkward rig, and turned back to the cliff. It took him more than an hour to carry it back up to Kith-Kanan, but the hour of toil seemed to warm and vitalize him.

His brother showed no change. Sithas dribbled some water into Kith's mouth, just enough to wet his tongue and throat. He also washed away the blood that had caked on the elf's frostbitten face. There was even some water left over, since Kith's frozen waterskin had begun to melt from the heat of the sun.

"What now, Kith?" Sithas asked softly.

He heard a sound from somewhere and looked anxiously around. Again came the noise, which sounded like rocks falling down a rough slope.

Then he saw a distinct movement across the valley. White shapes leaped and sprang along the sheer face, and for a moment, he thought they flew, so effectively did they defy gravity. More rocks broke free, crashing and sliding downward. He saw that these nimble creatures moved upon hooves.

He had heard about the great mountain sheep that dwelled in the high places, but never had he observed them before. One, obviously the ram, paused and looked around, raising his proud head high. Sithas glimpsed his immense horns, swirling from the creature's forehead.

For a moment, he wondered at the presence of these great beasts as he watched them press downward. They reached the foot of the cliff, and then the ram bounded through the powder, plowing a trail for the others.

"The water!" Sithas spoke aloud to himself. The sheep needed the water, too!

Indeed, the ram was nearing the shallow stream. Alert, he looked carefully around the valley, and Sithas, though he was out of sight, remained very still. Finally the proud creature lowered his head to drink. He stopped frequently to look around, but he drank for a long time before he finally stepped away from the small hole in the snow.

Then, one by one, the females came to the water. The

ram stood protectively beside them, his proud head and keen eyes shifting back and forth.

The group of mountain sheep spent perhaps an hour beside the water hole, each of the creatures slaking its thirst. Finally, with the ram still in the lead, they turned back along the tracks and reclimbed the mountain wall.

Sithas watched them until they disappeared from view. The magnificent creatures moved with grace and skill up the steep face of rock. They looked right at home here—so very different from himself!

A soft groan beside him pulled his attention instantly back to Kith-Kanan.

"Kith! Say something!" He leaned over his twin's face, rejoicing to see a flicker of vitality. Kith-Kanan's eyes remained shut, but his mouth twisted into a grimace and he was gasping for breath.

"Here, take a drink. Don't try to move."

He poured a few drops of water onto Kith's lips, and the wounded elf licked them away. Slowly, with obvious pain, Kith-Kanan opened his eyes, squinting at the bright daylight before him.

"What . . . happened?" he asked weakly. Abruptly his eyes widened and his body tensed. "The giants! Where . . . ?"

"It's all right," Sithas told him, giving him more water. "They're dead—or gone, I'm not sure which."

"Arcuballis?" Kith's eyes widened and he struggled to sit up, before collapsing with a dull groan.

"He's . . . gone, Kith. He attacked the first giant, got clubbed over the head, and fell."

"He must be down below!"

Sithas shook his head. "I looked. There's no sign of his body—or of any of the giants, either."

Kith moaned, a sound of deep despair. Sithas had no words of comfort.

"The giants . . . what kind of beasts do you think they were?" asked Sithas.

"Hill giants, I'm sure," Kith-Kanan said after a moment's pause. "Relatives of ogres, I guess, but bigger. I wouldn't have expected to see them this far south."

"Gods! If only I'd been faster!" Sithas said, ashamed.

"Don't!" snapped the injured elf. "You warned me—gave me time to get my sword out, to get into the fight." Kith-Kanan thought for a moment. "When—how long ago was it, anyway? How much time has passed since—"

"We've been up here for two nights," said Sithas quietly. "The sun has nearly set for the third time." He hestitated, then blurted his question. "How badly are you hurt?"

"Bad enough," Kith said bluntly. "My skull feels like it's been crushed, and my right leg seems as if it is on fire."

"Your leg?" Sithas had been so worried about the blow to his brother's head that he had paid little attention to the rest of his body.

"It's broken, I think," the elf grunted, gritting his teeth against the pain.

Sithas's mind went blank. A broken leg! It might as well be a sentence of death! How would they ever get out of here with his twin thus crippled? And winter had only begun! If they didn't get out of the mountains quickly, they could be trapped here for months. Another snowfall would make travel by foot all but impossible.

"You'll have to do something about it," Kith said, though it took several moments before the remark registered in Sithas's mind.

"About what?"

"My leg!" The injured elf looked at his twin sharply, then toughened his voice. Almost without thinking, he used the tones of command he had become accustomed to when he led the Wildrunners.

"Tell me if the skin is broken, if there's any discoloration--any infection."

"Where? Which leg?" Sithas struggled to focus his thoughts. He had never been so disoriented before in his life.

"The right one, below the knee."

Gingerly, almost trembling, Sithas pulled the blankets and cloaks away from his brother's feet and legs. What he saw was terrifying.

The ugly red swelling had almost doubled the size of the limb from the knee to the ankle, and Kith's leg was bent outward at an awkward angle. For a moment, he cursed himself, as if the injury was his own fault. Why hadn't he thought to examine his brother two days earlier, when Kith had first been injured? Had he twisted the wound more when he moved the fallen elf into the shelter of the rocky niche?

"The—the skin isn't broken," he explained, trying to keep his voice calm. "But it's red. By the gods, Kith, it's blood-red!"

Kith-Kanan grimaced at the news. "You'll have to straighten it. If you don't, I'll be crippled for life!"

The Speaker of the Stars looked at his twin brother, the sense of helplessness growing inside him. But he saw the pain in Kith-Kanan's eyes, and he knew he had no choice but to try.

"It's going to hurt," he warned, and Kith nodded silently, gritting his teeth.

Cautiously he touched the swollen limb, and then instantly recoiled at Kith's sharp gasp of pain. "Don't stop," hissed the wounded elf. "Do it—now!"

Gritting his teeth, Sithas grasped the swollen flesh. His fingers probed the wound, and he felt the break in the bone. Kith-Kanan cried aloud, gasping and choking in his pain as Sithas pulled on the limb.

Kith shrieked again and then, mercifully, collapsed into unconsciousness. Desperately Sithas tugged, forcing his hands and arms to do these things that he knew must be causing Kith-Kanan unspeakable pain.

Finally he felt the bones slip into place.

"By Quenesti Pah, I'm sorry, Kith," Sithas whispered, looking at his brother's terribly pale face.

Quenesti Pah . . . goddess of healing! The invocation of that benign goddess brought his mind around to the small vial his mother had given them before they departed. From Miritelesina, she had said, high priestess of Quenesti Pah. Frantically Sithas dug through the saddlebag, finally discovering the little ceramic jar, plugged with a stout cork.

He popped the cork from the bottle's mouth and immediately recoiled at the pungent scent. Smearing some of the salve on his fingers, he drew off the cloak and spread the stuff on Kith's leg, above and below the wound. That done, he covered his brother with the blankets and leaned back against the stone wall to wait.

Kith-Kanan remained unconscious throughout the impossibly long afternoon as the sun sank through the pale blue sky and finally disappeared behind the western ridge. Still, no sign of movement came from the wounded elf. If anything, he seemed even weaker.

Gently Sithas fed his brother drops of water. He wrapped him in all of their blankets and lay down beside him.

He fell asleep that way, and though he awoke many times throughout the brutally cold night, he stayed at Kith-Kanan's side until dawn began to brighten their valley.

Kith-Kanan showed no sign of reviving consciousness. Sithas looked at his brother's leg and was appalled to see a streak of red running upward, past his knee and into his thigh. What should he do? He had never seen an injury like this before. Unlike Kith-Kanan, he hadn't been confronted by the horrors of battle or by the necessity of self-sufficiency in the wilds.

Quickly the elf took the rest of the cleric's salve and smeared it onto the wound. He knew enough about blood poisoning to realize that if the venomous infection could not be arrested, his brother was doomed. With no way left to treat Kith-Kanan, however, all Sithas could do was pray.

Once again the water in their skins was frozen, and so he made the arduous trek down the narrow pathway from the ledge to the valley floor. The trough in the snow made by his passage on the previous day remained, for the wind had remained blessedly light. Thus he made his way to his snow-rimmed water hole with less difficulty than the day before.

But here he encountered a challenge: The bitter cold of the night had frozen even the rapidly flowing water beneath the snow. He chopped and chipped with his sword, finally exposing a small trickle, less than two inches deep. Only by stretching himself full-length in the snow, and immersing his hand into the frigid waters could he collect enough to carry back to their high campsite.

As he rose from the water hole, he saw the trail of the sheep across from him and remembered the magnificent creatures. Suddenly he was seized by an inspiration. He thought of his bow and arrows, still up on the ledge with Kith-Kanan. How could he conceal himself in order to get close enough to shoot? Unlike Kith-Kanan, he was not an expert archer. A close target would be essential.

He gave up his ponderings in the effort of making his way back to the ledge. Here he found no change in Kith-Kanan, and all he could do was force his brother once again to take a few drops of water between his lips.

Afterward, he strung his bow, checking the smooth surface of the weapon for flaws, the string for knots or frays. As he did so, he heard a clattering of hooves even as he stewed in his frustration. Once again led by the proud ram, the mountain sheep descended from their slope across the valley and made their way to the faint trickle of water. They took turns drinking and watching, with the ram remaining alert.

Once, when the creature's eyes passed across the cliff where Sithas and Kith lay motionless, the animal stiffened. Sithas wondered if he had been discovered and wrestled with a compulsion to quickly nock an arrow and let it fly in the desperate hope of hitting something.

But he forced himself to remain still, and finally the ram relaxed its guard. Sithas sighed and clenched his teeth in frustration as he watched the creatures turn and plow through the snow back toward their mountain fastness. The powdery drifts came to the shoulders of the large ram, and the sheep floundered and struggled until they reached the secure footing of the rocky slope.

The rest of the day passed in frigid monotony. That night was the coldest yet, and Sithas's own shivering kept him awake. He would have been grateful for even such an uncomfortable sign of life from his brother, but Kith-Kanan remained still and lifeless.

The fourth morning on the ridge, Sithas could barely bring himself to emerge from beneath the cloaks and blankets. The sun rose over the eastern ridge, and still he lay motionless.

Then urgency returned, and he sat up in panic. He sensed instinctively that today was his last chance. If he could not feed himself and his brother, they would not experience another dawn.

He grabbed his bow and arrows, strapped his sword to his back, and allowed himself the luxury of one woolen cloak from the pile that sheltered Kith-Kanan. He made his way down the cliff with almost reckless haste. Only after he nearly slipped fifty feet above the valley floor did he calm himself, forcing his feet to move with more precision.

He pushed toward the water hole, feeling sensation return to his limbs and anticipation and tension fill his heart. Finally he reached the place opposite where the sheep came to drink. He didn't allow himself to ponder a distinct possibility: What if the sheep didn't return here today? If they didn't, he and his brother would die. It was a simple as that.

Urgently he swept a shallow excavation in the snow, fearful that the sheep might already be on their way. He swung his eyes to the southern ridge, to the slope the sheep had descended on each of the two previous days, but he saw no sign of movement.

In minutes, Sithas cleared the space he desired. A quick check showed no sign of the sheep. Trembling with tension, he freed his bow and arrows and laid them before him in the snow. Next he knelt, forcing his feet into the powdery fluff behind him. He took the cloak he had brought and lay it before him, before stretching, belly down, on top.

The last thing was the hardest to do. He pulled snow from each side into the excavation, burying his thighs, buttocks, and torso. Only his shoulders, arms, and head remained exposed.

Feeling the chill settle into his bones as he pressed deeper into the snowy cushion, he twisted to the side and pulled still more of the winter powder onto him. His bow, with several arrows ready, he covered with a faint dusting of snow directly in front of him.

Finally he buried his head, leaving an opening no more than two inches in diameter before his face. From this tiny slot, he could see the water hole and he could get enough air to breathe. At last his trap was ready. Now he had only to wait.

And wait. And wait some more. The sun passed the zenith, the hour when the sheep had come to water on each of the previous days, with no sign of the creatures. Cold numbness crept into Sithas's bones. His fingers and toes burned from frostbite, which was bad enough, but gradually he became aware that he was losing feeling in them altogether. Frantically he wiggled and stretched as much as he could within the limitations of his confinement.

Where were the accursed sheep?

An hour of the afternoon passed, and another began. He could no longer keep any sensation in his fingers. Another few hours, he knew, and he would freeze to death.

But then he became aware of strange sensations deep within his snowy cocoon. Slowly, inexplicably, he began to grow warm. The burning returned to his fingertips. The snow around his body formed a cavity, slightly larger than Sithas himself, and he noticed that this snow was wet. It packed tightly, giving him room to move. He noticed wetness in his hair, on his back.

He was actually warm! The cavity had trapped his body heat, melting the snow and warming him with the trapped energy. The narrow slot had solidified before him, and it was with a sense of exhilaration that he realized he could wait here safely for some time.

But the arrival of twilight confirmed his worse fears—the sheep had not come to drink that day. Bitter with the sense of his failure, he tried to ignore the gnawing in his belly as he gathered more water and made the return to the ledge, arriving just as full darkness settled around them.

Had the sheep seen his trap? Had the flock moved on to some distant valley, following the course of some winter migration? He could not know. All he could was try the same plan tomorrow and hope he lived long enough for the effort.

Sithas had to lean close to Kith-Kanan just to hear his brother's breathing. "Please, Kith, don't die!" he whispered. Those words were the only ones he spoke before he fell asleep.

His hunger was painful when he awoke. Once again the day was clear and still, but how long could this last? Grimly he repeated his process of the previous day, making his way to the streambank, settling himself in with his bow and arrows, and trying to conceal any sign of his presence. If the sheep didn't come today, he knew that he would be too weak to try on the morrow.

Exhausted, despairing, and starving, he passed from consciousness into an exhausted sleep.

Perhaps the snow insulated him from sound, or maybe

his sleep was deeper than he thought. In any event, he heard nothing as his quarry approached. It wasn't until the sheep had reached the water hole that he woke suddenly. They had come! They weren't twenty feet away!

Not daring to breathe, Sithas studied the ram. The creature was even more magnificent up close. The swirled horns were more than a foot in diameter. The ram's eyes swept around them, but Sithas realized with relief that the animal did not notice his enemy up close.

The ram, as usual, drank his fill and then stepped aside. One by one the ewes approached the small water hole, dipping their muzzles to slurp up the icy liquid. Sithas waited until most of the sheep had drank. As he had observed earlier, the smallest were the last to drink, and it was one of these that would prove his target.

Finally a plump ewe moved tentatively among her larger sisters. Sithas tensed himself, keeping his hands under the snow as he slowly reached forward for his bow.

Suddenly the ewe raised her head, staring straight at him. Others of the flock skittered to the sides. The elf felt two dozen eyes fixed upon his hiding place. Another second, he suspected, and the sheep would turn in flight. He couldn't give them that opportunity.

With all of the speed, all of the agility at his command, he grasped his bow and arrows and lurched forward from his hiding place, his eyes fixed on the terrified ewe. Vaguely he sensed the sheep spinning, leaping, turning to flee. They struggled through the deep snow, away from this maniacal apparition who rose apparently from the very earth itself.

He saw the ram plunge forward, nudging the ewe that stood stock-still beside the water hole. With a panicked squeal, she turned and tried to spring away.

As she turned, for one split second, she presented her soft flank to the elven archer. Even as he struggled to his feet, Sithas had nocked his arrow. He pulled back the string as his target became a blur before him. Reflexively he let the missile fly. He prayed to all the gods, desperate for a hit.

But the gods were not impressed.

The arrow darted past the ewe's rump, barely grazing her skin, just enough to spur the frightened creature into a maddened flight that took her bounding out of range even as

Sithas fumbled with another arrow. He raised the weapon in time to see the ram kick his heels as that great beast, too, sprinted away.

The herd of mountain sheep bounded through the deep snow, springing and leaping in many different directions. Sithas launched another arrow and almost sobbed aloud in frustration as the missile flew over the head of a ewe. Mechanically he nocked another arrow, but even as he did so, he knew that the sheep had escaped.

For a moment, a sensation of catastrophe swept over him. He staggered, weak on his feet, and would have slumped to the ground if something hadn't caught his attention.

A small sheep, a yearling, struggled to break free from a huge drift. The animal was scarcely thirty feet away, bleating pathetically. He knew then he had one more chance— perhaps the *last* chance—for survival. He held his aim steady, sighting down the arrow at the sheep's heaving flank. The animal gasped for breath, and Sithas released the missile.

The steel-tipped shaft shot true, its barbed head striking the sheep behind its foreleg, driving through the heart and lungs in a powerful, fatal strike.

Bleating one final time, a hopeless call to the disappearing herd, the young sheep collapsed. Pink blood spurted from its mouth and nostrils, foaming into the snow. Sithas reached the animal's side. Some instinct caused him to draw his sword, and he slashed the razor-sharp edge across the sheep's throat. With a gurgle of air, the animal perished.

For a moment, Sithas raised his eyes to the ledge across the valley. The ewes scampered upward, while the ram lingered behind, staring back at the elf who had claimed one of his flock. Sithas felt a momentary sense of gratitude to the creature. His heart filled with admiration as he saw it bound higher and higher up the sheer slope.

Finally he reached down and gutted the carcass of his kill. The climb back to Kith-Kanan would be a tough one, he knew, but suddenly his body thrummed with excitement and energy.

Behind him, atop the ridge, the ram cast one last glance downward and then disappeared.

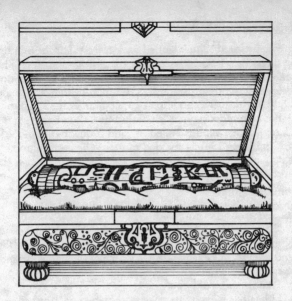

❧ 13 ❧

Fresh Blood

Sithas cut a slice of meat from his kill on the valley floor, tearing bites from the raw meat, uncaring of the blood that dribbled across his chin. Smacking greedily, he wolfed down the morsel before he carried the rest of the carcass up the steep trail to their ledge. He found Kith-Kanan as still as when he had left him, but now, at least, they had food—they had hope!

The lack of fire created a drawback, but it didn't prevent Sithas from devouring a large chunk of meat as soon as he got it back to the ledge. The blood, while it was still warm, he dribbled into his unconscious brother's mouth, hoping that the warmth and nourishment might have a beneficial effect, however minimal.

Finally sated, Sithas settled back to rest. For the first time in days, he felt something other than bleak despair. He had stalked his game and slain it—something he had never done before, not without beaters and weapon-bearers and guides. Only his brother's condition cast a pall over the situation.

For two more days, Kith's condition showed no signs of change. Gray clouds rolled in, and a dusting of snow fell around them. Sithas trickled more of the ewe's blood into Kith's mouth, hiked down for water several times a day, and offered prayers to Quenesti Pah.

Then, toward sunset of their seventh day on the ledge, Kith groaned and moved. His eyes fluttered open and he looked around in confusion.

"Kith! Wake up!" Sithas leaned over his twin, and slowly Kith-Kanan's eyes met his own. At first they looked dull and lifeless, but even as Sithas watched they grew brighter, more alert.

"What—how did you . . . ?"

Sithas felt weak with relief and helped his brother to sit up. "It's okay, Kith. You'll be all right!" He forced more confidence into his tone than he actually felt.

Kith's eyes fell upon the carcass, which Sithas had perched near the precipice. "What's that?"

"Mountain sheep!" Sithas grinned proudly. "I killed it a few days ago. Here, have some!"

"Raw?" Kith-Kanan raised his eyebrows but quickly saw that there was no alternative. He took a tender loin portion and tore off a piece of meat. It was no delicacy, but it was sustenance. As he chewed, he saw Sithas watching him like a master chef savoring the reaction to a new recipe.

"It's good," Kith-Kanan said, swallowing and tearing off another mouthful.

Excitedly Sithas told him of stalking his prey—about his two wasted arrows and the lucky break that helped him make his kill.

Kith chuckled with a heartiness that belied his wounds and their predicament.

"Your leg," Sithas said concernedly. "How does it feel today?"

Kith groaned and shook his head. "Need a cleric to work on it. I doubt it'll heal enough to carry me."

Sithas sat back, suddenly too tired to go on. Alone, he *might* be able to walk out of these mountains, but he didn't see any way that Kith-Kanan could even get down from this exposed, perilous ledge.

For a while, the brothers sat in silence, watching the sun set. The sky domed over them, pale blue to the east and overhead but fading to a rose hue that blended into a rich lavender along the western ridge. One by one stars winked into sight. Finally darkness crept across the sky, expanding from the east to overhead, then pursuing the last lingering strips of brightness into the west.

"Any sign of Arcuballis?" asked Kith hopefully. His brother shook his head sadly.

"What do we do now?" Sithas asked.

To his dismay, his brother shook his head in puzzlement. "I don't know. I'm don't think I can get down from here, and we can't finish our quest on this ledge."

"Quest?" Sithas had almost forgotten about the mission that had brought them to these mountains. "You're not suggesting we still seek out the griffons, are you?"

Kith smiled, albeit wanly. "No, I don't think *we* can do much searching. *You*, however, might have a chance."

Now Sithas gaped at his twin. "And leave you here alone? Don't even think about it!"

The wounded elf gestured to stem Sithas's outburst. "We *have* to think about it."

"You won't have a chance up here! I won't abandon you!"

Kith-Kanan sighed. "Our chances aren't that great any way you look at it. Getting out of these mountains on foot is out of the question until spring. And the months of deep winter are still before us. We can't just sit here, waiting for my leg to heal."

"But what kind of progress can I make on foot?" Sithas gestured to the valley walls surrounding them.

Kith-Kanan pointed to the northwest, toward the pass that had been their goal before the storm had driven them to this ledge. The gap between the two towering summits was protected by a steep slope, strewn with large boulders and patches of scree. Strangely, snow had not collected there.

"You could investigate the next valley," the elf suggested. "Remember, we've explored much of the range already."

"That's precious little comfort," Sithas replied. "We flew over the mountains before. I'm not even sure I could climb that pass, let alone explore beyond it."

Kith-Kanan studied the steep slope with a practiced eye. "Sure you could. Go up on the big rocks off to the side there. Stay away from those smooth patches. They look like easy going, but it's sure to be loose scree. You'd probably slip back farther than you climbed with each step. But if you stay on the good footing, you could make it."

The wounded elf turned his eyes upon his skeptical brother and continued. "Even if you don't find the griffons, perhaps you'll locate a cave, or better yet some herdsman's hut. Whatever lies over that ridge, it can't be any more barren than this place."

The Speaker of the Stars squatted back on his haunches, shaking his head in frustration. He had looked at the pass himself over the last few days and privately had decided that he would probably be able to climb it. But he had never considered the prospect of going without his brother.

Finally he made a decision. "I'll go—but just to have a look. If I don't see anything, I'm coming straight back here."

"Agreed." Kith-Kanan nodded. "Now maybe you can hand me another strip of lamb—only this time, I'd like it cooked a little more on the rare side. That last piece was too well done for my taste."

Laughing, Sithas used his dagger to carve another strip of raw mutton. He had found that by slicing it very thin he could make the meat more palatable—at least, more easily chewed. And though it was still cold, it tasted very, very good.

* * * * *

Kith-Kanan sat up, leaning against the back wall of the ledge, and watched Sithas gather his equipment. It was nearly dawn.

"Take some of my arrows," he offered, but Sithas shook his head.

"I'll leave them with you, just in case. . . ."

"In case of what? In case that ram comes looking for revenge?"

Suddenly uncomfortable, Sithas looked away. They both knew that if the hill giants returned, Kith-Kanan would be helpless to do more than shoot a few arrows before he was overcome.

"Kith . . ." He wanted to tell his brother that he wouldn't leave him, that he would stay at his side until his wounds had healed.

"No!" The injured elf raised a hand, anticipating his brother's objections. "We both understand—we *know*— that this is the only thing to do!"

"I—I suppose you're right."

"You *know* I'm right!" Kith's voice was almost harsh.

"I'll be back as soon as I can."

"Sithas—be careful."

The Speaker of the Stars nodded dumbly. It made him feel like a traitor to leave his brother like this.

"Good luck, Brother." Kith's voice came to Sithas softly, and he turned back.

They clasped hands, and then Sithas leaned forward to embrace his brother. "Don't run off on me," he told Kith, with a wry smile.

An hour later, he was past the water hole, where he had stopped to refill his skin. Now the pass loomed before him like an icy palisade—the castle wall of some unimaginably monstrous giant. Carefully, still some distance away from the ascent, he selected a route up the slope. He stopped to rest several times before reaching the base, but before noon, he began the rugged climb.

All the time he remained conscious of Kith-Kanan's eyes on his back. He looked behind him occasionally, until his brother became a faint speck on the dark mountain wall. Before he started up the pass, he waved and saw a tiny flicker of motion from the ledge as Kith waved back.

The pass, up close, soared upward and away from him like a steep castle wall, steeper than it had looked from the safe distance of their campsite. The base was a massive, sloping pile of talus—great boulders that, over many centuries, had been pried loose by frost or water to tumble and crash down the mountainside. Now they teetered precariously on top of each other, and powdery snow filled the gaps between them.

Sithas strung his bow across his back, next to his sword. His cloak he removed and tied around his waist, hoping to maintain full freedom of movement.

He picked his way up the talus slope, stepping from rock to rock only after testing each foothold for security. Once several rocks tumbled away beneath him, and he sprang aside just in time. Always he gained altitude, pulling himself up the sheer face with his leather-gloved hands. Sweat dripped into his eyes, and for a moment, he wondered how, in the midst of this snow-swept landscape, could he get so Abyss-cursed hot? Then a swirl of icy wind struck him, penetrating his damp tunic and leggings and bringing an instant shiver to his bones.

Soon he reached the top. Here he encountered long stretches of loose scree, small stones that seemed to slip and slide beneath each footfall, carrying him backward four feet for every five of progress.

Kith-Kanan, of course, had been right. He was *always* right! His brother knew his way around in country like this, knew how to survive and even how to move and explore, to hunt and find shelter.

Why couldn't it have been Sithas to suffer the crippling injury? A healthy Kith-Kanan would have been able to care for both of them, Sithas knew. Meanwhile, he wrestled with overwhelming despair and hopelessness, and he was not yet out of sight of their base camp!

Shaking off his self-pity, Sithas worked his way sideways, toward steeper, but more solid, shoulders of bedrock. Once his feet slipped away, and he tumbled twenty or thirty feet down the slope, only stopping himself by digging his hands and feet into the loose surface. Cursing, he checked his weapons, relieved to find them intact. Finally he reached a solid rock, with a small shelf shaped much like a chair, where he collapsed in exhaustion.

A quick look upward showed that he had made it perhaps a quarter of the way up the slope. At this rate, he would be stranded here at nightfall, a prospect that terrified him more than he wanted to contemplate.

Resolutely he started upward again, this time climbing along rough outcrops of rock. After only a few moments, he realized that this was by far the easiest climbing yet, and his spirits rose rapidly.

Stepping upward in long strides, he relished a new sense of accomplishment. The valley floor fell away below him; the heavens—and more mountains—beckoned from above. He no longer felt the need for rest. Instead, the climb seemed to energize him.

By midafternoon, he had neared the top of the pass, and here the route narrowed challengingly. Two huge boulders teetered on the slope, with but a narrow crack of daylight between them. One, or both, could very easily roll free, carrying him back down the mountainside if they didn't crush him between them first.

No other route presented itself. To either side of the massive rocks, sheer cliffs soared upward to the pinnacles of the two mountains. The only way through the pass lay between those two precarious boulders.

He didn't hesistate. He approached the rocks and saw that the gap was wide enough to allow him to pass—just barely. He entered the aperture, climbing upward across loose rock.

Suddenly the ground beneath his feet slipped away, and his heart lurched. He felt one of the huge boulders shift with a menacing rumble. The rock walls to either side of him pressed closer, narrowing by an inch or so. Then the rock seemed to settle into place, and he felt no more movement.

With a quick burst of speed, he darted upward, scrambling out of the narrow passage before the rocks could budge again. His momentum carried him farther up the last hundred yards of so of the ascent until finally he stood upon the summit of the pass.

Trees! He saw patches of green among the snowfields, far, far below. Trees, which meant wood, which meant fire! The slope before him, while steep and long, was nowhere near as grueling as the one he had just climbed. He glanced over his left shoulder at the sun, estimating two remaining hours of daylight.

It would have to be enough. He would have a fire tonight, he vowed to himself.

He plunged recklessly downward, sometimes riding a small, tumbling pillow of snow, at other times leaping through great drifts to soft landings ten or fifteen feet below.

Exhausted, sweat-soaked, and bone-weary, he finally reached a clump of gnarled cedars far down in the basin. Now, at last, his spirits soared. He used the last illumination of daylight to gather all of the dead limbs he could find. He piled the firewood before an unusually thick trio of evergreens, where he had decided to make his camp.

A mere touch of his steel dagger to the flint he carried in his belt-pouch brought a satisfactory spark. The dry wood kindled instantly, and within minutes, he relished the comfort of a crackling blaze.

*　*　*　*　*

Was this the curse of the gods, thought Kith-Kanan, the punishment for his betrayal of his brother's marriage? He leaned against the cliff wall and shut his eyes, wincing not in pain but in guilt.

Why couldn't he have simply died? That would have made things so much easier. Sithas would have been free to perform the quest instead of worrying about him like a nervous nursemaid worries about a feverish babe.

In truth, Kith-Kanan felt more helpless than a crawling infant, for he didn't have even that much mobility.

He had watched Sithas make his way up the slope until his twin had disappeared from sight. His brother had moved with grace and power, surprising Kith with the speed of his ascent.

But as long as Kith-Kanan lay here upon this ledge, he knew Sithas would be tied to this location by their bond of brotherhood. He would explore their immediate surroundings, perhaps, but would never bring himself to travel far beyond.

All because I'm so damned *stupid!* Kith railed at himself. They had made inadequate preparations for attack! They had both dozed off. Only the sacrifice of brave Arcuballis had given the first warning of the hill giants.

Now his griffon was gone, no doubt dead, and he himself was impossibly crippled. Sithas searched alone and on foot. It seemed inevitable to Kith-Kanan that their quest would be a failure.

* * * * *

Sithas dried his clothes and boots, every stitch of which had been soaked by sweat or melting snow, by the crackling fire. It brightened his night, driving back the high mountain darkness that had previously stretched to infinity on all sides, and it warmed his spirits in a way that he wouldn't have thought possible a few hours earlier.

The fire spoke to him with a soothing voice, and it danced for him in sultry allure. It was like a companion, one who could listen to his thoughts and give him pleasure. And finally the fire allowed him to cook a strip of his frozen meat.

That morsel, seared for a few minutes on a forked stick that Sithas plunged into the flames, emerged from the fire covered with ash, blackened and charred on the outside and virtually raw in the center. It was unseasoned, tough, imperfectly preserved . . . and it was unquestionably the most splendid meal that the elf had ever eaten in his life.

The three pines served as a backdrop to his campsite. Sithas scraped away the small amount of snow here and cleared for himself a soft bed of pine needles. He stoked the fire until he had to back away from the blazing heat.

That night he slept for a few hours, and then awoke to fuel his fire. A mountainous pile of coals radiated heat, and the ground provided a soft and comfortable cushion until the coming of dawn.

Sithas arose slowly, reluctant to break the reverie of warmth and comfort. He cooked another piece of meat, more patiently this time, for breakfast. By the time he finished, sunlight was bathing the bowl-shaped depression around him in its brilliant light. He had made a decision.

He would bring Kith-Kanan to this valley. He didn't know how yet, but he was convinced that this was the best way to insure his brother's recovery.

His course plotted, he gathered up his few possessions and lashed them to his body. Next he took several minutes to gather a stack of firewood—light, sun-dried logs that would burn steadily. He trimmed the twigs off of these so that he could bundle them tightly together. This bundle he then lashed to his back.

Finally he turned his face toward the pass. The slope before him still lay in shadow, as it would for most of the day. Retracing his tracks of the previous afternoon, he forced his way through the deep snow, back toward the summit of the pass.

It took him all morning, but finally he reached the summit. He paused to rest—the climb had been extremely wearying—and sought out the speck of color that he knew would mark Kith-Kanan's presence on the ledge in the distance. He had to squint, for the sunlight reflecting from the snow-filled bowl brutally assaulted his eyes.

He couldn't see the ledge, though he recognized the water hole where he had collected their drinking water. What was that? He saw movement near the stream, and for a moment, he wondered if the sheep had returned. His eyes adjusted to the brightness, and he understood that these could not be sheep. Large humanoid shapes lumbered through the snow. Shaggy fur seemed to cover them in patches, but the "fur" proved to be cloaks cast over broad shoulders.

They moved in single file, some ten or twelve of them, as they crossed the valley floor, taking no notice of the depth of the snow.

With a sickening realization, Sithas understood what was happening: The hill giants had returned, and they were making their way toward Kith-Kanan.

↭ 14 ↭

Immediately following

Sithas studied the hill giant that led the column of the
brutes, perhaps two miles away and a thousand feet below
him. The monster gestured to its fellows, pointing upward.
Not toward Sithas, the elf realized, but toward . . . the
ledge! His brother's camp! The dozen giants trudged
through the snow of the valley floor, making their way in
that direction.

Sithas tried to spot his twin, but the distance was too
great. Wait . . . there! Kith-Kanan, he realized, must also
have seen the giants, for the wounded elf had pulled a dark
cloak over himself and was now pressed against the far
wall of the ledge. His camouflage seemed effective and
would make him virtually invisible from below as the

giants headed toward the cliff.

The column of giants waded the stream. The one in the lead gestured again, this time indicating the path in the snow that Sithas had made in his travels back and forth for water. Another giant indicated a different track, the one made by Sithas on the previous day.

That slight gesture gave him a desperate idea. He acted quickly, casting around until his eyes fell upon a medium-sized boulder resting in the summit of the pass and cracked loose from the bedrock below. Seizing it in both of his hands, grunting from the exertion, he lifted the stone over his head. The last of the giants had crossed the stream, and now the file of huge, grotesque creatures was nearing the cliff wall.

Sithas pitched the boulder as hard and as far as he could. The rock plummeted down the steep, rock-strewn pass. Then it hit, crashing into another boulder with a sharp report before bouncing and smashing again and again down the mountain pass. Breathlessly Sithas watched the giants. They *had* to hear the commotion!

Indeed they did. Suddenly the twelve monsters whirled around in surprise. Sithas kicked another rock, and that one too clattered down the pass, rolling between the two huge boulders that he had slipped between on the previous day's climb.

Now the beasts halted, staring upward. Breathlessly Sithas waited.

It worked! He saw the first giant gesturing wildly, pointing toward the summit of the pass, toward Sithas! Kith-Kanan was left behind as the entire band of the great brutes turned and broke into a lumbering trot, pursuing the elf they probably thought they had "discovered" trying to sneak through the pass.

Sithas watched them advance toward him. They plunged through the deep snow in giant strides, each stride taking them farther from Kith-Kanan. Sithas wondered if his brother was watching, if he had seen the clever diversion created by his twin. He lay still, peering around a boulder as the monsters approached the bottom of the pass.

Now what could he do? The giants had almost reached the base of the pass. He looked behind him. Everywhere the valley was blanketed by deep snow. Wherever he went, he would leave a trail so obvious that even the thick-witted hill giants would have no difficulty in following him.

His attention returned to the immediate problem. He saw, with sharp panic, that the giants had disappeared from view. Moments later he understood: They were so close to the pass now that the steepness of the slope blocked his vision.

His head seemed fogged by fear, his body tensed with the anticipation of combat. The thought almost brought a smile to his lips. The prospect of facing a dozen giants with his puny sword struck him as ludicrous indeed! Yet by the same token, that prospect seemed inevitable, so that his amusement quickly gave way to stark terror.

Carefully he crept forward and looked down the pass. All he saw were the two monstrous boulders that had bracketed his ascent of the pass on the day before. As yet there was no sign of the giants.

Should he confront them at those rocks? No more than one at a time could pass through the narrow aperture. Still, with a brutally honest assessment of his own fighting prowess, he knew that one of them was all it would take to squash his skull like an eggshell. Also, he remembered the precarious balance of those boulders. Indeed, one of them had shifted several inches merely from the weight of his touch.

That recollection gave him an idea. The elf checked his longsword, which was lashed securely to his back. Quickly he unlashed the bundle of firewood and dropped the sticks unceremoniously to the ground. He hefted the longest one, which was about as long as his leg but no thicker than his arm. Still, it would have to do.

Without pausing to consider, Sithas, in a running crouch, crossed through the saddle and started down the slope toward the two rocks. He could see several of the giants through the crack now, and realized with alarm that they were nearly halfway up the steep-sided pass.

In a slide of tumbling scree, Sithas crashed into one of the boulders and felt it lurch beneath his weight. But then it settled back into its place, and he couldn't force it to move farther. Turning to the second rock, he pushed and heaved at it and was rewarded by a fractional shifting of its massive bulk. However, it, too, seemed to be nestled in a comfortable spot and would not move any farther.

Desperately Sithas slid downward through the crack between the boulders. The elf reached beneath the base of the one he judged to be the loosest and began to dig and chop with his piece of firewood.

He pried a large stone loose, and it skittered down the slope. Immediately he began prying at a different rock. A bellow of surprise reached him from below, and he knew that he didn't have much time. He didn't look behind him. Instead, he scrambled back upward between the rocks. He pitched his body against the rock he had worked so hard to loosen and was rewarded by a slight teetering. Then a shower of gravel sprayed from beneath it to tumble into the faces of the approaching giants.

The leader of the monsters bellowed again. The creature was a bare fifty yards below Sithas now and bounding upward with astonishing speed.

After one last, futile push at the rock, Sithas knew that he would have to abandon that plan. His time had run out. Drawing his sword, he dropped through the narrow crack again, prepared to meet the first giant at the mouth of the opening. Grimly he resolved to draw as much blood as possible before he perished.

The beast came toward him, its face split by a garish caricature of a grin. Sithas saw the tiny bloodshot eyes and the stubs of teeth jutting like tusks from its gums. Its huge lips flapped with excitement as the brute prepared to squash the life from this impudent elf.

The thing held one of those monstrous clubs such as the giants had employed in their earlier attack. Now that weapon lashed outward, but Sithas ducked back into the niche, feeling the rock tremble next to him from the force of the blow. He darted outward and stabbed quickly with his steel blade. A sense of cruel delight flared within him as the weapon scored a bloody gash on the giant's forehead.

With a cry of animal rage, the giant lunged upward, dropping its club and reaching with massive paws toward Sithas's legs. The elf skipped backward, scrambling up and away. As he did, he stabbed downward, driving his blade clear through the monster's hand.

Howling in pain, the giant twisted away, shrinking back down the slope to clutch its bleeding extremity. Sithas had no time to reconnoiter, however. The next monster had already caught up. This one had apparently learned from his comrade's errors, for it thrust its heavy club into the crack and stayed out of reach.

Sithas twisted away with a curse as the crude weapon nearly crushed his left wrist. The giant reached in, and Sithas scrambled upward. But then a loose patch of scree caused him to lose his footing, and he slipped downward toward that leering, hate-filled face.

He saw the monstrous lips spread in a leering grin, darkened stubs of ivory teeth ready to tear at his flesh. Sithas kicked out, and his boot cracked into the beast's huge, wart-covered nose.

Desperately Sithas kicked again, pushing himself upward and catching one boot on an outcrop of the rock wall beside him. The giant reached up to catch him, but the elf remained just out of his reach, barely a foot or so above him.

With determination, the broad-shouldered brute pressed into the narrow crack between the boulders. The force of his body pushed the stones outward slightly.

Yet that seemed to be enough. The monster's hand clutched Sithas's foot. Even as the elf kicked and flailed frantically, one of the rocks teetered precariously on the brink of a fall.

The Speaker of the Stars braced his back against one of the rocks and pressed both of his boots against the other. Calling for the blessings of every god he could think of, he pushed outward, straining and gasping to move the monstrous weight.

Slowly, almost gradually, the huge boulder toppled forward. The giant stared upward, his beady eyes nearly bulging out of his skull as the huge load slid forward, then began to roll downward. Tons of rock crushed the life from the brute as the boulder broke free.

His foothold suddenly gone, Sithas slid downward in the wake of the crashing stone. He felt a sickening crunch in the earth and looked up to see the other rock also break free to crash toward the valley floor a thousand feet below. Desperately the elf sprang to one side, feeling the ground shake as the huge stone tumbled past him.

The sounds of the rockslide grew and echoed, seeming to shake the bedrock of the world. Sithas pressed his face into the ground, trying to cling with his hands as the entire wall of the pass fell away. The thunderous volume overwhelmed him, and he expected to be swept away at any second.

But now the gods looked kindly on the Speaker of the Stars, and though the cliff wall a scant twelve inches from his hand plunged below, the rock to which Sithas clung remained fixed, miraculously, to the ridge.

The world crashed and surged around Sithas for what seemed like hours, though in reality it was no more than a few minutes. When he finally opened his eyes, blinking away the dust and grime, he looked down at a scene of complete devastation.

A dust cloud had settled across the formerly pristine snowfields, casting the entire valley in a dirty gray hue. The surface of the cliff gaped like a fresh scar where scree and talus, even great chunks of bedrock, had torn away. He could see none of the twelve giants, but it seemed inconceiveable that any of them could have lived through that massive, crushing avalanche.

The pass was now even steeper than it had been when he climbed it, but the entire surface was clear of snow, and the rock that remained was solid mountain. Thus he had little difficulty in picking his way painstakingly down the thousand feet of descent to the valley floor.

Near the bottom, he came upon the body of one of the giants. The creature was half-buried in rubble and covered with dust.

Sithas stepped carefully along the slope, using handholds to maintain his balance, until he reached the motionless body of the giant. The creature hung over a sharp outcrop of rock, looking like a rag doll that someone had casually cast aside. When the elf reached the monster, he examined it more closely.

He saw that it wore boots of heavy fur and a tunic of bearskin. The creature's beard was long but sparsely grown, adding to the straggled and unkempt appearance of its face. The great mouth hung slackly open, and its long, floppy tongue protruded. Several broken teeth studded its gums alongside a single well-formed tusk of ivory in front. Sithas found himself feeling a spontaneous reaction of compassion as he looked at the pathetic visage.

His reaction changed instantly to alarm when the giant moved, reaching out with one trunklike arm toward him. The elf stepped nervously backward, his longsword in his hand.

Then the giant groaned, smacking his lips and snorting in discomfort before finally forcing open the lid of one blank, bloodshot eye. The eye stared straight at the elf.

Sithas froze. His instincts, as soon as the beast had moved, had urged him to drive his keen steel blade into the creature's throat or its heart.

However, some inner emotion, surprising the elf with its strong compulsion, had held his hand. The blade remained poised before the giant's face, a foot from the end of its blunt and swollen nose, but Sithas didn't drive it home.

Instead, he studied the creature as it opened its other eye. The two orbs crossed ludicrously as it appeared to study the keen steel so close to its face. Slowly the bloodshot orbs came into focus. Sithas sensed the giant tensing, and he knew that he should slay it, if it wasn't already too late! Misgivings assailed him.

Still he held firm. The giant scowled, still trying to understand what had happened, what was going on. Finally the realization came, with a reaction that took Sithas completely by surprise. The monster yelped—a high-pitched gasp of fright—and tried to squirm backward, away from the elf and the weapon.

A large boulder blocked its retreat, and the beast cowered against the rock, raising its massive fists as if to ward away a blow. Sithas took a step forward, and when the beast cried out again, he lowered his blade, bemused by the strange behavior.

Sithas made a casual gesture with his sword. The giant raised its hands to protect its face and grunted something in a crude tongue. Again Sithas was struck by the one perfect tooth bobbing up and down amongst the otherwise ragged gums.

The problem remained of what to do with it. Letting the brute just wander away seemed like an unacceptable risk.

Yet Sithas couldn't kill it out of hand, now that it cowered and gibbered at him. It didn't seem like much of a threat anymore, despite its huge size.

"Hey, One-Tooth. Stand up." The elf gestured with his blade, and after several moments, the giant climbed hesitantly to its feet.

The creature loomed ten feet or more tall, with a barrel-sized chest and stout, sinew-lined limbs. One-Tooth gaped pathetically at Sithas as the elf nodded, pleased. He gestured again with his sword, this time down the pass, toward the valley.

"Come on, you lead the way," he instructed the giant. They started down the mountain, with Sithas keeping his sword ready.

But One-tooth seemed perfectly content to shuffle along ahead of the elf. On the ground, Sithas found it a great boon to follow in the footsteps of the giant, rather than break his own trail through the snow. Following an elaborate pantomime, he showed One-Tooth how to drag his feet when he walked, thus making a deeper and smoother path for the elf.

He directed the giant toward the ledge where Kith-Kanan lay helpless. At the bottom, before they picked their way up the steep, treacherous trail, Sithas turned back to the giant.

"I want *you* to carry him," he explained. He cradled his arms as if he was carrying an infant and pointed to the ledge above them. "Do you understand?"

The giant squinted at the elf, his eyes shrinking to tiny dots of bloodshot concentration. He looked upward.

Then his eyes widened, as if someone had just opened the shutters to a dark, little-used room. His mouth gaped happily, and the tooth bobbed up and down in enthusiastic comprehension.

"I hope so," Sithas muttered, not entirely confident about what he was doing.

Now the elf led the way, working his way up the narrow trail until he reached the ledge that had sequestered his brother.

"Well done, Brother!" Kith-Kanan was sitting upright, his back against the cliff wall and his face creased by a grin of amazed delight. "I saw them coming, and I figured that was the end!"

"That thought crossed my mind as well," admitted Sithas.

Kith looked at him with an admiring expression Sithas had never seen in his brother's eyes before. "You could have been killed, you know."

Sithas laughed self-consciously, feeling a warm sense of pride. "I can't let you have all the fun."

Kith smiled, his eyes shining. "Thanks, Brother." Clearing his throat, he nodded at One-Tooth. "But what is this—a prisoner or friend? And what idea do you have now?"

"We're going to the next valley," Sithas replied. "I couldn't find a horse, so you'll have to ride a giant!"

✒ 15 ✒

Winter, in the Army of Ergoth

The rains beat across a sea of canvas, a drumming, monotonous cadence that marked time during winter on the plains. Gray skies stretched over the brown land, encloaked by air that changed from fog to downpour to icy mist.

If only it would freeze! This was the wish of every soldier in the army who had to stand guard, conduct drills, or make the arduous treks to distant woods for firewood or lumber. A hard frost would soldify the viscous earth that now churned underfoot, miring wagon wheels and making the simple act of walking an exhaustive struggle.

Sentries stood shivering on guard duty around the ring of the great human encampment. The great bulk of Sithelbec was practically invisible in the gray anonymity of the twilit gloom. The fortress walls loomed strong; they had been tested at the cost of more than a thousand men during recent months.

Darkness came like a lowering curtain, and the camp became still and silent, broken only by the fires that dotted the darkness. Even these blazes were few, for all sources of firewood within ten miles of the camp had already been picked clean.

Amid this darkness, an even darker figure moved. General Giarna stalked toward the command tent of High General Barnet. Trailing him, trying to control her terror, followed Suzine.

She didn't want to be here. Never before had she seen General Giarna as menacing as he seemed tonight. He had summoned her without explanation, his eyes distant . . . and hungry. It was as if he barely knew that she was present, so intent were his thoughts on something else.

Now she understood that his victim was to be Barnet.

General Giarna reached the high general's tent and flung aside the canvas flap, boldly entering. Suzine, more cautiously, came behind him.

Barnet had been expecting company, for he stood facing the door, his hand on the hilt of his sheathed sword. The three of them were alone in the dim enclosure. One lamp sputtered on a battered wooden table, and rain seeped through the waterlogged roof and sides of the tent.

"The usurper dares to challenge his master?" sneered the white-haired Barnet, but his voice was not as forceful as his words.

"Master?" The black-armored general's voice was heavy with scorn. His eyes remained vacant, and focused on something very far away. "You are a failure—and your time is up, old man!"

"Bastard!" Barnet reacted with surprising quickness, given his age. In one smooth movement, his blade hissed from its scabbard and lashed toward the younger man's face.

General Giarna was quicker. He raised one hand, encased in its black steel gauntlet. The blade met the gauntlet at the wrist, a powerful blow that ought to have chopped through the armor and sliced off the general's hand.

Instead, the sword shattered into a shower of silver splinters. Barnet, still holding the useless hilt, gaped at the taller Giarna and stepped involuntarily backward.

Suzine groaned in terror. Some unbelievably horrible power pulsed in the room, a thing that she sensed on a deeper level than sight or smell or touch. Her knees grew weak beneath her, but somehow she forced herself to stand.

She knew that Giarna *wanted* her to watch, for this was to be a lesson for her as much as a punishment for Barnet.

The old man squealed—a pathetic, whimpering sound—as he stared at something in the dark eyes of his nemesis. Giarna's hands, cloaked in the shiny black steel, grasped Barnet around the neck, and the high general's sounds faded into strangled gasps and coughs.

Barnet's face expanded to a circle of horror. His tongue protruded, and his jaw flexed soundlessly. His skin grew red—bright red, like a crimson rose, thought Suzine. Then the man's face darkened to a bluish, then ashen, gray.

Finally, as if his corpse was being seared by a hot fire, Barnet turned black. His face ceased to bulge, slowly shrinking until the skin pressed tight around the clear outlines of his skull. His lips stretched backward, and then split and dried into mummified husks.

His hands, Suzine saw, had become veritable claws, each an outline of white bone, with bare shreds of skin and fingernails clinging to the ghastly skeleton.

Giarna cast the corpse aside, and it settled slowly to the floor, like an empty gunny sack that catches the undercurrents of air as it floats downward.

When the general finally turned back to Suzine, she gasped in mindless dread. He stood taller now. His skin was bright, flushed.

But his eyes were his most frightening aspect, for now they fixed upon her with a clear and deadly glow.

*   *   *   *   *

Later, Suzine stared into her mirror, despairing. Though it might show ten thousand signs, to her it was still devoid of that which meant all to her. She no longer knew if Kith-Kanan was even alive, so far distant had he flown.

In the ten days since General Giarna had slain Barnet, the army camp had been driven into furious activity. An array of great stone-casting catapults took shape along the lines. Building the huge wooden machines was slow work, but by the end of winter, twoscore of the war machines would be ready to rain their destruction upon Sithelbec.

A hard ground freeze had occurred during the days immediately following the brutal murder, and this had eliminated the mud that had impeded all activity. Now great parties of human riders scoured the surrounding plains, and the few bands of Wildrunners outside Sithelbec's walls had been eliminated or driven to the shelter of the deepest forests.

Wearily Suzine turned her thoughts to her uncle, Emperor Quivalin Soth V. The mirror combed the expanse of the frozen plain to the west, and soon she found what Giarna had directed her to seek: the emperor's great carriage, escorted by four thousand of his most loyal knights, was trundling closer to the camp.

She went to seek her commander and found him belaboring the unfortunate captains of a team sent to bring lumber from a patch of forest some dozen miles away.

"Double the size of your force if you need to!" snarled General Giarna, while six battle-scarred officers trembled before him. "But bring me the wood by tomorrow! Work on the catapults must cease until we get those timbers!"

"Sir," ventured the boldest, "it's the horses! We drive them until near collapse. Then they must rest! It takes two days to make the trip!"

"Drive them until they collapse, then—or perhaps you consider horseflesh to be more valuable than your own?"

"No, General!" Badly shaken, the captains left to organize another, larger, lumbering expedition.

"What have you learned?" General Giarna whirled upon Suzine, fixing her with his penetrating stare.

For a moment, Suzine looked at him, trying to banish her trembling. The Boy General reminded her, for the first time in a long time, of the vibrant and energetic officer she had first met, for whom she had once developed an infatuation. What did the death of Barnet have to do with this? In some vile way, it seemed to Suzine that the man had *consumed* the life force of the other, devoured his rival, and found the deed somehow invigorating.

"The emperor will arrive tomorrow," she reported. "He makes good time, now that the ground is frozen."

"Splendid." The general's mind, she could see, was already preoccupied with something else, for he turned that sharp stare toward the bastion of Sithelbec.

*   *   *   *   *

If Emperor Quivalin noticed any dark change in General Giarna, he didn't say anything to Suzine. His carriage had rolled into the camp to the cheers of more than a hundred thousand of his soldiers. The great procession rumbled around the full circumference of the circular deployments before arriving at the tent where the Boy General kept his headquarters.

The two men conferred within the tent for several hours before the ruler and the commander emerged, side by side, to address the troops.

"I have appointed General Giarna as High General of the Army," announced Quivalin, to the cheers of his men, "following the unfortunate demise of former High General Barnet.

"He has my full confidence, as do you all!" More cheers. "I feel certain that, with the coming of spring, your force will carry the walls of the elven fortress and reduce their defenses to ashes! For the glory of Ergoth, you will prevail!"

Adulation rose from the troops, who surged forward to get a close look at the mighty ruler. A sweeping stare from their general, however, held them in their tracks. A slow, reluctant silence fell over the mass of warriors.

"The collapse of my predecessor, due to exhaustion, was symptomatic of the sluggishness that previously pervaded this entire army—a laxness that allowed our enemy to reach its fortress months ago," said General Giarna. His voice was level and low, yet it seemed to carry more ominous power than the emperor's loud exhortations.

Murmurs of discontent rose in many thousands of throats. Barnet had been a popular leader, and his death hadn't been satisfactorily explained to the men. Yet the stark fear they felt for the Boy General prevented anyone from audibly muttering open displeasure.

"Our emperor informs me that additional troops will be joining us, a contingent of dwarves from the Theiwar Clan of Thorbardin. They are skilled miners and will be put to work digging excavations beneath the walls of the enemy defenses. "Those of you who are not engaged in preparations for the attack will begin tomorrow a vigorous program of training. When the time comes to attack, you will be ready! And for the glory of our emperor, you will succeed!"

❧ 16 ❧

two Weeks later, early Winter

---

the firelight reflected from the walls of the cave like dancing sprites, weaving patterns of warmth and comfort. A haunch of venison sizzled on a spit over the coals, while Sithas's cloak and leggings dried on a makeshift rack.

"No tenderloin of steer ever tasted so sweet or lay so sumptuously on the palate," announced Kith-Kanan, with an approving smack of his lips. He reached forward and sliced another hot strip from the meat that slow-roasted above the coals.

Sithas looked at his brother, his eyes shining with pride. Unlike the sheep, which he admitted had been slain by dumb luck as much as anything, he had stalked this deer through the woods, lying in wait for long, chilly hours, until the timid creature had worked its way into bow range. He had aimed carefully and brought the animal down with one shot to the neck.

"I have to agree," Sithas allowed as he finished his own piece. He, too, carved another strip for eating. Then he cut several other juicy morsels, piling them on a flat stone that served as a platter, before lifting the spit from the fire.

He turned to the mouth of the shallow cave, where winter's darkness closed in. "Hey, One-Tooth," he called. "Dinner time!"

The giant's round face, split by his characteristic massive grin, appeared. One-Tooth squinted before reaching his massive paw into the cave. His eyes lit up expectantly as Sithas handed him the spit.

"Careful—it's hot. Eat hearty, my friend." Sithas watched in amusement as the giant, who had learned several words of the common tongue—'hot' being high on the list—picked tentatively at the dripping meat.

"Amazing how friendly he got, once we started feeding him," remarked Kith-Kanan.

Indeed, once the hill giant had satisified himself that the elf wasn't going to slay him, One-Tooth had become an enthusiastic helper. He had carried Kith down the narrow trail from the ledge with all the care that a mother shows to her firstborn babe. The weight of the injured elf hadn't seemed to slow the hill giant at all as Sithas led him back over the steep pass and into this valley.

The trip had been hard on Kith-Kanan, with each step jarring his injured leg, but he had borne the punishment in silence. Indeed, he had been amazed and delighted at the degree of control with which Sithas had seized the reins of their expedition.

It had taken another day of searching, but finally the Speaker of the Stars had discovered this shallow cave, its entrance partially screened by boulders and brush. Lying in the overhang of a rock-walled riverbank, the cave itself was dry and spacious, albeit not so spacious that the giant didn't have to remain outside. A small stream flowed within a dozen feet of its mouth, assuring a plentiful supply of water.

Now that they had reached this forested valley, Sithas had been able to rig a splint for Kith-Kanan's wound.

Nevertheless, it galled the leader of the Wildrunners, who had always handled his own problems, to sit here in forced immobility while his brother, the Speaker of the Stars, did the hunting, wood-gathering, and exploration, as well as the simpler jobs like fire-tending and cooking.

"This is truly amazing, Sithas," Kith said, indicating their rude shelter. "All the comforts of home."

The cave was shallow, perhaps twenty feet deep, with a ceiling that rose almost five feet. Several dense clumps of pines and cedars grew within easy walking distance.

"Comforts," Sithas agreed. "And even a palace guard!"

One-Tooth looked attentive, sensing that they were talking about him. He grinned again, though the juice dribbling from his huge lips made the effect rather grotesque.

"I have to admit, when you first told me that I was going to ride a giant, I thought the cold had penetrated a little too far between your ears. But it worked!"

They had set up a permanent camp here, agreeing tacitly between them that without Arcuballis they were stuck in these mountains at least for the duration of the winter.

Of course, they were haunted by awareness of the distant war. They had discussed the nature of Sithelbec's defenses and concluded that the humans probably wouldn't be able to launch an effective assault before summer. The stout walls ought to stand against a long barrage of catapult attacks, and the hard earth would make tunneling operations difficult and time-consuming. All they could do now was wait and hope.

Sithas had gathered huge piles of pine boughs, which made fairly comfortable beds. A fire built at the mouth of the cave sent its smoke billowing outward, but radiated its impressive heat throughout their shelter. It made the cave into a very pleasant shelter, and—with the presence of One-Tooth—Sithas no longer feared for his brother's safety if he had to be left alone. They both knew that soon enough, Sithas would have to set out on foot to seek the griffons.

Now they sat in silence, sharing a sense of well-being that was quite extraordinary, given the circumstances. They had shelter and warmth, and now they even had extra food! Lazily Sithas rose and checked his boots, careful not to singe their fur-covered surface. He turned them slightly to warm a different part of their soggy surface. Immediately steam began to arise from the soaked leather. He returned to his spot and flopped down on his own cloak. He looked at his brother, and Kith-Kanan sensed that he wanted to say something.

"I think you've got enough food here to last you for a while," Sithas began. "I'm going to search for the griffons."

Kith nodded. "Despite my frustration with this—" he indicated his leg—"I think that's the only thing to do."

"We're near the heart of the range," Sithas continued, with a nod. "I figure that I can head out in one direction, make a thorough search, and get back here within a week or ten days. Even with the deep snow, I'll be able to make some progress. I'll stop back and check on you and let you know what I've found. If it's nothing, I'll head out in a different direction after that."

"Sounds like a reasonable plan," Kith-Kanan agreed. "You'll take the scroll from Vedvedsica, of course."

Sithas had planned on this. "Yes. If I find the griffons, I'll try to get close enough to use the spell."

His brother looked at him steadily. Kith-Kanan's face showed an expression Sithas was not accustomed to. The injured elf spoke. "Let me do something before you go. It might help on your journey."

"What?"

Kith wouldn't explain, instead requesting that his brother bring him numerous supple pine branches—still green, unlike the dried sticks they used for firewood. "The best ones will be about as big around as your thumb and as long as possible."

"Why? What do you want them for?"

His brother acted mysterious, but Sithas willingly gathered the wood as soon as daylight illuminated the valley. He spent the rest of the day gathering provisions for the first leg of his trek, checking his own equipment, and stealing sidelong glances at his brother. Kith-Kanan pretended to ignore him, instead whittling away at the pine branches, weaving them into a tight pattern, even pulling threads from his woolen cloak to lash the sticks together firmly.

Toward sunset, he finally held the finished creations up for Sithas's inspection. He had made two flat objects, oval in shape and nearly three feet long by a foot wide. The sticks had been woven back and forth into a grid pattern.

"Wonderful, Kith—simply amazing. I've never seen anything like them! But . . . what are they?"

Kith-Kanan smiled smugly. "I learned about them during that winter I spent in the Wildwood." For a moment, his smile tightened. He couldn't remember that time without thinking of Anaya, of the bliss they had shared, and of the strange fate that had claimed her. He blinked and went on. "They're called 'snowshoes.' "

Instantly Sithas saw the application. "I lash these to my boots, right?" he guessed. "And then walk around, leaving footprints in the snow like a giant?"

"You'll be surprised, I promise. They'll let you walk on top of the snow, even deep powder."

Indeed, Sithas wasted no time pulling on his boots and affixing the snowshoes to them with several straps Kith had created by tearing a strip from one of their cloaks. He tripped and sprawled headlong as he left the cave but quickly dusted himself off and started into the woods on a test walk.

Though the snowshoes felt somewhat awkward on his feet and forced him to walk with an unusually wide-spread gait, he trotted and marched and plodded through the woods for nearly an hour before returning to the cave.

"Big feet!" One-Tooth greeted him outside, where he had left the giant.

"Good feet!" Sithas replied, reaching up to give the giant a friendly clap on the arm.

Kith awaited him expectantly.

"They're fantastic! I can't believe the difference they make!"

Kith was forced to admit, as he looked at his exhilarated brother, that Sithas no longer seemed to need the assistance of anyone to cope with the rigors of the high mountain winter.

Determined to begin his quest well rested, Sithas tried to force himself to sleep. But though he closed his eyes, his mind remained alert. It leaped from fear to hope to anticipation in a chaotic whirling dance that kept him wide awake as the hours drifted past. He heard One-Tooth snoring at the cave mouth and saw Kith slumbering peacefully on the other side of the fire.

Finally, past midnight, Sithas slept. And when he did, his dreams were rich and bright, full of blue skies swarming with griffons.

* * * * *

Yellow eyes gleamed in the woods, staring at the fading fire in the mouth of the cave. The dire wolf crept closer, suppressing the urge to growl.

The creature saw and smelled the hill giant slumbering at the mouth of the cave. Though the savage canine was huge—the size of a pony, weighing more than three hundred pounds—it feared to attack the larger hill giant.

Too, the fire gave it pause. It had been burned once before, and remembered well the terrifying touch of flame.

Silently the wolf slinked back into the woods. When it was safely out of hearing of the cave, it broke into a patient lope, easily moving atop the snow.

But there was food in the cave. During the lean winter months, fresh meat was a rare prize in this mountain fastness. The wolf would remember, and as it roamed the valleys, it would meet others of its kind. Finally, when the pack had gathered, they would return.

* * * * *

Sithas's first expedition, to the west, lasted nearly four weeks. He pressed along snow-swept ridges and through barren, rock-boundaried vales. He saw no life, save for the occasional spoor of the hardy mountain sheep or the flying speck of an eagle soaring in the distance.

He traveled alone, having persuaded One-Tooth—only after a most intricate series of contortions, pantomimes, threats, and pleas—to remain behind and guard Kith-Kanan. Each day his solitude seemed to weigh heavier on him and become an oppressive, gnawing despair.

Winds tore at him every day, and as often as not, his world vanished behind a shroud of blowing snow. The days of clear weather that had followed Kith's injury, he now realized, had been a fortunate aberration in the typical weather patterns of the high mountains. Winter closed in with a fury, shrouding him in snow and hail and ice.

He pressed westward until at last he stood upon a high ridge and saw ground falling to foothills and plains beyond. He would find no mountainous refuge of griffons in this direction. The route he followed back to Kith-Kanan and One-Tooth diverged somewhat from the trail he had taken westward, but this, too, proved fruitless.

He found his brother and the hill giant in good spirits, with a plentiful supply of meat. Though Kith could not yet bear his weight on his leg, the limb seemed to be healing well. Given time, it would regain most of its prior strength.

After a night of warmth and freshly cooked meat, Sithas began his search to the north. This time his quest took even longer, for the Khalkist Range extended far along this axis. After twenty-five days of exploring, however, he saw that he had left the highest summits of the range behind. Though the trail northward was mountainous and the land uninhabited, he could see from his lofty vantage that it lacked the towering, craggy summits that had been so vividly described in Kith-Kanan's dream. It seemed safe to conclude that the valley of the griffons did not lie farther north.

His return to camp took another ten days and carried him through more lofty, but equally barren, country. The only significant finds he made were several herds of deer. He had stumbled across the creatures by accident and watched them race away, plunging through the deep snow. It was with a sensation approaching abject hopelessness that he plodded over the last ridge and found the camp nestled in its cave and remaining very much as he had left it.

One-Tooth was eager to greet him, and Kith-Kanan looked stronger and healthier, though his leg was still awkwardly splinted. His brother was working on an intricately carved crutch, but as yet he hadn't tried walking with it.

By now the food supply had begun to run short, so Sithas remained for several days, long enough to stalk and slay a plump doe. The deer's carcass yielded more meat than either of his previous kills, and when he returned to camp with the doe, he was surprised to find Kith waiting at the cave mouth—*standing* and waiting.

"Kith! Your leg!" he asked, dropping the deer and stepping quickly to his brother's side.

"Hurts like all the fires of the Abyss," Kith grunted, but his teeth, though clenched, forced his mouth into a tight smile. "Still, it can hold me up, with the help of my crutch."

"Call you Three-Legs now," observed One-Tooth dryly.

"Fair enough!" Kith agreed, still gritting his teeth.

"I think this calls for a celebration. How about some melted snow and venison?" proposed Sithas.

"Perfect," Kith-Kanan agreed.

One-Tooth drooled happily, sharing the brothers' elation. The trio enjoyed an evening of feasting. The giant was the first to tire, and soon he was snoring noisily in his accustomed position outside the mouth of the cave.

"Are you going back out?" Kith asked quietly after long moments of contented silence.

"I have to," Sithas replied. They both knew that there was no other alternative.

"This is the last chance," Kith-Kanan observed. "We've come up from the south, and now you've looked to the north and the west. If the valley doesn't lie somewhere to the east, we'll have to face the fact that this whole adventure might have been a costly pipe dream."

"I'm not prepared to give up yet!" Sithas said, more sharply than he intended. Truthfully, the same suspicions had lurked in his own subconscious for many days. What if he found no sign of the griffons? What if they had to march back to Silvanost on foot, a journey that would take months and couldn't begin until snowmelt in late spring? And what if they returned, after all this time, empty-handed?

So it was that Sithas began his eastward search with a taut determination. He pushed himself harder than ever before, going to reckless lengths to scale sheer passes and traverse lofty, precipitous ridges. The mountains here were the most rugged of any in the range, and any number of times they came very close to claiming the life of the intrepid elf.

Every day Sithas witnessed thundering avalanches. He learned to recognize the overhanging crests, the steep and snow-blanketed heights that gave birth to these crushing snowslides. He identified places where water flowed beneath the snow, gaining drinking water when he needed it but avoiding a potential plunge through the ice that, by soaking him in these woodless heights, would amount to a sentence of death by freezing.

He slept on high ridges, with rocks for his pillow and bed. He excavated snow caves when he could and found that the warmth of these greatly improved his chances of surviving the long, dark nights. But once again he found nothing that would indicate the presence of griffons—indeed, of *any* living creatures—among these towering crags.

He pressed for two full weeks through the barren vales, climbing rock-studded slopes, dodging avalanches, and searching the skies and the ridges for some sign of his quarry. He pressed forward each day before dawn and searched throughout the hours of daylight until darkness all but blinded him to any spoor that wasn't directly in front of his nose. Then he slept fitfully, anxious for the coming of daylight so that he could resume his search.

However, he was finally forced to admit defeat and turned back toward the brothers' camp. A bleak feeling of despair came over him as he made camp on a high ridge. It was as he rearranged some rocks to form his sleeping place that Sithas saw the tracks: like a cat's, only far bigger, larger than his own hand with the fingers fully outstretched. The rear, feline feet he identified with certainty, and now the nature of the padded forefeet became clear, too. They might have been made by an incredibly huge eagle, but Sithas knew this was not the case. The prints had been made by the great taloned griffon.

*　*　*　*　*

Kith-Kanan squirmed restlessly on his pine-branch bed. The once-soft branches had been matted into a hard and lumpy mat by more than two months of steady use, and no longer did they provide a pleasant cushion for his body. As he had often done before—indeed, as he did a hundred or a thousand times each day--he cursed the injury that kept him hobbled to this shelter like an invalid.

He noticed another sound that disturbed his slumber—a rumble like a leaky bellows in a steel-smelting plant. The noise reverberated throughout the cave.

"Hey, One-Tooth!" Kith snapped. "Wake up!"

Abruptly the sound ceased with a snuffling gurgle, and the giant peered sleepily into the cave.

"Huh?" demanded the monstrous humanoid. "What Three-Legs want now?"

"Stop snoring! I can't sleep with all the racket!"

"Huh?" One-Tooth squinted at him. "Not snoring!"

"Never mind. Sorry I woke you." Smiling to himself, the wounded elf shifted his position on the rude mattress and slowly boosted himself to his feet.

"Nice fire." The giant moved closer to the pile of coals. "Better than village firehole."

"Where is your village?" asked Kith curiously. The giant had mentioned his small community before.

"In mountains, close to tree lands."

This didn't tell Kith much, except that it was at a lower altitude than the valley they now inhabited, a fact that was just as well, considering his brother's ongoing exploration of the highlands.

"Sleep some more," grunted the giant, stretching and yawning. His mouth gaped, and the solitary tusk protruded until One-Tooth smacked his lips and closed his eyes.

The giant had made remarkable progress in learning the elven tongue. He was no scintillating conversationalist, of course, but he could communicate with Kith-Kanan on a remarkable number of day-to-day topics.

"Sleep well, friend," remarked Kith softly. He looked at the slumbering giant with genuine affection, grateful that the fellow had been here during these months of solitude.

Looking outward, he noticed the pale blue of the dawn sky looming behind One-Tooth's recumbent form.

Damn this leg! Why did he have to suffer an injury now, just when his skills were most needed, when the entire future of the war and of his nation were at stake?

He had regained some limited mobility. He could totter, albeit painfully, around the mouth of the cave, getting water for himself and exercising his limbs. Today, he resolved, he would press far enough to get a few more pine branches for his crude and increasingly uncomfortable bed.

But that was nothing compared to the epic quest undertaken by his brother! Even as Kith thought about making the cave a little more cozy, his brother was negotiating high mountain ridges and steep, snow-filled valleys, making his camp wherever the sunset found him, pressing forward each day to new vistas.

More than once, Kith had brooded on the fact that Sithas faced great danger in these mountains. Indeed, he could be killed by a fall, or an avalanche, or a band of wolves or giants—by any of countless threats—and Kith-Kanan wouldn't even know about it until much time had passed and he failed to return.

Growling to himself, Kith limped to the cave mouth and looked over the serene valley. Instead of inspiring mountain scenery, however, all he saw were steep, gray prison walls, walls that seemed likely to hold him here forever.

What was his brother doing now? How fared the search for the griffons?

He limped out into the clear, still air. The sun touched the tips of the peaks around him, yet it would be hours before it reached the camp on the valley floor.

Grimacing with pain, Kith pressed forward. One-Tooth's forays for wood and water had packed down the snow for a large area around their cave, and the elf crossed the smooth surface with little difficulty.

He reached the edge of the packed snow, stepping into the spring mush and sinking to his knee. He took another step, and another, wincing at the effort it took to move his leg.

Then he froze, motionless, his eyes riveted to the snow before him. His hand reached for a sword that he was not wearing.

The tracks were clear in the soft snow. They must have been made the night before. A pack of huge wolves, perhaps a dozen or more, had run past the the cave in the darkness. Luckily he could see no sign of them now as he carefully backed toward the cave.

He remembered the fire they had built the night before and imagined the wolves sidling past, fearful of the flames. Yet he knew, as he studied the silent woods, that sooner or later they would return.

❧ 17 ❧

the next day

Sithas reached upward, pulling himself another eight inches closer to his goal. Sweat beaded upon his forehead, fatigue numbed his arms and legs, and a dizzying expanse of space yawned below him. All of these factors he ignored in his grim determination to reach the crest of the ridge.

The rocky barrier before him loomed high, with sheer sides studded with cracked and jagged outcrops of granite. A month ago, he reflected as he paused to gasp for breath, he would have called the climb impossible. Now it represented merely another obstacle, one that he would treat with respect yet was confident that he would successfully overcome.

High hopes surged in his heart, convincing him to keep

on climbing. This *had* to be the place! The night before, those tracks on the ledge had seemed so clear, such irrefutable proof that the griffons lived somewhere nearby. Now doubts assailed him. Perhaps his mind played tricks on him, and this torturous climb was simply another exercise in futility.

Beyond this steep-walled ridge, he knew, lay a stretch of the Khalkist Mountains that he had not yet explored. The region sprawled, a chaos of ridges, glaciers and valleys. Finally he pulled himself up over the rocky summit of the divide. He looked into the deep valley beyond, squinting against the bright sunlight. He no longer wore his scarf protectively across his face. Four months of exposure to wind, snow, and sun had given his skin the consistency and toughness of leather.

No movement greeted his eyes, no sign of life in the wide and deep vale. Yet before him—and far, far below—he saw a wide expanse of dark green forest. Amidst these trees, he glimpsed a sparkling reflection that he knew must be a pond or small lake, and unlike any other body of water he had seen for the last two months, this one was *unfrozen!*

He scrambled over the top of the ridge, only to be confronted by a precipitous descent beyond. Undismayed, he followed the knifelike crest, until at last he found a narrow ravine that led downward at an angle. Quickly, almost recklessly, Sithas slid down the narrow chute. Always he kept his eyes on the heavens, searching for any sign of the magnificent half-lion, half-eagle beasts that he sought.

Would he be able to tame them? He thought of the scroll he had carried during these weeks of searching. When he paused to rest, he removed it and examined its ivory tube. Uncorking the top, he checked to see that the parchment was still curled, well protected, within. From somewhere, a nagging doubt troubled him, and for the first time, he wondered if the enchantment would work. How could mere words, read from such a scroll, have an effect on creatures as proud and free as the griffons? He could only hope that Vedvedsica had spoken the truth.

The ravine provided him good cover and a relatively easy descent that carried him steadily downward for thousands of feet. He moved carefully, taking precautions that his footsteps didn't trigger any slide of loose rock. And though he saw no sign of his quarry, he wanted to make every effort to ensure that it was *he* who discovered *them*, rather than the other way around.

It took Sithas several hours to make the long, tedious descent. Steep walls climbed to his right and left, sometimes so close together that he could reach out his hands and touch each side of the ravine simultaneously. Once he came to a sharp drop-off, some twelve feet straight down. Turning to face the mountain, he lowered himself over the precipice, groping with his feet until he found a secure hold. Very carefully, he braced himself and sought lower grips for his hands. In this painstaking fashion, he negotiated the cliff.

The floor of the passage wound back and forth like a twisting corridor, and sometimes Sithas could see no more than a dozen feet in front of him. At such times, he moved with extra caution, peering around the bend before proceeding ahead. Thus it was that he came upon the nest.

At first he thought it to be an eagle's eyrie. A huge circle of twigs, sticks, and branches rested on a slight shoulder of the ravine. Steep cliffs dropped away below it. A hollow in the middle of the nest had obviously been smoothed out, creating a deep and sheltering lair that was nearly six feet across. Three small feathered creatures moved there, immediately turning to him with gaping beaks and sharp, demanding squawks.

The animals rose, spreading their wings and bleating with increased urgency. Their feathers, Sithas saw, were straggly and thin; they looked incapable of flight. Their actions seemed like those of fledglings, yet already the young griffons were the size of large hawks.

Sithas peeked carefully over the lip of a boulder. The tiny griffons, he saw, had collected themselves into a bundle of feathers and fur, talons and beaks. They hissed and spat, the feathers along the napes of their eagle necks bristling. At the same time, feline tails lashed back and forth in excitement and tension.

For several moments, the elf dared not draw a breath or even open his mouth. So powerful was the sense of triumph sweeping over him that he had to resist the temptation to shout his delight aloud.

He forced himself to keep still, hiding in the shadow of the huge rock, trying to restrain the pounding of his heart.

He had found the griffons! They lived!

Of course, these nestlings were not the proud creatures he sought, but the nearness of the flock was no longer a matter of doubt. It remained only a matter of time before he would discover the full-grown creatures. How many were there? When would they return? He watched and waited.

For perhaps half an hour, he remained immobile. He searched the skies above, even as he shrank against the wall of the ravine and tried to conceal himself from overhead view.

With sudden urgency, he pulled the ivory scroll tube from his backpack. Unrolling the parchment, he studied the symbols of enchantment. It would require concentration and discipline, he saw, in order to pronounce the old elvish script, which was full of archaic pronunciations and mystical terminology. He allowed his tongue to shape the unusual sounds, practicing silently.

"*Keerin—silvan! . . . Thanthal ellish, Quimost . . . Hothist kranthas, Karin Than-tanthas!*"

Such a simple spell. Perhaps it was madness to expect success from it. It certainly seemed rash, now that he stood here, to face a multitude of savage carnivores with nothing more than these words to protect him.

Again his restlessness returned, and finally he had to move. With as much stealth as he could muster, Sithas worked his way up the slope of the ravine. He sought a place with a commanding view of the valley. His instincts told him that the events of the rest of this day would prove the worth of the entire quest. Indeed, they might measure the worth of his entire life.

He found a broad shoulder of the ridge, an open ledge that nevertheless lay in the shadow of an overhanging shelf of rock. From here, he believed, he could see all of the valley below him, but he could not be seen, or attacked, from above.

He settled down to wait. The sun seemed to hang motionless in the sky, mocking him.

He dozed for a while, lulled by the warmth of the sun and perhaps drained by his own tension. When he awoke, it was with abrupt alarm. He thought momentarily that he had entered a bizarre dream.

Blinking and shaking his head, Sithas saw a tiny spot of movement, no more than a speck of darkness against the clear sky. From the great distance, he knew that whatever he saw must be very large indeed. He saw a pair of broad wings supporting a body that seemed to grow with each passing moment. He stared, but could see nothing else beyond this lone scout.

The streamlined bird shape swooped into a low dive, settling toward the ridge across the valley. Even at this great distance, Sithas saw the leonine rear legs descend, supporting the griffon's weight on the ground while it used its wings to slowly settle its forefeet. He could plainly see the creature's size and sense its raw, contained power. Another flying beast hove into view, and then several more, all of them settling beside the first. From this far away, he might have been looking at a flock of blackbirds settling toward a farmer's field lush with ripening corn. But he knew that each of the griffons was larger than a horse.

The beasts returned to their valley, flying in a great flock and shrieking their delight at the homecoming. They sounded like great eagles, though louder and fiercer than even those proud birds. The flock spread across a mile or more, darkening the sky with their impressive presence.

They settled along the jagged ridge and gathered upon nearby summits, still miles away from Sithas. The many rocky knobs disappeared beneath slowly beating wings and smooth, powerful bodies seeking comfortable perches. For the first time, Sithas became aware of many nests, all along the ridges and slopes of his side of the valley, as dozens of fledglings squawked and squirmed in their nests. So splendidly were they camouflaged that he hadn't noticed the presence of several within a hundred feet of his vantage point.

Now several of the adults took to the air again, springing into the valley with long, graceful dives, allowing their hind legs to trail out behind them in sleek, streamlined efficiency. As they drew closer, Sithas could see long strips of red meat dangling from their mouths. Birdlike, they would tend to the feeding of their young.

The rest of the flock followed, once again filling the sky with the steady pulse of their wingbeats. They numbered in the hundreds, perhaps half a thousand, though Sithas did not take the time to count. Instead, he knew that he had to act boldly and promptly.

With quick, certain gestures, he unfurled the scroll and took a look at the bizarre, foreign-looking symbols. Gritting his teeth, he stepped boldly outward, to the lip of the precipice, raising the scroll before him. Now he felt totally naked and exposed.

His movement provoked a stunning and instant reaction. The valley rang with a chorus of shrill cries of alarm as the savage griffons spotted him and squalled their challenges. The ones in the lead, those carrying food for the young, immediately dove to the sides, away from the elven interloper. The rest tucked their wings and dove straight toward the Speaker of the Stars.

Terror choked in Sithas's throat. Never had he faced such a terrible onslaught. The griffons rocketed closer with astonishing speed. Huge talons reached toward him, eager to tear the flesh from his limbs.

He forced himself to look down at the scroll, thinking that his voice would never even be heard in this din!

But he read the words anyway. His voice came from somewhere deep within him, powerful and commanding. The sounds of the old elvish words seemed suddenly like the language he had known all his life. He spoke with great strength, his tone vibrant and compelling, betraying no sign of the fear that threatened to overwhelm him.

"Keerin—silvan!"

At this first phrase, a silence descended so suddenly that the absence of sound struck Sithas almost like a physical force, knocking him off his feet. He sensed that the griffons were still diving, still swooping toward him, but their shrill cries had been silenced by his first words. This enhanced his confidence.

"Thanthal ellish, Quimost."

The words seemed to flame on the scroll before him, each symbol erupting into life as he read it. He did not dare to look up.

"Hothist kranthas, Karin Than-tanthas!"

The last of the symbols flared and waned, and now the elf looked up, boldly seeking the griffons with his eyes. He would meet his death bravely or he would tame them.

The first thing he saw was the hate-filled visage of a diving griffon. The monstrous creature's beak gaped, and both the eagleclaws of its front legs and the lion talons of its rear limbs reached toward Sithas, ready to tear him asunder.

But then suddenly it veered upward, spreading its broad wings and coming to rest upon the shelf of rock directly before the tall form of Sithas, Speaker of the Stars, scion of the House of Silvanos.

"Come to me, creatures of the sky!" Sithas cried. An awe-inspiring sense of power swept over him, and he raised his arms, his hands clenched into fists held skyward.

"Come, my griffons! Answer the call of your master!"

And come to him they did.

The flock, dramatically spellbound, swirled around him and settled toward places of vantage on the towering ridges nearby. One of these approached the elf, creeping along the crest of rock. Sithas saw a slash of white feathers across its brown breast, and his spirits soared in sudden recognition.

"Arcuballis!" he cried as the griffon's head rose in acknowledgment. The great creature lived and had somehow found a home with this flock of his kin!

The proud griffon sprang to Sithas, rearing before him and spreading his vast wings. The elf saw a gouge along one side of Arcuballis's head where the giant's club had cracked him. Sithas was surprised at the joy he felt at the discovery of his brother's lifelong steed, and that joy, he knew, would pale compared to Kith-Kanan's own delight.

The others, too, moved toward him—with pride and power, but no longer did they seem to be threatening. Indeed, curiosity seemed to be their dominant trait.

By the gods, he had done it! His quest had succeeded! Because of his elation, the distant war seemed already all but won.

❧ 18 ❧

that day, late winter

The dire wolves attacked suddenly, bursting from the concealment of trees that grew within a hundred feet of the cave mouth. Kith-Kanan and One-Tooth had planned their defense, but nevertheless, the onslaught came with surprising speed.

"There! Hounds come!" shouted the giant, first to see the huge, shaggy brutes.

Kith-Kanan seized his bow and pulled himself to his feet, cursing the stiffness that still impaired the use of his leg.

The largest of the dire wolves led the charge. A nightmarish brute, with murderous yellow eyes and a great, bristling mane of black fur, the beast sprinted toward the cave, while others of its pack followed in its wake. It snarled, curling its

---

black, drooling lips to reveal teeth as long as Kith's fingers.

The dire wolves had the same narrow muzzles, alert, pointed ears, and fur-coated bodies and tails of normal wolves. However, they were much larger than their more common cousins, and of far more fearsome disposition. A dozen erupted from the trees in the first wave, and Kith saw more of the dim gray shapes lurking in the woods beyond.

The elf propped himself up against a wall. With mechanical precision, he launched an arrow, nocked another, and fired again. He released a dizzying barrage of missiles at the loping canines. The razor-sharp steel of the arrowheads cut through fur and sinew, gouging deep wounds into the bristling canines, but even the bloodiest cuts seemed only to enrage the formidable creatures.

One-Tooth lumbered forward, his club raised. The hill giant grunted and swung, but his target skipped to one side. Whirling, the dire wolf reached with hungry fangs for the giant's unprotected calf, but One-Tooth leaped away with surprising quickness. Instead of lunging after the giant, the monster darted toward Kith-Kanan as a snarling trio of its fellow wolves took up the assault on the hill giant.

The elf smoothly raised his bow and let fly another arrow. Though the missile scored a bloody gash on the beast's flank it didn't seem to appreciably affect its charge. One-Tooth whirled in a circle, clearing the menacing forms away from himself, and then swung desperately, knocking the rear legs of one large monster to the side. The wolf crashed to the ground and then sprang away.

The wolves began to circle One-Tooth. Kith-Kanan shot at yet another wolf, and another, dropping each with arrows to the throat. A wolf turned from the giant, loping toward the elf, and Kith brought it down—but not before driving three arrows into its chest, and even then the beast didn't stop until it had practically reached him.

Once again they came in a rush, a nightmarish image of snarling lips, glistening fangs, and gleaming, hate-filled eyes. The elf shot his arrows one after the other, scarcely noting the effect of one before the next was nocked. The giant bashed at the shaggy beasts, while they in turn tore at his legs, ripping gory wounds with their fangs.

The packed snow around the cave mouth was covered

with gray bodies, and great patches of it were stained crimson by the spilled blood of the slain wolves. One-Tooth stumbled, nearly going down amid the viciously snarling attackers. A wolf leaped for the giant's neck, but the elven archer killed it in midair with a single arrow to the heart.

Then Kith-Kanan reached for another arrow and realized he had used them all. Grimly drawing his sword, he pushed himself away from the wall and limped toward the beleaguered giant. He felt terribly vulnerable without the rock wall behind him, but he couldn't leave the courageous hill giant to die by himself.

Then suddenly, before Kith reached the melee, the wolves sprang away from the giant and darted back to the shelter of the trees, leaving a dozen of their number behind, dead.

"Where go hounds?" demanded the hill giant, shaking his fist after the wolves.

"I don't know," admitted the elf. "I don't think *I* scared them away."

"Good fight!" One-Tooth beamed at Kith-Kanan, wiping a trunklike wrist below his running nose. "Big hounds—mean, too!"

"Not so mean as we are, my friend," Kith noted, still puzzled by the sudden retreat of the wolves just when their victory had seemed assured.

Kith-Kanan was relieved to see that One-Tooth's wounds, while bloody, were not deep. He showed the giant how to clean them with snow, meanwhile keeping his eyes nervously on the surrounding pines.

He heard the disturbance in the air before One-Tooth did, but both of them instinctively looked up at the sky. They saw them coming from the east—a horizon full of great soaring shapes, with proudly spread wings and long, powerful bodies.

"The griffons!" Kith cried, whooping with glee. The giant stared at him as if he had lost his mind while he danced about the clearing, waving and shouting.

The great flock settled across the valley floor, squawking and growling over the best perches. Sithas came to earth, riding one of the griffons, and Kith-Kanan recognized his mount immediately.

"Arcuballis! Sithas!"

His brother, equally elated, leaped to the ground. The twins embraced, too full of emotion for words.

"Big lion-bird," grunted One-Tooth, eyeing Arcuballis carefully. "Rock-nose bring home."

"Bring home—to your village?" asked Kith.

"Yup. Lion-bird hurt. Rock-nose feed, him fly away."

"The giants must have taken him with them that night they first attacked us," Kith-Kanan guessed. "They nursed him back to health."

"And then he escaped, and found the flock in the wild. He was with them when I finally discovered their nests," Sithas concluded.

Sithas related the tale of his search and the discovery of the flock. "I left the nestlings and several dozen females who had been feeding them in the valley. The rest came with me."

"There are *hundreds*," observed Kith-Kanan, amazed.

"More than four hundred, I think, though I haven't made an exact count."

"And the spell? It worked like it was supposed to?"

"I thought they were going to tear me apart. My hands were shaking so much I could hardly hold the scroll," Sithas exaggerated. "I read the incantation, and the words seemed to flame off the page. I had just finished the spell when the first one attacked."

"And then what?"

"He just landed in front of me, as if he was waiting for instructions. They *all* settled down. That's when I saw Arcuballis. When I mounted him and he took to the air, the others followed."

"By the gods! Let's see the humans try to stand against us *now!*" Kith-Kanan practically crowed his excitement.

"How have you fared? Not without some trouble, I see." Sithas indicated the pile of dead wolves, and Kith told him about the attack.

"They must have heard you coming," Kith speculated.

"Let's get back to the city. A whole winter has passed!" Sithas urged.

Kith turned toward the cave, suddenly spotting One-Tooth. The giant had observed—at first with interest, but then with ill-concealed concern—the exchange between the brothers.

It surprised the elf to realize the depth of the bond that had developed between them.

"Three-Legs fly away?" One-Tooth looked at Kith, frowning quizzically.

Kith didn't try to explain. Instead, he clasped one of the giant's big hands in both of his own. "I'll miss you," he said quietly. "You saved my life today—and I'm grateful to have had your friendship and protection."

"Good-bye, friend," said the giant sadly.

Then it was time for the elves to mount the griffons and to turn their thoughts toward the future . . . toward home.

PART III:
WINDRIDERS

19

Early Spring, Year of the Bear, 2213 (PC)

*The forestlands of Silvanost stretched below like a shag-*gy green carpet, extending to the far horizons and beyond. Huge winged shadows flickered across the ground, marking the path of the griffons. The creatures flew in great **V**-shaped wedges, several dozen griffons in each wedge. These formations spread across more than a mile.

Kith-Kanan and Sithas rode the first two of the mighty beasts, flying side by side toward their home. The forest had stretched below them for two days, but now, in the far distance, a faint glimmer of ivory light appeared. They soared faster than the wind, and swiftly that speck became identifiable as the Tower of the Stars. Soon the lesser towers of Silvanost came into view, jutting above the treetops like a field of sharp spires.

As they left the wilderness behind, Kith-Kanan thought fondly of the giant they had grown to know. One-Tooth had waved to them from the snow-filled valley until the fliers had vanished from sight. Kith-Kanan still remembered his one tusklike tooth bobbing up and down in a forlorn gesture of farewell.

They followed the River Thon-Thalas toward the island that held the elven capital. The griffons streamed into a long line behind them, and several of them uttered squawks of anticipation as they descended. Five hundred feet over the river, they raced southward, and soon the whole city sprawled below them.

The creatures shrieked and squalled, alarming the good citizens of Silvanost so much that, for several minutes, there existed a state of general panic, during which time most elves assumed that the war had come home to roost via some arcane and potent human ensorcelment.

Only when the two blond-haired elves were spotted did the panic turn to curiosity and wonder. And by the time Sithas and Kith-Kanan had circled the palace grounds and then led their charges in a gradual downward spiral toward the Gardens of Astarin, the word had spread. The emotions of the Silvanesti elves exploded into a spontaneous outpouring of joy.

Nirakina was the first to meet the twins as the great creatures settled to the ground. Their mother's eyes flowed with tears, and at first she could not speak. She took turns kissing each of them and then holding them at arm's length, as if making sure that they were alive and fit.

Beyond her, Sithas saw Tamanier Ambrodel, and his spirit was buoyed even higher. Lord Ambrodel had returned from his secret mission to Thorbardin. Loyally, he had stayed discreet about what he had learned. Now he might have decisive news about a dwarven alliance in the elven war.

"Welcome home, Your Highness," Ambrodel said sincerely as Sithas clasped the lord chamberlain's shoulders.

"It's good to see you here to greet me! We will talk as soon as I can break away." Ambrodel nodded, the elf's narrow face reflecting private delight.

Meanwhile, the griffons continued to descend into the gardens, and across the gaming fields, and even into many of the nearby vegetable plots. They shrieked and growled, and the good citizens of the city gave them wide berth. Nevertheless, each griffon remained well behaved once it landed, moving only to preen its feathers or to settle weary wings and legs. When they had all landed, they squatted comfortably on the ground and took little note of the intense excitement surrounding them.

Kith-Kanan, with a barely noticeable limp, took his mother's arm as Hermathya and a dozen courtiers emerged from the Hall of Audience. Lord Quimant walked, with a quick stride, at their head.

"Excellency!" he cried in delight, racing forward to warmly embrace the Speaker of the Stars.

Hermathya approached a good deal more slowly, greeting her husband with a formal kiss. Her greeting was cool, though her relief was obvious even through her pretense of annoyance.

"My son!" Sithas said excitedly. "Where is Vanesti?"

A nursemaid stepped forward, offering the infant to his father.

"Can this be him? How much he's changed!" Sithas, with a sense of awe, took his son in his arms while the crowd quieted. Indeed, the elfin child was much larger than when they had departed, nearly half a year earlier. His blond hair grew thick upon his scalp. As his tiny eyes looked toward his father, Vanesti's face broke into a brilliant smile.

For several moments, Sithas seemed unable to speak. Hermathya came to him and very gently took the child. Turning away from her husband, her gaze briefly met Kith-Kanan's. He was startled by the look he saw there. It was cool and vacant, as if he did not exist. It had been many weeks since he had thought of her, but this expression provoked a brief, angry flash of jealousy—and, at the same time, a reminder of his guilt.

"Come—to the palace, everyone!" Sithas shouted, throwing an arm around his brother's shoulders. "Tonight there will be feast for all the city! Let word be spread immediately! Summon the bards. We have a tale for them to hear and to spread across the nation!"

The news carried through the city as fast as the cry could pass from lips to ears, and all the elves of Silvanost prepared to celebrate the return of the royal heirs. Butchers slaughtered prime pigs, casks of wine rumbled forth from the cellars, and colorful lanterns swiftly sprouted, as if by magic, from every tree, lamppost, and gate in the city. The festivities began immediately, and the citizenry danced in the streets and sang the great songs of the elven nation.

Meanwhile, Sithas and Kith-Kanan joined Lord Regent Quimant and Lord Chamberlain Tamanier Ambrodel in a small audience chamber. The regent looked at the chamberlain with some surprise and turned to Sithas with a questioning look. When the Speaker of the Stars said nothing, Quimant cleared his throat and spoke awkwardly.

"Excellency, perhaps the lord chamberlain should join us after the conclusion of this conference. After all, some of the items I have to report are of the most confidential nature." He paused, as if embarrassed to continue.

"Indeed, in this nearly half a year that you have been absent, I must report that the lord chamberlain has not in fact been present in the capital. He only returned recently, from his family estates. Apparently matters of his clan's business interests took precedence over affairs of state."

"Tamanier Ambrodel has my complete confidence. Indeed," Sithas replied, "we may find that he has reports to make as well."

"Of course, my lord," Quimant said quickly, with a deep bow.

Quimant immediately started to fill them in on the events that had occurred during their absence.

"First, Sithelbec still stands as strong as ever." The lord of Clan Oakleaf anticipated Kith-Kanan's most urgent question. "A messenger from the fortress broke through the lines a few weeks past, bringing word that the defenders have repulsed every attempt to storm the walls."

"Good. It is as I hoped," Kith replied. Nevertheless he was relieved.

"However, the pressure is increasing. We have word of a team of dwarven engineers—Theiwar, apparently—aiding the humans in excavating siegeworks against the walls. Also, the number of wild elves throwing in their lot with

Ergoth is increasing steadily. There are more than a thousand of them, and apparently they have been formed into a 'free elf' company."

"Fighting their own people?" Sithas was aghast at the notion. His face reddened with controlled fury.

"More and more of them have questioned the right of Silvanost to rule them. And an expedition of the wild elves of the Kagonesti arrived here shortly after you left to plead for an end to the bloodshed."

"The ignoble scum!" Sithas rose to his feet and stalked across the chamber before whirling to face Quimant. Vivid lines of anger marred his face. "What did you tell them?"

"Nothing," Quimant replied, his own face displaying a smug grin. "They have spent the winter in your dungeon. Perhaps you'd care to speak to them yourself."

"Good." Sithas nodded approvingly. "We can't have this kind of demonstration. We'll make an example of them to discourage any further treachery."

Kith-Kanan faced his brother. "Don't you want to—at the very least—hear what they have to say?"

Sithas looked at him as if he spoke a different language. "Why? They're traitors, that's obvious! Why should we—"

"*Traitors?* They have come here to talk. The traitors are those who have joined the enemy out of hand! We *need* to ask questions!"

"I find it astonishing that *you*, of all of us, should take this approach," Sithas said softly. "You are the one who has to carry out our plans, the one whose life is most at risk! Can you not understand that these . . . *elves*"—Sithas spat the word as if it were anathema—"should be dealt with quickly and ruthlessly!"

"If they are indeed traitors, of course! But you can take the trouble to hear them first, to find out if they are in fact treacherous or simply honest citizens living in danger and fear!"

Sithas and Kith-Kanan glowered at each other like fierce strangers. Tamanier Ambrodel quietly watched the exchange. He had offered no opinion on any topic as yet, and he felt that this was not the time to interject his view. Lord Quimant, however, was more forthright.

"General, Excellency, please . . . there are more details.

Some of the news is urgent." The lord stood and raised his hands.

Sithas nodded and collapsed into his chair. Kith-Kanan remained standing, turning expectantly toward the lord regent.

"Word out of Thorbardin arrived barely a fortnight ago. The ambassador, Than-Kar of the Theiwar clan, reported it to me in a most unpleasant and arrogant tone. His king, he claims, has ruled this to be a war between the humans and elves. The dwarves are determined to remain neutral."

"*No* troops? They will send us *nothing?*" Kith-Kanan stared at Quimant, appalled. Just when he had begun to see a glimmer of hope on the military horizon, to get news like this! Nothing could be more disastrous. The general slowly slumped into his chair, trying unsuccessfully to fight a rising wave of nausea.

Shaking his head in shock, he looked at his brother, expecting to see the same sense of dismay written across Sithas's face. Instead, however, the speaker's eyes had narrowed in an inscrutable expression. Didn't he *understand?*

"This is catastrophic!" Kith-Kanan exclaimed, angry that the Speaker didn't seem to grasp this basic fact. "Without the dwarves, we are doomed to be terribly outnumbered in every battle. Even with the griffons, we can't prevail against a quarter of a million men!"

"Indeed," Sithas agreed calmly. Finally he spoke to Ambrodel. "And your own mission, my lord, does that bear this information out?"

Lord Quimant gave a start when he realized that Sithas was addressing Ambrodel.

"Rather dramatically not, Excellency," Ambrodel replied softly. Kith-Kanan and Lord Quimant both stared at the chamberlain in mixed astonishment.

"I regret the subterfuge, my lords. The Speaker of the Stars instructed me to reveal my mission to no one, to report only to him."

"There was no reason to say anything—not until now," Sithas said. Once again, the others felt that commanding tone in his voice that brought all discussion to an abrupt halt. "If the lord chamberlain will continue . . . ?"

"Of course, Your Excellency." Ambrodel turned to include them all in his explanation. "I have wintered in the dwarven kingdom of Thorbardin. . . ."

"What?" Quimant's jaw dropped. Kith-Kanan remained silent, but his lips compressed into a tight smile as he began to appreciate his brother's wiliness.

"It had been the Speaker's assessment, very early on, that Ambassador Than-Kar was not doing an appropriately thorough job of maintaining open and honest communication between our two realms."

"I see," Quimant said, with a formal nod.

"Indeed, as events have developed, our esteemed leader's assessment has been proven to be accurate."

"Than-Kar has deliberately sabotaged our negotiations?" demanded Kith.

"Blatantly. King Hal-Waith has long backed our cause, as it was presented to him by Dunbarth Ironthumb upon that ambassador's return home. Than-Kar's original mission had been to report to us the king's intent to send twenty-five thousand troops to aid our cause."

"But I saw no sign of these troops on the plain. There is no word of them now, is there?" Kith-Kanan probed.

Quimant shook his head. "No—and certainly reports would have reached Silvanost had they marched during the winter."

"They did *not* march, not then," continued Ambrodel. "The offer of aid came with several conditions attached, conditions which Than-Kar reported to his king that we were unwilling to accept."

"Conditions?" Now Kith was concerned. "What conditions?"

"Fairly reasonable, under the circumstances. The dwarves recognize you as overall commander of the army, but they will not allow their own units to be broken up into smaller detachments—and dwarven units will work only under dwarven leaders."

"Those commanders presumably answerable to me under battle conditions?" Kith-Kanan asked.

"Yes." Ambrodel nodded.

The elven general couldn't believe his ears. Dwarven fighting prowess and tactical mastery were legendary. And twenty-five thousand such warriors . . . why, if they fought alongside a griffon cavalry, the siege of Sithelbec might be lifted in a long afternoon of fighting!

"There were some other minor points, also very reasonable. Bodies to be shipped to Thorbardin for burial, dwarven holidays honored, a steady supply of ale maintained, and so on. I do not anticipate any objection on your part."

"Of course not!" Kith-Kanan sprang to his feet again, this time in excitement. Then he remembered the obstruction presented by Than-Kar, and his mood darkened. "Have you concluded the deal? Must we still work through the ambassador? How long—"

Ambrodel smiled and held up his hands. "The army was mustering as I left. For all I know, they have already emerged from the underground realm. They would march, I was promised, when the snowmelt in the Kharolis Mountains allowed free passage." The chamberlain shivered as he remembered the long, dark winter he spent there. "It *never* gets warm in Thorbardin! You're always damp and squinting through the dark. By the gods, who knows how the dwarves can stand living underground?"

"And the ambassador?" This time Sithas asked the question. Once again those lines of anger tightened his face as he pondered the extent of Than-Kar's duplicity.

"King Hal-Waith would consider it a personal favor if we were to place him under arrest, detaining him until such time as the next dwarven mission arrives. It should be here sometime during the summer."

"Any word on numbers? On their march route?" Tactics already swirled through Kith-Kanan's head.

Ambrodel pursed his lips and shook his head. "Only the name of the commander, whom I trust will meet with your approval."

"Dunbarth Ironthumb?" Kith-Kanan was hopeful.

"None other."

"That *is* good news!" That dignified statesman had been the brightest element of the otherwise frustrating councils between Thorbardin, Silvanesti, and Ergoth. The ambassador from the dwarven nation had retained a sense of humor and self-deprecating whimsy that had lightened many an otherwise tedious session of negotiation.

"Where am I to join him?" Kith-Kanan asked. "Shall I take Arcuballis and fly to Thorbardin itself?"

Ambrodel shook his head. "I don't think you could. The gates remain carefully hidden."

"But surely *you* could direct me! Didn't you say that you have been there?"

"Indeed," the chamberlain agreed with a nod. He coughed awkwardly. "But to tell you the truth, I never saw the gates, nor could I describe the approach to you or to anyone."

"How did you get in, then?"

"It's a trifle embarrassing, actually. I spent nearly a month floundering around in the mountains, seeking a trail or a road or any kind of sign of the gate. I found nothing. Finally, however, I was met in my camp by a small band of dwarven scouts. Apparently they keep an eye on the perimeter and were watching my hapless movements, wondering what I was up to."

"But you must have entered through the gate," Kith said.

"Indeed," nodded Ambrodel. "But I spent the two days of the approach—two very *long* days, I might add—stumbling along with a blindfold over my eyes."

"That's an outrage!" barked Quimant, stiffening in agitation. "An insult to our race!"

Sithas, too, scowled. Only Kith-Kanan reacted with a thin smile and a nod of understanding. "With treachery among their own people, it only seems a natural precaution," the elven general remarked. That lessened the tension, and Ambrodel nodded in reluctant agreement.

"Excellency," inquired Quimant, with careful formality. It was obvious that the lord regent was annoyed by not having been apprised of the secret negotiations. "This is indeed a most splendid development, but was it necessary to retain such a level of secrecy? Perhaps I could have aided the cause had I been kept informed."

"Indeed, quite true, my good cousin-in-law. There was no fear that the knowledge would have been misplaced in you—save this one: In your position as regent, you are the one who has spent the greatest amount of time with Than-Kar. It was essential that the ambassador not know of this plan, and I felt that the safest way to keep you from a revealing slip—inadvertent, of course—was to withhold the knowledge from you. The decision was mine alone."

"I cannot question the Speaker's wisdom," replied the noble humbly. "This is a most encouraging turn of events."

* * * * *

Kith left the meeting in order to arrange for the postings around the city. He wanted all Silvanost to quickly learn of the call for volunteers. He intended to personally interview and test all applicants for the griffon cavalry.

Sithas remained behind, with Quimant and Ambrodel, to attend to matters of government. "As to the city, how has it fared in our absence?"

Quimant informed him of other matters: Weapons production was splendid, with a great stockpile of arms gathered; refugees from the plains had stopped coming to Silvanost—a fact that had greatly eased the tensions and crowding within the city. The higher taxes that Sithas had decreed, in order to pay for the war, had been collected with only a few minor incidents.

"There has been some violence along the waterfront. The city guard has confronted Than-Kar's escorts on more than one occasion. We've had several elves badly injured and one killed during these brawls."

"The Theiwar?" guessed Sithas.

"Indeed. The primary troublemakers can be found among the officers of Than-Kar's guard, as if they *want* to create an incident." Quimant's disgust with the dwarves was apparent in his sarcastic tone.

"We'll deal with them . . . when the time is right. We'll wait till Kith-Kanan forms his cavalry and departs for the west."

"I'm certain he'll have no shortage of volunteers. There are many noble elves who had resisted the call to arms, as it applies to the infantry," said Lord Quimant. "They'll leap at the chance to form an elite unit, especially with the threat of conscription hanging over their heads!"

"We'll keep news of Thorbardin's commitment secret," Sithas added. "Not a word of it is to leave this room. In the meantime, tell me about the additional troops for the infantry. How fares the training of the new regiments?"

"We have five thousand elves under arms, ready to march when you give the command."

"I had hoped for more."

Quimant hemmed and hawed. "The sentiment in the city is not wholly in favor of the war. Our people do not seem to grasp the stakes here."

"We'll *make* them understand," growled Sithas, looking to the lord as if he expected Quimant to challenge him. His wife's cousin remained silent on that point, however.

Instead, Quimant hesitantly offered another suggestion. "We do have another source of troops," he ventured. "However, they may not meet with the Speaker's satisfaction."

"Another source? Where?" Sithas demanded.

"Humans—mercenaries. There are great bands of them in the plains north of here and over to the west. Many of them bear no great love for the emperor of Ergoth and would be willing to join our service—for a price, of course."

"Never!" Sithas leaped to his feet, livid. "How can you even suggest such an abomination! If we cannot preserve our nation with our own troops, we do not deserve victory!"

His voice rang from the walls of the small chamber, and he glared at Quimant and Ambrodel, as if daring a challenge. None was forthcoming, and slowly the Speaker of the Stars relaxed.

"Forgive my outburst," he said, with a nod to Quimant. "You were merely making a suggestion. That I understand."

"Consider the suggestion withdrawn." The lord bowed to his ruler.

*　*　*　*　*

The recruits for the griffon-mounted cavalry were sworn in during a sunny ceremony a week after the brothers had arrived in the city. The event was held on the gaming fields beyond the gardens, for no place else in the city provided enough open space for the great steeds and their proud newly appointed riders to assemble.

Thousands of elves turned out to watch, overflowing the large grandstands and lining the perimeter of the fields. Others gathered in the nearby towers, many of which rose a hundred feet or more into the air, providing splendid vantage.

"I welcome you, brave elves, to the ranks of an elite and decisive force, unique in our grand history!" Kith-Kanan addressed the recruits while the onlookers strained to hear his words.

"We shall take to the sky under a name that bespeaks our speed. Henceforth we shall be known as the Windriders!"

A great cheer arose from the warriors and the spectators.

As Quimant had predicted, many scions of noble families had flocked to the call to arms once they learned of the nature of the elite unit. Kith-Kanan had disappointed and angered a great number of them by selecting his troops only after extensive combat tests and rigorous training procedures. Sons of masons, carpenters, and laborers were offered the same opportunities as the proud heirs of the noble houses. Those who were not truly desirous of the honor, or were unwilling or incapable of meeting the high standards established by Kith-Kanan, quickly fell away, consigned to the infantry. At the end of the brutal week of tests, the elven commander had been left with more than a thousand elves of proven courage, dedication, and skill.

"You will train in the use of the light lance, the elven longbow, and the steel-edged longsword. Lances will be wielded in the air or on the ground."

He looked over the assembled elves. They stood, a pair flanking each griffon, wearing shiny steel helms with long plumes of horsehair. The Windriders wore supple leather boots and smooth torso armor of black leather. They were a formidable force, and the training to come would only enhance their abilities.

Brass trumpets blared the climax of the ceremony, and each of the Windriders received a steel-edged shortsword, which would be worn throughout the training. They would have to learn fast, Kith-Kanan had warned his new recruits, and he knew that they would.

He looked to the west, suddenly restless. It won't be long, now, he told himself.

Soon the siege of Sithelbec would be broken—and how long after that would it be before the war was won?

❧ 20 ❧

MIDSPRING, 2213 (PC)

kith-kanan couldn't sleep. he went for a walk in the Gar-
dens of Astarin, relieved that the griffons had all been
moved to the sporting fields. There the creatures rested and
enjoyed the fresh meat that the palace liverymen hastily
had butchered and carted over to them.

For a time, the elf lost himself in the twists and turns of
the elegant gardens. The soothing surroundings took him
back to his youth, to untroubled days and, later, to passionate nights. How many times, he reflected, had he and Hermathya met among this secluded foliage?

Anxiously he tried to shrug off the memories. Soon he
and Arcuballis would take to the air, leaving this city and
its temptations behind. The mere sight of her was a source

of deep guilt and discomfort to him.

As if circumstances mirrored his thoughts, he turned a corner and encountered his brother's wife, walking in quiet contemplation. Hermathya looked up, but if she was at all surprised to encounter him, her face didn't reveal anything.

"Hello, Kith-Kanan." Her smile was deep and warm—and suddenly, it seemed to Kith, reckless.

"Hello, Hermathya." He was certainly surprised to see her. The rest of the palace was dark, and the hour was quite late.

"I saw you come to the garden and came here to find you," she informed him.

Alarms bells went off in his mind as he gazed at her. By the gods, how beautiful she was! No woman he had ever known aroused him like Hermathya. Not even Anaya. He could tell, by the smoldering look in her eyes, that her thoughts were similar.

She took a step toward him.

The instinct to reach out and crush her to him, to pull her into his arms and touch her, was almost overpowering. But at the same time, he had sordid memories of their last tryst and her unfaithfulness to his brother. He wanted her, but he dare not weaken again—especially now, after all that he and Sithas had been through together.

Only with a great effort of will did Kith-Kanan step back, raising his hands to stop her approach.

"You are my brother's wife," he said, somewhat irrelevantly.

"I was his wife last autumn," she spat, suddenly venomous.

"Last autumn was a mistake. Hermathya, I loved you once. I think of you now more than I care to admit. But I will not betray my brother!" Again, he added silently. "Can you accept this? Can we be members of the same family and not torment each other with memories of a past that ought to be buried and forgotten?"

Hermathya suddenly clasped her hands over her face. Her body wracking with sobs, she turned and ran, swiftly disappearing from Kith-Kanan's sight.

For a long time afterward, he stared at the spot where she had stood. The image of her body, of her face, of her exquisite presence, remained vivid in his mind, almost as if she was still there.

*   *   *   *   *

Three days later, Kith was ready to embark. His plan of battle had been made, but there remained many things to be done. The Windriders wouldn't fly to the west for another six weeks. Under the tutelage of their new captain, Hallus, they had to train rigorously in the meantime.

"How long do you think it will take to find Dunbarth?" asked Sithas when he, his mother, and Tamanier Ambrodel came to see Kith-Kanan off.

Kith shrugged. "That's one reason I'm leaving right away. I have to hook up with the dwarves and fill them in on the timetable, then get to Sithelbec before the Windriders."

"Be careful," his mother urged. The color had come back into her face since the brothers' return, and for the past several weeks she had seemed as merry and robust as ever. Now she struggled not to weep.

"I will," Kith promised, holding her in his arms. They all hoped the war would end quickly but understood that it might be many months, even years, before he could return.

The door to the audience chamber burst open, and the elves whirled, surprised and then amused. Vanesti stood there.

Sithas's son, not yet a year old, toddled toward them with an unsteady gait and a broad smile across his elven features. In his hand, he brandished a wooden sword, slashing at imagined enemies to the right and left until his own momentum toppled him to the floor. The sword abandoned, he rose and approached Kith-Kanan unsteadily.

"Pa-pa!" cried the tiny elf, beaming.

Kith blushed and stepped aside. "*There's* your papa," he said, indicating Sithas.

Kith-Kanan noted how much Vanesti had changed during the course of their winter in the mountains. Conceivably the war could drag on for several more years. The toddler would be a young boy by the next time he saw him.

"Come to Uncle Kith, Vanesti. Say good-bye before I ride the griffon!"

Vanesti pouted briefly, but then he wrapped his uncle in a hug. Lifting the tiny fellow up and holding him, Kith felt a pang of regret. Would he ever be able to settle down and have children of his own?

Once again Kith-Kanan and Arcuballis took off on an important mission. The vast forestlands of Silvanesti sprawled beneath them. Far to the south, Kith caught an occasional glimpse of the Courrain Ocean, which stretched past the horizon with a limitless expanse.

Soon he came to the plains, and they continued to soar high above the sea of grass that stretched to the limits of his vision. He knew that, northward, his embattled Wildrunners still held their fortress against the pressing human horde. Soon he would join them.

He spotted the snowy crests of the Kharolis Mountains jutting into the sky. For a full day, Kith watched the imposing heights grow closer, until at last he flew above the wooded valleys that extended from the heart of the range and he was encircled on all sides by great peaks.

Here he began his search in earnest. He knew that the kingdom of Thorbardin lay entirely underground, with great gates providing access from the north and south. The snowmelt had long passed from the forested valleys to the high slopes. The gate, he reasoned, would occupy a lower elevation, both for enhanced concealment and easier access.

He searched along these valleys every day from first to last light, seeking a sign of the passage of the dwarven army. The land consisted of almost entirely uninhabited wilderness, so he reckoned that the march of twenty thousand heavy-booted dwarves would leave some kind of obvious trail.

For days, his search was fruitless. He began to chafe at the lost time. Borne by his speedy griffon, he crossed the range two full times, but never did he find the evidence he sought. His search took him through all of the high valleys and much of the lower foothills. He decided, in desperation, that he would make his last sweep along the very northern fringe of the range, where the jagged foothills petered out into low slopes and finally the flat and expansive plains.

Frequent rainstorms, often accompanied by thunder and lightning, hampered his search. He spent many miserable afternoons huddled with Arcuballis under whatever shelter they could find while hail and rain battered the land. He wasn't surprised, for spring weather was notoriously violent on the plains, yet the forced delays were extremely dispiriting.

Nearly two weeks into his search, he was working his way to the north, following a broad zigzag from east to west. The sun was high that day, so much so that he could see his shadow directly below him. Finally the shadow ebbed away toward the east, matching the sun's descent in the west. Still he had seen no sign of his quarry.

It was near sunset when something caught his eye.

"Let's go, old boy—down there," he said, unconsciously voicing the command that he simultaneously relayed to Arcuballis through subtle pressure from his knees on the griffon's tawny flanks. The creature tucked his wings and swooped low, flying along a shallow stream that marked a broad, flat valley bottom.

At one place, however, the river spilled over a ten-foot shelf of rock, creating a bright and scenic waterfall. It wasn't the beauty of the scene that had caught Kith-Kanan's eye, however.

The elf noticed that the brush lining the streambanks was flattened and trampled; indeed, there was a swath some twenty feet wide. The matted brush and grass extended in an arc from the streambed above the falls to the waterway.

Kith-Kanan could see no other sign of passage anywhere in this broad, meadow-lined valley, nor were there any groves of trees that might have concealed a trail. Arcuballis came to rest on a large boulder near the streambank. Kith swiftly dismounted, leaving the griffon to preen his feathers and keep an eye alert for danger while the elf explored the terrain.

The first thing he noticed was the muddy streambank. Higher up, where the earth was slightly drier, he saw something that made his heart pound.

Bootprints! Heavy footgear had trod here, and in great numbers. The prints indicated their wearers were heading down the valley after emerging from the streambed. Of course! The dwarves had taken great pains to keep the entrance to their kingdom a secret, and now Kith understood why there had been no road, nor even a heavily used path, leading to the north gate of Thorbardin.

The dwarves had marched along the streambed!

"Come on—back into the sky!" he shouted, rousing Arcuballis.

The creature crouched low to allow Kith to leap into the wide, deep saddle. The elf lashed himself in with one smooth motion and kicked the griffon's flanks sharply.

Instantly Arcuballis sprang from the rock, his powerful wings driving downward to carry them through the air. As the griffon began to climb, Kith-Kanan nudged him with his knees, guiding him low above the stream.

They glided along the course of the stream while Kith-Kanan searched the ground along either bank for more signs. Thank the gods for that waterfall! Dusk soon cast long shadows across the valley, and Kith-Kanan realized that he would have to postpone his search until the morrow.

Nevertheless, it was with high spirits that he directed Arcuballis to land. They camped beneath an earthen overhang on the banks of the stream, and the griffon snatched nearly a dozen plump trout from the water with lighting grasps of his eagle-clawed forefeet. Kith-Kanan feasted on a pair of these while the griffon enjoyed his share.

The next morning Kith again beat the morning sun into the sky, and within an hour, he had left the foothills behind. The mountain stream he followed joined another gravel-bottomed watercourse, and here it became a placid brook, silt-bottomed and sluggish.

Here, too, there were signs that the dwarven column had emerged to march overland.

Now Kith-Kanan urged Arcuballis ahead, and the griffon's wings carried them to a lofty height. The trail became a wide rut of muddy earth, clearly visible even from a thousand feet in the air. The griffon followed the path below while the elf's eyes scanned the horizon. For much of the day, all he could see was the long brown trail vanishing into the haze of the north.

Kith-Kanan began to worry that the dwarves had already

reached Sithelbec. Certainly they were tough and capable fighters, but even in their compact formations, they would be vulnerable to the sweeping charges of the human cavalry if they fought without the support of auxiliary forces.

It was late afternoon before he finally caught sight of his goal and knew that he was not too late. The marching column stretched as straight as a spear shaft across the plains, moving toward the north. Kith urged the griffon downward, picking up speed.

As he flew closer, he saw that the figures marched with military precision in a long column that was eight dwarves wide. How far into the distance the troops extended he could not be certain, though he flew overhead for several minutes after he had observed the tail of the column before he could even see its lead formations.

Now he was spotted from below. The tail of the column split and turned, while companies of short, stocky fighters broke to the right and left, quickly swinging into defensive postures. As Arcuballis dove lower, he saw the bearded faces, the metal helms with their plumes of feathers or hair, and, most significantly, the rank of heavy crossbows raised to fire!

He pulled back on the reins and brought Arcuballis into a sharp climb, hoping he was out of range and that the dwarves wouldn't shoot without first identifying their target.

"Ho! Dwarves of Thorbardin!" he called, soaring about two hundred feet over the ranks of suspicious upturned faces.

"Who are you?" demanded one, a grizzled captain with a shiny helmet plumed by bright red feathers.

"Kith-Kanan! Is that you?" cried another gruff voice, one that the elf recognized.

"Dunbarth Ironthumb!" the elf shouted back, waving at the familiar figure.

Happy and relieved, he brought the griffon through a long, circling dive. Finally Arcuballis came to rest on the ground, though the griffon pranced and squawked nervously at the troops arrayed before him.

Dunbarth Ironthumb clumped toward him, a wide smile splitting his full, gray-flecked beard. Unlike the other officers of his column, the dwarf wore a plain, unadorned breastplate and a simple steel cap.

Kith sprang from the saddle and seized the stalwart dwarf in a bear hug. "By the gods, you old goat, I thought I'd never find you!" he declared.

"Humph!" snorted Dunbarth. "If we'd wanted to be found, we would have posted signs! Still, what with the storms we've been dodging—floods, lightning, even a black funnel cloud!—it's a lucky thing you did find us. Why were you looking?"

The grizzled dwarf raised his eyebrows in curiosity, waiting for Kith to speak.

"It's a long story," the elf explained. "I'll save it for the campfire tonight."

"Good enough," grunted Dunbarth. "We'll be making camp after another mile." The dwarven commander paused, then snapped his fingers in sudden decision.

"To the Abyss with it! We'll make camp here!"

Dunbarth made Kith-Kanan laugh easily. The elf commander ate the hardtack of the dwarves around the fire, and even took a draft of the cool, bitter ale that the dwarves hold so dear but which elves almost universally find to be unpleasant to the palate.

As the fire died into coals, he spoke with Dunbarth and a number of that dwarf's officers. He told them of the mission to capture the griffons and of the forming of the Windriders. His comrades took heart from the tale of the flying cavalry that would aid them in battle.

He also described, to mutters of indignation and anger, the complicity of Than-Kar and his brother's plans to arrest the ambassador and return him to King Hal-Waith in chains.

"Typical Theiwar treachery!" growled Dunbarth. "Never turn your back on 'em, I can tell you! He never should have been entrusted with a mission of such importance!"

"Why was he?" Kith inquired. "Don't let it go to your head, but you were always a splendid representative for your king and your people. Why did Hal-Waith send a replacement?"

Dunbarth Ironthumb shook his head and spat into the fire. "Part of it was my own fault, I admit. I *wanted* to go home. All that talking and diplomacy was getting on my nerves—plus, I'd never spent more than a few months on the surface at a time. I was in Silvanost for a full year, you'll remember, not counting time on the march."

"Indeed," Kith-Kanan said, nodding. He remembered Tamanier Ambrodel's remarks about that elf's long months underground. For the first time, he began to understand the adjustment these subterranean warriors must make in order to undertake an aboveground campaign. Growing up, working and training—all their lives were spent underground.

Surprising emotion choked his throat, for suddenly he realized the depth of the commitment that had brought forth the dwarven army. He looked at Dunbarth and hoped that the dwarf understood the strength of his appreciation.

Dunbarth Ironthumb gruffly cleared his throat and continued. "We have a tricky equilibrium in Thorbardin, I'm sure you appreciate. We of the Hylar Clan control the central realms, including the Life-Tree."

Kith-Kanan had heard of that massive structure, a cave city all of its own carved from the living stone of a monstrous stalagmite. He nodded his understanding.

"The other clans of Thorbardin all have their own realms—the Daergar, the Daewar, the Klar, and the Theiwar," continued Dunbarth. The old dwarf sighed. "We are a stubborn people, it is well known, and sometimes hasty to anger. In none of us are these traits so prevalent as among the Theiwar. But also there is a level of malevolence, of greed and scheming and ambition, among our pale-skinned brethren that is not to be found among the higher dwarven cultures. The Theiwar are much distrusted by the rest of the clans."

"Then why would the king appoint a Theiwar as ambassador to Silvanesti?" Kith-Kanan asked.

"Alas, they are all those things I said, but so too are the Theiwar numerous and powerful. They make up a large proportion of the kingdom's population, and they cannot be excluded from its politics. The king must select his ambassadors, his nobles, even his high clerics from the ranks of *all* the clans, including the Theiwar."

Dunbarth looked the elf squarely in the eye. "King Hal-

Waith thought, mistakenly it would appear, that the crucial negotiations with the elves had been concluded with my departure from your capital. Therefore he took the chance of appointing a Theiwar to replace me, having in mind another important task for me and knowing that the Theiwar Clan would make a considerable disturbance if they were once again bypassed for such a prominent ambassadorship."

"I think you start to get the picture," Dunbarth continued. "But now to matters that lie before us, instead of behind. Do you have plans for a summer campaign?"

"The wheels are already in motion," Kith explained. "And now that I have caught up with you, we can put the final phase of the strategy into motion."

"Splendid!" Dunbarth beamed, all but licking his lips in anticipation.

Kith-Kanan went on to outline his battle plan, and the dwarven warrior's eyes lit up as every detail was described.

"If you can pull it off," he grunted in approval after Kith-Kanan had finished, "it will be a victory that the bards will sing about for years!"

They spent the rest of the evening making less momentous conversation, and around midnight, Kith-Kanan made his camp among the army of his allies. At dawn, he was up and saddling Arcuballis, preparing to leave. The dwarves were awake, too, ready to march.

"Less than three weeks to go," said Dunbarth, with a wink.

"Don't be late for the war!" chided Kith. Moments later, the sunlight flickered from the griffon's wing feathers a hundred feet above the dwarven column.

Arcuballis soared into the sky, higher and higher. Yet it was many hours before Kith saw it, a blocklike shape that looked tiny and insignificant from his tremendous height. He would reach it by dark. It was Sithelbec, and for now at least, it was home.

✍ 21 ✍

Late Spring, in the Army of Ergoth

Long rows of makeshift litters filled the tent, and upon them, Suzine saw men with ghastly wounds—men who bled and suffered and died even before she could begin to treat them. She saw others with invisible hurts—warriors who lay still and unseeing, though often their eyes remained open and fixed. Oil lanterns sputtered from tent poles, while clerics and nurses moved among the wounded.

Men groaned and shrieked and sobbed pathetically. Others were delirious, madly babbling about pastoral surroundings they would in all likelihood never see again.

And the stench! There were the raw smells of filth, urine, and feces, and the sweltering cloud of too many men in too small an area. And there were the smells of blood, and of rotting meat. Above all, there remained an ever-pervasive odor of death.

For months, Suzine had done all that she could for the wounded, nursing them, tending their injuries, providing them what solace she could. For a time, there had been fewer and fewer wounded as those who had been injured in the battles of the winter had been healed or perished or were sent back to Ergoth.

But now it was a new season, and it seemed that the war had acquired a new ferocity. Just a few days earlier, Giarna had hurled tens of thousands of men at the walls of Sithelbec in a savage attempt to smash through the barricades. A group of the wild elves had led the way, but the elves within the fortress had fallen upon their kin and the humans who followed with a furious vengeance. More than a thousand had perished in the fight, while these hundreds around her represented just a portion of those who had escaped with varying degrees of injuries.

Most of the suffering were humans, but there were a number of elves—those who fought against Silvanesti—and Theiwar dwarves as well. The Theiwar, under the stocky captain Kalawax, had spearheaded one assault, attempting to tunnel under the fortress walls. The elves had anticipated the maneuver and filled the tunnel, jammed tightly with dwarves, with barrels full of oil, which had then been set alight. Death had been fast and horrible.

Suzine went from cot to cot, offering water or a cool cloth upon a forehead. She was surrounded by filth and despair, but she herself bore hurts that could not be seen but which nevertheless cut deeply into her spirit.

So Suzine felt a kinship with these hapless souls and gained what little comfort she could by caring for them and tending their hurts. She remained throughout most of this long night, knowing that Giarna was tormented by the failure of his attack, that he might seek her out. If he found her, he would hurt her as he always did, but here he would never come.

The hours of darkness passed, and gradually the camp fell into restless silence. Past midnight, even those men in the most severe pain collapsed into tentative slumber. Weary to the point of collapse, praying that Giarna already slept, she finally left the wounded to return to her own shelter.

Outside the hospital tent waited her two guards, the men-at-arms who escorted her when she moved about the camp. Actually they were a pair of the Kagonesti elves who had joined ranks with the army in the hope that it offered them a chance to gain independence for their people. Oddly, she had come to enjoy the presence of the softspoken, competent warriors in their face paint, feathers, and dark leather garb.

Suzine had wondered how such elves could rationalize their fight, since it was waged with great terror against their own people. Several times she had asked the Kagonesti about their reasons, but only once had she gotten an honest answer—from a young elf she was caring for, who had been wounded in one of the attempts to storm the fortress walls.

"My mother and father have been taken as slaves to work in the iron mines north of Silvanost," he had told her, his voice full of bitterness. "And my family's farm was seized by the Speaker's troops when my father was unable to pay his taxes."

"But to go to war against your own people . . ." she had wondered.

"Many of my people have been hurt by the elves of Silvanost. *My* people are the Kagonesti and the elves of the plains! Those who live in that crystal city of towers are no more my kin than are the dwarves of Thorbardin!"

"Do you wish to see the elven nation destroyed?"

"I only wish for the wild elves to be left alone, to regain our freedom, and to have nothing to do with the causes of governments that have made our lands a battleground!" The elf had gasped his beliefs with surprising vehemence, struggling to sit up until Suzine eased him back down.

"If the Emperor of Ergoth treats us ill after this war is won, then shall we struggle against him with the same fortitude! But until that time, the human army is our only hope of throwing off the yoke of Silvanesti oppression!"

She had been deeply disturbed by the elf's declarations, for it did not fit her idea of Kith-Kanan to hear such tales of injustice and discrimination. Surely he didn't know of the treatment accorded to Kagonesti by his own people!

Thus she had convinced herself of his innocence and

looked upon the Kagonesti elves with pity. Those who had joined the human army she befriended and tried to ease their troubled hurts.

Now her two guards held open her tent flap for her and waited silently outside. They would stand there until dawn, when they would be relieved. As always, this knowledge gave her a sense of security, and she lay down, totally exhausted, to try to get some sleep.

But though she lay wearily upon her quilt, she couldn't sleep. An odd sense of excitement took hold of her emotions, and suddenly she sat up, aroused and intrigued.

Instinctively she went to her mirror. Holding the crystal on her dressing table, she saw her own image first, and then she concentrated on setting her mind free.

Immediately she espied that handsome elven face, the visage she had not looked upon for nearly eight months. Her heart leaped into her throat and she stifled a gasp. It was Kith-Kanan.

His hair flew back from his face, as though tossed by a strong wind. She remembered the griffon, only this time, instead of flying away from her, he was returning!

She stared at the mirror, breathless. She should report this to her general immediately. The elven general was returning to his fortress!

Yet at the same time, she sensed a decision deep within her. The return of Kith-Kanan stirred her emotions. He looked magnificent, proud and triumphant. How unlike General Giarna! She knew she would say nothing about what she had seen.

Swiftly, guiltily, she placed the mirror back inside of its velvet-lined case. Almost slamming the engraved ivory lid in her haste, she hid the object deep within her wardrobe trunk and returned to her bed.

Suzine had barely stretched out, still tense with excitement, when a gust of wind brushed across her face. She sensed that the flap of her tent had opened, though she could see nothing in the heavy darkness.

Instantly she felt fear. Her elven guards would stand firm against any illicit intruder, but there was one they would not stop—did not dare stop—for he held their fates in his hands.

Giarna came to her then and touched her. She felt his touch like a physical assault, a hurt that would leave no scar that could be seen.

How she hated him! She despised everything that he stood for. He was the master slayer. She hated the way he used her, used everyone around him.

But now she could bear her hatred because of the knowledge of a blond-haired elf and his proud flying steed—knowledge which, even as General Giarna took her, she found solace in, knowledge that was hers alone.

* * * * *

Kith-Kanan guided Arcuballis through the pitch-dark skies, seeking the lanterns of Sithelbec. He had passed over the thousands of campfires that marked the position of the human army, so he knew that the elven stronghold lay close before him. He needed to find the fortress before daylight so that the humans wouldn't learn of his return to the plains.

There! A light gleamed in the darkness. And another!

He urged Arcuballis downward, and the griffon swept into a shallow dive. They circled once and saw three lights arranged in a perfect triangle, glimmering on the rooftop. That was the sign, the signal he had ordered Parnigar to use to guide him back to the barracks.

Indeed, as the griffon spread his wings to set them gently atop the tower, he saw his trusted second-in-command holding one of the lights. The other lantern-bearers were his old teacher, Kencathedrus, and the steadfast Kagonesti elf known as White-lock.

The two officers saluted smartly and then clasped their commander warmly.

"By the gods, sir, it's good to see you again!" said Parnigar gruffly.

"It is a pleasure and a relief. We've been terribly worried!" Kencathedrus couldn't help but sound a little stern.

"I have a good excuse. Now let's get me and Arcuballis out of sight before first light. I don't want the troops to know I've returned—not yet, in any event."

The officers looked at him curiously but held their questions in check while arrangements were made with a stable-master to secure Arcuballis in an enclosed stall. Meanwhile, Kith-Kanan, concealed by a flowing, heavy robe, slipped into Kencathedrus's chamber and awaited the two elven warriors. They joined him just as dawn was beginning to lighten the eastern horizon.

Kith-Kanan told them of the quest for the griffons, describing the regiment of flying troops and the coming of the dwarves and detailing his battle plans.

"Two weeks, then?" asked Parnigar, scarcely able to contain his excitement.

"Indeed, my friend—after all this time." Kith-Kanan understood what these elves had been through. His own ordeals had been far from cheery. Yet how difficult it must have been for these dynamic warriors to spend the winter and the spring and the first few weeks of summer cooped up within the fortress.

"Fresh regiments are on the march to Sithelbec. The Windriders will leave in a few days, making their way westward. The dwarves of Thorbardin, too, are preparing to move into position."

"But you wish your own presence to remain secret?" asked Kencathedrus.

"Until we're ready to attack. I don't want the enemy to suspect any changes in our defenses. When the attack develops, I want it to be the biggest surprise they've ever had."

"Hopefully the *last* surprise," growled Parnigar.

"I'll stay here for a week, then fly west at night to arrange the rendezvous with the forces arriving from Silvanost. When I return, we'll attack. Until then, conduct your defenses as you have in the past. Just don't allow them to gain a breach."

"These old walls have held well," Parnigar noted. "The humans have tried to assault them several times and always we drove them back over the heaped bodies of their dead."

"The spring storms, in fact, did us more harm than all the human attacks," Kencathedrus added.

"I flew through some of them," Kith-Kanan said. "And I heard Dunbarth speak of them."

"Hail crushed two of the barns. We lost a lot of our livestock." Kencathedrus recounted the damage. "And a pair of tornadoes swept past, doing some damage to the outer wall."

Parnigar chuckled grimly. "*Some* damage to the wooden wall—and a lot of damage to the human tents!"

"True. The destruction outside the walls was even worse than within. I have never seen weather so violent."

"It happens every year, more or less," Parnigar, the more experienced plainsman, explained. "Though this spring was a little fiercer than most. Old elves tell of a storm three hundred years ago when a hundred cyclones came roaring in from the west and tore up every farm within a thousand miles."

Kith-Kanan shook his head, trying to imagine such a thing. It even dwarfed war! He turned his attention to other matters. "How about the size of the human army? Have they been able to replace their losses? Has it grown or diminished?"

"As near as we can tell—" Parnigar started to answer, but Kith-Kanan's former teacher cut him off.

"There's *one* addition they've had, it shames me to admit!" Kencathedrus barked. Parnigar nodded sorrowfully as the captain of the Silvanesti continued.

"*Elves!* From the woods! It seems they're content to serve an army of human invaders, caring naught that they wage war against their own kingdom!" The elf, born and bred amid the towers of Silvanost, couldn't understand such base treachery.

"I have heard this, to my surprise. Why are they party to this?" Kith-Kanan asked Parnigar.

The Wildrunner shrugged. "Some of them resent the taxes levied upon them by a far-off capital, with the debtors taken for servitude in the Clan Oakleaf mines. Others feel that trade with the humans is a good thing and opens opportunities for their children that they didn't have before. There are thousands of elves who feel little if any loyalty to the throne."

"Nevertheless, it is gravely disturbing," Kith-Kanan sighed. The problem vexed him, but he saw no solution at the present.

"You'll need some rest," noted Kencathedrus. "In the meantime, we'll tend to the details."

"Of course!" Parnigar echoed.

"I knew that I could count on you!" Kith-Kanan declared, feeling overwhelmed by a sense of gratitude. "May the future bring us the victory and the freedom that we have worked so hard for!"

He took the officers up on their offer of a private bunk and enjoyed the feel of a mattress beneath his body for the first time in several weeks. There was little more he could do at the moment, and he fell into a luxurious slumber that lasted for more than twelve hours.

✒ 22 ✒

Clan Oakleaf

The mouth of the coal mine gaped like the maw of some insatiable beast, hungry for the bodies of the soot-blackened miners who trudged wearily between the shoring timbers to disappear into the darkness within. They marched in a long file, more than a hundred of them, guarded by a dozen whip-wielding overseers.

Sithas and Lord Quimant stood atop the steep slope that led down into the quarry. The noise from below pounded their ears. Immediately below them, a slave-powered conveyor belt carried chunks of crushed ore from a pit, where other slaves smashed the rock with picks and hammers, to the bellowing ovens of the smelting plant. There more laborers shoveled coal from huge black piles into the roaring heat of the furnaces. Beyond the smelting sheds rose the smoke-spewing stacks of the weaponsmiths, where raw, hot steel was pounded into razor-edged armaments.

Some of the prisoners wore chain shackles at their ankles. "Those are the ones who have tried to escape," Lord Quimant explained. Most simply marched along, not needing any physical restraint, for they had been broken as slaves in a deeper, more permanent sense. Each of these trudged, eyes cast downward, almost tripping over the one ahead of him in the line.

"Most of them become quite docile," the lord continued, "after a year or two of labor. The guards encourage this. A slave who cooperates and works hard is generally left alone, while those who show rebelliousness or a reluctance to work are . . . disciplined."

One of the overseers cracked his whip against the back of a slave about to enter the mines. This fellow had lagged behind, opening a gap between himself and the worker in front of him. At the flick of the lash, he cried out in pain and stumbled forward. Even from his height, Sithas saw the red welt spread across the slave's back.

In his haste, the slave stumbled, then crawled pathetically to his feet under another flurry of lashes from the guard.

"Watch now. The rest of them will step quite lively."

Indeed, the other slaves did hasten into the black abyss, but Sithas didn't think such cruelty was warranted.

"Is he a human or an elf?" wondered the Speaker.

"Who—oh, the tardy one?" Quimant shrugged. "They get so covered with dust that I can't really tell. Not that it makes much difference. We treat everybody the same here."

"Is that wise?" Sithas was more disturbed than he thought he would be about the brutality he saw here.

Lord Quimant had attempted to dissuade Sithas from visiting the Clan Oakleaf estates and mines, yet the Speaker had been determined to take the three-day coach ride to Quimant's family's holdings. Now he began to wonder if perhaps Lord Quimant had been right to want to spare him the sight. He had too many disturbing reservations about the Oakleaf mines. Yet at the same time, he had to admit he needed the steel that came from these mines and the blades that were cast by the nearby smithies.

"Actually, it's the humans who give us the most trouble. After all, the elves are here for ten or twenty years, whatever the sentence happens to be for their crime. They know they must suffer that time, and then they'll be free."

Indeed, the Speaker of the Stars had sentenced a number of citizens of Silvanost to such labor—for failure to pay taxes, violence or theft against a fellow elf, smuggling, and other serious transgessions. The whole issue had seemed a good deal simpler in the city, when he could simply dismiss the offending elf and rarely, if ever, think of him again.

"So this is their miserable fate," he said quietly.

Quimant continued. "The humans, you know, are here for life—of course, a foreshortened life, in any event. And you know how reckless they are anyway. Yes, indeed, humans are the ones who give us the most problems. The elves, if anything, help to keep them in line. We encourage their little acts of spying on one another."

"Where do all the humans come from?" inquired Sithas. "Surely they haven't all been sentenced by elven courts."

"Oh, of course not! These are mostly brigands and villains, nomads who live to the north. They trouble the elves and kender of the settled lands, so we capture them and set them to work here."

Quimant shook his head, thinking before he continued. "Imagine—a paltry four or five decades to grow up, experience romance, try to make a success of your life, and leave children behind you! It's amazing they do so well, when you consider what little time they have to work with!"

"Let's go back to the manor," said Sithas, suddenly very weary of the harsh spectacle before him. Quimant had arranged for a splendid banquet after dark, and if they remained here any longer, Sithas was certain that he would lose his appetite.

* * * * *

The ride back to Silvanost seemed to Sithas to take much longer than the trip into the country. Still, he felt relieved to leave the Oakleaf estates behind.

The banquet had been a festive affair. Hermathya, the pride of Oakleaf, and her son Vanesti had been the stars of the evening. The affair lasted far into the night, yet Quimant and Sithas made an early start for the city on the following morning. Hermathya and the boy remained behind, intending to visit the clanhold for a month or two.

The first two days of the trip had seemed to drag on forever, and now they had reached the third and final day of the excursion. Sithas and Quimant traveled in the luxurious royal coach. Huge padded couches provided them with room to recline and stretch. Velvet draperies could be closed to block off dust and weather . . . or intrusive ears and eyes. Each of the huge wheels rested on its own spring mechanism, smoothing the potholes of the crushed gravel trail.

Eight magnificent horses, all large palominos, trotted at the head of the vehicle, their white manes and long fetlocks smoothly combed. Metal trim of pure gold outlined the shape of the enclosed cabin, which was large enough to hold eight passengers.

The two lords traveled with an escort of one hundred elven riders. Four archers, in addition to their driver, rode atop the cabin, out of sight and hearing of the pair of elves within.

Sithas sat shrouded in gloom. His mind would not focus. He considered all the progress that had been made toward a counterattack. The training of the Windriders was nearly complete. In a few days, they would fly west to begin their part in Kith-Kanan's great attack. The final rank of elven infantry—four thousand elves of Silvanost and the nearby clanholds—had already departed. They should reach the vicinity of Sithelbec at the same time as the Windriders.

Even these prospects did not brighten his mood. He imagined the satisfying picture of the dwarven ambassador Than-Kar captured and brought to the Speaker of the Stars in chains, but that prospect only reminded him of the prisoners of the Oakleaf mines.

Slave pits! With *elven* slaves! He accepted the fact that the mines were necessary. Without them, the Silvanesti wouldn't be able to produce the vast supply of arms and weapons needed by Kith-Kanan's army. True, there were good stockpiles of weapons, but a few weeks of intensive fighting could deplete those reserves with shocking speed.

"I wonder," he said, surprising himself and Quimant by speaking aloud. "What if we found another source of labor?"

The lord blinked at the Speaker in surprise. "But how? Where?"

"Listen to this." Sithas began to envision a solution, speaking his thoughts as they occurred to him. "Kith-Kanan still needs reinforcements on the ground. By Gilean, we were only able to send him four thousand troops this summer! And that left the capital practically empty of able-bodied males."

"If Your Majesty will remember, I cautioned against such a number. The city itself is laid bare. . . ."

"I still have my palace guard—a thousand elves of the House Protectorate, their lives pledged to the throne." Sithas continued. "We will form the slaves—the *elven* slaves—from your mines into a new company. Swear them to the Wildrunners for the duration of the war, their sentences commuted to military duty."

"They number a thousand or more," Quimant admitted cautiously. "They are hardened and tough. It's perhaps true that they would make a formidable force. But you can't close down the mines!"

"We will replace them with human prisoners captured on the battlefield!"

"We *have* no prisoners!"

"But Kith's counterattack begins in less than two weeks' time. He'll break the siege and rout the humans, and he's bound to take many of them as captives." Unless Kith's plan is a failure, he thought. Sithas wouldn't allow himself to consider that possibility.

"It may just work," Quimant noted, with a reluctant nod. "Indeed, if his attack is a great success, we might actually increase the number of, ah . . . laborers. Production could improve. We could open new mines!" He warmed to the potential of the plan.

"It's settled, then," Sithas agreed, feeling a great sense of relief.

"What about Than-Kar, Excellency?" inquired Quimant after several more miles of verdant woodlands slipped by.

"It will be time for retribution soon." Sithas paused. "You

know that we intercepted his spy with a message detailing the formation of the Windriders."

"True, but we never discovered who the message was intended for."

"It was being carried west. It was sent to the Ergoth general, I'm certain." Sithas was convinced that the Theiwar had joined with the humans in a bid for dominance of the dwarven nation. "I'll keep Than-Kar in suspense until Kith is ready to attack, so he doesn't find out that we're onto his treachery until it's too late for him to send another warning to the west."

"A fine trap!" Quimant imagined the scene. "Surround the dwarves in their barracks with your guard, disarm them before they can organize, and like magic, you have him as your prisoner."

"It's too bad I promised to return him to King Hal-Waith," noted Sithas. "I'd like nothing better than to send *him* to your coal mines."

Suddenly they leaned toward the front of the cabin as the coach slowed. They heard the coachman calling out to the horses as he hauled back on the reins.

"Driver? What's the delay?" inquired the Speaker, leaning out the window. He saw a rider—an elf, wearing the breastplate of the House Protectorate—galloping toward them from the front of the column.

The elf wasn't a member of the escort, Sithas realized. He saw the foam-flecked state of the horse and the dusty, bedraggled condition of the rider, and knew that the fellow must have come a long way.

"Your Majesty!" cried the elven horseman, reining in and practically falling out of the saddle beside the speaker's carriage door. "The city—there's trouble! It's the dwarves!"

"What happened?"

"We kept a watch over them as you ordered. This morning, before dawn, they suddenly burst out of the inns where they were quartered. They took the guards by surprise, killed them, and headed for the docks!"

"Killed?" Sithas was appalled—and furious. "How many?"

"Two dozen of the House Protectorate," replied the messenger. "We've thrown every soldier in the city into the fray, but when I left six hours ago they were slowly fighting their way to the riverbank."

"They need boats," guessed Quimant. "They're making a break for the west."

"They sniffed out my trap," groaned Sithas. The prospect of Than-Kar escaping the city worried him, mostly because he feared the dwarf would somehow be able to warn the humans about the Windriders.

"Can the house guards hold until we get there?" demanded the Speaker.

"I don't know."

"Dwarves hate the water," observed Quimant. "They won't try a crossing at night."

"We can't take that chance. Come in here," he ordered the rider, throwing open the coach door. "Driver, to the city! As fast as you can get us there!"

The gilded carriage and its escort of a hundred mounted elves thundered toward distant Silvanost, raising a wide plume of dust.

* * * * *

"They've made it to the river, and even now they seize boats along the wharf!" Tamanier Ambrodel greeted Sithas on the Avenue of Commerce, the wide roadway that paralleled the city's riverfront.

"Open the royal arsenal. Have every elf who can wield a sword follow me to the river!"

"They're already there. The battle has continued all day." The royal procession had arrived in the city with perhaps two hours of light remaining.

Sithas leaped from the coach and took the reins of a horse that had been saddled for him on Tamanier's orders. He quickly donned a chain mail shirt and hefted the light steel shield that bore the crest symbolizing the House of Silvanos.

In the meantime, the riders from his escort had dismounted, readying for conflict.

"They've barricaded themselves into two blocks of warehouses and taverns, right at the waterfront. It seems they're having some difficulties getting their boats rigged," explained the lord chamberlain.

"How many have we lost?" asked the speaker.

"Nearly fifty killed, most in the first few hours of the fight. Since then we've been content to keep them bottled up until you got here."

"Good. Let's root them out now."

Surprisingly, that thought gave him a sense of grim satisfaction. "Follow me!" Sithas cried, turning the prancing stallion down the wide Avenue of Commerce. The elves of his guard followed him. He inspected detachments that held positions down several streets that led toward the wharf. Just beyond these companies, Sithas could see hastily erected wooden barricades. He imagined the white, wide eyes of Theiwar dwarves peering between the gaps of these crude defenses.

"They're there," a sergeant assured Sithas. "They don't show themselves until we attack. Then they give a good accounting of themselves. Our archers have picked off more than a few of them."

"Good. Attack when you hear the trumpets."

Sithas himself led the band of his personal guard toward White Rose Lane before leading them down a narrow thoroughfare that was the most direct route to the waterfront.

As he had suspected, the dwarves were prepared to meet them here as well. He saw several large fishing boats lashed to the wharf, while bands of dwarves wrestled several more into place. A sturdy line of dwarves blocked the street before him, a rank four deep, armed with crossbows, swords, and stubby dwarven pikes. A barrier of barrels, planks, and huge coils of rope stood before them.

Behind these, Sithas saw the dwarven ambassador himself. Than-Kar, squinting in the uncomfortable glow of afternoon sunlight, cursed and shouted at his guards as they tried to pull the largest of the boats against the quay.

"Charge!" Sithas cried, his voice hoarse. "Break them where they stand!" Three trumpeters blared his command. A roar arose from the elves gathered along the nearby streets and lanes. Sithas spurred his charger forward.

A piece of paving stone had worked its way loose over many winters of frost and springtimes of rain. Now it lay on White Rose Lane, looking for all the world like the rest of the securely cemented stones that made up the smooth surface of the street.

But when the right forehoof of Sithas's mount came to rest for a fraction of a second upon it, the treacherous stone skidded away, twisting the hoof of the charging horse. Bones snapped in the animal's leg, and it collapsed with a shriek of pain, hurling the Speaker of the Stars from the saddle. At the same time, a full volley of steel-tipped cross-bow quarrels whistled through the air, whirring over Sithas's head. He took no note of the missiles as he crashed headlong into the roadway. His sword blade snapped in his hand, and his face exploded in pain. Groaning, he struggled to rise.

The elves of the royal guard, seeing their ruler collapse before them and not knowing that his fall had been caused by a loose paving stone, cried out in fury and rage. They charged forward, swords raised, and began to clash with the dwarves who blocked their path. Steel rang on steel, and shouts of agony and triumph echoed from the surrounding buildings.

Sithas felt gentle hands on his shoulders. Though he could barely move, someone turned him onto his back. With a shock, the Speaker of the Stars looked up to see that the sky had become a haze of red smoke. Then a kerchief dabbed at his head and cool water washed his brow. His eyes cleared, and he saw the anxious faces of several of his veteran guards. The red haze, he realized, had been caused by the blood that still spurted from the deep gashes on his forehead and cheeks.

"The fight," he gasped, forcing his lips and tongue to move. "How does the fight go?"

"The dwarves stand firm," grunted an elf, cold fury apparent in his voice. Sithas recognized the fellow as Lashio, a longtime sergeant-major who had been one of his father's guards.

"Go! I'll be all right! Break them! They must not escape!"

Lashio needed no urging. Seizing his sword, he sprang toward the melee. "Don't try to move, Excellency. I've sent for the clerics!" A nervous young trooper tried to dab at Sithas's wounds, but the Speaker angrily brushed the fellow's ministrations away.

Sitting up, Sithas tried to ignore the throbbing in his head. He looked at the hilt of his shattered weapon, still clutched in his bleeding hand. In fury, he tossed the ruined piece away.

"Give me your sword!" he barked at the guardsman.

"B-But, Excellency . . . please, you're hurt!"

"Are you in the habit of disobeying orders?" Sithas snarled.

"No, sir!" The young elf bit his lip but passed his weapon, hilt first, to the Speaker of the Stars without further delay.

Unsteadily Sithas climbed to his feet. The throbbing in his head pounded into a crescendo, and he had to grit his teeth to prevent himself from crying out in pain. The din of the battle raging nearby was nothing compared to the pain inside his head.

His unfortunate horse lay beside him, moaning and kicking. From the grotesque angle of its foreleg, Sithas knew that the animal was beyond saving. Deliberately he cut its throat with the sword, watching sadly as its lifeblood spurted across the pavement, splattering his boots.

Slowly his head began to clear, as if the shock of the horse's death penetrated the haze of his own wounds. He looked down the narrow lane and saw the mass of his royal guard, still pressing against the line of Than-Kar's bodyguards. Sithas realized that he could do nothing in that direction.

Instead, he looked up the street and saw a nearby tavern, the Thorn of the White Rose. The melee in the street raged just beyond its doors. Sithas remembered the place. It was a large establishment, with sleeping rooms and kitchen as well as the typical great room of a riverfront tavern. Instinctively he knew that it would suit his purpose.

He started to hurry toward the door. Shouting to those members of his guard who were in the back of the fight, unable to reach the dwarves because of the press of their comrades and the narrow confines of the lane.

"Follow me!" he called, pushing open the door. Several dozen of his guardsmen, led by Lashio, turned to answer his call.

The startled patrons of the bar, all of whom were standing at the windows to watch the fight in the street, turned in astonishment as their blood-streaked ruler stumbled in. Sithas paid them no note, instead leading his small company past the startled bartender, through the kitchen, and out into the alley behind the place.

A lone dwarf stood several paces away, apparently guarding this route of approach. He raised his steel battle-axe and shouted a hoarse cry of alarm. It was the last sound he made as the Speaker of the Stars lunged at him, easily dodging the heavy blow of his axe to run him through.

Immediately Sithas and his small band raced from the alley onto the docks. The dwarves fought to reach their boats as bands of the royal guardsmen surged onto the waterfront from other nearby streets and alleys.

A black-bearded dwarf confronted Sithas. The elf saw that his attacker wore a breastplate and helm of black steel, but it was his eyes that caught Sithas's attention: wide and vacant, like the huge white circles of a madman, pure Theiwar.

Snarling his frustration—for he saw Than-Kar, behind this dwarf, scrambling into one of the boats—Sithas charged recklessly forward.

But this foe proved far more adept than the Speaker's previous opponent. The Theiwar's keen-edged battle-axe bashed Sithas's longsword aside, and only a desperate roll to the side saved the elf from losing his right forearm. He bounced to his feet in time to ward off a second blow, and for a few moments, the two combatants poked and stabbed ineffectively, each searching for an opening.

Sithas thrust again, grimly pleased to see panic flash in the Theiwar's otherwise emotionless eyes. Only a desperate twist to the side, one that dropped the dwarf to his knees for a moment, saved him from the elf's deadly steel. With surprising quickness, however, the dwarf sprang to his feet and parried Sithas's next blow.

Then the elf had to ward off several hard slashes as the dwarf drove him backward for several steps. Sithas caught his heel on a coil of rope and tripped, but recovered in time to parry a savage blow. Steel rang against steel, but his strong arm held firm.

Then, behind the black-armored warrior, the dwarven ambassador raised his head and gave a sharp call. The dwarves on the dock immediately fell back toward the boats, and this gave Sithas his opening.

The elf reached down and grasped the coil of rope. With a grunt of exertion, he hurled it at the carefully retreating Theiwar. The dwarf raised his axe to knock the snakelike strands aside, and Sithas darted forward.

His blade penetrated the dwarf's skin at the throat, just above his heavy breastplate. With a gurgling cry of pain, the warrior stumbled, his wildly staring eyes growing cold and vacant.

As his fallen foe slumped to the docks, Sithas leaped over the body, racing toward the boat where Than-Kar frantically gestured to his guards. The Speaker of the Stars reached the edge of the quay as the craft began to drift into the river. For a moment, he considered leaping after it.

A second look at the boat full of dwarves changed his mind. Such a leap would accomplish nothing but his own death. Instead, he could only watch in dismay as the Theiwar dwarf and his bodyguards, propelled by a timely breeze, made their way smoothly to the far bank of the Thon-Thalas River and the road to the west beyond.

☙ 23 ❧

a Week Later, Sithelbec

Kith-kanan remained in Sithelbec for a week, keeping within the small officer's cabin for the whole time. He met with Parnigar, Kencathedrus, and other of his trusted officers. All were cautioned to secrecy on their leader's plan. Indeed, Kith made a point of asking Parnigar to keep the news from his wife, who was human.

Kith had plenty of time to rest as well, but his sleep was troubled by recurring dreams. Often in the past he had dreamed of Anaya, the lost love of his life, and more recently the alluring vision of Hermathya had haunted him, often banishing Anaya from his thoughts.

Now, since he had come to Sithelbec, a third woman intruded herself in his dreams—the human woman who had saved him from General Giarna when he had been captured. The trio of females waged a silent but forceful war in his subconscious. Consequently his periods of true sleep were few in number.

Finally the week was over, and in the middle of a dark night, he left the fortress upon the back of Arcuballis. This time his flight was short, a mere fifteen miles to the east. He made for the wide clearing, surrounded by a dense ring of forest, that he had established.

He was pleased when the Windriders, under the young, capable Captain Hallus, arrived on schedule. Four thousand elves of Silvanost had also camped here, providing him with substantial reinforcement. Sithas left fresh orders and flew back to the fortress before darkness broke. Few realized he had ever been gone.

It only remained to see whether Dunbarth and his dwarves would fulfill their part of the bargain, but Kith-Kanan had few worries on this score. One more day had to pass before their deadline.

*   *   *   *   *

Kencathedrus and Parnigar had done their work well. Kith-Kanan emerged from the captain's room at sunset to find the fortress of Sithelbec alive with tension and subdued excitement. Troops cleaned their weapons or oiled their armor. The elven horsemen fed and saddled their mounts, preparing for the sortie that was coming. Archers checked their bowstrings and gathered stores of extra arrows beside their positions.

Kith-Kanan walked among them, stopping to clap a warrior on the shoulder here or to ask a quiet question there. Word of his return spread through the fortress, and the activities of the Wildrunners took on a dramatic degree of purpose and determination.

Rumors spread like smoke on the wind. The Wildrunners would make a grand attack! An elven army gathered on the plains beyond the fortress! The morale of the human army had crumbled. They would be routed if faced with a vigorous sortie!

Kith-Kanan made no attempt to dispute these rumors.

Indeed, his tight-lipped demeanor served to heighten the tension and anticipation among his troops. The long siege, barely a month short of a year, had brought the Wildrunners to a such state that they would willingly risk their lives to end the confinement.

The general made his way to the high tower of the fortress. Darkness still shrouded the plains, and the elves burned no lamps, even within the walls. Their nightvision allowed them to move around and organize without illumination.

At the base of the tall structure, Kith found Parnigar, waiting as he had been ordered to, with a young elf. The latter didn't wear the accoutrements of the warrior, but instead was wrapped in a soft cloth robe. He wore doeskin boots, no helmet, and his eyes were bright as Kith-Kanan approached.

"This is Anakardain," introduced Parnigar. The young elf saluted crisply, and Kith-Kanan acknowledged the gesture, signaling Anakardain to relax.

"Has Captain Parnigar informed you of my needs?" he inquired quickly.

"Indeed, General." Anakardain nodded enthusiastically. "I am honored to offer my humble skills in this task."

"Good. Let's get to the top of the tower. Captain?" Kith turned back to Parnigar.

"Yes, sir?"

"Have Arcuballis brought to the tower top. When I need to mount, I won't have time to come down to the stables."

"Of course!" Parnigar turned to get the griffon, while the two elves entered the base of the tower and made their way up the long, winding stairway to the top. Anakardain, Kith sensed, wanted to ask a hundred questions, but he remained silent, which Kith-Kanan greatly appreciated at this particular moment.

They emerged onto the high tower's parapet with the sky, still dark, looming overhead. They could see a red glow where the crimson moon, Lunitari, had just set over the western horizon. The white moon, Solinari, was a thin crescent in the east. The only other illumination above them came from millions of stars, while it seemed that an equal number of campfires burned in the great ring of the human army surrounding them.

The fortress of Sithelbec was a dark sprawl around them. The stars boded well, Kith-Kanan thought. It was important that they have a clear day for the implementation of his plan.

"This is where you desire my spell?" inquired Anakardain, finally breaking the silence.

"Yes—to the limits of your range."

"It will be seen for twenty miles," promised the young mage.

A shape, rising through the air, emerged from the darkness, and Anakardain flinched backward nervously as Arcuballis came to rest on the parapet beside them. Kith chuckled, easing the young elf's tension as he took the griffon's bridle and led him onto the high platform.

Other elves, including Parnigar and a small detachment of archers, joined them. One of the troopers carried a shining trumpet, and even through the darkness, the instrument seemed to radiate a golden sheen. A faint glimmer of rosy sky marked the eastern horizon by now, and they watched as it gradually extended over their heads. One by one the stars winked out of sight, overtaken by the greater brightness of the sun.

Now Kith-Kanan could look down and see the fortress come alive around him. The Wildrunner cavalry, three hundred proud elves, gathered before the huge wooden gates that provided the main entrance and egress from the fort. Those gates had not been opened in eleven months.

Behind the riders, companies of elven infantry gathered in a long column. Some of these collected in the alleys and passages leading to the main avenue, for there wasn't enough open space for all of the troops, some ten thousand in number, to form up before the gates. The infantry included units of pike and longbow, plus many with sword and shield. The elves stood or paced restlessly.

The plans for the attack had been made carefully. Kencathedras himself rode a prancing charger before the gates. Though the proud veteran had wished to ride forth with the first wave of cavalry, Kith-Kanan had ordered him to remain behind until the infantry joined the fight.

This way, Kencathedrus would be able to direct each unit

to begin its charge, and Kith hoped they would avoid a great traffic jam at the gates themselves.

The next hour was the longest of Kith-Kanan's life. All of the pieces were in place, all the plans had been laid. All that they could do now was to wait, and this was perhaps the most difficult task of all.

The sun, with agonizing slowness, reached the eastern horizon and slowly crept upward into the sky. The long shadow of the high tower stretched across the closest section of the human camp west of the fortress. As the sun climbed, it dazzled everyone—humans and elves alike— with its fiery brilliance.

The general studied the human camp. Wide, muddy avenues stretched among great blocks of tents. Huge pastures, beyond the fringes of the tents, held thousands of horses. Closer to the fortress walls, a ring of ditches, trenches, and walls of wooden spikes had been erected. More piles of logs had been gathered at the fringes of the camp, dragged from the nearest forests, some ten miles away, and collected for a variety of uses.

These siege towers had been constructed over the winter. Though the humans preferred to let hunger and confinement do their work for them, obviously their patience had begun to wear thin. These great wooden structures had many portals from which archers could shower their missiles over Sithelbec's walls. Huge wheels supported the towers, and Kith knew that eventually they would rumble forward to try to take the fortress by storm. Only the high cost of such an attack had stayed the human hand thus far.

Signs of activity began to dot the human camp as breakfast fires were lit and wagons of provisions pulled by draft horses struggled along the muddy lanes. The sun crested the wall of the fortress. The elves could count on the fact that the humans to the west would be blinded by that bright orb.

The time, Kith-Kanan knew, had finally come.

"Now!"

The general barked that one word, and the trumpeter instantly raised his horn to his lips. The loud bray of the call rang from atop the tower, blaring stridently across the fortress and ringing harshly against the ears of the slowly awakening human army.

A deep rumble shook the fortress as gatesmen released the great stone counterweights and the massive fortress gates swung open with startling swiftness. Immediately the elven riders kicked their steeds, startling the horses into explosive bursts of speed. Shouts and cries of excitement and encouragement whooped through the air as the riders surged forth.

Still the trumpet brayed its command, and now the elven infantry rushed from the gates, emerging from the dust cloud raised by the stampeding horses. Kencathedrus, his lively mount prancing with excitement, indicated with his sword each company of foot soldiers, and, in turn, they followed but a pace or two behind the unit that rushed before.

In the camp of the humans, the surprise was almost palpable, jerking men from breakfast idylls, or for those who had had duty during the night, from sleep. Eleven months of placid siege-making had had the inevitable effect of lessening readiness and building complacency. Now the peace of a warm summer's morning exploded with the brash violence of war.

The cavalry led the elven charge while the companies of foot soldiers spread into lines and advanced behind the horsemen. The lead horses reached the ditch the humans had excavated around the fortress and charged through the obstacle. Properly manned, it would have been a formidable barrier, but the elven lances pierced the few humans who stood up to challenge them as the horses charged up the steep dirt sides.

The elven lancers thundered through the ditch and then smoothly spread their column into a broad line. Lances lowered, they charged into a block of tents, spearing and trampling any humans who dared oppose them.

Trumpet calls echoed from the companies of the Ergothian Army, but to the elven commander, the tones held a frantic, hysterical quality that accurately reflected the confusion sweeping through the vast body of men. A group of swordsmen gathered, advancing shield-to-shield into the face of the thundering cavalry.

The elven horses kicked and bucked. Riders stabbed with their lances. Some of the wooden shafts splintered as their tips met the hard steel of human shields, but others drove the sharp points between the shields into soft human flesh beyond. One powerful elf thrust his lance forward so hard that it penetrated a shield, sticking the soldier beyond into the ground like an insect might be pinned to a board for display.

That rider, like so many others, drew his sword following the loss of his lance. The tight ranks of horse, crowded in among the tangle of tents and supply wagons, inevitably broke into smaller bands, and a dozen skirmishes raged through the camp.

Elven riders hacked and chopped around them as the humans scrambled to put up a defense. A rider decapitated one foe while his horse trampled another. Three humans rushed at his shield side, and he bashed one of them to the ground. Whirling, the horse reared and kicked, knocking another of the men off his feet. As the steed's forefeet fell, the elf's sword, in a lightning stroke, caught the remaining footman in the throat. With a gurgling gasp, he fell, already forgotten as his killer looked for another target.

There was no shortage of victims amid that vast and teeming camp. Finally the humans started to gather with some sense of cohesion. Swordsmen collected in units of two or three hundred, giving the horsemen wide berth until they could face them in disciplined ranks. Other humans, the herdsmen, gathered the horses from the pastures and hastened to saddle them. It would be some minutes before human cavalry could respond to the attack, however.

Archers, in groups of a dozen or more, started to send their deadly missiles into the elven riders. Fortunately the horses moved so quickly and the camp around them was so disordered that this fire had little effect. Bucking, plunging horses trampled some of the canvas tents and kicked the coals from the numerous fires among the wreckage. Soon equipment, garb, and tents began to smolder, and yellow flames licked upward from much of the ruined camp.

* * * * *

"Where is that witch?" demanded General Giarna, practically spitting his anger. He spouted questions, orders, and demands at a panicked group of officers "Quickly! Get the horses saddled! Organize archers north and south of the breach! Alert the knights! Gods curse your slowness!"

Beside him, Kalawax, the Theiwar commander, watched shrewdly. "This was unexpected," he murmured.

"Perhaps. It will also be a disaster for the elves. They have given me the opportunity I have so long desired, to meet them in the open field!"

Kalawax said nothing. He merely studied the human leader, his Theiwar eyes narrowed to slits. Even so, the whites showed abnormally large to either side of his pupils.

Suzine was forgotten for the moment.

"General! General!" A mud-splattered swordsman lurched through the crowd of officers and collapsed to his knees. "We attacked the elven line at the ditch, but they stopped us! My men, all killed! Only—"

Further words choked away as the general's black-gloved hand seized the gagging messenger. Giarna squeezed, and there was the sound of bones snapping.

Casting the corpse aside, General Giarna fixed each of his officers with a black, penetrating gaze. To a man, they were terrified to the core.

"Move!" barked the commander.

The officers scattered, each of them racing to obey.

*　*　*　*　*

More trumpets blared, and companies of humans swarmed from across the vast encampment, charging toward the elves who stood in a semicircle before the fortress gates. The companies of Wildrunner infantry, led by Kencathedrus, met the first of these attackers with shields and swords. The clash of metal and screaming of the wounded added to the cacophony.

The humans around the fort still outnumbered the elves by ten to one, and Kith-Kanan had only committed a quarter of the defenders to this initial sortie. Nevertheless, small bands of humans acquitted themselves well, hurling their bodies against the shredding blades of the elves.

"Stand firm there!" shouted Kencathedrus, urging his horse into a gap where two elves had just fallen.

The captain maneuvered his steed into the breach while

his blade struck down two men who tried to force their way past him. Swords smashed against shields. Men and elves slipped in the mud and the blood. Now the ditch served as a defensive line for two of the elven companies. Cursing and slashing, the humans charged into the muddy trough, only to groan and bleed and die beneath the swords of the elves.

Elven archers showered the human troops with a deadly rain of steel-tipped hail. The ditch became a killing ground as panicked men turned to flee, tangling themselves among the fresh troops that the human commanders were casting into the fray.

Beyond the ditch, the elven cavalry of three hundred riders plunged and raced among thirty thousand humans. But more and more fires erupted, sending clouds of black smoke wafting across the field, choking noses and throats and blocking vision.

Greedy flames licked at the walls of one tent, and suddenly the blaze crackled upward. Wreckage fell inward, revealing several rows of neat casks, the cooking and lamp oil for this contingent of the human army. One of the casks began to blaze, and hot oil cascaded across the other barrels. A rush like a hot, dry wind surged from the tent, followed by a dull thud of sound. Instantly fiery oil sprayed outward. A cloud of hellfire mushroomed into the sky, wreathed in black smoke.

Instantly the inferno spread to neighboring tents. A hundred men, doused by the liquid death, screamed and shrieked for long moments before they dropped, looking like charred wood.

From his vantage on the tower, Kith-Kanan watched the battle rage through the camp. Though chaos reigned on the field, he could see that the sortie had affected only a relatively small portion of the human camp. The enemy had begun to recover from the surprise attack, and fresh regiments surged against the elven horsemen, threatening to cut them off from any possible retreat.

"Sound the recall—now!" Kith-Kanan barked.

The trumpeter blared the signal even as Kith finished his command. The notes rang across the field, and the elven riders immediately turned back toward the gates.

At the ditch, Kencathedrus and his men stood firm. A

thousand human bodies filled the trench, and there wasn't an elven blade that didn't drip with gore. The infantry opened a gap in their line for the riders to thunder through as an increasing rain of arrows held the humans at bay.

Even as this was happening, Kith turned his eyes to the south, looking along the horizon for some sign that the next phase of his strategy could begin. The time was ripe.

There! He saw a row of banners fluttering above the grass, and soon he discerned movement.

"The dwarves of Thorbardin!" he cried, pointing.

The dwarves came on in a broad line, trotting as fast as their stocky legs could carry them. A throaty roar burst from their throats, and the legion of Thorbardin hastened into a charge.

The humans were pressing the elven forces at the gates of Sithelbec. From his vantage, Kith-Kanan watched with grim satisfaction as his Wildrunners managed to beat back attack after attack. To the south, some of the humans had now realized the threat lumbering forward against their backs.

* * * * *

"Dwarves!" The cry raced through the human camp, quickly reaching General Giarna. Kalawax, beside him, gaped in astonishment, his already pallid complexion growing even more pale.

"The dwarven legion! Hylar, from Thorbardin!" More reports, from the throats of hoarse messengers, were brought back to the general in his command tent. "They drive against the south!"

"I knew *nothing* of this!" squawked Kalawax, unconsciously backing away from Giarna. The dwarf's earlier aplomb had vanished with this new turn of events "My spies have been tricked. Our agents in Silvanost have worked hard to prevent this!"

"You have *failed!*"

Giarna's words carried with them a sentence of doom. His eyes, black and yawning, seemed to flare for a moment with a deep, parasitic fire.

His fist lashed out, pummeling the Theiwar on the side of

his head. But this was no ordinary blow. It connected squarely, and the dwarf's thick skull erupted. The general's other hand seized the corpse by the neck. His face flushed, and his eyes flared with an insane pleasure. In another moment, he cast the Theiwar—now a dried and shriveled husk—to the side.

Kalawax was already forgotten as the general absently wiped his hand on his cloak, focusing on the problem of how to stem this most recent attack.

*　*　*　*　*

"For Thorbardin! For the king!"

A few human companies of swordsmen raced to block the surging waves of dwarves, but most of the Army of Ergoth was preoccupied with the elven sortie. Dunbarth Ironthumb led the way. A man raised a sword, holding his shield across his chest, and then chopped savagely downward at the dwarven commander. Dunbarth's battle-axe, held high, deflected the blow with a ringing clash. In the next instant, the dwarven veteran slashed his weapon through a vicious swing, cutting underneath the human's shield. The man shrieked in agony as the axe sliced open his belly.

"Charge! Full speed! To the tents!"

Dunbarth barked the commands, and the dwarves renewed their advance. Those humans who tried to stand in the way quickly perished, while others dropped their weapons and fled. Some of these escaped, while others fell beneath the volley of crossbow fire leveled by the dwarven missile troops.

Dunbarth led a detachment along a row of tents, chopping at the guy lines of each, watching the rude shelters collapse like wilting flowers. They came upon a supply compound, where great pots of stew had been abandoned, still simmering. Seizing everything flammable, they tossed weapons and harnesses, even carts and wagons, onto the coals. Quickly searing tongues of flame licked upward, igniting the equipment and marking the spot of the dwarven advance.

"Onward!" cried Dunbarth, and again the dwarves

moved toward Sithelbec.

The human troops didn't react quickly to this new threat. Small bands perished as the stocky Hylar swept around them, and the waves of the attackers gave little time for the humans to muster a stand.

The sheer numbers of the defenders gave the humans an edge. Soon Dunbarth found some brave human contesting every forward step he tried to take. His axe rose and fell, and many an Ergothian veteran perished beneath that gory blade. But more and more of the humans stepped up.

"Stand firm!" cried Ironthumb.

Now the dwarves hacked and chopped in tight formation in the middle of a devastated human camp. A thousand men rushed against their left, met by the sharp clunk of crossbows and a volley of steel-tipped death. Hundreds fell, pierced by the missiles, and others turned to flee.

Swords met axes in five thousand duels to the death. The dwarves fought with courage and discipline, holding their ranks tight. They maimed and killed with brutal efficiency, but they were well matched by the courageous humans who pressed them in such great numbers.

But it was those numbers that would have to tell the tale. Slowly Dunbarth's force contracted into a great ring. Amid the cries and the clanging and the shouting and screaming, Dunbarth slowly realized the tactical situation.

The dwarven legion was surrounded.

ꝛ 24 ꝛ

Late Morning, Battle of Sithelbec

kith-kanan watched the courageous stand of the dwarves with a lump of admiration burning in his throat. Dunbarth's magnificent charge had taken the pressure off the elves at the gate, and now Kencathedrus's force could surge forward again, expanding their perimeter against the distracted humans.

Attacked from two sides, the Army of Ergoth wavered and twitched like a huge but indecisive beast set upon by a swarm of stinging pests. Great masses of human foot soldiers stood idle, waiting for orders while their comrades perished in desperate battles a few hundred yards away.

But now a sense of purpose seemed to settle across the humans. The tens of thousands of horses had been saddled.

The riders, especially the light horsemen of General Giarna's northern wing, had reached their steeds and were ready for battle.

Unlike the humans on foot, however, the cavalry did not race piecemeal into the fray, setting themselves up for defeat. Instead, they collected into companies and regiments and finally into massive columns. The riders surged around the outside of the melee, gathering and positioning themselves for one crucial charge.

The elves of the sortie force could save themselves by a quick return to the fortress. The dwarves, however, were isolated amid the wreckage of the south camp and had no such fallback. Lacking pikes, they would be virtually helpless against the onslaught Giarna was almost ready to unleash.

Kith-Kanan turned to Anakardain, who had remained at his side throughout the battle. "Now! Give the signal!" commanded the general.

The elven mage pointed a finger toward the sky. "*Exceriate! Pyros, lofti!*" he cried.

Instantly a crackling shaft of blue light erupted from his pointing hand, hissing upward amid a trail of sparks. Even in the bright sunlight, the bolt of magic stood out clearly, visible to all on the battlefield.

And, Kith devoutly hoped, to those who waited some twenty miles away—waited for this very signal.

For several minutes after the flare, the battle raged, unchecked. Nor was there any sign that might alter this, though Kith-Kanan kept his eyes glued to the eastern horizon. The sun hung midway between that horizon and the zenith of noon, though it seemed impossible that the battle had raged for barely three hours.

Now the human cavalry galloped from the pastures, an impressive mass of horsemen under the tight control of a skilled commander. They surged around the trampled encampment, veering toward the embattled dwarves.

Finally Kith-Kanan, still staring to the east, saw what he had been looking for: a line of tiny winged figures, a hundred feet above the ground and heading fast in this direction. Sunlight glinted from shiny steel helms and sparkled from deadly lance heads.

"The charge—sound it again!" barked the elven general to his trumpeter.

Another blare sounded across the field, and for a moment, the momentum of battle paused. Humans looked upward in surprise. Their officers, in particular, were puzzled by the command. The elven and dwarven troops, hard-pressed now, seemed to be in no position to execute an offensive.

"Again—the charge!"

Again and again the call brayed forth.

Kith-Kanan watched the Windriders as the soaring line approached nearer and nearer, within two or three miles of the field. The elven general picked up his shield and checked to see that his sword hung loosely in his scabbard.

"Take over the command," Kith told Parnigar, at the same time grabbing the reins of Arcuballis and stepping to the griffon's side.

The Wildrunner captain stared at his general. "Surely you're not going out there! We need you here. Your plan is working! Don't jeopardize it now!"

Kith shook his head, casting off the arguments. "The plan has a life of its own now. If it fails, sound the recall and bring the elves back into the fortress. Otherwise, continue to give them support from the archers on the walls—and be ready to bring the rest of them out if the humans start to break."

"But, General!" Parnigar's next objections died away as Kith-Kanan swung into his high leather saddle. Obviously he would not be deterred from his actions.

"Good luck to you," finished the captain, grimly looking over the field where thousands of humans still surged in attack.

"Luck has been with us so far," Kith replied. "May she stay with us just for a little longer."

Now the Windriders, still flying in their long, thin ranks, slowly nosed into shallow dives. They hadn't yet been sighted by the humans on the ground, who had no reason to expect attack from the air.

Again the bugler brayed his charge. Arcuballis sprang from the tower, his powerful wings carrying Kith-Kanan into line with the other Windriders. At this cue, the griffons shrieked their harsh challenge, a jarring noise that cut cleanly through the chaos of the battle. Talons extended, beaks gaping, they howled downward from the heavens.

The whole pulse of the battle ceased as the shocking vision swept lower. Men, elves, and dwarves alike gaped upward.

Cries of alarm and terror swept through the human ranks. Units of men who had until now maneuvered in tightly disciplined formations suddenly scattered into uncontrolled mobs. The shadows of the griffons passed across the field, and again the beasts shrilled their savage war cries.

If the reaction by the humans to the sudden attack was dramatic and pronounced, the effect upon the horses was profound. At the first sound of the approaching griffons, all cohesion vanished from the cavalry units. Horses bucked and pitched, whinnied and shrieked.

The Windriders passed over the entire battlefield a hundred feet above the ground. Occasionally a human archer had the presence of mind to launch an arrow upward, but these missiles always trailed their targets by great distances before arcing back to earth, to land as often as not among the human ranks.

Elven archers along the walls of Silthelbec showered their stunned opponents with renewed volleys as their captains sensed the battle's decisive moment.

"Again—once back, and we'll take to the ground!" Kith-Kanan cried, edging Arcuballis into a dive. The unit followed, and each griffon tucked its left wing, diving steeply and turning sharply to the left.

The creatures swung through a hundred-and-eighty-degree arc, losing about sixty feet of height. Now the cries of the elven riders joined those of the griffons as they raced over the human army. Bugles blared from the fortress walls and towers and from the ranks of the sortie force. Throaty dwarven cheers erupted from Dunbarth's veterans, and the legion of Thorbardin quickly broke its defensive position, charging into the panicked humans surrounding them.

The elves of the sortie force, too, charged through the ditch into the humans who had been pressing them with such intensity. Columns of elves burst from the open gates of Sithelbec, reinforcing their comrades.

Kith-Kanan selected a level field, a wide area of pasture between the western and southern human camps, for a landing site and brought the griffons to earth there. His first target would be the brigade of armored knights that were struggling to regain control of their mounts.

The griffons barely slowed as they tucked their wings and sprang forward, propelled by their powerful leonine hindquarters while their deadly foreclaws reached forward as if eager to shred the flesh of the foe.

The single line of griffons, their riders still holding their lances forward, ripped into the bucking, heaving mass of panicked horses. No charge of plate-mailed knights ever struck with such killing force. Lances punctured armor and horses fell, gored by the claws of the savage griffons, and then the elven swords struck home.

Kith-Kanan buried his lance in the chest of a black-armored knight as the human's horse bucked in terror. He couldn't see the man's face behind the closed shield of his dark helmet, but the steel tip of his weapon erupted from his victim's back in a shower of blood. Arcuballis sprang, his claws tearing away the saddle of the heavy war-horse as the terrified animal crashed to the ground.

His lance torn away by the force of the charge, Kith drew his sword. A knight plunged nearby, desperately struggling to control his mount; Kith-Kanan stabbed him in the back. Another armored warrior, on foot and wielding a massive morning star, swung the spiked ball at Arcuballis. The griffon reared back and then pounced on the man, tearing out his throat with a single powerful strike of his beak.

A chaotic jumble of shrieks and howls and moans surged around Kith, mingling with the pounding of hooves and the clash of sharp steel against plate mail. But even the superior armor of the humans couldn't save them. With no control over their mounts, they could do little more than hold on and try to escape the maelstrom of death. Very few of them made it.

"To the air!" Kith cried, spurring Arcuballis into a powerful upward leap. Shattered knights covered the ground below them while the thundering mass of their horses stampeded right through a line of human archers who couldn't get out of the way in time. All around Kith-Kanan, the other griffons sprang into the air, and with regal grace, the Windriders once again soared across the field. Slowly they climbed, forming again into a long line, flying abreast.

As the griffon's wings carried him upward, Kith looked across the field. In the distances rolled great clouds of dust. Some twenty thousand horses had already stampeded away from the battle, and these plumes marked their paths of flight. Human infantry fled from the tight ranks of the dwarven legion, while the elven reinforcements drove terrified humans into panic. Many of the enemy had dropped their weapons and thrown up their hands, pleading and begging for mercy.

Kith-Kanan veered toward the Ergothian foot soldiers, the line of Windriders following in precise formation. He took up his bow and carefully nocked an arrow. He let the missile fly, watching it dart downward and penetrate the shoulder of one of the foot soldiers. The fellow toppled forward, his helmet rolling in the mud, and Kith-Kanan got a jolt when he espied the long blond hair cascading around his body. Other arrows found targets among this company as the griffons passed overhead, and the general noticed with surprise these other men, too, all had blond hair.

One of them turned and launched an arrow upward, and a nearby griffon shrieked, pierced through the wing. The animal's limb collapsed, and the beast tipped suddenly to the side, plummeting to the earth among the Ergothian archers. The rider died from the force of the crash, but this didn't stop the soldiers from hacking and chopping at his body until only a gory mess remained.

Kith shot another arrow, and a third, watching grimly as each took the life of one of these blond savages. Only when the humans had been riddled with losses did the Windriders consider the death of their comrade avenged. As they soared away, Kith-Kanan was struck by the narrow face of one of his victims, lying faceup in the mud. Diving lower, he saw a pointed ear and blond hair.

Elves! His own people fighting for the Army of the Emperor of Ergoth! Growling in anger, he urged Arcuballis upward, the rest of his company following. With terrible purpose, he looked across the mud-and-blood-strewn field for an appropriate target.

He saw one group of horsemen, perhaps two thousand strong, that had rallied around a streaming silver banner—the ensign of General Giarna himself, Kith knew. Instantly he veered toward this unit as the general was urging his reluctant troops into a renewed charge. The griffons flew low, no more than ten feet off the ground, and the creatures shrilled their coming.

Unaffected by the curses of their commanding general, the human riders allowed their horses to turn and scatter, unwilling to face the griffon cavalry. Kith-Kanan urged Arcuballis onward, seeking the general himself, but the man had vanished among the dusty, panicked ranks of his troops. He might already have been trampled to death, for all Kith-Kanan knew.

The Windriders flew across the field, landing and attacking here and there, wherever a pocket of the human army seemed willing to make a stand. Often the mere appearance of the savage creatures was enough to break a formation, while occasionally they crashed into the defending ranks and the griffons tore with talons and beaks while their elven riders chopped and hacked with their lethal weapons.

The elves on the ground and their dwarven allies raced across the field, encouraging the total rout of the human army. More and more of the humans held up their hands in surrender as they concluded that escape was impossible. Many of the horses were stampeded, riderless, away from the field, lost to the army for the forseeable future. A great, streaming column of refugees—once a proud army but now a mass of panicked, terrified, and defeated men—choked the few roads and scarred new trails across the prairie grasslands.

When the Windriders finally came to earth before the gates of Sithelbec, they landed only because there were no more enemies left to fight. Huge columns of human prisoners, guarded by the watchful eyes of elven archers and dwarven axemen, stood listlessly along the walls of the fortress. Amidst the smoke and chaos of the camps, detachments of the Wildrunners poked and searched, uncovering more prisoners and marking stockpiles of supplies.

"General, come quickly!" Kith-Kanan looked up at the

cry, seeing a young captain approaching. The elf's face was pale, and he gestured toward a place on the field.

"What is it?" Sensing the urgency in the young soldier's request, Kith hurried behind him. In moments, he knew the reason for the officer's demeanor.

He found Kencathedrus lying among the bodies of a dozen humans. The old elf's body bled from numerous ugly wounds.

"We beat them today," gasped Kith-Kanan's former teacher and weaponmaster, managing a weak smile.

"Didn't we, though?" The general took his friend's head in his hands, looking toward the nearby officer. "Get the cleric!" he hissed.

"He's been here," objected Kencathedrus. Kith-Kanan could read the result in the wounded elf's eyes: There was nothing that even a cleric could do.

"I've lived to see this day. It makes my life as a warrior complete. The war is all but won. You must pursue them now. Don't let them escape!"

Kencathedrus gripped Kith's arm with surprising strength, nearly raising himself up from the ground. "Promise me," he gasped. "You will not let them escape!"

"I promise!" whispered the general. He cradled Kencathedrus's head for several minutes, even though he knew that he was dead.

A messenger—a Kagonesti scout in full face paint— trotted up to Kith-Kanan to make a report. "General, we have reports of enemy activity in the north camp."

That part of the huge circular human camp had seen the least fighting. Kith nodded at the scout and gently laid Kencathedrus's body on the ground. He rose and called to a nearby sergeant-major.

"Take three companies and sweep through the north camp," he ordered. He remembered, too, that General Giarna and his horsemen had escaped in that direction. He gestured to several of his Windriders. "Follow me."

﹡ 25 ﹡

afternoon, Battle of Sithelbec

Suzine watched the battle in her glass. Here in her tent in the northern camp, she did not feel the brunt of battle so heavily. Though the men here had raced to the fight and suffered the same fate as the rest of the army, the camp itself had not yet experienced the wholesale destruction that marked the south and west camps of the humans.

She had seen the Windriders soaring from the east, had watched their inexorable and unsuspected approach against her general's army, and she had smiled. Her face and her body still burned from Giarna's assaults, and her loathing for him had crystallized into hatred.

Thus when the elf commander had led the attack that sundered the army around her, she had felt a sense of joy, not dismay, as if Kith-Kanan had flown with no other purpose than to effect her own personal rescue. Calmly she had watched the battle rage, following the elven general in her mirror.

When he led the charge against Giarna's remnant of the great cavalry brigades, she had held her breath, part of her hoping he might come upon the human general and strike him dead, another part wishing that Giarna would simply flee and leave the rewards of victory to the elven forces. Even when her elven guards fled from their posts, she had taken no note.

Now she heard marching outside her tent as the elves of the sortie force moved through the north camp looking for human survivors. Suzine heard some men surrender, pleading for their lives; she heard others attack with taunts and curses, and finally screams and moans as they fell.

The battle coursed around her, washing the tent city in smoke and flame and pain and blood. But still Suzine remained within her tent, her eyes fixed upon the golden-haired figure in her mirror. She watched Kith-Kanan, mounted upon the leaping, clawing figure of his great beast, slash and cut his way through the humans who tried to challenge him. She saw that the elven attack moved steadily closer to her. Now the Wildrunners fought a mere thousand yards to the south of her tent.

"Come to me, my warrior!" she breathed.

She willed him to come to her with all of her heart, watching in her glass as Kith-Kanan hacked the head from a burly human axeman.

"I am here!" Suzine desperately wanted Kith-Kanan to sense her presence, her desire, her—did she dare believe it?—love.

The opening of her tent flap interrupted her reverie. It was *him!* It *must* be! Her heart afire, she whirled, and only when she saw Giarna standing there did brutal reality shatter her illusion. As for Giarna, he looked past her violently, at the image of the elven commander in the mirror.

The human general stepped toward her, his face a mask of fury, more like a beast's than a man's. It sent an icy blade of fear into the pit of Suzine's stomach.

When Giarna reached her and seized her arms, each in

one bone-crushing hand, that blade of fear twisted and slashed within her. She couldn't speak, couldn't think; she could only stare into those wide, maddened eyes, the lips flecked with spittle, stretched taut to reveal teeth that seemed to hunger for her soul.

"You betrayed me!" he snarled, throwing her roughly to the ground. "Where did these flying beasts come from? How long have they been waiting, ready to strike?" He knelt and punched her roughly, splitting her lip.

He glanced at the mirror on the table. Now, her concentration broken, the image of Kith-Kanan had faded, but the truth of her obsession had been revealed.

The general's black-gauntleted hand pulled a dagger from his belt, and he pressed it between her breasts, the point puncturing her gown and then brushing the skin beneath it.

"No," he said, at the very moment when she expected to die. "That would be too merciful, too cheap a price for your treachery."

He stood and glared down at her. Every instinct of her body told her to scramble to her feet, to fight him or to run! But his black eyes seemed to hypnotize her to the ground, and she couldn't bring herself to move.

"Up, slut!" he growled, kicking her sharply in the ribs and then reaching down to seize her long red hair. He pulled her to her knees, and she winced, closing her eyes, expecting another blow to her face.

Then she sensed a change within the small confines of the tent, a sudden wash of air against her face . . . the increase in the sounds of battle beyond . . .

Giarna cast her aside, and she looked at the door to the tent.

There he was!

Kith-Kanan stood in the opened tent flap. Beyond him lay bodies on the ground, and she caught a glimpse of men and elves hacking against each other with swords and axes. The tents in her line of view smoked and smoldered, some spewing orange flame.

The golden-haired elf stepped boldly into the darkened tent, his steel longsword extended before him. He spoke harshly, his blade and his words directed at the human general.

"Surrender, human, or die!" Kith-Kanan, obviously not recognizing the commander of the great human army in the semidarkness of the tent, took another step toward Giarna.

The human general, his dagger still in his hand and his body trembling with rage, stared soundlessly at the elf for a moment. Kith-Kanan squinted and crouched slightly, ready for close-quarter fighting. As he studied his opponent, recognition dawned, memories of that day of captivity a year before, when the battle had gone against the elves.

"It's *you*," the elf whispered.

"And it is fitting that *you* come to me now," replied the human general, his voice a strangled, triumphant snarl. "You will not live to enjoy the fruits of your victory!"

In a flash of motion, the man's hand whipped upward. In the same instant, he reversed his grip on the dagger, flipping its hilt from his hand and catching the tip of the foot-long blade in his fingertips.

"Look out!" Suzine screamed, suddenly finding her voice.

Giarna's hand lashed out, flinging the knife toward Kith's throat. Like a silver streak, the blade flashed through the air, true toward its mark.

Kith-Kanan couldn't evade the throw, but he could parry it. His wrist twitched, a barely perceptible movement that swung the tip of his sword through an arc of perhaps six inches. That was enough; the longsword hit the knife with a sharp clink of metal, and the smaller blade flipped over the elf's shoulder to strike the tent wall and fall harmlessly to the ground.

Suzine scrambled away from Giarna as the man drew his sword and rushed toward the elf. Kith-Kanan, eight inches shorter and perhaps a hundred pounds lighter than the human general, met the charge squarely. The two blades clashed with a force that rang like cymbals in the confines of the tent. The elf took one step back to absorb the momentum of the attack, but Giarna was stopped in his tracks.

The two combatants circled, each totally focused on the other, looking for the slightest hint, the twitch of an eye or a minute shifting of a shoulder, that would warn the other of an intended lunge.

They slashed at each other, then darted out of the way

and just as quickly slashed again. Neither bore a shield. Consummate swordsmen both, they worked their way around the spacious tent. Kith-Kanan tipped a dressing screen in front of the human. The man leaped over it. Giarna drove the elf backward, hoping to trip him on Suzine's cot. Kith sensed the threat and sprang to the rear, clearing the obstacle and then darting to the side, driving against the human's flank.

Again the man parried, and the two warriors continued to circle, each conserving his strength, neither showing the weariness of the long day's battle. Where Giarna's face was a mask of twisted hatred, however, the elf's remained an image of cool, studied detachment. The man struck with power that the elf could not hope to match, so Kith-Kanan had to rely on skill and control for each parry, each lightning thrust of his own.

The woman glanced back and forth, her eyes wide with horror alternating with hope.

They were too equal in skill, she saw, and given this fact, Giarna's size and strength inevitably would vanquish the elf. An increasing sense of desperation marked Kith's parries and attacks. Once he stumbled and Suzine screamed. Only Giarna's heavy boot, as it caught in a fold of her rug, prevented his blade from tearing through the elf's heart.

Nevertheless, he managed to cut a slash in Kith's side, and the elf grunted in pain as he regained his balance. Suzine saw a tightness in his expression that hadn't been there before. It could be called the beginnings of fear. Once he glanced toward the door, as if he hoped for assistance from that quarter.

Only when he did that did Suzine notice the sudden quiet that seemed to have descended across the camp. The fight outside had moved beyond them. Kith-Kanan had been left behind.

She saw Giarna drive Kith backward with a series of ringing blows, and she knew she had to do something! Kith sprang forward, desperation apparent in each of his swinging slashes. Giarna ducked away from each blow, giving ground as he searched for the fatal opening.

There! The elf overreached himself, leaning too far forward in an attempt to draw blood from his elusive target.

Giarna's sword came up, its tip, glistening from Kith's moist blood, held for just a moment as the elf followed through with his reckless swing.

Kith tried to twist away, raising his left arm so that he would take the wound in his shoulder, but Giarna simply raised that deadly spike and drove it toward the elf's neck.

The sound of shattering glass was the next thing that Suzine knew. She didn't understand how she came to hold the frame of her mirror in her hands, didn't comprehend the shards of glass scattered across the rug. More glass, she saw, glinted upon Giarna's shoulders. Blood spurted from long slashes in his scalp.

The human leader staggered, reeling from the blow to his head, as Kith-Kanan twisted away. He looked at the woman, gratitude shining in his eyes—or was that something deeper, more profound, more lasting, that she wished to see there?

The elf's blade came up, poised to strike, as Giarna shook his head and cursed, wiping the blood from his eyes. His back to the door, he stared at the elf and the woman, his face once again distorted by his monstrous hatred.

Kith-Kanan stepped to Suzine's side, sensing the man's hatred and protecting her from any sudden attack.

But there would be no attack. Groggy, bleeding, surrounded by enemies, Giarna made a more pragmatic decision. With one last burning look at the pair, he turned and darted through the tent flap.

Kith-Kanan started forward but stopped when he felt Suzine's hand on his arm.

"Wait," she said softly. She touched the bloodstained tunic at his side, where Giarna's sword had cut him.

"You're hurt. Here, let me tend your wound."

The weariness of the great battle finally arose within Kith-Kanan as he lay upon the bed. For the first time in more months than he cared to remember, he felt a gentle sensation of peace.

* * * * *

The war almost ceased to exist for Kith-Kanan. It became distant and unreal. His wound wasn't serious, and the woman who tended him was not only beautiful but also had been haunting his dreams for weeks.

As the Army of Ergoth scattered, Parnigar took command of the pursuit, skillfully massing the Wildrunners to attack concentrations of the enemy wherever they could be found. Kith-Kanan was left to recuperate and paid little attention to his lieutenant's reports of progress.

They all knew the humans were beaten. It would be a matter of weeks, perhaps months now, before they were driven back across the border of their own empire. Windriders sailed over the plains, dwarves and elves marched, and elven cavalry galloped at will.

And back at the nearly abandoned fortress, the commander of this great army was falling in love.

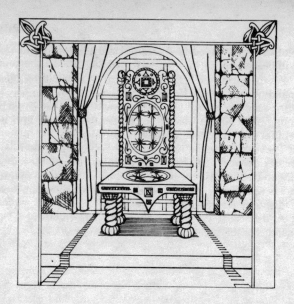

❧ 26 ❧

Late Summer, Year of the Bear

Already the cool winds presaging autumn swirled northward from the Courrain Ocean, causing the trees of the great forestlands to discard their leaves and prepare for the long dormancy of winter. The elves of Silvanesti felt the winds, too, throughout the towns and estates and even in the great capital of Silvanost.

The city was alive with the great jubilation of victory. Word from the front told of the rout of the human army. Kith-Kanan's army was on the offensive. The elven general had sent columns of Wildrunners marching swiftly across the plains, fighting the pockets of human resistance.

The dwarven league did its part against the humans, while the Windriders swept down from the skies, shattering the once-proud Ergothian regiments, capturing or killing hundreds of humans, and scattering the rest to the four winds. Most bands of desperate survivors sought nothing more than flight back to the borders of Ergoth.

Great camps of human prisoners—tens of thousands— now littered the plains. Many of these Kith-Kanan sent to the east upon the orders of his brother, where the human prisoners were condemned to spend their lives in the Clan Oakleaf mines. Others were assigned to rebuild and strengthen the fortress of Sithelbec and repair the damage to settlements and villages ravaged by two years of war.

These should be the greatest days of my life! Sithas brooded over the reports from his great emerald throne. He was reluctant to leave the Hall of Audience for the brightness of the garden or the city despite the beautiful late afternoon sky.

An hour ago he had ordered his courtiers and nobles to leave him alone. He was disconsolate, despite the most recent missive from Kith-Kanan—borne by a Windrider courier, the news less than a week old—which had continued favorable reports of victory.

Perhaps he would have been relieved to talk to Lord Quimant—no one else seemed to understand the pressures of his office—but that nobleman had left the city more than a week earlier to assist in the administration of the new prisoner slaves at his family's mines in the north. He had no clear idea when he would return.

Sithas's mind ran over his brother's latest communication. Kith reported that the central wing of the Army of Ergoth, which had tried to march home by the shortest and most direct route, had since ceased to exist. The entire force had been eradicated when the Wildrunners gathered and attacked the central wing, causing massive casualties.

There was no longer much of a southern wing, either. Its soldiers had suffered the highest toll in the initial counterattack. And the smaller northern wing, with its thousands of light horsemen and fast-moving infantry under the shrewd General Giarna, had been scattered into fragments that desperately sought refuge among the clumps of forest and rough country that fringed the plains.

Why, then, could Sithas not share in the exultation of the

Silvanost citizenry?

Perhaps because reports had been confirmed of Theiwar dwarves joining with the fleeing remnants of Giarna's force, even though their cousins, the Hylar, fought on the side of the elves. Sithas had no doubt that the Theiwar were led by the treacherous general and Ambassador Than-Kar. Such internecine dwarven politics served to further confuse the purposes of this war.

Neither was there any doubt now that large numbers of renegade elves fought on the side of Ergoth. Elves and dwarves and humans fighting against elves and dwarves! Quimant continued to advocate the hiring of human mercenaries to further reinforce Kith-Kanan's armies. This was a step that Sithas was not prepared to take. And yet . . .

The immediate victory didn't seem to offer an end to the differences among the elves. Would Silvanesti ever be pure again? Would involvement in this war break down the barriers that separated elvenkind from the rest of Krynn?

Even the name of the war itself, a name he had heard uttered in the streets of the city, even murmured from the lips of polite society, underscored his anguish. Following the summer's battles and the lists of the dead, it had become the universal sobriquet for the war, too commonly known to be changed even by the decree of the Speaker of the Stars.

The Kinslayer War.

The name left a bitter taste on his tongue, for to Sithas, it represented all that was wrong about the cause they fought against. Blind, misguided elves throwing in their lot with the human enemy—they forfeited their right to any kinship!

More serious to Sithas, in a personal sense, was the nasty rumor now making the rounds of the city, a preposterous allegation. The scurrilous gossip had it that Kith-Kanan himself had taken a human woman for a consort! No one, of course, dared present this news to Sithas directly, but he knew that the others believed and whispered the ludicrous tale.

He had ordered members of the House Protectorate to disguise themselves as workers and artisans and to enter the taverns and inns frequented by the citizens. They were to listen carefully, and if they overheard anyone passing this rumor, the culprit was to be immediately arrested and brought to the palace for questioning.

"Pa-pa?"

The voice brightened his mood as nothing else could. Sithas turned to see Vanesti toddling toward him, carrying— as always—the wooden sword Kith-Kanan had made for him before departing for Sithelbec.

"Come here, you," the Speaker of the Stars said, kneeling before the throne and throwing wide his arms.

"Pa-pa!" Vanesti, his beaming face framed by long golden curls, hastened his pace and immediately toppled forward, landing on his face.

Sithas scooped the tyke into his arms and held him, patting him on the back until his crying ceased. "There, there. It doesn't hurt so bad, does it?" he soothed.

"Ow!" objected the youth, rubbing his nose.

Sithas chuckled. Still carrying his son, he started toward the royal door that led to the Gardens of Astarin.

* * * * *

Quimant returned two days later and came to see Sithas as the Speaker sat alone in the Hall of Audience.

"Your plan has worked miracles!" reported the lord. If he noticed his ruler's melancholy air, he didn't call attention to it. "We have tripled the number of slaves and can work the mines around the clock now. In addition, the freed elves have marched off to the plains. They make a very formidable company indeed!"

"The war may be over by the time they reach the battlefield," sighed Sithas. "Perhaps I have simply freed a number of malefactors for nothing."

Quimant shook his head. "I've heard the reports. Even though the Wildrunners are pushing the humans westward, I wouldn't expect a complete end to the war before next summer."

"Surely you don't think the Army of Ergoth will reassemble now that the Windriders are pursuing them?"

"Not reassemble, no, but they will break into small bands. Kith-Kanan's army will find many of them, but not all. Yes, Excellency, I fear we will still have an enemy to contend with a year from now—perhaps even longer."

Sithas cast off the notion as unthinkable. Before the debate proceeded further, however, a guard appeared at the hall's door.

"What is it?" inquired the Speaker.

"Lashio has captured a fellow, a stonemason, in the city. He was spreading the—er, the tale about General Kith-Kanan."

Sithas bolted upright in his throne. "Bring him to me! And summon the stablemaster. Tell him to bring a whip!"

"Your Majesty?"

The words came from behind the guard, who stepped aside and let Tamanier Ambrodel enter. The noble elf approached and bowed formally. "May I have a private word with the Speaker?"

"Leave us," Sithas told the guard. When only Quimant and himself were present, he gestured Tamanier to speak.

"I wish to prevent you from allowing a grave injustice," Ambrodel began.

"*I* dispense the justice here. What business is it of yours?" demanded Sithas.

Ambrodel flinched at the Speaker's harsh tone but forged ahead. "I am here at your mother's request."

"What is the nature of this 'injustice'?"

"It concerns your punishment of this elf, this mason. Your mother, as you know, has received letters from Kith-Kanan separate from the official missives he sends to you. It seems that he communicates to her on matters that he does not care to discuss . . . with others."

Sithas scowled.

"Kith-Kanan *has* taken a human woman as his companion. He has written your mother about her. Apparently he is very much smitten."

Sithas sagged backward in the monstrous throne. He wanted to curse at Tamanier Ambrodel, to call him a liar. But he couldn't. Instead, he had to accept the unthinkable, no matter how nightmarish the knowledge.

He suddenly felt sick to his stomach.

* * * * *

Sithas labored for hours over the letter he tried to write to his brother. He attempted a number of beginnings.

Kith-Kanan, my Brother,

I have word from mother of a woman you have taken from the enemy camp. She tells me that the human saved your life. We are grateful, of course.

He could go no further. He wanted to write, *Why? Why? Don't you understand what we're fighting for?* He wanted to ask why victory had come to smell like failure and defeat.

Sithas crumpled up the parchment and hurled it into the fireplace. The realization hit him brutally.

He no longer had anything to say to his brother.

❧ 27 ❧

Early Winter, last day of 2213 (PC)

The blizzard swept over the iceberg-dotted ocean and around the snow-swept flanks of the Kharolis Mountains. It roared over the plains, making life a bitter and icy nightmare for the armies of both sides.

Those forces—human, elven, and dwarven—ceased all maneuvers and combat. Wherever the blast caught them, the brigades and regiments of the Wildrunners sought what little shelter they could and made quarters for the winter. Their Ergothian enemies, in even smaller bands, occupied towns, farm outposts, and wilderness camps in a desperate attempt to shelter themselves from nature's onslaught.

The Windriders, together with a large detachment of the dwarven legion, were more fortunate. Their camp occupied the barns and cabins of a huge farm, abandoned by its human tenants during the rout of the Ergothian Army. Here they found livestock for the griffons and bins of grain from which elven and dwarven cooks prepared a hard bread that, while bland and tough, would sustain the troops for several months.

The rest of Kith-Kanan's army occupied a multitude of camps, more than forty, across an arc of the plains stretching some five hundred miles.

On this brutally cold day, Kith made an inspection of the Windriders' camp. He pulled his woolen scarf closer about his face. It wouldn't entirely block the wind, but perhaps it would keep his ears from becoming frostbitten. In a few minutes, he would reach the shelter of the dwarven lodge, where he would meet with Dunbarth. After that, the warm fire of his own house . . . and Suzine.

The Wildrunners had succeeded in driving the remnants of the Ergothian Army hundreds of miles to the west. Throughout the campaign, Suzine had ridden with Kith on his griffon and lain with him in his tent. Zestful and hardy in a way that was unlike elven females, Suzine had adopted his life as her own and made no complaints about fighting conditions or the vicissitudes of weather.

The Army of Ergoth had left thousands of corpses behind on the plains. The bravest of the human warriors had taken shelter in tracts of forestland, where the Windriders couldn't pursue. Most of their fellows streamed home to Daltigoth. But these stubborn remnants, mostly light horsemen from the northern wing of the Ergothian Army, fought and held out.

Trapped within the forests, the horsemen couldn't use their strengths of speed and surprise. Out of necessity, the human army began waging a relentless campaign of guerrilla warfare, striking in small groups, then falling back to the woods. Ironically the elves among them had proven particularly adept at organizing and utilizing these scattershot tactics.

After months of hard pursuit and small victories in countless skirmishes, Kith-Kanan was preparing for a sweeping attack that might have expelled the hated enemy from the elven lands altogether. The Wildrunner infantry had assembled, ready to drive into the tracts of forest and expunge the Ergothian troops. Elven cavalry and the Windriders would fall upon them after they were forced into the open.

Then the early blows of winter had paralyzed military operations.

In his heart, the elven general felt scant disappointment that circumstances would force him to remain in the field at least until spring. He was content in the large, well-heated cottage that he had requisitioned, his due as commander. He was content in the arms of Suzine. How she had changed his life, revitalized him, given him a sense of being that extended beyond the present! It was ironic, he reflected, that it was war between their people that had brought them together.

The long, low shape of the dwarven lodge emerged before him, and he knocked on the heavy wooden door, setting aside thoughts of his woman until later. The portal swung open, and he stepped into the dim, cavelike log house that the dwarves had erected as their winter shelter. The temperature, while warmer than the outside air, was quite a bit cooler than that which was maintained in the elven shelters.

"Come in, General!" boomed Dunbarth, amid a crowd of his veterans gathered around a platform in the middle of the lodge.

Two nearly naked dwarves gasped for breath on the stage before hurling themselves at each other. One of them swiftly picked his opponent up and flipped him over his shoulder, whereupon the dwarven crowd erupted into cheers and boos. More than a few pouches, bulging with gold and silver coins, changed hands.

"At least you don't lack for diversion," remarked Kith-Kanan with a smile, settling beside the dwarf commander at a low bench that several other dwarves had swiftly vacated for him.

Dunbarth chuckled. "It'll do until we can get back to the *real* war. Here, I've had some wine heated for you."

"Thanks." Kith took the proffered mug while Dunbarth hefted a foaming tankard of ale. How the dwarves, who marched with a relatively small train of supplies, maintained a supply of the bitter draft was a mystery to Kith, yet every time he visited this winter shelter he found them drinking huge quantities of the stuff.

"And how do our elven comrades weather the storm?" inquired the dwarven commander.

"As well as could be expected. The griffons seem unaffected for the most part, while the Windriders and other elves have sufficient shelter. It could be a long winter."

"Aye. It could be a long war, too." Dunbarth made the remark in a lighthearted tone, but Kith-Kanan didn't think he was joking.

"I don't think so," the elf countered. "We have the remnants of the humans trapped to the west. Surely they can't move any more than we can in the midst of this storm!"

The dwarf nodded in silent agreement, so the elf continued. "As soon as the worst of the winter passes, we'll head into the attack. It shouldn't take more than two months to push the whole mass of them off the plains and back within the borders of Ergoth where they belong!"

"I hope you're right," replied the dwarven general sincerely. "Yet I'm worried about their commander, this Giarna. He's a resourceful devil!"

"I can handle Giarna!" Kith's voice was almost a growl, and Dunbarth looked at him in surprise.

"Any word from your brother?" inquired the dwarf after a moment's pause.

"Not since the storm set in."

"Thorbardin is disunited," reported his companion. "The Theiwar agitate for a withdrawal of dwarven troops, and it seems they might be winning the Daergar Clan over to their side."

"No wonder, with their own 'hero' joining ranks with the Army of Ergoth!" The reports had been confirmed in late autumn: After Sithas had driven him from Silvanost, Than-Kar had delivered his battalion over to General Giarna. The Theiwar dwarves had helped protect the retreating army during the last weeks of the campaign before winter had stopped all action.

"A shameful business, that," agreed Dunbarth. "The lines of battle may be clear on the field, but in the minds of our people, they begin to grow very hazy indeed."

"Do you need anything here?" inquired Kith-Kanan.

"You wouldn't have a hundred bawdy dwarven wenches, would you?" asked Dunbarth with a sly grin. He winked at the elf. "Though perhaps they would merely sap our fighting spirits. One has to be careful, you know!"

Kith laughed, suddenly embarassed about his own circumstances. The presence of Suzine in his house was common knowledge throughout the camp. He felt no shame about that, and he knew his troops liked the human woman and that she returned their obvious affection. Still, the thought of her being regarded as his "bawdy wench" he found disturbing.

They talked for a while longer of the pleasures of homecomings and of adventures in more peaceful times. The storm continued unabated, and finally Kith-Kanan remembered that he needed to finish his rounds before returning to his own house. He bade his farewells and continued his inspection of the other elven positions before turning toward his cottage.

His heart rose at the prospect of seeing Suzine again, though he had been gone from her presence for mere hours. He couldn't bear the thought of this winter camp without her. But he wondered about the men. Did they see her as a "wench" as Dunbarth seemed to? As some sort of camp follower? The thought would not go away.

A bodyguard, an immaculate corporal in the armor of the House Protectorate, threw open the door of his house as he approached. Kith quickly went inside, enjoying the warmth that caressed him as he shook off his snow-covered garb.

He passed through the guardroom—once the parlor of the house, but now the garrison for a dozen men-at-arms, those trusted with the life of the army commander. He nodded at the elves, all of whom had snapped to attention, but he quickly passed through the room into the smaller chambers beyond, closing the interior door behind him.

A crackling blaze filled the fireplace before him, and the aroma of sizzling beef teased his nostrils. Suzine came into his arms and he felt completely alive. Everything would wait until the delights of reunion had run their course. Without speaking, they went to the hearth and lay down before the fire.

Only afterward did they slowly break the spell of their silence.

"Did you find Arcuballis in the pasture?" Suzine asked, lazily tracing a finger along Kith-Kanan's bare arm.

"Yes. He seems to prefer the open field to the barn," the elf replied. "I tried to coax him into a stall, but he stayed outside, weathering the storm."

"He's too much like his master," the human woman said tenderly. Finally she rose and fetched a jug of wine that she had warmed by the fireplace. Huddled together under a bearskin, they each enjoyed a glass.

"It's odd," said Kith-Kanan, his mood reflective. "These are the most peaceful times I've ever spent, here beside the fire with you."

"It's not odd," replied the woman. "We were meant to know peace together. I've seen it, *known* it, for years."

Kith didn't dispute her. She had told him how she used to watch him in the mirror, the enchanted glass that she had crashed over Giarna's skull to save his life. She carried the broken shards of the glass in a soft leather box. He knew that she had seen the griffons before the battle yet hadn't told her commander about this crucial fact. Often he had wondered what could have made her take such a risk for one—an enemy!—she had met only once before.

Yet as the weeks became months, he had ceased to ask these questions, sensing—as did Suzine—the rightness of their lives together. She brought to him a comfort and serenity that he thought had been gone forever. With her, he felt a completeness that he had never before attained, not with Anaya nor Hermathya.

That she was a human seemed astonishingly irrelevant to Kith. He knew that the folk of the plains, be they elf or dwarf or human, had begun to see the war break the barriers of racial purity that had so long obsessed them. He wondered, for a brief moment, whether the elves of Silvanost would ever be able to appreciate the good humans, people like Suzine.

A schism was growing, he knew, among his folk. It divided the nation just as certainly as it would inevitably divide his brother and himself. Kith-Kanan had made up his mind which side he was on, and in that decision, he knew that he had crossed a line.

This woman with him now, her head resting so softly upon his shoulder, deserved more than to be considered a general's "bawdy wench." Perhaps the fumes from the fire wafted too thickly through the room, muddling his thoughts. Or perhaps their isolation here on the far frontiers of the kingdom brought home to Kith the truly important things in his life.

In any event, he made up his mind. Slowly he turned, feeling her stir against his side. Sleepily she opened an eye, brushing aside her red hair to smile at him.

"Will you become my wife?" asked the general of the army.

"Of course," replied his human woman.

PART IV:

KINSLAYER

✒ 28 ✒

from *The River of Time,*
the Great Scroll of Astinus,
Master Historian of Krynn

The Kinslayer War spewed blood across the plainslands for nearly forty years. It was a period of long, protracted battles, of vast interludes of retrenchment, of starvation, disease, and death. Savage blizzards froze the armies camped in winter, while fierce storms—lightning, hail, and cyclonic winds—ripped capriciously through the ranks of both sides during the spring season.

From the historian's perspective, there is a dreary sameness to the war. Kith-Kanan's Wildrunners pursued the humans, attacked them, seemed to wipe them out, and then even more humans took the places of the slain.

General Giarna maintained complete control of the Ergothian troops, and though his losses were horrendous, he bore them without regret. The pressure of his sudden attacks chipped away at the elves, while reinforcements balanced out the general's losses. A stalemate evolved, with the forces of Silvanesti winning every battle, but with the humans always averting complete defeat.

Despite this monotonous pattern, the course of the war had several key junctures. The Siege of Sithelbec must be considered a decisive hour. It seemed the last chance for General Giarna to attain an undiluted victory. But the Battle of Sithelbec turned the tide and will always be ranked among the turning points of the history of Krynn.

Throughout, the life of one individual best illustrates the tragedy and the inevitability of the Kinslayer War. This is the human wife of Kith-Kanan, Suzine des Quivalin.

Relative of the great Emperor Quivalin V, as well as his heirs (a total of three Quivalin rulers presided over the war), her presence in the army of her nation's enemy served to solidify the human resolve. Disowned by her monarch, sentenced in absentia to hang by her former lover, General Giarna, she took to the elven cause with steadfast loyalty.

For over thirty-five years, the greater part of her life, she remained true to her husband, first as his lover and later as his companion and adviser, always as his wife. She was never accepted by the elves of Silvanesti; her husband's brother never even acknowledged her existence. She bore Kith-Kanan two children, and the half-elves were raised as elves among the clans of the Wildrunners.

Yet the elven army, like its society, changed over the years. Even as human blood entered the royal elven veins, the human presence came to be accepted as a part of the Wildrunner force. The pure racial lines of the eastern elves became irrelevant in the mixed culture of the west. Even as they fought for the cause of Silvanesti, Kith-Kanan's elves lost the distinction of the war's purpose as seen by Sithas.

And the battles raged on and seemingly built to an inevitable climax, only to have the elusive moment of decision once again slip out of reach.

Beyond these key moments, however, and certainly surpassing them in oddity, was the peculiar end of the war itself. . . .

❧ 29 ❧

Early Spring, Year of the Cloud Giant, 2177 (PC)

The sprig that had once made such a proud sapling now towered over Kith-Kanan, a stalwart oak of some sixty feet in height. He gazed at it but could summon little emotion. He found that the memory of Anaya had faded over the distance of time. Nearly four decades of combat, of battles against the elusive armies of Ergoth, had worn away at his life. It seemed that treasured thoughts of a time before the war had been the first memories to disappear. Mackeli and Anaya might have been aquaintances of a friend, elves he had heard described and seen illustrated but had never actually met.

Even Suzine. He had a hard time now remembering her as she used to be. Her hair, in earlier days lush and fiery red, was now thin and white. Once supple grace had become slow and awkward movement, her once beautiful young body arthritic and stiff. Her sight and hearing had begun to fail. While he, with his elven longevity, was still a young adult, she had become an elderly woman.

He had flown here early this morning, partly in order to avoid her—to avoid all of those who gathered at the forest camp, an hour's flight by griffon from here, for the war conference. This was the eighth such council between himself and his brother. They met about once every five years. Most of the gatherings occurred, like this one, halfway between Silvanost and Silthelbec. Kith-Kanan couldn't bear the thought of returning to the elven capital, and Sithas preferred to avoid a journey all the way to the war zone.

These quintennial conferences had begun as grand outings, an opportunity for the general and his family, together with his most trusted captains, to embark on a journey away from the tedious rigors of war. By now, they were anathema to Kith, as predictable in their own way as the battlefield.

His brother's family and retinue had made an art out of shunning the human woman whom Kith-Kanan had married. Suzine was always invited to the banquets and feasts and celebrations. Once there, however, she was pointedly ignored. Some elves, such as his mother, Nirakina, had defied the trend, showing kindness and courtesy to Kith's wife. Nirakina's husband of the past thirty years, Tamanier Ambrodel, who came from the plainslands himself, tried to lessen the prejudice that fell upon her.

But Hermathya and Quimant and the others had shown her only contempt, and over the years, Suzine had tired of facing their antagonism. Now she avoided the large gatherings, though she still traveled with Kith-Kanan to the conference site.

Kith looked away from the tree, as if guilty about his thoughts, which now turned to his children. Suzine had borne him two half-elves, and he knew that they should bring him joy.

Ulvian, son of Kith-Kanan! That one, it would seem, was destined to rule some day. Was he not the eldest son of the elven hero who had led his army faithfully for all the years of the Kinslayer War? Despite the rapid growth to adult-hood that was a mark of his half-human ancestry, how could he fail to show the wisdom and bravery that had been his father's traits of survival for all these years? So far, those traits hadn't been evident. The lad showed a lack of ambition bordering on indolence, and his arrogant and supercilious nature had alienated anyone who had tried to be his friend.

Or Verhanna, his daughter. Blessed image of her mother? She was in danger of becoming, with her constant tantrums and her litany of rude demands, a living reminder of the divisive war that had become a way of life for him and for all of the elven peoples.

The Kinslayer War. How many families had been divided by death or betrayal? No longer was this a war between elves and humans, if it had ever been that. The population of Silvanesti couldn't support the level of warfare, so now, in addition to the stalwart dwarves, huge companies of human mercenaries fought alongside his Wildrunners. They were well paid for serving the elven standards.

At the same time, many elves, especially the Kagonesti, driven from the nation by the demanding decrees of the Speaker of the Stars, had fled to the human banner. Dwarves, particularly of the Theiwar and Daergar clans, had also enlisted to serve the Emperor of Ergoth.

This was a strange admixture of alliances. How often had elf slain elf, human fought human, or dwarf butchered dwarf? Each battle brought new atrocities, as likely as not visited by fighters of one race against enemies of the same background.

The war, once fought along clear and precise lines, had become an endlessly feeding monster, for the numberless enemy seemed willing to pay any price to win, and the skilled and valiant troops of Kith-Kanan purchased victory after victory on scores of battlefields with the precious coin of their own blood. Yet ultimate victory—a settlement of the war itself—remained elusive.

With a sigh, Kith-Kanan rose to his feet and crossed wearily to Arcuballis. He would have to get back to the camp, he knew. The conference was due to begin in an hour. The griffon leaped into the sky while the rider mused sadly about the time when his life had been shadowed by the growth of a tree in the forest.

* * * * *

"We have chased the humans across the plains every summer! We kill a thousand of them, and five thousand come to take their places!" Kith-Kanan loudly complained about the frustrating cycle of events.

Sithas, Lord Quimant, and Tamanier Ambrodel had come from the capital city to attend this council. For his part, Kith-Kanan had brought Parnigar and Dunbarth Ironthumb on his journey across the plains. Other members of their respective parties—including Hermathya, Nirakina, Suzine, and Mari, Parnigar's newest human wife—now enjoyed the shade of awnings and trees around the fringes of the great meadow where they camped.

Meanwhile, the two delegations engaged in heated discussion within an enclosed tent in the middle of the clearing. Two dozen guards stood, out of earshot, around the shelter.

The most savage of the spring storms were still some weeks away, but a steady drizzle soaked the tent and added to the gray futility of the mood.

"We crush an army in battle, and another army marches at us from another direction. They know they cannot defeat us, yet they keep trying! What kind of creatures are they? If they kill five of my Windriders at the cost of a thousand of their own soldiers, they hail it as a victory!"

Kith-Kanan shook his head, knowing that it *was* a human victory whenever his griffon cavalry lost even one precious body. The Windriders numbered a bare hundred and fifty stalwart veterans now, scarcely a third of their original number. There were no more griffons to ride, nor trained elven warriors to mount them. Yet the tide of humans flowing across the plains seemed to grow thicker every year.

"What kind of beings *are* these that they could spill so much blood, lose so many lives, and still carry forward their war?" Sithas demanded, exasperated. Even after forty years of warfare, the Speaker of the Stars couldn't fathom the motivations of the humans or their various allies.

"They breed like rabbits," observed Quimant. "We have no hope of matching their numbers, and our treasury runs dry simply to maintain the troops that we have."

"Knowing that this is true and doing something about it are two different things," Sithas retorted.

The council lapsed into glum silence. There was a depressing familiarity to their predicament. The national attrition caused by the war had become readily apparent thirty years earlier.

"The winter, at least, has been mild," suggested Parnigar, trying to improve their mood. "We lost very few casualties to cold or snow."

"Yes, but in the past, such winters have given us the heaviest spring storms!" answered Kith-Kanan. "And the summers are always bloody," he concluded.

"We could send peace feelers to the emperor," suggested Tamanier Ambrodel. "It may be that Quivalin the Seventh is more amenable than his father or grandfather."

Parnigar snorted. "He's been ruler for four years. In that time, we've seen, if anything, an increase in the pace of Ergoth's attacks! They butcher their prisoners. This past summer, they began poisoning wells wherever they passed. No, Quivalin the Seventh is no peacemonger."

"Perhaps it is not the emperor's true will," suggested Quimant, drawing another snort from Parnigar. "General Giarna has made an empire for himself of the battlefield. He would be reluctant to relinquish it—and what better way to sustain his power than to ensure that the war continues?"

"There *is* the matter of General Giarna," grunted Dunbarth, with an uncharacteristic scowl. "He presses forward with every opportunity, more brutal than ever. I don't think he'd desist even if given the order. War has become his life! It *sustains* him!"

"Surely after all these years . . . ?" Tamanier wondered.

"The man doesn't *age!* Our spies tell us he looks the same as he did forty years ago, and he has the vitality of a young man! His own troops hate and fear him, but there are worse ways to insure the obedience of your subordinates."

"We have taken the extreme step of sending assassins after him, a brigade comprised of humans and elves both." Kith related the tale of the assassination attempt. "None survived. From what we have pieced together, they reached Giarna in his tent. His personal security seemed lax. They attacked with daggers and swords but couldn't even injure him!"

"Surely that's an exaggeration," suggested his brother. "If they got that close, how could they not have been successful?"

"General Giarna has survived before, under circumstances where I would have expected him to die. He has been showered with arrows. Though his horse may be slain beneath him, he gets away on foot. He has fought his way out of deadly ambushes, leaving dozens of dead Wildrunners behind him."

"Something unnatural is at work there," pronounced Quimant. "It's dangerous to think of peace with such a creature."

"It is dangerous to *fight* such a creature as well," remarked Parnigar pointedly. Quimant understood the intent of the remark. Parnigar had done nearly a half century of fighting, after all, while Quimant's family had spent those years raking in a fortune in munitions profits. But the lord coolly ignored the warrior's provocation.

"We cannot talk of peace, yet!" emphasized Sithas. He turned to his brother. "We need something that will allow us to bargain from a position of strength."

"Do you mean to suggest that you'd be willing to bargain?" asked Kith-Kanan, surprised.

Sithas sighed. "You're right. You've all been right, but for years, I've refused to believe you. But it has begun to seem inconceivable that we can win a complete victory over the humans. Still, we cannot maintain this costly war forever!"

"I must inform you," interjected Dunbarth, clearing his throat. "Though I have stalled my king for several years now, his patience will not last forever. Already many dwarves are agitating for us to return home. You must realize that King Pandelthain is not so suspicious of humans as was King Hal-Waith."

And you, old friend—you deserve the chance to go home, to rest and retire. Kith-Kanan kept that thought to himself. Nevertheless, the changes wrought by age in Dunbarth were more apparent than any that were manifest in the elves. The dwarf's beard and hair were the color of silver. His once husky shoulders had a frail look to them, as if his body was a mere shell of its former self. The skin of his face was mottled and wrinkled.

Yet his eyes still shined with a merry light and keen perceptiveness. Now, as if he followed Kith's thoughts, he turned to the elven general and chuckled. "Tell 'em, young fellow. Tell 'em what we've got up our sleeves."

Kith nodded. The time was right.

"We have word that the humans are planning a trap against the Windriders. They will lure the griffons into an archery ambush. We want to amass the Wildrunners, using all the mercenaries, garrison forces, and dwarves—our entire army. We want to come at them from the north, east, and south. If we hit them hard and we keep the advantage of surprise, we'll achieve the kind of setback that will force them to the bargaining table."

"But Sithelbec—you'd leave the fortress unscreened?" Sithas asked. In the course of the Kinslayer War, the siege of those high palisades had become an epic tale, and a bustling military city had blossomed around the walls. The place had a tremendous symbolic as well as practical importance to the Silvanesti cause, and a sizable proportion of the Wildrunners were permanently garrisoned there.

"It's a risk," Kith-Kanan admitted. "We will move quickly, striking before the humans can learn our intentions. Then the Windriders will act as the bait of the trap, and while the enemy is distracted, we will strike."

"It's worth a try," urged Parnigar, supporting his general's plan. "We can't keep chasing shadows year after year!"

"Some shadows are more easily caught," observed Quimant acidly. "The human women, for example."

Parnigar leaped to his feet, knocking his chair over backward and lunging toward the lord.

"Enough!" The Speaker of the Stars reached out and pushed the warrior back toward his chair. Even in his rage, Parnigar heeded his ruler.

"Your insulting remark was uncalled for!" barked Kith-Kanan, staring at Quimant.

"True," Sithas agreed. "But neither would it be invited if you and your officers kept your loyalties a little more clear in your own heads!"

Kith-Kanan flushed with anger and frustration. Why did it always come down to this? He glared at Sithas as if his twin was a stranger.

A noise at the tent flap pulled their attention away from the conference. Vanesti, Ulvian, and Verhanna, the children of the royal twins, erupted into the tent with impertinent boldness. Hermathya followed.

Kith-Kanan met her eyes and froze, suddenly numb. By the gods, he had forgotten how beautiful she was! Furious and guilty, he nonetheless watched her furtively. She cast him a sideways glance, and as always, he saw the beckoning in her eyes. That only furthered his pain. Never again, he knew, would he betray his brother. And now there was the matter of his own wife.

"Uncle Kith!" Vanesti irritated his father by running directly to his uncle. The young elf stopped quickly and then pantomimed a formal bow.

"Come here. Stop acting like the court jester!" Kith swept his nephew into an embrace, keenly aware of the eyes of his own children upon him. Ulvian and Verhanna, though younger than Vanesti, had matured much more quickly because of their half-human blood. Already young adults, they looked disdainfully upon such adolescent outbursts of emotion.

Perhaps, too, they sensed the bitter contrast in their relationship with their own uncle. There had never been an "Uncle Sithas!" or a "Come here, children!" between them. They were half-human and consequently had no place in the Speaker's royal family.

Perhaps they understood, but they didn't forgive.

"This reminds me of a final matter for discussion," Sithas said stiffly. He relaxed when Vanesti left Kith's side to stand with Ulvian and Vehanna beside the open door flap of the tent.

"Vanesti is due to begin his training in the warrior arts. He has disdained the academies in the city and has prevailed upon me to make this request: Will you take him as your squire?"

For a moment, Kith-Kanan sat back, acutely aware of Vanesti's hopeful gaze. He couldn't suppress a surge of affection and pride. He liked the young elf and felt that he would be a good warrior—good at whatever he attempted, for that matter. Yet he couldn't entirely ignore another feeling.

The proposition reminded him of Ulvian. Kith had sent his son to Parnigar, as squire to that most able soldier. The young half-elf had proven so intractable and shiftless that, with deep regret, Parnigar had been forced to send him back to his father. The failure had stung Kith-Kanan far more than it had disturbed Ulvian.

Yet when he looked at the young form of Vanesti, so much like a younger version of Kith-Kanan himself, he knew what his answer must be.

"It would be my honor," Kith replied seriously.

* * * * *

The aging woman watched the image of the elf in the mirror. The glass was cracked and patched, with several slivers missing. It had, after all, been reconstructed from shards. Five years earlier, she had hired a legion of skilled elven artisans to take those broken pieces, guarded by Suzine for years, adding crafts of their own to restore the glass to some measure of its former power.

It seemed that, with the distance that had grown between herself and her husband, she had little left to do in life but observe the course of things around her. The mirror gave her the means to do so, without forcing her to leave her carriage and be exposed to the subtle humiliations of the Silvanesti elves.

Suzine flushed as she thought of Hermathya and Quimant, whose cutting remarks had hurt her decades earlier when she had allowed them to penetrate her emotions. Yet even those barbs had been easier to take than the aloof silence of Sithas, her own brother-in-law, who had barely acknowledged her existence!

Of course, there was goodness to be found in elvenkind, too. There was Nirakina, who had always treated her as a daughter, and Tamanier Ambrodel, who had offered friendship. But now age had impaired even those relationships. How could she feel like a daughter to Nirakina when the four-centuries old elfwoman seemed like a spry young woman beside the aging Suzine? And her hearing made conversation difficult, so that even Tamanier Ambrodel had to shout his remarks, often repeating them two or three times. She found it less embarrassing to simply avoid these two good souls.

So she remained in this enclosed coach that Kith-Kanan had given her. The large vehicle was comfortably appointed, even to the point of containing a soft bed—a bed that was always hers alone.

For what must have been the millionth time, she wondered about the course her life had taken, about the love she had developed for an elf who would inevitably outlive her by centuries. She couldn't regret that decision. Her years of happiness with Kith-Kanan had been the finest of her life. But those years were gone, and if she didn't regret her choice of nearly four decades earlier, neither could she bury the unhappiness that was now her constant companion.

Her children were no comfort. Ulvian and Verhanna seemed embarrassed by their mother's humanness and shunned her, pretending to be full-blooded elves insofar as they could. But she felt pity for them as well, for their father had never shown them the affection that would have been due his proper heirs—as if he himself was secretly ashamed of their mixed racial heritage.

Now that she was too old to ride a horse, her husband carted her around in this carriage. She felt like so much baggage, a cargo that Kith-Kanan was determined to see properly delivered before he proceeded with the rest of his life. How long could she remain like this? What could she do to change her lot in her waning years?

Her mind drifted to the enemy—to her husband's enemy and her own. General Giarna frightened her now more than ever before. Often she had observed him in the repaired glass, shocked by the youthful appearance and vigor of the man. She sensed in him the power of something much deeper than she had first suspected.

Often she remembered the way Giarna had slain General Barnet. It was as if he had sucked the life out of him, she remembered thinking. That, she now knew, was exactly what he had done. How many more lives had the Boy General claimed over the years? What was the true cost of his youthfulness?

Her mind and her mirror drifted back to Kith-Kanan. She saw him in the conference. He was close enough to her that she could see him very clearly indeed. The elf's image grew large in her mirror, and then she looked into his eyes, *through* his eyes. She stared, as she had learned to do years before, into his subconscious.

She looked past the war, the constant fear that she found within him, to gentler things. She sought the image of his three women, for she was used to seeing the elfwomen Anaya and Hermathya there. Suzine sought the image of herself—herself as a young woman, alluring and sensual. That image had grown more difficult to find of late, and this added to her sorrow.

This time she could find no remembrance of herself. Even the spritely Anaya was gone, her image replaced by the picture of a tall, slender tree. Then she came upon Hermathya and sensed the desire in Kith's mind. It was a new sensation that suddenly caused the mirror to glow, until Suzine turned her face away. The mirror faded into darkness as tears filled her eyes.

Slowly, gently, she placed the mirror back into its case. Trying to stem the trembling of her hands, she looked about for her coachman. Kith-Kanan wouldn't return for several hours, she knew.

When he did, she would be gone.

🍃 30 🍃

midspring, 2177 (pc)

The lord-major-chieftain supreme of hillrock stretched his brawny arms, acutely aware that his muscles were not so supple as they had once been. Placing a huge hand to his head, he stroked blunt fingers through hair that seemed to grow thinner by the week.

Squinting against the setting sun, he looked about his pastoral community of large one-room dwellings hewn from the rock of this sheltered valley. To the east towered the heights of the Khalkist Mountains, while to the west, the range settled into the flatlands of the Silvanesti plain.

For three decades, he had ruled as lord-major-chieftain supreme, and they had been good years for all of his people. Good years, but past now. Poking his broad tongue against the single tooth that jutted proudly from his lower gum, the lord-major exercised his mind by attempting to ponder the future.

A nagging urge tugged at him, desirous of pulling him away from peaceful Hillrock. He couldn't put his finger on the reasons, but the hill giant who had once been called One-Tooth now felt a need to leave, to strike out across those plains. He was reluctant to answer this compulsion, for he had the feeling that once he left, he would never return. He couldn't understand this compulsion, but it grew more persistent every day.

Finally the hill giant gathered his wives together, cuffing and cursing them until he had their attention.

"I go away!" he said loudly.

The formalities completed, he hefted his club and started down the valley. Whatever the nature of the longing that drew him to the plains, he knew that he would find its source in an elf who had once been his friend.

*　*　*　*　*

The conference broke up in awkward farewells. Only Hermathya displayed emotion, screaming and rebuking Sithas for his decision to send Vanesti to the battlefield. The Speaker of the Stars coolly ignored his wife, and she collapsed into spasms of weeping. She desperately hugged the young elf, to his acute embarrassment, and then retired to her coach for the long journey back to Silvanost.

Few had noted Suzine's departure late on the previous day. Kith-Kanan was puzzled by her leaving, though he assumed she had reason to return to Sithelbec. In truth, he was also a little relieved. The presence of his human wife put strain on any communication with Sithas, and Suzine's absence had made the subdued farewell banquet a little easier to endure.

Still, it was unlike her to depart so abruptly without advising him, so he couldn't totally banish his concern. This concern mounted to genuine anxiety when, ten days later, they finally arrived at the fortress and learned that the general's wife hadn't been seen. Nor had she sent any message.

He dispatched Windriders to comb the plains, seeking a

sign of Suzine's grand coach. However, true to Kith's prediction, the spring storm season began early, and thunderstorms blanketed the grasslands with hail and torrential rains. Winds howled unchecked across hundreds of miles of prairie. The search became all but impossible and had to be suspended for all intents and purposes.

In the meantime, Kith-Kanan threw himself into the choreography of his great battle plan. The forces of the Wildrunners mustered at Sithelbec, preparing to march westward, where they would hit the human army before General Giarna even realized they had left the region of the fortress.

Intelligence about the enemy was scarce and unreliable. Finally Kith called upon the only scout he could count on to make a thorough reconnaissance: Parnigar.

"Take two dozen riders and get as close as you can," ordered Kith-Kanan, knowing full well that he was asking his old friend to place his life at grave risk. But he had no real alternative.

If the veteran resented the difficult order, he didn't let on. "I'll try to get out and back quickly," he replied. "We want to get the campaign off to an early start."

"Agreed," Kith noted. "And be careful. I'd rather see you come back empty-handed than to not come back at all!"

Parnigar grinned, then grew suddenly serious. "Has there been any word about—I should say 'from'—Suzine?"

Kith sighed. "Not a thing. It's as if the world gobbled her up. She slipped away from the conference that afternoon. I brought Vanesti back to the camp as my squire and found her gone."

"These damned storms will run their course in another few weeks," said the scout, "but I doubt you'll be able to send fliers out before then. No doubt she's holed up safe on some farmstead. . . . "

But his words lacked conviction. Indeed, Kith-Kanan had lost optimism and didn't know what to believe anymore. All indications were that Suzine had left the camp of her own free will. Why? And why wasn't he more upset?

"You mentioned your squire." Parnigar smoothly changed the subject. "How's the young fellow working out?"

"He's eager, I've got to grant him that. My armor hasn't gleamed like this in years!"

"When we march . . . ?"

"He'll have to come along," Kith replied. "But I'll keep him to the rear. He doesn't have enough experience to let him near the fighting."

"Aye," grunted the old warrior before disappearing into the storm.

* * * * *

"This will do, driver. I shall proceed on foot."

"Milady?" The coachman, as he opened the door for Suzine, looked at her in concern. "The Army of Ergoth has scouts all over here," he said. "They'll find you for sure."

I'm counting on that. Suzine didn't verbalize her reply. "Your dedication is touching, but, really, I'll be fine."

"I think the general would be—"

"The general will not be displeased," she said firmly.

"Very well." His reluctance was plain in his voice, but he assisted her in stepping to the ground. The carriage rested at the side of a muddy trail. Several wide pathways led into the woods around them.

She was grateful for the smoothness of the trail. Neither her eyes nor her legs were up to a rigorous hike. She turned toward the coachman who had carried her so faithfully across the plains for more than a week. Her mirror, now resting in the box on her belt, had shown her where to go, allowing her to guide them around outposts of human pickets. The only other possession she carried was in a pouch at her belt: a narrow-bladed knife. She wouldn't be coming back, but she couldn't tell the driver that.

"Wait here for two hours," she said. "I'll be back by then. I know these woods well. There are some old sights I would like to see."

Nodding and scowling, the driver climbed back onto his seat and watched until the woods swallowed her up. She hurried along the trail as fast as her aging legs would carry her, but even so, it took her more than an hour to cover two miles. She moved unerringly past many forks in the path, certain that the mirror had shown her the right way.

Shortly after she passed the end of her second mile, an armored crossbowman stepped into the path before her.

"Halt!" he cried, leveling his weapon. At the same time, he gaped in astonishment at the lone old woman who approached the headquarters of the Army of Ergoth.

"I'm glad you are here to greet me," she said pleasantly. "Take me to see General Giarna."

"You want to see the general?"

"We're . . . old friends."

Shaking his head in amazement, the guard nevertheless led Suzine a short way farther down the trail, entering a small clearing. The top of the meadow was almost completely enclosed by a canopy of tall elms—protection against detection from the air, Suzine knew.

"The general's in there." The man gestured to a small cottage near the clearing's edge. Two men-at-arms flanked the doorway, and they snapped to attention as Suzine walked up to them.

"She wants to see the general," explained the crossbowman, with a shrug.

"Should we search her?" The question, from a muscular halberdier, sent a shiver down Suzine's stooped spine. She felt acutely conscious of the dagger in her pouch.

"That won't be necessary." Suzine recognized the deep voice from within the cottage. The watchmen stood aside, allowing Suzine to step through the door.

"You have come back to me."

For a moment, Suzine stood still, blinking and trying to see in the dim light. Then the large black-cloaked figure moved toward her, and she knew him—knew his sight, his smell, and his intimidating presence.

With a sense of dull wonder, she realized that the tales she had heard, the images of her mirror, were all true. General Giarna stood before her now. She knew that he must be at least seventy years old, but *he looked the same as he had forty years earlier!*

He stepped closer to her. She felt the revulsion and fear she had known forty years earlier when he had approached her, had *used* her. Slowly her fingers closed around the weapon in her pouch. The man loomed over her, looking down with a slightly patronizing smile. She stared into his eyes and saw that same hollowness, the same sense of *void*, that she remembered with such vivid terror.

Then she pulled out the knife and threw back her arm. Why is he laughing? She wondered about that even as she drove the point of the weapon toward the unarmored spot at his throat. Giarna made no attempt to block her thrust.

The blade struck his skin but snapped as the weapon broke at the hilt. The useless shard of metal fell to the floor as Suzine blinked, incredulous.

General Giarna's throat showed not the tiniest hint of a wound.

* * * * *

It wasn't until Parnigar returned with his company of scouts that Kith-Kanan received any vital information regarding the enemy's positions. Wearing sodden trail clothes from the nine-day reconnaissance, the veteran captain reported to Kith-Kanan as soon as he returned to the fort.

"We pushed at the fringes of their position," he reported. "Their pickets were as thick as flies on a dead horse. They got two of my scouts, and the rest of us barely slipped out of their grasp."

Kith shook his head, wincing. Even after forty years of war, the death of each elf under his command struck him like a personal blow.

"We couldn't get into the main camp," explained Parnigar. "There were just too many guards. But judging by the density of their patrols, I have to conclude they were guarding the main body of Giarna's force."

"Thanks for taking the risk, my friend," said Kith-Kanan finally. "Too many times I have asked you."

Parnigar smiled wearily. "I'm in this fight to the end—one way or another!" The lanky warrior cleared his throat hesitatantly. "There's . . . something else."

"Yes?"

"We found the Lady Suzine's coachman on the outskirts of the human lines."

Kith-Kanan looked up in sudden fear. "Was he—is he alive?"

"Was." Parnigar shook his head. "He'd been taken by

their pickets, then escaped after a fight. Badly wounded in the stomach, but he made it to the trail. We found him there."

"What did he tell you?"

"He didn't know where she was. He had dropped her beside the trail, and she followed a path into the woods. We checked out the area. Guards were thicker than ever there, so I think the headquarters must have been somewhere nearby."

Could she be heading back to Giarna? Kith-Kanan sensed Parnigar's unspoken question. Surely she wouldn't betray Kith-Kanan.

"Can you show me where this place is?" asked the elven commander urgently.

"Of course."

Kith sighed sympathetically. "I'm sorry that you must travel again so quickly, but perhaps . . ."

Parnigar waved off the explanation. "I'll be ready to ride when you need me."

"Go to your quarters now. Mari's been waiting for you for days," Kith-Kanan ordered, realizing that Parnigar still dripped from his drenched garments. "She's probably got dry clothes all ready to get you dressed."

"I doubt she wants to *dress* me!" Parnigar chuckled knowingly.

"Off to your wife now, before she grows old on you!" Kith's attempt at humor felt lame to both of them, though Parnigar forced a chuckle as he left.

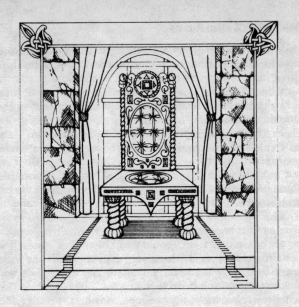

✎ 31 ✎

Late Spring, Silvanost

Hermathya looked at herself in the mirror. She was beautiful and she was young . . . yet for what purpose? She was alone.

Tears of bitterness welled in her eyes. She rose and whirled away from her table, only to be confronted by her bed. That canopied, quilted sleeping place mocked her every bit as harshly as did the mirror. For decades, it had been hers alone.

Now even her child had been sent away. Her anger throbbed as hot as ever, the same rage that had turned the two-week journey back to the city into a silent ordeal for Sithas. He endured her fury and didn't let it bother him, and Hermathya knew that he had won.

Vanesti was gone, serving beside his uncle on the front lines of danger! *How* could her husband have done this? What kind of perverse cruelty would cause him to torture his wife so? She thought of Sithas as a stranger. What little closeness they had once enjoyed had been worn thin by the stresses of war.

Her thoughts abruptly wandered to Kith-Kanan. How much like Sithas he looked—and yet how very different he was! Hermathya looked back upon the passion of their affair as one of the bright moments of her life. Before her name had been uttered as the prospective bride of the future Speaker of the Stars, her life had been a passionate whirl.

Then the announcement had come—Hermathya, daughter of the Oakleaf Clan, would wed Sithas of Silvanos! She remembered how Kith-Kanan had begged—he had *begged!*—her to accompany him, to run away. She had laughed at him as if he were mad.

Yet the madness, it now seemed, was hers. Prestige and station and comfort meant nothing, she knew, not when compared to the sense of happiness that she had thrown away.

The one time since then when Kith-Kanan and she had come together illicitly flared brightly in her mind. That episode had never been repeated because Kith-Kanan's guilt wouldn't allow it. He had avoided her for years and was awkward when they were brought together through necessity.

Shaking her head, she fought back the tears. Sithas was in the palace. Hermathya would go to him and make him bring their son back home!

She found her husband in his study, perusing a document with the Oakleaf stamp, in gold, at the top. He looked up when she entered, and blinked with surprise.

"You must call Vanesti back," she blurted, staring at him.

"I will not!"

"Can't you understand what he means to me?" Hermathya fought to keep her voice under control. "I *need* him here with me. He's all I've got!"

"We've been over this. It will do the lad good to get out of the palace, to live among the troops! Besides, Kith will take good care of him. Don't you trust him?"

"Do *you*?" Hermathya uttered the insinuation without thinking.

"Why? What do you mean?" There had been something in her tone. Sithas leapt from his chair and stared at her accusingly.

She turned away, suddenly calm. She controlled the discussion now.

"What did you mean, do *I* trust him?" Sithas's voice was level and cold. "Of course I do!"

"You have been gullible before."

"I know that you loved him," the Speaker added. "I know of your affair before our marriage. I even know that he pleaded with you to go with him when he flew into exile."

"I should have gone!" she cried, whirling suddenly.

"Do you still love him?"

"No." She didn't know whether this was a lie or not. "But he loves me."

"That's nonsense!"

"He came to me in my bedroom long ago. He didn't leave until the morning." She lied about the room because it suited her purpose. Her husband wouldn't know that it was *she* who had gone to *him*.

Sithas stepped closer to her. "Why should I believe you?"

"Why should I lie?"

His open hand caught her across the cheek with a loud smack. The force of his blow sent her tumbling backward to the floor. With a burning face, she stood up, her eyes spitting fire at him.

"Vanesti will stay on the plains," Sithas declared as she turned and fled. He turned to the window, numb, and stared to the west. He wondered about the stranger his brother had become.

* * * * *

"You believed that you could come here to *kill* me?" General Giarna looked at Suzine with mild amusement. The old woman backed against the closed door of his cottage. She had picked up the broken blade of her knife, but the weapon felt useless and futile, for it couldn't harm her enemy.

Thunder rumbled outside as another storm swept across the camp.

"Your death would be the greatest thing that could happen to Krynn!" She spoke bravely, but her mind was locked by fear. How could she have been so stupid as to come here alone, thinking she could harm this brutal warrior? Instead, she had become his prisoner.

Her heart quailed as she remembered the man's dark tortures, his means of gaining information from his captives. And no captive had ever possessed such valuable information as the wife of his chief enemy.

Now the general laughed heartily, placing his hands on his hips and leaning backward like a young man. "My death, you should know, is not so easily attained."

Suzine stared at him.

"Do you remember the last night of General Barnet?"

She would never forget that awful, shriveled corpse, cast aside by General Giarna like an empty shell, drained of all its life.

"My powers come from places you cannot *begin* to understand!"

He paced in agitation, looking at her.

"There are gods who care for people of power, gods whose names are only whispered in the dead of night, for fear of frightening the children!"

General Giarna whirled again, his brow furrowed in concentration. "There is Morgion, god of disease and decay. I tell you, he can be *bought*! I pay him in lives, and he saves his curse from my flesh! And there are others—Hiddukel, Sargonnas! And of course—" his voice dropped to a whisper; his body quivered, and he looked at Suzine—"the Queen of Darkness, Takhisis herself! They say that she is banished, but that's a lie. She is patient and she is generous. She bestows her powers on those who earn her favor!

"It is the power of *life*, in all its aspects! It allows me to be strong and young, while those around me grow old and die!"

Now he stared directly at her, and there seemed to be genuine anguish in his voice. "*You* might have shared this with me! You were a woman of power. You would have made a fitting partner for me! Who knows, one day we might have ruled Ergoth itself!"

"Your madness consumes you," Suzine replied.

"*It is not madness!*" he hissed. "*You* cannot kill me. No human can kill me! Nor a dwarf, nor an elf. *None* may slay me!"

General Giarna paced restlessly. A steady beat of rain suddenly began pounding on the roof, forcing him to raise his voice. "Not only do I remain young and vigorous, but I am also *invulnerable!*" He looked at her sideways, slyly. "I even had my men capture a griffon so that I might devour it and take over its aura. Now not even one of those beasts— the bane of this long war!—can claim my blood.

"But enough of this talk," said Giarna, suddenly rough. He took her arm and pulled her to a chair, throwing her into it.

"My spies tell me that the Wildrunners prepare an attack. They will move on my headquarters here because they have learned of our plans to ambush the griffons."

Suzine looked at him dumbly.

"No doubt you know the route of march they will take when they come west. You will tell me. Be sure of this, you *will* tell me. I will simply move my ambush and consummate the victory that has eluded me for so long."

Fear pulsed hotly in Suzine's mind. She did know! Many nights she had been present during battle planning between Parnigar and Kith-Kanan. The other officers had ignored her, assuming that she wasn't listening, but out of curiosity, she had paid attention and absorbed most of the details.

"The only question is"—Giarna's voice was a deep bass warning—"will you tell me now or afterward?"

Her mind focused with exceptional clarity. She heard the rain beating steadily against the wooden frame of the house. She thought of her children and her husband, and then she knew.

There *was* a way—an escape for her! But she had to act fast, before she had second thoughts.

Her bleeding fingers, still clutching the knife blade, jerked upward. Giarna saw the movement, an expression of mild annoyance flickering across his face. The crone already knew she couldn't harm him!

Him. In that instant, he recognized his mistake as the

keen edge sliced through Suzine's own neck. A shower of bright blood exploded from the torn artery, covering the general as the old woman slumped to the ground at his feet.

* * * * *

One-Tooth plodded through yet another thunderstorm. His march, already an epic by hill giant standards, had taken him through the foothills of his beloved mountains and across hundreds of miles of flatlands.

How did people ever *live* around here? He wondered at a life without the comforting rocky heights. He felt vulnerable and naked on these open prairies of grass.

Of course, his journey was made easier by the fact that such inhabitants as he encountered fled in panic at his approach, giving him a free sampling of whatever food had been bubbling on the stove or whatever milk might be chilling in the damp cellar.

The giant still didn't know why he had embarked upon this quest or what his ultimate destination would be. But his feet swung easily below him, and the miles continued to fall behind. He felt young again, more spry than he had in decades.

And he was propelled by an inchoate sense of destiny. When his march ended, that was where his destiny would be found.

🌿 32 🌿

One Week Later

Rain lashed at the griffon and its rider, but the pair pressed on through the storm. Though the day was hours old, the horizon around them remained twilit and dim, so heavy was the gray blanket of clouds. Arcuballis flew low, seeking a place to land, cringing still closer to the earth against sudden blasts of lightning that seemed to warn them from the sky.

Finally Kith-Kanan found it—the small house in the center of the farmstead, down the trail where the coachman had seen Suzine disappear. Parnigar had showed him the trail two miles back, but he had flown past the clearing twice. So closely entwined were the overhanging branches that he hadn't even noticed it.

The trailhead was more than two miles away, and she couldn't have walked much farther than this. Yet there seemed to be nothing else besides anonymous woods for several miles in all directions. This *had* to be the place.

Arcuballis dove quickly to earth, dropping like a stone between the limbs of the broad elms. The griffon landed in a crouch, and Kith's sword was in his hand.

The door to the small house stood partially open, slamming and banging against its frame as the wind gusts shifted direction. The yard around the house was churned to mud, mired by the hooves of countless horses. Blackened pits showed where great cookfires had blazed, but now these were simply holes filled with sodden ash.

Cautiously Kith-Kanan dismounted and approached the house. He pushed the door fully open and saw that it consisted of one main room—and that room was now a shambles. Overturned tables, broken chairs, a pile of discarded uniforms, and a collection of miscellaneous debris all contributed to the disarray.

He began to pick through debris, kicking things with his boots and moving big pieces with his free hand, always holding his longsword at the ready. He found little of worth until, near the back corner, his persistence was rewarded.

A tingle of apprehension ran along his spine as he uncovered a wooden box he recognized instantly, for it was the one Suzine had used to store her mirror. Kneeling, he pulled it from beneath a moldy saddle blanket. He opened the top, and his reflection stared back at him. The mirror had remained intact.

Then as he looked, the image in the glass grew pale and wavery, and suddenly the picture became something else entirely.

He saw a black-cloaked human riding a dark horse, leading a column of men through the rain. The human army was on the march. He could recognize no landmarks, no signposts in the murky scene. But he knew that the humans were moving.

Obviously the planned ambush of the Windriders was suspected and now would have to be cancelled. But where did the humans march? Kith had a sickening flash of Sithelbec, practically defenseless since most of the garrison had marched into the field with the Wildrunners. Could General Giarna be that bold?

A more hideous thought occurred to him. Had Suzine betrayed him, revealing their battle plans to the human commander? Did the enemy march somewhere unknown to set up a *new* ambush? He couldn't bring himself to believe this, yet neither could he ignore the evidence that she had been here at the human command post.

Where was Suzine? In his heart, he knew the answer.

Grimly he mounted Arcuballis and took off. He made his way back to the east, toward the spearhead of his army, which he had ordered to march westward in an attempt to catch the human army in its camp. Now he knew that he had to make new plans—and quickly.

It took two days of searching before the proud griffon finally settled to earth, in a damp clearing where Kith had spotted the elven banner.

Here he found Parnigar and Vanesti and the rest of the Wildrunner headquarters. This group marched with several dozen bodyguards, trying to remain in the approximate center of the farflung regiments. Because of the weather, the march columns were separated even more than usual, so that the small company camped this night in relative isolation.

"They've broken camp," announced Parnigar, without preamble.

"I know. Their base camp is abandoned. Have you discovered where they've gone?"

Kith's worst fears were confirmed by Parnigar's answer. "East, it looks like. There are tracks leading in every direction, as always, but it looks like they all swing toward the east a mile or two out of the camps."

Again Kith-Kanan thought of the ungarrisoned fortress rising from the plains a hundred miles to the east.

"Can we attack?" asked Vanesti, unable to restrain himself any longer.

"You'll stay here!" barked Kith-Kanan. He turned to Parnigar. "In the morning, we'll have to find them."

"What? And leave me here alone? In the middle of nowhere?" Vanesti was indignant.

"You're right," Kith conceded with a sigh. "You'll have to

come. But you'll also have to do what I tell you!"

"Don't I always?" inquired the youth, grinning impishly.

* * * * *

General Giarna slouched in his saddle, aware of the tens of thousands of marching soldiers surrounding him. The Army of Ergoth crept like a monstrous snake to the east, toward Sithelbec. Outriders spread across a thirty-mile arc before them, seeking signs of the Wildrunners. Giarna wanted to meet his foe in open battle while the weather was unchanged, hoping that the storm would neutralize the elves' flying cavalry. The Windriders had made his life very difficult over the years, and it would please him to fight a battle where the griffons wouldn't be a factor.

Even in his wildest hopes, he hadn't reckoned on weather as dismal as this. A day earlier, a tornado had swept through the supply train, killing more than a thousand men and destroying two weeks' worth of provisions. Now many columns of his army blundered through the featureless landscape, lost. Every day a few more men were struck by lightning, crippled or killed instantly.

The general didn't know that, even as he marched to the east, the elven army trudged westward, some twenty-five miles to the north. The Wildrunners sought the encampment of the human army. Both forces blundered forward in disarray, passing within striking range of each other, yet not knowing of their enemy's presence.

General Giarna looked to his left, to the north. There was something out there! He *sensed* it, though he saw nothing. His intuition informed him that the presence that drew him was many miles away.

"There!" he cried, suddenly raising a black-gloved hand and pointing to the north. "We must strike northward! Now! With all haste!"

Some companies of his army heard the command. Ponderously, under the orders of their sergeants-major, they wheeled to the left, preparing to strike out toward the north, into the rain and the hail—and, soon, the darkness. Others didn't get the word. The ultimate effect of the maneuver spread the army across twice as much country as

Giarna intended, opening huge gaps between the various brigades and adding chaos to an already muddled situation.

"Move, damn you!" The general cried, his voice taut. Lightning flashed over his head, streaks of fire lancing across the sky. Thunder crashed around them, sounding as if the world was coming apart.

Still the great formations continued their excruciating advance as the weary humans endeavored to obey Giarna's hysterical commands.

He couldn't wait. The scent drew him on like a hound to its prey. He wheeled his horse, kicking sharp spurs into the black steed's flanks. Breaking away from the column of his army, he started toward the north ahead of his men.

Alone.

* * * * *

Warm winds surged across the chill waters of the Turbidus Ocean, south of Ergoth, collecting moisture and carrying it aloft until the water droplets loomed as monumental columns of black clouds, billowing higher until they confounded the eyes of earthbound observers by vanishing into the limitless expanse of the sky.

Lightning flashed, beginning as an occasional explosion of brightness but increasing in fierceness and tempo until the clouds marched along to a staccato tempo, great sheets of hot fire slashing through them in continuous volleys. The waters below trembled under the fury of the storm.

The winds swirled, propelled by the rising pressure of steam. Whirlwinds grew tighter, shaping into slender funnels, until a front of cyclones roared forward, tossing the ocean into a chaotic maelstrom of foam. Great waves rolled outward from the storm, propelled by lashing torrents of rain.

And then the storm passed onto land.

The mass of clouds and power roared northward, skirting the Kharolis Mountains as it veered slightly toward the east. Before it lay the plains, hundreds of miles of flat, sodden country, already deluged by thunder and rain.

The new storm surged onto the flatlands, unleashing its winds as if it knew that nothing could stand in its path.

* * * * *

A soaking Wildrunner limped through the brush, raising his hand to ward off the hail and wipe rain away from his face. Finally he broke into a clearing and saw the vague outlines of the command post. Finding it had been sheer luck. He was one of two dozen men who had been sent with the report, in the hopes that one of them would reach Kith-Kanan.

"The Army of Ergoth," he gasped, stumbling into the small house that served as the general's headquarters. "It approaches from the south!"

"Damn!" Kith-Kanan instantly saw the terrible vulnerability of his army, stretched as it was into a long column marching east to west. Wherever the humans hit him, he would be vulnerable.

"How far?" he asked quickly.

"Five miles, maybe less. I saw a company of horsemen—a thousand or so. I don't know how many other units are there."

"You did well to bring me the news immediately." Kith's mind whirled. "If Giarna is attacking us, he must have something in mind. Still, I can't believe he can execute an attack very well—not in this weather."

"Attack them, uncle!"

Kith turned to look at Vanesti. His fresh-faced nephew's eyes lit with enthusiasm. His first battle loomed.

"Your suggestion has merit," he said, pausing for a moment. "It's one thing that the enemy would never suspect. His grasp of the battle won't be much greater than mine, if I'm on the offensive. And furthermore, I have no way to organize any kind of defense in this weather. Better to have the troops moving forward and catch the enemy off balance."

"I'll dispatch the scouts," Parnigar noted. "We'll inform every company that we can. It won't be the whole army, you realize. There isn't enough time, and the weather is too treacherous."

"I know," Kith agreed. "The Windriders, for one, will have to stay on the ground." He looked at Arcuballis. The great creature rested nearby, his head tucked under one wing to protect himself from the rain.

"I'll take Kijo and leave Arcuballis here." The prospect made him feel somehow crippled, but as the storm increased around him, he knew that flight would be too dangerous a tactic.

He could only hope that his enemy's attack would be equally haphazard. In this wish, he was rewarded, for even as the fight began, it moved out of the control of its commanders.

* * * * *

The two armies blundered through the rain. Each stretched along a front of several dozen miles, and great gaps existed in their formations. The Army of Ergoth lumbered north, and where its companies met elves, they fought them in confusing skirmishes. As often as not, they passed right through the widely spaced formations of the Wildrunner Army, continuing into the nameless distance of the plains.

The Wildrunners and their allies struck south. Like the humans, they encountered their enemy occasionally, and at other times met no resistance.

Skirmishes raged along the entire distance, between whatever units happened to meet each other in the chaos. Human horsemen rode against elven swords. Dwarven battle-axes chopped at Ergothian archers. Because of the noise and the darkness, a company might not know that its sister battalion fought for its life three hundred yards away, or that a band of enemy warriors had passed across their front a bare five minutes earlier.

But it didn't matter. The real battle took shape in the clouds themselves.

✿ 33 ✿

Nightfall, Midsummer, Year of the Cloud Giant

Hail thundered through the woods, pounding trees into splinters and bruising exposed flesh. The balls of ice, as big across as gold pieces, quickly blanketed the ground. The roar of their impact drowned all attempts at communication.

Kith-Kanan, Vanesti, and Parnigar halted their plodding horses, seeking the minimal shelter provided by the overhanging boughs of a small grove of elms. They were grateful that the storm hadn't caught them on the open plains. Such a deluge could be extremely dangerous without shelter. Their two dozen bodyguards, all veterans of the House Protectorate, took shelter under neighboring trees. All the elves were silent, wet, and miserable.

They hadn't seen another company of Wildrunners in several hours, nor had they encountered any sign of the enemy. They had blundered through the storms for the whole day, lashed by wind and rain, soaked and chilled, fruitlessly seeking sign of friend or foe.

"Do you know where we are?" Kith asked Parnigar. Around them, the pebbly residue of the storm had covered the earth with round, white balls of ice.

"I'm afraid not," the veteran scout replied. "I *think* we've maintained a southerly heading, but it's hard to tell when you can't see more than two dozen feet ahead of you!"

All of a sudden Kith held up a hand. The hailstorm, with unsettling abruptness, had ceased.

"What is it?" hissed Vanesti, looking around them, his eyes wide.

"I don't know . . ." Kith admitted. "Something doesn't *feel* right."

The black horse exploded from the bushes with shocking speed, its dark rider leaning forward along the steed's lathered neck. Sharp hooves pounded the ice-coated earth, sending slivers of crushed hailstones flying with each step. The attacker charged past two guards, and Parnigar saw the glint of a sword. The blade moved with stunning speed, slaying both elven bodyguards with quick chops.

"We're attacked!" Parnigar shouted. The veteran scout seized his sword and leaped into his saddle, spurring the steed forward.

Kith-Kanan, followed by Vanesti, ducked around the broad tree trunk just in time to see Parnigar collide with the attacker. The brutal impact sent the elf's mare reeling sideways and then tumbling to the ground. The horse screamed as the elven warrior sprang free, crouching to face the black-cloaked human on his dark war-horse.

"Giarna!" hissed Kith-Kanan, instantly recognizing the foe.

"Really?" gasped Vanesti, inching forward for a better look.

"Stay *back!*" growled the elven general.

The black steed abruptly reared, lashing out with its forehooves. One of them caught Parnigar on the skull, and the elf fell heavily to the ground.

Frantically Kith looked toward his bow, tied securely to his saddlebags on the other side of the broad tree. Cursing, he drew his sword and darted toward the fight.

With savage glee, the human rider leaped from his saddle, straddling Parnigar as the stunned elf struggled to move. As Kith ran toward them, the human thrust his sword through the scout's chest, pinning him to the ground with the keen blade.

Parnigar flopped on his back, stuck to the earth. Blood welled around the steel blade, and the icy pebbles of hail beneath him quickly took on a garish shade of red. In moments, his struggles faded to weak twitching, and then to nothing.

By that time, Kith had lunged at the black swordsman. The elf slashed with his sword but gaped in surprise as the quick blow darted *past* Giarna. The man's fist hammered into Kith-Kanan's belly, and the elf grunted in pain as he staggered backward, gasping for air.

With a sneer, the human pulled out his blade, turning to face two more Wildrunners, Kith's bodyguards, who charged recklessly forward. His sword flashed once, twice, and the two elves dropped, fatally slashed across their throats.

"Fight *me*, you bastard!" growled Kith-Kanan.

"That is a pleasure I have long anticipated!" General Giarna's face broke into a savage grin. His teeth appeared to gleam as he threw his head back and laughed maniacally.

A quartet of veteran Wildrunners, all loyal and competent warriors of the House Protectorate, rushed General Giarna from behind. But the man whirled, his bloody sword cutting an arc through the air. Two of the guards fell, gutted, while the other two stumbled backward, horrified by their opponent's quickness. Kith-Kanan could only stare in shock. Never had he seen a weapon wielded with such deadly precision.

The retreating elves moved backward too slowly. Giarna sprang after them, leaping like a cat and stabbing one of them through the heart. The other elf rushed in wildly. His head sailed from his body following a swathlike cut that the human made with a casual flick of his wrist.

"You monster!" The youthful scream caught Kith-

Kanan's attention. Vanesti had seized a sword from somewhere. Now he charged out from behind the elm trunk, lunging toward the murderous human general.

"No!" Kith-Kanan cried out in alarm, rushing forward to try to reach his nephew. His boot caught on a treacherous vine and he sprawled headlong, looking up to see Vanesti swinging his sword wildly.

Kith scrambled to his feet. Each of his movements seemed grotesquely slow, exaggerated beyond all reason. He opened his mouth to shout again, but he could only watch in horror.

Vanesti lost his balance following his wild attack, stumbling to the side. He tried to deflect the human's straight-on stab, but the tip of General Giarna's blade struck Vanesti at the base of his rib cage, penetrating his gut and slicing through his spine as it emerged from his back. The youth gagged and choked, sliding backward off the blade. He lay on his back, his hands clutching at the air.

* * * * *

The lord-major-chieftain supreme of Hillrock pressed forward, trudging resolutely through weather the like of which he had never experienced before. Hailstones pummeled him, rain lashed his face, and the wind roared and growled in its futile efforts to penetrate the hill giant's heavy wolfskin cloak, a cloak he had worn proudly for forty years.

Yet One-Tooth plodded on, grimly determined to follow the compulsion that had drawn him here. He would see this trek through to its end. The burning drive that had led him this far seemed to grow more intense with each passing hour, until the giant broke into a lumbering trot, so anxious was his feeling that he neared his goal.

As he moved across the plains, a strange haze seemed to settle over his mind. He began to forget Hillrock, to forget the giantesses who were his wives, the small community that had always been his home. Instead, his mind drifted to the heights of his mountain range, to one snow-blanketed winter valley long ago and a small, fire-warmed cave.

* * * * *

Later, elves who had lived for six hundred years swore that they had never before seen such a storm. The weather erupted across the plains with a violence that dwarfed the petty squabbles of the mortals on the ground.

The thunderheads grew in frenzy, an explosive, seething mass of power that transcended anything in human or elven memory. The storms lashed the plains, striking with wind and fire and hail.

At nightfall, when darkness gathered across the already sodden plains on the night of the summer solstice, Solinari gleamed full and bright, high above the clouds, but no one on earth could see her.

Lightning erupted, hurling crackling bolts to the ground. Great cyclones of wind, miles across, whirled and roared. They spiraled and burst, a hundred angry funnel clouds that shrieked over the flat plains, leveling everything in their path.

The great battle of armies never occurred. Instead, a howling dervish of tornadoes formed in the west and roared across the plains, scattering the two forces before them, leaving tens of thousands of dead in their wake.

The most savage of the tornadoes swirled through the Army of Ergoth, scattering food wagons, killing horses and men, and sending the remnants fleeing in all directions.

But if the human army suffered the bulk of the death toll, the Wildrunners suffered the greatest destruction. Huge columns of black clouds, mushrooming into the heights of the distant sky, gathered around the great stone block of Sithelbec. Dark and forboding, they collected in an awful ring about the city.

For hours, a dull stillness pervaded the air. Those who had sought shelter in Sithelbec fled, fearing the unnatural calm.

Then the lightning began anew. Bolts of energy lashed the city. They crackled into the stone towers of the fortress, exploding masonry and leaving the smell of scorched dust in the air. They seared the blocks of wooden buildings around the wall, and soon sheets of flame added to the destruction.

Like a cosmic bombardment, crackling spears of explosive electricity thundered into the stone walls and wooden roofs. Crushing and pounding, pummeling and bruising, the storm maintained its pressure as the city slowly collapsed into ruin.

*　*　*　*　*

Kith realized that he was screaming, spitting his hatred and rage at this monstrous human who had dogged his life for forty years. He threw caution aside in a desperate series of slashes and attacks, but each lunge found Giarna's sword ready with a parry—and each moment of battle threatened to open a fatal gap in the elf's defenses.

Their blades clanged together with a force that matched the thunder. The two opponents hacked and chopped at each other, scrambling over deadfalls, pushing through soaking thornbushes, driving forward in savage attacks or careful retreats. The rest of the House Protectorate bodyguards rushed, in a group, to their leader's defense. The human's blade was a deadly scythe, and soon the elves bled the last of their lives into the icy, hail-strewn ground.

It became apparent to Kith that Giarna toyed with him. The man was unbeatable. He could have ended the fight at virtually any moment, and he seemed completely impervious to Kith's blows. Even when, in a lucky moment, the elf's blade slashed against the human's skin, no wound opened.

The man continued to allow Kith to rush forward, to expend himself on these desperate attacks, and then to stumble back, seemingly inches ahead of a mortal blow.

Finally he laughed, his voice a sharp, cruel bark.

"You see now that, for all your arrogance, you cannot live forever. Even elven lives must come to an end!"

Kith-Kanan stepped back, gasping for breath and staring at the hated enemy before him. He said nothing as his throat expanded, gulping air.

"Perhaps you will die with as much dignity as your wife," suggested Giarna, musing.

Kith froze. "What do you mean?"

"Merely that the whore thought she could do what all of your armies have been unable to do. She tried to kill me!"

The elf could only stare in shock. Suzine! By the gods, why would she attempt something so mad, so impossible?

"Of course, she paid the price for her stupidity, as you will do as well! My only regret was that she took her own life before I could draw the information I needed from her."

Kith-Kanan felt a sense of horror and guilt. Of course she had done this. He had left her no other way in which to aid him!

"She was braver and finer than we will ever be," he said, his voice firm despite his grief.

"Words!" Giarna snorted. "Use them wisely, elf. You have precious few left!"

Vanesti lay on the ground, so still and cold that he might have been a pale patch of mud. Near him, Parnigar lay equally still, his eyes staring sightlessly upward, his fingers curled reflexively into fists. His warm blood had melted the hailstones around him, so that he lay in an icy crimson pool.

Marshaling his determination, Kith charged, recklessly slashing at his opponent in a desperate bid to break his icy control. But Giarna stepped to the side, and Kith found himself on his back, looking up into gaping black holes, the deadened eyes of the man who would be his killer. The elf tried to scramble away, to spring to his feet, but his cloak snagged on a twisted limb beside him. Kith kicked out, then fell back, helpless.

Trapped between two logs, Kith-Kanan couldn't move. Desperately, feeling a rage that was nonetheless overpowering for its helplessness, he glared at the blade that was about to end his life. Giarna stood over him, slowly raising the bloodstained weapon, as if the steel intended to savor the final, fatal thrust.

The crushing blow of a club knocked Giarna to the side before the killing blow could fall. Stuck behind the deadfall, Kith couldn't see where the blow had come from, but he saw the human stumble, watched the great weapon swing through his field of vision.

Snarling with rage, Giarna whirled, ready to slay whatever impertinent foe distracted him from his quarry. He felt no fear. Was he not impervious to the attack of elf, dwarf, or human?

But this was no elf. Instead, he stared upward at a creature that towered over his head. The last thing Giarna saw before the club crushed his skull and scattered his brains across the muddy ground was a lone white tooth, jutting proudly from the attacker's jaw.

*   *   *   *   *

"He's alive," whispered Kith-Kanan, scarcely daring to breathe. He kneeled beside Vanesti, noting the slow rise and fall of his nephew's chest. Steam wisped from his nostrils at terrifyingly long intervals.

"Help little guy?" inquired One-Tooth.

"Yes." Kith smiled through his tears, looking with affection at the huge creature who must have marched hundreds of miles to find him. He had asked him why, and the giant had merely shrugged.

One-Tooth reached down and grasped the bundle that was Vanesti. They wrapped him in a cloak, and now Kith rigged a small lean-to beneath the shelter of some leafy branches.

"I'll light a fire," said the elf. "Maybe that will draw some of the Wildrunners."

But the soaked wood refused to burn, and so the trio huddled and shivered through the long night. Then in the morning, they heard the sound of horses pushing along a forest trail.

Kith wormed his way through the bushes, discovering a column of Wildrunner scouts. Several veterans, recognizing their leader, quickly approached him, but they had to overcome their fear of the hill giant when they came upon the scene of the savage fight.

Gingerly they rigged a sling for the youth and prepared to make the grueling ride to Sithelbec.

"This time you'll come home with me," Kith told the giant. In the thinning mist, they started toward the east. Not for several days, until they met more survivors of his army—some who had had word from the fortress—did they learn that the home they marched to had been reduced to a smoldering pile of rubble.

❧ Epilogue ❧

autumn, 2177 (PC)

Shapeless blocks of stone jutted into the sky, framed by the burned-out timbers that outlined walls, gates, and other structures of wood. Sithelbec lay in ruins. The tornadoes and lightning had razed the fortress more effectively than any human attack could have done. The surviving Wildrunners collected on the plains around the wreckage, nursing their wounded and trying to piece together the legacy of the disaster.

Only gradually did they become aware that the humans were gone. The Army of Ergoth had broken and fled, driven by nature to do what forty years of elven warfare had been unable to accomplish. The surviving humans streamed toward the lush farmlands of Daltigoth, the war forgotten.

The Theiwar dwarves—those who survived—fled back to Thorbardin. And the elves who had fought for the human cause returned to the woodlands, there to strive for survival in the ruins left by the storms of spring.

Dunbarth Ironthumb organized the ranks of his Hylar legion, most of whom had been fortunate enough to find riverbank caves that had sheltered them during the worst of the storm.

"It's back to good, old-fashioned rock walls and a stone ceiling over my head!" announced the gruff veteran, clasping Kith-Kanan's hand before he embarked on the long march.

"You've earned it," said the elf sincerely. For a long time, he watched the receding column of stocky figures until it disappeared into the mists to the south.

Sithas journeyed to the plains once more, two months after the great storm. He came to get his son, to bring him home. Vanesti would live, though, barring a miracle, he would never stand on his own legs.

The twins stood before the ruins of Sithelbec. The city was a blackened patch of earth, a chaotic jumble of charred timbers and broken, twisted stone.

The Speaker of the Stars met his brother's eyes.

"Tamanier Ambrodel has gone to Daltigoth. He, together with an ambassador from Thorbardin—a *Hylar* ambassador—will arrange a treaty. We will see the swords sheathed once and for all."

"Those swords that remain," said Kith quietly. He thought of Parnigar and Kencathedrus—and Suzine—and all the others who had perished in the course of this war.

"This war has changed many things—perhaps everything," observed Sithas quietly. Hermathya told me! his mind screamed silently. He wanted to accuse his brother, to set this discussion on the solid ground of truth, but he couldn't.

Kith nodded, silent.

These lands, Sithas thought, with a look at the wreckage around him. Were they worth clinging to? They had been held at a cost in lives that was beyond measuring. Yet what had they won?

Humans would never be totally banished from the western lands, the Speaker knew. Kith-Kanan would certainly allow those who had fought for his cause to remain. And the elves who had opposed them—what would be their fate? Permanent banishment? Sithas didn't want to think of further strife, further suffering inflicted upon his people. Yet at the same time, he was opposed to further changes.

There was only one way now to preserve the purity of Silvanesti. Just as the infected limb of a diseased person must be removed to save the whole, so must the infected society of his nation be cut away to preserve the sanctity of Silvanesti.

"I'm granting you the lands extending from here to the west," announced Sithas firmly. "They are no longer part of Silvanesti. You may do with them as you like."

"I have thought about this," replied Kith, his voice a match for his brother's strength. His words surprised Sithas, for he had thought his announcement would be unanticipated. Yet Kith-Kanan, too, seemed to sense that they were no longer part of the same world.

"I will build my new capital to the west, among the forested hills." Qualinesti, he thought, though he didn't say the name aloud. To himself, he vowed that it would be a land of free elves, a place that would never go to war for the sake of some mistaken purity.

As the two brothers parted, the clouds remained leaden over the storm-lashed plains. The elves, once one nation, henceforth became two.